PALADIN

SALLY SLATER

PERFECT
ANALOGY

Published by Perfect Analogy Publishing.

First Edition

For information about special discounts for bulk purchases or author interviews and appearances please contact Perfect Analogy Publishing at info@perfect-analogy.com.

ISBN-10: 0-9894633-5-4

ISBN-13: 978-0-9894633-5-5

www.perfect-analogy.com

DEDICATION

To my readers on Wattpad, for believing in Paladin and in me.

ACKNOWLEDGEMENTS

You often hear writers say that writing is a lonely business, but I guess I got lucky, because when I wrote I was never alone. Thank you to the entire Wattpad community for keeping me company on every step of this crazy journey. Without Wattpad, there would be no Paladin.

Special thanks to Daniel Taylor, AKA my geography and character name consultant, and to Hayley John, who made my amazing cover.

Thanks also to my awesome publishers at Perfect Analogy for making my publishing dream a reality.

Thanks to my boyfriend for being my biggest supporter and putting up with my insane writing hours. Now grow your beard.

Finally, thanks to my mom for inspiring my love of reading and letting me sneak-read under the covers. I couldn't have asked for a better editor.

PROLOGUE

S AM PACED ANXIOUSLY outside the Duke of Haywood's solar. The duke, Sam's father, had not had the chance to properly scold her the night before since he couldn't very well scold her in front of all his esteemed guests. But before she'd gone off to bed, he'd instructed her to meet him on the morrow for, as he put it, a "brief discussion." Sam knew the conversation was bound to be neither brief nor a discussion. She was in for a one-sided rant.

Gathering her courage, she knocked on the great oak door to her father's bedroom. "Come in!" her mother, Duchess Tsalene of Haywood, called out in her thick Rhean accent.

Sam exhaled a breath in relief. The duke was infinitely more reasonable when his wife was present. Sam drew her shoulders back, pushed open the door, and stepped inside.

With its damask-covered walls, mahogany carved furniture, and massive double fireplace, the solar had a romantic elegance that reflected her mother's eclectic tastes more than her father's unimaginative aesthetic. As was customary, the duchess had her own suite of rooms in the western tower of the castle, but she rarely used them, choosing instead to share quarters with her husband.

The Duke of Haywood reclined in a throne-like chair by the mantle of the fireplace. "Samantha," he drawled, drawing out the syllables of her name as though to nettle her. He knew she preferred Sam.

She dipped into a curtsy. "Your Grace." Then she went to her mother, who sat on the edge of the canopied bed. "Mother," Sam said warmly, pressing a kiss to her mother's cheek.

The duchess made a clicking sound with her tongue. "La,

daughter, show your father some affection. You wouldn't want him to get jealous."

Sam rolled her eyes. The duchess was the only person capable of inspiring jealousy in the duke. "I'm quite sure he prefers I don't," Sam said.

The duke cleared his throat. "*He* is standing right here and prefers not to be spoken for." He gave his wife a long look before returning his attention to Sam. "How did you sleep?" he asked awkwardly.

It was an olive branch, and Sam was smart enough to take it. "Well, father. Thank you."

"Excellent, excellent." He gave his wife another long look.

The duchess did not return his gaze, instead looking down at her turquoise-varnished nails. Sam began to grow nervous.

"Samantha," the duke said, "take a seat beside your mother."

Sam obliged, smoothing her skirts underneath her. The duke stared at her for a long moment, not saying anything. Even her mother began to fidget.

"I'm sorry!" Sam burst out when she couldn't stand the silence anymore. "I'm sorry about last night. I should never have provoked Lord Crawford."

"What's this?" asked the duke, his eyebrows narrowing. "You *provoked* Lord Crawford?"

Sam blinked. "He didn't mention it to you?" She had poured her drink down Lord Crawford's shirt when he'd gotten a little fresh, and she'd been sure he would blab to her father.

The duke glowered at her. "No he did not, but perhaps he should have." He turned toward his wife. "You see, Tsalene, this is exactly the sort of behavior I'm talking about."

"I said I was sorry!" Sam said.

Her mother took Sam's hands into her own. "Your father didn't ask you here to apologize."

Now Sam was well and truly nervous. The last time her mother had spoken to her with such gravity was to tell her that Old Tom, the former castle steward, had passed. "Why am I here, then?"

"To talk about the future," said her father. "*Your* future."

Sam folded her arms over her chest. "I don't see what there is to talk about. I already know my future. Find a suitable husband, marry, and produce an heir. I understand." Sam didn't like her future, but she'd made peace with it. What other choice did she have?

The duke raised a skeptical eyebrow. "Do you? Because it seems like you're doing everything in your power to obstruct it."

"I have no idea what you're talking about."

"Don't be obtuse, Samantha!" he snapped. "Provoking Lord Crawford, of all people?"

Sam returned his glare. "Lord Crawford is a fool."

"He is young, handsome, and wealthy. A catch by most ladies' standards."

She lifted her chin defiantly. "I'm not most ladies."

"That doesn't excuse your ridiculous behavior!" he yelled.

"Richard," her mother cut in with a note of warning. The duke closed his mouth. Squeezing Sam's hands, her mother said, "What your father is trying to say is that it's time for you to take the prospect of marriage seriously."

"High time," the duke said, moving towards the bed so as to loom over her. "You're sixteen years of age, Samantha. You can't keep running around with your hair all amok and dirt on your face, waving your silly sword. You're a *lady*, for the Gods' sake. Act like one."

"All right," Sam said in placating tones. "I'll pay my appearance more mind and make an effort to be more courteous." Assuming the matter was settled, she rose from the bed.

The duke put his hands on her shoulders and shoved her back down. "This conversation isn't over." He glanced at his wife, who gave him a slight nod. "We've given you too much leeway for too long. You have till your next birthday to find a husband, or we'll find one for you."

Her mouth fell open. "You can't be serious."

"I am entirely serious, Samantha. Enough is enough."

Without another word, Sam shot up from the bed and stormed out of the duke's solar, slamming the door behind her. She strode across the long corridor, down several flights of stairs, and out of the castle, shoving past the guards without so much as a "pardon me." Her father wanted to marry her off to some lordling stranger before she turned seventeen? Faith in blood, her seventeenth birthday was less than six months away!

She felt betrayed—not by her father, as she expected this sort of nonsense from him, but by her mother for going along with it. Sam would have thought that her mother, of all people, would stand up for her. True, her mother had married at her age, but she'd married for love. Shouldn't she want the same for her daughter instead of forcing her to meet some arbitrary deadline?

Needing time alone to think, Sam walked till the notched turrets of Castle Haywood disappeared from view and the light of the afternoon sun filtered red-tinted through the trees. When she could hear the sound of moving water, she forked left, heading onto the winding forest road that bisected the land between Haywood and Catania. She'd traveled this road hundreds, maybe thousands of times, in search of the one place that always gave her sanctuary: the small clearing that was her mother's secret spot, or had been, till she had shared it with Sam.

When Tsalene of Rhea first came to Haywood, a new bride and a stranger in a strange land, she'd found this place, a hidden alcove surrounded by coppice and a babbling brook. She'd dug a hole in the soft ground and planted a seed taken from her homeland. Now, twenty years later, it was a firm cherry tree with drooping branches that bore cascades of pale pink blossoms. Tsalene had dubbed it the Goddess Tree in tribute to Rhea's patron goddess, Emese the Great Mother, and when she came out here, she would pray beneath its flowering boughs.

Sam sagged against the Goddess Tree, closed her eyes, and prayed. *Emese, if you're listening, help me . . .* She paused, uncertain of what kind of help to pray for. Finding a good husband? Someone who made her parents happy? Someone who loved her? Someone she loved?

Sam didn't *want* a husband, not really. In her heart of hearts, she wanted more. She just didn't know what "more" looked like.

A twig snapped, and Sam's eyes flew open while a startled yip escaped her lips.

Husky laughter floated across the breeze. "It's only me," her mother said, emerging from the brush. "I didn't mean to scare you."

"I wasn't scared. You just surprised me."

"Of course. My fearless daughter," her mother said with gentle mockery, a smile transforming her exotic features from merely striking to beautiful. She might claim that Sam had inherited her smile, but the duchess's smile had an air of mystery that Sam's lacked, as though it guarded a thousand secrets.

"What are you doing here?" Sam asked, her anger still raw.

Her mother wiped a stray leaf from her gown and crossed to the Goddess Tree, running her fingers over the bark. "I came to find you." She sat down against its trunk and patted the ground beside her. "Come sit by me." Begrudgingly, Sam did as she was told, settling her skirts around her ankles. Together, they sat beneath the Goddess Tree, watching the cherry blossoms fall in silence.

Her mother spoke first. "You're angry with me."

Sam saw no point in holding back. "Aye. It's bloody unfair, is what it is."

Her mother sighed. "There are many things in this world that are unfair, Sam. You are the sole heir to a great and noble family, and so you must marry and carry on your father's line. All of us are born with a Gods-given purpose in life, and whether or not it's what we'd choose for ourselves has no bearing."

"So that's it, then?" Sam asked bitterly. "I'm to marry whomever my father chooses for me and spend the rest of my days stitching embroidery and minding the babes?"

Her mother arched a sable eyebrow. "I think I should be offended. Do you think that is all I do?"

Sam blushed. "No, it's just—" She took a deep breath. "This life is what you *wanted*. It's not what I want."

"What I wanted?" Her mother gave a one-sided smile. "I am happy now, far happier than I ever imagined. But if I'd had my choice, I would have followed a different path."

"You would have?" Sam asked, surprised. Her mother had never said anything of the like before.

"Oh, yes," her mother said. "You and I are not so different. When I was your age, I wanted to be a great warrior, like my sister Nasrin."

Sam's mouth fell open. "Your sister was a warrior?"

"*Is* a warrior. Or she was when I last saw her, Gods, more than twenty years ago now. It is not so uncommon in Rhea for a woman to take up a weapon, though there are few who devote their lives to it." She nudged Sam with her elbow. "Who do you think convinced your father to teach you to fight?"

Sam shrugged. "I thought he enjoyed the excuse to wallop me with a stick." Although nowadays, it was usually the other way around.

Her mother chuckled. "It does seem like that sometimes, doesn't it? My father was my teacher, too, you know."

"Your father taught you the sword?" Sam asked, delighted.

"He tried," her mother said, laughing. "I didn't have Nasrin's talent. Or yours. And he never hesitated to tell me as much."

The corners of Sam's mouth kicked up. "That must have rankled."

"In the end, it didn't matter. Nasrin joined the Convent of the Sun, and as my father's only other daughter, it fell on me to marry, and marry well." She played idly with a fallen petal. "My father wanted to ally the family with a foreign lord, one with great military power. He chose Richard for me."

Sam scrunched her face in confusion. The Duke and Duchess of Haywood were the most famous love match of their generation. "But that's—"

"Not the story you've heard?" her mother said. "Or one I've ever told you. All of Thule knows the story of our accidental first meeting in the king's private gardens. It was no accident—my father orchestrated the whole thing. He *is* Rhea's finest military strategist, after all."

Sam digested this. "Does Father know?"

Her mother grinned. "I told him the day after we consummated our marriage. He didn't speak to me for an entire week after that. He forgave me, though, because by then I'd fallen in love with him, and he with me." Her grin vanished. "I did not know, or dare hope, I'd love the man I'd marry. But I did my duty, and the Gods saw fit to give me a husband worth loving, and to give me you, my most precious daughter. You'll see. The Gods will reward you, too."

"Maybe," Sam said, unconvinced.

Her mother pushed to her feet and offered Sam her hand. "Let's go home. Today is a day for celebrating, not for arguing." She glanced up at the sky. "And we best go quickly. It's going to rain."

As if to emphasize her warning, a distant roll of thunder shook the ground. Sam clasped her mother's hand and stood up. When had the sky become so dark? It wasn't the dark of evening, but the dark gray of a fast-approaching storm.

They pressed back towards the main forest road as fast as they were able, without a care for the thorny thicket. Thunder rumbled again, closer now. Sam had counted ten seconds between this boom of thunder and the last. The storm was minutes away. When dots of water began to speckle the forest path, they ran.

A violent crack of lightning rent the sky, and it began to rain in earnest. Mid-stride, Sam slipped on a wet rock, ripping her skirts at the knee. "Great," she muttered, brushing off dirt and grime. The skin underneath was bloody.

Her mother kneeled down in the mud beside her, hissing in sympathy. She, like Sam, was soaked to the bone, her gown plastered to her body and her hair hanging in lank, wet strands. "Can you walk?"

Sam nodded, easing herself off the ground. "It's just a bad scrape." She put her full weight onto the offending leg, and winced. "I think."

Her mother lifted her face to the sky, allowing rain to splash down her cheeks. "We'll go slowly. We can withstand a little water." She rose and slung Sam's arm around her shoulder. Grateful, Sam leaned into her, and together they hobbled down the road.

The rain came down harder, and heavy fog settled over the forest, thick enough that Sam couldn't see more than an arm's length in front of her. She shivered, cold and a little afraid, though she was loathe to admit it.

Lightning split the sky with a sharp crack. Sam and her mother yelped in unison then traded guilty smiles. "It's very dark, isn't it?" her mother whispered.

"Aye," Sam whispered back. "Why are we whispering?"

"I don't know. It feels appropriate."

A nervous giggle escaped Sam's lips, and her mother looked at her crosswise. Sam wasn't much of a giggler.

They pressed on, slower now, while visibility worsened and the rain beat down on their heads. In theory, they were moving closer to the edge of the woods, but without the familiar turrets of Castle Haywood in sight, Sam felt miles and miles away.

Lightning flashed, cutting through the fog, and Sam's heart stuttered. She had seen something in that brief flash of light. Two red orbs and jagged yellow triangles. Eyes. And teeth.

She squeezed her mother's shoulder and said, as quietly as she could, "Something's out there."

"La, don't be silly. It's only your—"

"Hush!"

"—imagination," her mother said, too loudly. A low growl punctuated the air.

Sam's stomach clenched with fear. It wasn't her imagination, whatever *it* was. She squinted into the fog and glimpsed black fur and a long, glossy snout. Please let it be a wolf, she prayed silently. She watched its outline grow larger as it drew nearer. Please . . . just a really, really big wolf . . .

"Faith in blood," her mother swore. There was no hiding the fear in her voice.

They could see the creature clearly now, and smell it too—it stunk of wet fur and copper and rot. And it was no wolf. The creature was the size of a horse and had fur so black it seemed to consume the light. It was tall at the withers and gaunt like a greyhound, its ribcage visible where its coat was finest, with long, muscular hindquarters that tapered into monstrous claws. Its crimson eyes were flat and unintelligent—but hungry, so, so hungry as they bore down on Sam and her mother.

Those blood-red eyes could mean only one thing . . .

Demon.

Her hand brushed against her side, reaching for a sword that was not there. Gods, how she wished she had a weapon. "What do we do?" Sam asked her mother, trying to remain calm. Sam was all confidence and bluster with a sword in hand, but without one she was as vulnerable as anyone else.

Her mother closed her eyes and traced a circle over her left breast. "Great Goddess, let us survive this day." Her lids flew open and she looked at Sam, speaking with low urgency. "You need to run, Sam. Run as fast and as far as you can."

"What about you?"

"I will run in the opposite direction. It can't catch us both." She shoved at Sam's chest. "Run!"

Sam hesitated, staring at her mother's frightened face, and then broke into a limping run. Pain shot up her injured leg with each footfall and several times she nearly fell, but she did not look back. She heard nothing but the sound of the rain hitting the trees and her uneven breath. Was the demon close behind? Had it even followed her? She half-hoped that it had—the alternative was that it had chased after her mother.

A shrill scream pierced the air. Sam skidded to a stop. Mother. Heart pumping in her chest, she twisted and looked behind her. No sight of the demon.

The scream came again, long and loud, a mix of pain and terror. Her heart leapt into her throat. Please, Gods, let her be okay. With a final prayer, she turned and ran in the direction of the scream.

She found her mother stumbling in the rain, wet hands clutching her side. "Sam," her mother said in a voice that was paper thin. "I told you to run, you foolish child."

"You said you would run, too," Sam accused as she rushed to her mother. Hot tears pricked the back of her eyes, but she refused to cry.

Her mother's pale lips formed a wan smile. "I did run. And now I'm caught." Her hands were slick not with rain but with blood. She reached out and touched Sam's cheek with scarlet fingers. "But you are not caught yet. Run. Run!"

"I'm not going to leave you," Sam said through clenched teeth.

"Better to both die then?" Tsalene asked harshly, a spark returning to her eyes. She removed her other hand from her side, revealing the extent of her wound. "Don't throw away your life for a dying woman, Sam."

"Don't say that!" Sam covered her mother's wound with her own hands, felt the hot liquid against her palms. "You're not going to die. Just . . . hold on."

Her mother gripped her by the shoulders and shook. "Run, Sam! For the love of Emese, run!"

But it was too late; the demon lurched out from behind the cover of the trees. Blood dripped from a wound in its side. Had her mother done that? How?

Her mother sagged to her knees and wrapped her arms around Sam's legs for balance. "Run, child!"

Sam felt her own knees sag. "I can't," she said brokenly. The tears brimming in her eyes spilled over. "I'm afraid."

"For me?" Her mother smiled and like always it transformed her. "I do not fear the Afterlight. But it's not yet your time." The smile left her face and she became gray and drawn again. She lay her head on Sam's shoulder. "I'm sorry."

"For what?" Sam asked. Her mother didn't respond. "For what?" she asked again, panic creeping into her voice. "For what?"

The demon's growl filled her mother's silence.

"Stay away!" Sam shouted over her mother's slack form. She's not dead, Sam chanted in her head, as if wishing would make it so. She's not dead. She's not dead.

Gently, she tilted her mother's head back, cradling her neck. Her mother's eyes were closed, her mouth parted. Her pale faced glistened with tears. Sam ran her thumb over her mother's damp cheeks. The skin was cool—all the heat had drained out of it. Her fingers ran south to her mother's neck, where her pulse should be. Nothing.

"No," Sam whispered. And then she threw back her head and screamed. Fury like she'd never before felt consumed her, drowning out everything else. My mother is dead, echoed endlessly in the back of her head. But grief blended with anger and set her blood aflame.

Sam eased her mother's limp body to the ground and stood up, meeting the demon's crimson stare with her own defiant stare. Less than three yards away, it cocked its head to the side like an overgrown wolf pup, as if it couldn't quite figure her out.

"You killed my mother," she told the demon with a calm she didn't feel, "and now I'm going to kill you."

The demon's lips peeled back into a hungry, canine grin, and Sam bared her teeth in a semblance of a smile. "I *will* kill you," she promised, curling her fingers into claws. The demon snarled in response and pawed the ground with its foreleg.

A shred of rational thought managed to slip through the wall of her anger. She had no weapon or armor. She scanned the woods for something, *anything* she could use against the demon. A fallen branch rested on the ground near her feet. It would have to do. She snatched it up, tucking it under her arm like she would a thrusting spear.

The demon charged, and so did she.

It launched itself at her in a blur of black fur. She ran towards it, angling her makeshift spear towards the left side of its barrel chest, where she imagined its heart would be, if demons had hearts.

Before they connected, something heavy slammed into her side. The branch snapped in two as she landed in a sprawl on the ground. Dazed, she struggled up onto her elbows.

"Get behind me!" a man's voice shouted.

Sam's eyes swung towards the voice. A tall, starkly beautiful man stood in the middle of the forest path with his sword held aloft, his gaze trained on the demon. He was panting heavily, and some combination of rain and sweat had plastered his blond hair to his skull. "Get behind me, Gods damn it! *Move!*" He let out an exasperated huff. "Do you want to die?"

Her gaze shifted to her mother, laid out among the dirt and fallen leaves, back to the strange man, and then finally the demon. Swallowing a sob, Sam scrambled to her feet and wove her way through the brush till she was a few paces behind him.

He turned to glare at her. "Fighting a demon with a stick? Are you mad?"

Sam looked at him with a blank expression. "My mother is dead."

The sharp planes of his face softened for an instant and then hardened again. "You can grieve later. For now, focus on staying alive." He dug something out of his boot—a long knife—and tossed it at her feet. "Don't use it unless you have to. Leave the demon to me."

Sam nodded mutely and picked up the knife. She'd lost the white rage she'd been feeling. Now she just felt brittle and empty.

The man did not attack immediately—he observed, tilting his head back to take in the beast's full height. "It's big," he said quietly. "One of the biggest I've seen." He adjusted his grip on his sword and edged closer.

The demon gave him a considering look and then sniffed at the air, licking its chops. Ignoring the man, it ambled over to her mother's body and snuffled at her stomach, mottled red and brown where she'd bled through her gown. It lolled out the full length of its tongue and began lapping up the blood. Teeth flashed and sank into purpling skin.

Rage flared anew. "Get away from her!" Sam screamed. She sprinted toward the demon and rammed her knife into its side.

The demon reared onto its hind legs and roared, knocking Sam onto the ground. Claws scraped the ground, inches away from her face.

Hands slid under her arms and pulled her backwards and up. "You bloody idiot," the man fumed, shoving her behind him. "Stay. Back." He gave her another shove for good measure.

He drew his sword and faced the demon. Its eyes had gone wild, rolling in their sockets. The knife, Sam noted with grim satisfaction, was still buried in its ribcage. There was no way she'd let that *thing* eat her mother, dead or not.

The demon swiped at the man with its front paw. He held his ground and swung his sword. The blade struck talon, which must have been as hard as steel, or harder, since it didn't break. He swung again, before the demon could retract its claw. This time, the edge of his blade sliced clean through the demon's carpals, hacking paw from limb. Dark brown sludge spurted from the stump of its leg, reeking of rotten meat.

The beast let out an unearthly howl, but the loss of its limb did not slow it down. It stretched its neck forward, snapping at the man's throat. He ducked and rolled out of reach. He regained his footing and then lunged, jamming his sword into the demon's breast. The sword slid out covered in the same putrid brown sludge. Still, the demon did not die. It attacked with jaws open wide, closing on air as he skirted out of the way.

The demon sprung at him. He shifted to the side and leapt, raising his sword high over his head with both hands. He slashed down, hard and fast, blade whistling through the air. Skull split from spine, and the demon's severed head dropped to the ground.

It was dead.

So was her mother.

The man wiped his sword on the grass and returned it to its sheath. He rubbed his face with one hand. "Are you hurt?" he asked.

"My foot . . . It's sprained, I think. I fell, before." Before the demon. Before her mother had died. She hid her face with her hands and turned her back to him, so he couldn't see her tears.

A hand touched her shoulder. "It gets better."

She whipped around, let him see the angry tears. "Does it really?"

He hesitated. "No. No, it doesn't. It gets . . . easier." His hand fell from her shoulder. "I'm sorry, my lady. I don't have the right words. I'm just a man with a sword."

Sam made a sound that was half sob, half laugh. "I suppose I should thank you." She didn't say, *I wish you'd come earlier.* Instead, she asked, "Who are you?"

He drew himself up and swept an elegant bow. "Paladin Tristan Lyons, First of the Sword."

Sam gasped in spite of herself. "Demon slayer."

"Aye." An unreadable expression crossed his face. "I'm sorry I couldn't save her, too."

What was there to say to that? She couldn't say, *it's okay*—it wasn't. She couldn't blame him either. So Sam said nothing.

They stood in silence for a while, the rain falling in torrents around them. "You're shivering," he said finally. "We should get you home. Can you walk?"

She nodded. "My ankle's not so bad as that. What about my mother's—" She stopped short, unable to finish the sentence. "Will you bring her home, too?"

"Aye, my lady." With a backward glance at her, he walked over to her mother's body, unmoved from the forest floor where Sam had left her. He knelt down and scooped her mother into his arms. Her body hung like a wet rag doll, her head flung back at an unnatural angle, hair trailing in a snarled black curtain.

Bile rose in Sam's throat, and she looked away. That *corpse* wasn't her mother. It was a shell, nothing more.

My mother is dead.

And there was nothing she, Paladin Lyons, or even the Gods could do about it.

Her hands clenched into fists.

She couldn't change the past, but she could change the future.

CHAPTER 1

SAM HELD THE scissors at her neck and closed her eyes.

Snip, snip.

Twisted coils of sable hair fell to the floor of the inn. It's only hair, she told herself, hacking off another lock. Hair grew back. Although if all went as planned, it would be ages before she'd wear long hair again.

Sam turned towards the mirror and winced. The ducal court at Haywood had called Tsalene of Rhea an exotic butterfly, but Sam wasn't pretty and never had been. The only beauty she'd inherited from her mother was a poor imitation of her smile and her glorious mane of hair. The latter now lay on the floor in tangled snarls. Her new ear-length cut, no matter how nicely it curled, did her prominent nose no favors.

Sam removed her chemise, shoving it into her small travel sack of belongings. She snatched up the band of cloth from where she'd laid it down on the straw mattress and wrapped it around her small breasts. The binding was far from comfortable, but it was bearable. She pulled on a pair of tan breeches and a loose-fitting tunic, and then faced the mirror again, doing her best to emulate a man's relaxed posture.

A younger, softer version of the Duke of Haywood stared back at her. The Duke of Ice, they called him now, his heart hardened to stone by his wife's untimely death. Father and daughter shared the same intense yellow-green stare, but hers lacked his frost.

Do you even miss me, Father? She wondered how many days had passed before the duke had even noticed she was gone.

Sam had few regrets about leaving Haywood behind. Since the day of her mother's funeral, her father had been shut off and cold to her. Rather than suffer the sting of her father's indifference or fall into a depression, Sam had used the tragedy of her mother's death to fuel her. What was once a hobby became compulsion. Sam spent every spare hour training. She practiced with a sword on foot, on horseback, against pells and training dummies, and when she could, against people. She learned how to fight with a shield and how to defend herself without one. If she didn't have a blade in hand, she used bell clappers and lifted stones to strengthen her upper body. In the early mornings, she ran, weighted down by a heavy breastplate she'd stolen from the castle armory.

She touched her shorn hair, running her fingers through phantom locks. All of her training had been for this. For a chance to become her own hero.

It was now or never. The Paladins waited for no man.

And certainly for no woman.

After collecting her things, Sam paid the innkeeper and set out towards the northernmost part of Heartwine, the kingdom's capitol. She hadn't the luxury of a horse to call her own, so she traveled by foot, passing through the commercial quarter, where shops were stacked one on top of the other on either side of the street, and then over the footbridge into the Old City.

An ancient church stood at its epicenter, an architectural remnant of the Age of the First Men. Rows of houses spun out from the church like the radials of a spider web. Four-storied homes with timber frames leaned against each other, some leaning out over the streets. Above the tiled roofs of the houses rose the crenellated turrets of the royal palace, and beyond that lurked an enormous fortress. A sprawling structure of stone and brick, the fortress served as headquarters to the Paladins and gave residence to the High Commander himself. The Duke of Haywood had made clear his dislike for the living legend—a point in the High Commander's favor as far as Sam was concerned.

Drawing nearer, Sam could see a long line of boys extending past the latticed iron gates blocking the entrance to the fortress courtyard and well into the street. There must have been hundreds of boys, and it was early yet; there would surely be many more to come.

Quietly, Sam took her place at the end of the line, so anxious she was sick with it. Would anyone believe her charade, or would they see right through her? Every time someone glanced her way, her heart leapt into a gallop. She kept her mouth shut and her eyes on the ground to discourage anyone from talking to her.

The line moved steadily along, and Sam eventually passed through the massive iron gates into the courtyard. Around its perimeter was a two-tiered arcade with marble columns and rounded arches. Apart from a cobblestone circle in the center, the ground was covered with thick well-manicured grass.

A few yards in front of her, a thin, balding man with spectacles perched on the tip of his nose was recording names. A delicate white hand curled around a feather quill. He peered at her over his spectacles. "Name?"

"It's Sam." Her eyes flew wide. Too high, too high! She coughed noisily into her hand and said in lower tones, "Sam of Haywood."

Behind his glasses, his gaze narrowed in an assessing stare. She fidgeted under his scrutiny. "Is there an honorific I should note?" he asked.

She cleared her throat and gave the falsehood she had devised. "Lord Sam of Haywood, second son of Lord Hawkins." There was, of course, no such lord in Haywood. Or if there was, she'd never made his acquaintance.

The man wrote down her name in a looping scrawl. "And your weapon?"

"Weapon?" she repeated, not grasping his meaning.

He waved his quill with an impatient flick. "Your preferred weapon. Knives, bow-and-arrow, sword—"

"Sword. Definitely sword."

"Wonderful," the man said without inflection, scribbling "sword" beside her name. Once finished, he pointed toward the paved circle in the center of the courtyard, where most of the boys had gathered. "Wait over there."

She thanked him and started in that direction. Her steps grew heavier as she approached—by the Gods, she was nervous! Though she'd done nothing but stand in line for hours, and it was a rather brisk morning, sweat encircled her underarms and pooled in the space between her flattened breasts. The dampness of her binding cloth made her skin itch, but she couldn't very well scratch *there*.

She stopped a few feet back from the circle, gathering her courage and sizing up her competition. There were tall boys and short boys—though none as short as she—fat boys and skinny boys, boys in second-hand clothes and boys dressed in expensive fashion. Some, like her, stood alone while others stood in groups, talking and laughing.

"Watch where you stand," a voice said in her ear. Sam whirled around to face a boy around her own age, handsome in a haughty sort of way, with a patrician face, cool, gray eyes, and thin lips arranged in a frown. He wore his black hair in curls to his shoulders, and if those perfect ringlets were Gods-given, then snowflakes were green. "Fenric," he said by way of introduction. "You'll thank me later."

Her forehead creased. "Excuse me?"

"Look at the boy over there," he said, jerking his chin to the left. "You're *staring*. Don't be so obvious about it."

Annoyed by his audacity, she glared at him and then subtly returned her gaze to the same general vicinity.

"With the strange clothes and silver hair," Fenric breathed, his voice just above a whisper.

Once she knew what she was looking for, it was impossible to miss him. The others had given him a wide berth. His hair was long as a woman's, braided in a thick plait to his waist, and the color of spun silver. His clothes, however, long black robes that billowed out in a bell-shape around his ankles, were of a familiar Rhean make. This piqued her interest. Few traveled to Thule from her mother's homeland.

"That boy is no trainee," Fenric said conspiratorially. "He's a demon."

Sam snorted. "Are you addled? A demon? *Here*? In the Paladins' backyard?"

Fenric's face darkened. "I saw him—it—up close. It isn't human."

She stole a glance back at the boy Fenric had branded a demon. From her vantage point, he seemed human enough, though the distance obscured his features. "He doesn't look like a demon," she said, frowning. "And if he were, don't you think the Paladins would have done something?"

"Maybe they're testing us."

"Maybe," Sam said skeptically. She felt a twinge of pity for the silver-haired boy. "I appreciate your warning." She sketched a carefully practiced bow and excused herself from Fenric's presence. She felt his eyes on her as she walked away.

Boys continued to trickle in, filling up the courtyard. It wasn't till the sun was high overhead that the iron gates slammed shut.

A trumpet blared. The quiet rumble of voices swelled in volume and then subsided into a hush.

Long rows of men marched out beneath the soaring archways of the arcade, their strides in perfect rhythm. They wore red surcoats over their armor, the sigil of the Paladins—a golden hexagram surrounded by a perfect circle—emblazoned on their chests. The same sigil was carved into the pommels of their swords.

Sam let out a small gasp at the sight of them: Paladins in full formal attire.

They were magnificent to behold as they strode into the courtyard, the crimson tails of their surcoats streaming behind them. Among the boys, the rumbling started up again, a subtle crescendo.

The Paladins drew to a halt, and a tall man in the front row raised his hand for silence. Silence fell.

The paladin who had raised his hand stepped forward. Apart from his uncommon height, his appearance was unremarkable. He had a plain, forgettable face, the kind that people tended to skim over in a crowd. His hair was not quite blond, and not quite brown, his mouth was neither thin nor full, and his nose was straight and without character. His skin was lightly lined, like that of a middle-aged man who had aged well, or a younger man who had lived a life of labor.

Behind Sam, someone whispered in awed reverence, "Faith in blood, that's the High Commander."

Sam blinked back her surprise. That ordinary, unassuming man was the leader of the Paladins? She had imagined him to be bigger, broader, brighter, with the sort of towering presence expected of a hero. She'd imagined someone like Tristan Lyons. This man was so *normal*.

But then he spoke, and she was mesmerized. The bell of his tenor would make the Gods themselves weep.

"Welcome, new trainees," he said. He did not speak loudly but his voice still carried across the courtyard. "Welcome to the Paladins."

She sucked in air, reeling.

A small, amused smile played across his lips, as though he knew the effect of his voice. "The Paladins have defended Thule since the Age of the First Men. We are the thorn in Teivel's side, the bringers of hope to our people. There is no nobler duty, no greater honor, than to serve." His smile deepened. "But you know that already or you wouldn't be here."

Nervous laughter met his words. The smile slipped off his face, and the laughter died with it. "We are the best and bravest fighters in Thule. We come from all walks of life, but to the last man, we are warriors. Here, it is our mettle in battle that determines our worth. We live and die by the blade."

His gaze swept over them. "Not all of you can become paladins. Not all of you are fit to serve. It is not enough to be good. It is not enough to be great. Only the best men will be invited to join our ranks. You will have one year to prove your worth. That you are a worthy addition to our ranks. That you are worthy of the title, Paladin."

He gestured towards the iron gates at the entrance to the courtyard. "When you stepped through these gates, you made a commitment to Thule, and to the Gods themselves, to abide by our laws and to protect Thule's people." His lips twitched again into that small, amused smile. "But the Paladins are not without mercy. Leave now and you are free to go. Your commitment is forgotten."

Nobody moved.

The High Commander clapped his hands together. "Very well, then. Lord Astley, if you please."

The bald bespectacled man who had recorded her name scurried across the courtyard, a long roll of parchment paper in hand.

"Today, you become students in the art of war," the High

Commander said. "You will each be assigned to serve and train under a paladin mentor."

Sam swallowed a lump of nerves. Suddenly her clothes felt too tight.

"Lord Astley will call out your name and the name of your paladin," said the High Commander. He nodded at the small man. "You may begin."

Lord Astley cleared his throat. "Owain of Jigodin!" He looked down at his roll of parchment. "Paladin Johann Kemp!"

A tall boy with floppy brown hair that covered his eyebrows stumbled towards Lord Astley and the High Commander. One of the paladins stepped out of formation, grinned, and then slung an arm around the boy's shoulders.

"Fenric of Icetower!" Lord Astley continued. "Paladin Alan Savage!" She watched as Fenric went to meet his paladin, a man of swarthy complexion and flowing blue-black hair.

The names droned on for so long that Sam only listened with half an ear. Her mind began to wander, and some of the tension drained from her body.

"Sam of Haywood!" Lord Astley cried out. She jerked to attention.

Lord Astley's finger trailed along his parchment, searching for the corresponding name. "Paladin Tristan Lyons!" he shouted.

Her heart froze in her chest. Surely this was some sort of cosmic joke. The Gods wouldn't be so cruel.

Like a condemned criminal walking to the gallows, Sam made her way toward her new mentor.

There he stood, a ghost from her past. He had grown into himself in the two years since she'd last seen him. His face was harder and his golden hair cropped shorter, and he was more handsome than she remembered. His cobalt eyes met hers, widening before going cold and flat. Her belly tightened with nausea.

Paladin Tristan Lyons. The man who'd saved her and the reason she was here.

He would ruin everything.

CHAPTER 2

TRISTAN LYONS COULDN'T believe his bad luck. For years, he'd looked forward to the day he'd foster his first trainee. The lad would be cut from the same cloth as Tristan—accomplished at weaponry, incomparably strong, a mite more handsome than was good for him—and they would be as brothers. They would fight together, break bread together, whore together . . .

Instead, the Gods had seen fit to give him Sam of Haywood. Hadn't they had enough laughs at his expense?

A steady hum of conversation filled the fortress courtyard as trainees and paladins were introduced and began chatting. Tristan gritted his teeth. He would *not* be jealous.

The boy hadn't said a word since Lord Astley, the High Commander's sniveling worm of a secretary, had announced their pairing. At the sound of Tristan's name, his new trainee had gone white as a ghost and dropped half his belongings. What a sad, scrawny excuse for a boy. Sam of Haywood had no business being here.

When Tristan could take the strained silence no longer, he said, "Speak up, boy. Surely you have questions for me."

Sam bowed his head and gave it a slight shake.

Tristan fought back a growl. He needed a young man for a trainee, not a milksop. "Use words, boy, if you have them."

"Sam."

He stilled. "I beg your pardon?"

Something flashed in those yellow-green eyes. "My name is Sam, Paladin. Not *boy*."

So Sam of Haywood was not entirely without spirit. Good. In a stern voice, he said, "I'll call you whatever I please, *trainee*."

Sam tucked his head into his chest and nodded. He clasped his hands in front of him, the knuckles gone white.

Attempting kindness, Tristan said, "It's not too late, you know. You can still go home. A paladin's life isn't easy. No one here would judge you for it."

Sam unclasped his hands and jutted out his chin. There was something familiar about the boy's face, but Tristan couldn't place it. "I'm where I'm meant to be," Sam said simply.

Tristan looked at the undersized trainee with an ounce more respect. "So be it," he said. He offered his hand. "Paladin Tristan Lyons."

Sam stared at his extended hand like it was a dead fish. After a moment's hesitation, he clasped it with his own. The boy's hand, Tristan noted, was as callused as his, and his grip was firm. Perhaps there was hope for him yet. "Honored to serve, Paladin Lyons," Sam said softly.

"Tristan," he said without thinking.

Spots of color bloomed beneath Sam's cheeks.

"We're going to be spending a lot of time together, you and me," he explained, feeling awkward. "No reason to stand on ceremony."

"Okay, Tristan," Sam practically whispered.

Tristan pinched the bridge of his nose. One instant the boy showed glimpses of courage, and the next he was a scared rabbit. He'd need to toughen up if he had any hope of surviving past his first month. Forget about demons—his fellow trainees would eat him alive.

"Let's lay down the ground rules," Tristan said gruffly. "While we lodge in the capitol, I expect you to earn your keep. Breakfast is at dawn. Sleep through it if you want, but food won't be served again till midday. You'll do weapons training with the other train-ees straight after breakfast. Sleep through that and you'll answer to me." He paused to give Sam his best menacing glare. The boy looked suitably cowed. "Come, I'll show you to the armory."

Those yellow-green eyes gleamed with interest. "Will I get my own sword?"

Tristan chuckled in spite of himself. He remembered how eager he'd been as a trainee to get his hands on a real Paladin weapon. Gods, that seemed ages ago now. "That depends. Are you any good with one?"

Sam drew his shoulders back, scowling. "I'm good enough."

Surprise and then anger shot through him at his trainee's insolence. Sam had a sharp tongue, he'd give him that, but words were worthless in the heat of battle. "You heard the High Commander. 'Good enough' is never good enough here. You have to be the best."

His trainee flushed a deep red and looked down at his feet. When he looked up again, his jaw was set. "Who is the best?"

"What?"

"Who is the best?" Sam repeated. "You said I have to be the best. I'd like to know who currently holds that title."

"Me." Tristan shrugged. He wasn't boasting; it was plain truth. "I've never lost a duel, and I've slain more demons than men twice my age."

"Perfect," Sam said. "Then I'll just defeat you."

Tristan couldn't help himself. He burst into laughter. It wasn't a polite, mannerly chuckle either; he laughed long and loud, clutching at his belly.

"I don't see what's so funny," his trainee said stiffly.

Still chuckling, he answered, "You're mad. I'm First of the Sword. Do you know what that means? There are over ten thousand paladins in Thule, boy, and *not a one of them can beat me.* And you think *you* will be the first?"

Sam regarded him as though he were daft. "Well, not *today*. We've only just begun training."

Tristan guffawed. "I like that," he said once he managed to stop laughing. "We'd better get started, then, hadn't we?" He clapped Sam on the shoulder and pretended not to notice that the boy flinched.

"Pardon the interruption, Paladin Lyons," Lord Astley said, appearing behind Sam. "The High Commander wishes to speak with you."

Tristan glanced back and forth between the secretary and his trainee. Sam's face had paled again. "Now? Can it wait?"

Lord Astley peered at him over his spectacles. "No, Paladin, it cannot. He's waiting for you in his office."

He sighed. So much for getting started. "Lead the way, Astley." He motioned for Sam to follow him.

The High Commander's office was buried deep in the heart of the fortress. They traipsed up and down narrow stairways and rounded winding corridors. Daylight crept in through cross-like slits throughout the stone wall, illuminating their path. Tristan had walked these halls countless times and for him they no longer held surprises. Sam's eyes seemed as though they might explode from his head.

At the arched double doors marking the entrance to the office, they stopped. "You go on ahead," Lord Astley said. "I'll wait here with Haywood."

Tristan nodded his thanks and lifted the heavy brass knocker on the left door. Both doors drew open before he could let it thud.

"Paladin Lyons," came the High Commander's musical voice. "Tristan, my boy. Have a seat."

The High Commander reclined in a high-backed chair behind a large, angled desk. He was as self-possessed as ever, one leg draped over the other, thumbing through a stack of official looking papers.

Tristan ducked his head in acknowledgement and sat himself in the nearest chair. Most men were intimidated by the High Commander—and rightfully so, for he rivaled the king in power—but Tristan had spent more time in his company than almost any other living paladin. The leader of the Paladins was an intensely private man, and even Tristan, who knew him better than most, would never call him a close companion. But he'd trust him—and he had, many times—with his life.

"You're displeased with your new trainee," the High Commander said, still leafing through his papers.

"I never said that."

The High Commander glanced up, his mouth settling into a small smile. "You didn't have to. I've known you since you were a boy. I know how you think."

He wished he could say the same. "Sam of Haywood is . . . not what I'd expected," he said neutrally.

"You were hoping for someone like Danny."

Tristan winced, amazed that after all these years, the sound of his brother's name still pained him. "I was hoping for a trainee with a little more promise."

The High Commander waved his hand. "Sam is from Haywood, Tristan. There hasn't been a trainee from Haywood in more than a hundred years."

Tristan groaned. The long enmity between the High Commander and the Duke of Haywood was legendary. "I've already agreed to help you win an alliance with the duke."

A vague look of discomfort crossed the High Commander's face. "Circumstances may have changed."

Tristan leapt up onto his feet. "What do you mean, circumstances may have changed? We signed the agreement!"

The High Commander made a calming gesture. "Sit down, Tristan. The Duke of Haywood isn't what I brought you here to discuss."

He fought to keep his temper in check. Tristan was allowed some liberties with the High Commander, but there were limits. No one could sway the High Commander from his agenda.

Tristan bent in a stiff bow and reclaimed his seat. "What do you wish to discuss, High Commander?"

The High Commander's lips curved up for the briefest of moments, and then his pallid face grew grim. "Dark tidings and rumors from the West, my boy. If they are to be believed, another Age of Shadows may soon be upon us."

Tristan straightened in his chair. The Age of Shadows was the blackest time in Thule's history, a time when demons freely roamed the earth and men lived without law and order. It was said that ages come in cycles, but the Age of Shadows was one the world hoped never to repeat. "What have you heard?"

"Some truth, some lies, some in-between. Much of what the Sub Rosa has uncovered isn't concrete."

Tristan wrinkled his nose at the mention of the *Sub Rosa*, the Paladins' secret network of spies. They weren't bound to the same ethical standards as the rest of the Paladins, and he judged them for it. Freed from their vows once they became Sub Rosa, they let nothing get in the way of valuable information. Not even common decency.

"But the crux of it is this," the High Commander said, ignoring

Tristan's unspoken disapproval. "There are those who would see the end of us."

"The end of the Paladins? Why would anyone want to leave Thule defenseless?"

The High Commander chuckled musically. "You are such a simple man."

Tristan bristled, struggling to hide his offense.

"I don't mean that as an insult. It's what I've always liked about you. You are the best of us, Tristan, and not only because you're handy with a sword."

"What about you?" he blurted.

The High Commander's expression turned carefully blank. "I am what I have to be, for all our sakes."

They were the most honest words the High Commander had ever spoken to him. Tristan wasn't sure what to make of them. He pushed on. "You didn't answer my question. Why would anyone want to rid Thule of the Paladins?"

"Power," the High Commander said. "The easiest way to rule is through fear."

"That makes no sense. No one can control the demons. All we can do is watch and protect." Tristan shook his head. "Get rid of us, and Thule will descend into chaos."

The High Commander raised an eyebrow. "Leaving the opportunity for a new hero to rise and become Thule's savior."

"Thousands would die."

"Aye."

Tristan thought this over. When he'd spoken his vows, he'd sworn to fight demons, not men. He had no real interest in politics or power games, nor did he understand them. If he'd carved out a leadership position for himself among the Paladins, it was only because he fought well and hard and because he was naturally charismatic. People liked Tristan. They always had.

"Why are you telling me this?" he asked finally. "What do you want from me?"

The High Commander leaned back in his chair, folding his hands in his lap. "I want you to find them. The Uriel, they call themselves."

"And do what, once I've found these Uriel?"

"Nothing," the High Commander said. "We learn who they are and what they want and why."

"What about the Sub Rosa? Why me and not them?"

"Because I trust you, Tristan, and I can't trust them. I will not rest the fate of the Paladins in the hands of vow-less men." The High Commander's gaze roved over him. "And because when you first meet with the enemy, you always put forward your best man."

He should have been flattered. He was honored, truly . . . but . . . what the High Commander asked of him was unlike anything he'd ever done before. Faith in blood, all he wanted to do was kill demons! He had no interest in becoming entangled in men's affairs, nor any practice at it.

Tristan closed his eyes. "When do I leave?"

The High Commander smiled. "Soon, my boy. Not yet, but soon."

CHAPTER 3

SAM TRIED TO not let her anxiety show. Lord Astley was watching her like a hawk, making her all the more nervous. What secrets was the High Commander telling Tristan behind those enormous double doors? Had he somehow found out who she really was? Was he saying now to Tristan that his trainee was in reality a girl? And not just any ordinary girl—the daughter of His Grace, the seventeenth Duke of Haywood.

She still couldn't believe Tristan hadn't recognized her. Her riotous curls were gone and her slight curves were hidden, but she didn't think she looked *that* different. Maybe he didn't remember her. How funny it would be if the pivotal moment of her life hadn't warranted the faintest of his memories. Then again, Tristan probably had saved hundreds of lives—why should he remember hers?

What would he do if he *did* discover her true identity? Would he remember her then?

One side of the double doors swung open, and Tristan stepped out. Sam sucked in a harsh breath. Tristan's jaw was tightly clenched and his entire expression tense. He stood with rigid posture, staring at her but not seeing her. The vivid blue of his eyes had clouded over.

Her anxiety spiraled into full-blown panic. He knows. He has to know. "Tristan," she whispered. "I can explain."

His eyes cleared. "Explain what?" he asked, brow furrowing.

Praise the Gods above, he didn't know. As usual, she'd jumped to conclusions. Idiot, she scolded herself.

Fortunately, Sam didn't have to come up with a response because Lord Astley began clearing his throat.

"What is it, Astley?" Tristan asked, pinching the bridge of his nose.

"Did the High Commander explain to you about your trainee?"

Oh no. Sam squeezed her eyes shut. So they had found her out after all. How? She'd been so careful. She hadn't told a soul in Haywood where she was going or what she had planned.

Tristan regarded Lord Astley, then her, with suspicion. "He said nothing of note."

"Typical," the secretary said, lifting his nose and sniffing loudly. "You've been assigned another trainee."

"What!" Sam and Tristan exclaimed in unison.

"Do you mean to say there's been a mistake?" Tristan added, a touch too eagerly. Sam shot him a mutinous glare.

"You've misinterpreted me, Paladin Lyons. You've been assigned another trainee *in addition* to young Haywood, here."

Sam let out her breath in a whoosh of air. She wasn't going anywhere.

"But that's just not done," Tristan said. "It's always been one paladin and one trainee."

"Not anymore," Lord Astley said, unswayed. "Congratulations on starting a new tradition, Paladin."

"But why?"

The secretary thrust out his chest and squared his narrow shoulders. "High Commander's orders." He wilted under Tristan's unrelenting stare, dabbing at his forehead with his sleeve. "If you must know, one of the Paladins refused to accept his assigned trainee."

Tristan's mouth fell open. "We can *do* that?" Tristan asked. Sam scowled at him. She suspected he would toss her over if given half the chance, but he didn't have to be *so* obvious about it.

"No, you cannot," Lord Astley said with displeasure. "As was explained to Paladin Moreau in detail. He has since been discharged and his title has been revoked."

"Faith in blood," Tristan swore. "Who is this boy, Moreau's sworn enemy?"

The secretary coughed into his hand. "The boy is . . . unusual. But I assure you he is safe."

Tristan's eyebrows disappeared into his hairline. "Safe?"

"I'll bring him to you," Lord Astley said. "Unless, that is, you object?"

Tristan held up his hands. "I'm not Moreau."

"Glad you see it that way," Lord Astley said. He then turned and called out down the corridor, "Braeden, come here, lad."

There was a moment's pause, and then a tall, lithe figure stepped out of the shadows. Long black robes swirled in circles around his feet as he moved towards them. He kept his head bowed, hiding his face. Shocks of straight silver hair escaped from the confines of a topknot.

Sam's eyes widened in recognition. Only one trainee had hair that shade.

"Raise your head, boy," Tristan said. The boy hesitated, then slowly did as he was bade.

Sam's breath hitched. The boy's face was ordinary—hand-some, even—the healthy ochre of his skin stretching over high cheekbones and a square jaw. But his eyes . . . Slit pupils slashed through luminous crimson irises that swallowed most of the whites of his almond-shaped eyes. In the infinitesimal seconds that he blinked, he could pass for human. When his eyes were open, however, his gaze would draw a thousand questions.

Tristan started with the simplest one: "What are you?"

The boy met Tristan's stare. "My mother was a human, Paladin." The right side of his mouth quirked up. "Clearly my father was not."

Curiosity gave Sam the courage to speak. "What—what was he?"

An unholy smile split his face, more snarl than grin. "Daddy dearest was a demon."

She gasped. So Fenric had been right—or half right, anyway. Since when did demons procreate with humans? A half man, half demon was the stuff of legend.

Tristan, too, seemed startled by this revelation. "How is that even possible?"

He raised a single silver brow. "The usual way, I'd imagine." Sam snorted at the indelicate reply, and then her cheeks went red.

Tristan glared at the both of them. "You know what I mean, boy."

Braeden shrugged. "My mother's dead, or I'd have asked her myself."

Tristan seemed to struggle with himself; when he spoke again, his voice was strangled. "Are you *sure* you've got demon blood?"

The trainee laughed darkly. "I'm sure. I can prove it to you if my eyes aren't evidence enough."

"That's plenty, Braeden," Lord Astley said, his voice filled with warning.

Tristan frowned at the secretary. "I can take it from here, Astley. Leave us."

The secretary opened his mouth as though he were going to say something else, then changed his mind. He adjusted his spectacles so that they perched low on his nose and gave all three of them a stern look before scurrying away.

Tristan didn't speak again till Lord Astley was out of sight. "Braeden, is it?"

"Aye."

Tristan gave him a long once-over. "Do you want to be a paladin, Braeden?"

The half-demon's upper lip curled into a faint sneer. "Why else would I be here?"

"You tell me."

Braeden pushed his shoulders back, straightening to his full height. He was taller than Tristan by nearly half a head, though not as solid. "I bear no love for my demon father. I want to see every demon dead."

Sam shivered at the cold intensity in his words. He simmered with repressed violence, just beneath the surface; she could sense it. She took a few steps back, increasing the distance between them.

"Now let's get a few things straight," Tristan said, unaffected. "As long as the two of you are my trainees, you will treat me with the utmost respect. You are to obey my orders as if they came straight from the High Commander himself. Do we understand each other?"

Sam caught herself trading glances with the half-demon. Together, they nodded.

"Good."

That evening, after Sam and Braeden had been given a tour of the Paladins' extensive grounds and equipped with weaponry and armor, Tristan brought them to the central keep of the fortress, where they were to dine and sleep. They passed through the antechamber and into the great hall, a room large enough to fit a thousand men comfortably. Curved braces and beams of oak supported a high ceiling, and lush plum-colored carpeting covered much of the tiled floor. Archaic weaponry hung on the stone walls next to stained-glass windows, and mounted beside them were demon heads. Sam couldn't tell if they were real or statues. Either way, the effect was intimidating.

The first floor of the keep was near to full of people, paladins in their formal red jackets and gawping trainees in plain clothes. As they made their way toward the wide stone staircase at the back of the great hall, Sam felt the weight of stares coming from every direction. But she wasn't so paranoid to think she was their target. Nobody would wonder about the small too-pretty boy when there was a half-demon in their midst. And for that, she was obliged to him.

Tristan led Sam and Braeden up the stairs and through a maze of twisting hallways. "You two will be sharing this room," he said, pushing open a door at the end of the corridor. Sam glanced uneasily at Braeden. She had been hoping for her own private sleeping chambers; sharing a room would certainly complicate matters. It was going to be damned hard to maintain her charade day and night.

To Sam's relief, the room was outfitted with a separate bathroom and one of those newfangled flush privies. Using a chamber pot while a boy was in the room would jeopardize her identity, for obvious reasons. There were two beds—not featherbeds, but nicer than she'd slept in since she'd left Haywood—with enough distance between them to give a semblance of privacy.

"I'll be sleeping in the adjoining room," Tristan said, letting himself out through a door in the left wall. "I'll see you at training after breakfast. Don't be late."

Sam and Braeden sat on the edge of their respective beds, an awkward silence stretching between them. Braeden just looked at her with those eerie, inhuman eyes. She fought back a shudder.

"My eyes bother you, do they?"

"N-no," Sam stuttered, startled by the question. "Was I staring?"

"You were."

Sam winced at his bluntness. "Sorry, I didn't mean anything by it."

He turned his face away from hers. "It's okay. I'm used to it."

Sam wasn't sure what to say next, but decided on a version of the truth. "I haven't spent much time around boys my own age. You'll have to forgive any—" She paused, trying to find the right words. "—social inadequacies."

He laughed outright at that. "Said the human to the demon."

She recoiled, and he saw it. "Half," he said with a wry twist of his mouth. "I'm only half a monster."

She would *not* feel guilty. "My mother was killed by a demon," she burst out.

"So was mine."

She hadn't expected that, nor the pang of empathy that followed. "How . . . how did she die?"

His features knit into a dark expression. "She died giving birth to me."

Sam marveled at the self-loathing in his strange eyes. No one could possibly hate him as much as he hated himself. "I'm sorry," she said, for lack of ought else to say.

"Aye," said Braeden. "So am I, though not much good it does me." And with that, he abruptly stood up from his bed and headed into the privy.

Sam slid back onto her mattress, trying to sort through her chaotic thoughts. When her mother died, Sam had sworn she'd hunt down every demon, and Braeden had made no bones about what he was. But she was beginning to think she would be wrong to fixate on his demon half.

Shouldn't it matter that half of him was human?

Sam was awoken by the grumble of her stomach. "Is it breakfast yet?" she mumbled, but Braeden was already gone. She didn't mind that he had left without her; this way she could redo her binding and throw on fresh clothes without hiding in the privy.

Rubbing the sleep from her eyes, Sam dragged herself down to the great hall on the first floor of the fortress. Long tables with benches ran the length of the room. Before she could decide where to sit, she bumped into a familiar face. Fenric's hair hung in those same, too-perfect curls, his nose turned up as though he smelled something offensive.

"I saved you a seat," he said, and she had no choice but to join his table.

"I never properly introduced myself," Fenric said haughtily once they both were seated. "Lord Fenric Vane of Icetower. My father is Paladin Andrel Vane."

Sam digested this new piece of information. Andrel Vane was one of the most famous paladins of his generation. Fenric was Paladin royalty. "Sam of Haywood," she offered in return.

"You're rooming with *it*, aren't you?"

It took her a moment to process what, or rather, *who* he meant. "*His* name is Braeden," she found herself saying.

Fenric sneered at her. "Let's call him what he is. A demon."

Half a demon, she almost said, but instinctively held back. Fenric didn't seem the type to see things in halves. Her gaze wandered the hall, and she spotted Braeden, eating alone. She felt a stab of guilt.

She didn't have much time to feel guilty before the trainees were called out into the courtyard. Sam shoveled the last of her breakfast into her mouth and hurried after them.

Paladin Alan Savage—Fenric's mentor—waited for them outside. He was a fierce-looking man, tall and darkly handsome in spite of the deep scars running across his cheeks. With his long blue-black hair and pointed beard, he reminded Sam of a sea pirate—not that she'd ever met one.

Once all the trainees had gathered, he turned towards the front of the courtyard, indicating for them to follow him. By the iron gates, ten spherical gray stones were lined up on the grass in increasing size order. The tenth, largest stone was so large it was more boulder than stone.

Paladin Savage surveyed the trainees with a cool, dispassionate gaze. "Hmph," he said by way of greeting. "Lucky for you lot, today will be a test of brawn and not brains. The stone carry is one of our most ancient training methods, and one of the best. For those of you who have never tried your strength at the stone carry, it should be easy enough to understand. Nevertheless, I will demonstrate. All you have to do is pick up the stone"—Paladin Savage straddled his feet on either side of the smallest stone and squatted down, hugging his arms around its center and hoisting it high onto his chest—"and carry it to where Paladin Rendon is standing."

An older paladin with twinkling blue eyes and a twirling white mustache stood a hundred paces back. He gave them a jaunty wave.

"Then bring it back and set it down, like so." Paladin Savage dropped the stone with a thud. "Then you move on to the next stone, and the next stone after that, till it becomes too heavy." He looked around. "Any questions?"

Sam had known that joining the Paladins would push her strength to its limits. Thanks to regular weight training, she was exceptionally strong for a woman, and stronger than a lot of men. But in a contest of pure might against a man who trained as hard as she did, she'd lose. And she couldn't help notice she was the smallest among the trainees; the next shortest boy stood half a head taller. She hoped she didn't embarrass herself—or worse, give herself away.

The trainees queued up in a long line that wrapped around the courtyard. Sam waited towards the very back. Going near the end would give her an idea of what she needed to strive for. She couldn't afford to be the worst.

The first trainee to attempt the stone carry was a mountain of a boy with broad shoulders that belonged on a blacksmith. To no one's surprise, he lifted the first eight stones with nary a problem. The ninth proved a challenge—he nearly dropped it by Paladin Rendon—and the tenth refused to budge.

A fair number of boys were unable to lift the eighth and ninth stones, and some of the smaller boys failed on the seventh. A very few boys failed before that, but between Paladin Savage's harsh ridicule and the rest of the trainees' mockery, Sam decided right then and there she *had* to pick up the seventh stone. She didn't need any more reasons to make herself a target.

Finally, her turn arrived. She crossed over to the first, lightest stone. Behind her, she could hear snickering. Words like *scrawny* and *half-pint* were being bandied about, but *girl* was the only jab that affected her. She took a calming breath, reminding herself they didn't *actually* think she was a girl. They were just insulting her.

Sam shuffled her feet forward till the first stone rested between her ankles. Squatting till she was nearly parallel, she grasped the rock with straight arms and pulled it to chest height.

Hmph. It wasn't *that* heavy. Walking to Paladin Rendon and back took her no time at all.

But, as she soon discovered, there were significant jumps in weight between stones. I might fail, she realized as she stumbled the last few paces with the fifth stone.

She had to use her legs and back to get the sixth stone up, bringing it first into her lap, then driving her hips to kick it up above her abdomen. With slow, agonizing steps, she trudged over to Paladin Rendon and returned. Gods, that had been painful, and she had to do it all over again with a heavier stone.

Heart still thumping from her last effort, Sam got behind the seventh stone, settled into position and pulled.

It didn't move. Not an inch.

She didn't let go—to let go would be quitting—and shifted her weight onto her heels. She arched her back and tugged on the stone, to no avail.

"Give up!" someone shouted.

No. Gritting her teeth, Sam clamped her ankles and forearms around the stone and squeezed with everything she had. As she straightened, the stone inched off the ground. She pinched her legs together and re-bent her knees, forming a shelf. Taking a moment to center herself, she adjusted her grip and then pulled back explosively.

It was up.

She staggered forward, first with her right foot, then with her left. Her entire body screamed at her to stop, to quit, to let go of the weight. She pushed on, moving so slowly she was hardly moving at all.

It might have taken her an unreasonably long time, but her grip was sure and her feet kept plodding, and eventually, she made it. She dropped the stone with a sigh of relief and returned to her place in line.

Braeden was the last to go. Every trainee had been heckled during their turn, but the insults hurled at him went far beyond good-natured ribbing. Braeden, however, didn't so much as acknowledge their presence. Sam supposed whispers of *demon* and *monster* followed him everywhere. He was probably used to it.

He lifted the first stone as though it were no heavier than a pebble, hefting it up onto his shoulder and holding it in place with one hand. Only when he got to the ninth stone did he resort to using both arms, and even then, he made it look easy.

By the Gods, thought Sam, he's going to get the tenth stone.

The courtyard was silent as Braeden crouched behind the boulder of a stone that had foiled all of them. When he wrapped his arms around its girth, his hands didn't meet. He rocked back on his heels and then shot up, the stone tucked under his chin. Without any obvious effort, he completed the two hundred paces to Paladin Rendon and back.

"Demon," a voice hissed into the quiet. No one else said anything.

He should have stopped at the ninth, Sam thought, or at least feigned some difficulty on the tenth. The other boys didn't need any more reason to hate him, and from the sour look on his face, Paladin Savage was no warmer to the idea of a half-demon in their midst than the trainees.

Then again, were she in his shoes, would she not have done the same?

After the early morning's strength training, the trainees were separated into smaller groups. Sam and two dozen others went with Tristan, while Braeden stayed with Paladin Savage. Though she and Tristan hadn't exactly clicked, she didn't envy Braeden.

Tristan brought Sam's group to the inner ward of the fortress, a flat, grassy enclosure surrounded by four curtain walls. "All right, lads, line up," he ordered. The trainees shuffled till they stood in a single line, shoulder-to-shoulder. "Good, good," he said, taking their measure. "You lads look like a sturdy lot—" he paused, his gaze honing in on Sam "—for the most part."

Her hands clenched into fists. So much for the benevolent hero from her memories. This Paladin Lyons was a real louse.

He continued, "Now, today's just a warm up, boys, before the real work begins. I want to see what you've got. Grab a practice blade from over there"—Tristan pointed to a barrel full of wooden swords—"and find a partner."

There was an odd number of trainees, and to no one's surprise, including her own, it was Sam who was left without a partner. She'd expected as much: by a woman's standards, her arms were full and muscular, but next to Tristan and the other trainees, she looked pathetic and scrawny. There was no honor in fighting a weakling like her.

So what if they thought her weak? She'd proven herself at the stone carry and she'd prove herself again with a sword.

Tristan looked heavenwards and sighed. "I suppose there's no hope for it then." He tapped her on the shoulder with the flat of his sword. "Hello, partner."

Sam felt a grin tug at her lips; that he deigned to spar with her was a victory in and of itself. What better opportunity to prove herself than to best the Paladins' finest swordsman? But she hid her excitement, inclining her head in an almost-bow. "You honor me."

Tristan didn't seem impressed by her humble act. "Drop the practice sword, Sam."

What, had he already changed his mind? Her face fell. "Excuse me?"

"Drop the sword. When you practice with me, I want you to use a real blade."

Her mouth dropped open. "I get to use a real Paladin's sword?"

Tristan rolled his eyes. "For now," he said. "Take this." He unstrapped a sheathed sword from his hip and tossed it to her.

Sam tugged the sword free from its sheath. Up close, the weapon was even more spectacular than she'd imagined. The silver of the steel gleamed in the sun as she twisted it this way and that, and she ran her fingers along the Paladins' sigil, deeply etched into the pommel. It was the finest sword she'd ever had the privilege to hold.

"Are you *crying*?" asked Tristan, his expression aghast.

"N-no!" she sputtered, her cheeks reddening. She was a little overwrought, that was all.

Tristan pinched the bridge of his nose and let out a heavy sigh. "All right, Sam, let's get this over with. First to draw blood wins. Try not to embarrass yourself."

"I will, if you do the same," she shot back, before she could think better of it.

Tristan's mouth twisted. "Don't talk that way to your betters, boy."

A loud snort escaped her nose. She clamped her hands over her face, but it was too late. Tristan had clearly heard her.

Tristan made a strangled noise. "I'll tell you what," he said, after he'd calmed down enough to speak. "You win, and I'll let you keep that sword. If I win, you take a vow of silence for the rest of the day."

Sam had her own fair share of arrogance, but she wasn't fool enough to believe her swordsmanship equal to that of a paladin. Not yet, anyway. And yet she found herself saying, "It's a deal." She could hold her tongue if she needed to.

"Do I have your word on that?" he asked after a short pause.

Sam placed her hand over her heart.

Tristan slid his own sword free from its scabbard. "On my mark." He lifted his blade with a single-handed grip and gave her a definitive nod.

They'd begun.

Sam watched him warily. She'd have to attack first; if she had any hope of winning she'd have to rely on the element of surprise.

She lunged forward . . . and promptly tripped.

His free hand shot out to steady her. "Are you all right?" he asked. His voice was full of concern, but his dancing blue eyes betrayed his amusement.

Her skin heated with embarrassment. "I'm fine." Gathering the remnants of her pride, she straightened and plucked his hand from her elbow. She backed up a fair distance, and then she raised the hilt of her sword to her temple, her thumb curved under the blade. *Ready*, she signaled with a jerk of her head.

"This is pointless," Tristan muttered, but he readjusted his feet and weapon into a proper stance.

Careful not to trip over her own feet a second time, Sam crept forward in small stutter steps. As soon as she was within range, she lashed out with her sword, aiming for Tristan's shoulder. His blade met hers before she could see him move his arm. The force of his parry shook her hand to elbow, but she didn't lose her grip.

She struck again, harder this time. He deflected her swing effortlessly, as though she were attacking with a willow switch.

Damn it. She'd put her full weight into that blow.

Sam shuffled back, raising her weapon high above her head, the cross-guard cocked toward one ear. With a shout, Sam rotated the sword down with all her strength, hoping to throw Tristan off balance. Steel clanged against steel, but to her it felt like beating a stick against a stone wall.

Not one to give up, Sam swung at Tristan with a vicious chop. She tried every posture, every technique, every trick she'd learned: she thrust, she struck, she doubled, she feinted. She thwacked at his sword till the front of her shirt was soaked with sweat and she was panting for breath.

Tristan appeared to be unfazed. Bored, even.

Bastard.

"Stop smirking and attack already!" she snapped. That his skill so significantly outclassed hers rankled, but his patronizing behavior irritated her more.

Tristan made a great show of sighing. "I am yours to command," he said with mocking deference.

His hand tightened around the grip of his sword and he shifted his weight onto the balls of his feet.

It was over before she could blink.

Dumbfounded, she stared at her empty hands. Her precious sword lay in the grass, well out of reach. Tristan had disarmed her with a single stroke.

Gods, how mortifying.

"You lost," he said bluntly. A nicer man would have commended her for her efforts, but whatever Tristan's virtues, *nice* wasn't one of them.

That suited Sam just fine. Not only had he disarmed her, he'd done her pride serious injury. False platitudes would have been salt in the wound.

It wasn't that she had believed she could win, but she had thought she could fare better. She'd expected to put Tristan on the defensive once or twice, to make him work to earn his victory. She'd wanted to show him she was more than just some ninnyhammered noble who'd joined the Paladins on a lark. She'd wanted to impress him.

Instead, he probably thought she was a fool. And maybe she *was* a fool. Who was she, Lady Samantha of Haywood, to think she was worthy of the Paladins?

"You know," Tristan said, intruding on her self-pity, "your technique isn't half bad."

The compliment was just backhanded enough to ring true. "It's not?"

"Aye, your form is decent, if basic. Where you fall short is strength and speed. You have no power behind your sword, though I suppose for your size you have more than most." He clapped her on the shoulder, offering her a faint smile. "Well fought, Haywood."

You could have knocked her over with a feather. "Th—thank you," she said, thoroughly confused. "What about our bet?"

"Oh, aye, that's right," Tristan said, as though he'd forgotten all about it. "Best find yourself some parchment and a quill."

Her shoulders sagged. Whoever said the pen was mightier than the sword had never met Tristan.

CHAPTER 4

BRAEDEN PINNED THE dragonfly to the ground with his dagger and watched with mild interest as it struggled against the thin blade. The dragonfly had only three wings, two on its right side and one on its left. He felt little sympathy for the three-winged anomaly; its four-winged brethren would never have found themselves in such a predicament. He removed the dagger from its wing, but before it could launch itself into the air, he slit the dragonfly from abdomen to thorax.

Braeden scowled at the insect carcass. With his one pathetic enemy now dead, he was insufferably bored.

He propped up his elbows on his knees and rested his chin on his hands, watching the other trainees trade blows. Paladin Savage wove in and out, murmuring encouragements and chastisements in tandem. From afar, the paladin's catlike grace reminded Braeden of his former master. But the similarities ended there.

Braeden didn't know why he'd expected the Paladins to be different from anyone else. They listed neither virtue nor tolerance among their prerequisites; all a man needed was the ability to kill and the desire to act on it.

"Demon!" Paladin Savage had advanced on Braeden the moment the trainees had dispersed into smaller groups. He'd even gone so far as to draw his sword.

Braeden had showed empty palms and backed away slowly, as if from a rabid dog. "You mistake me, Paladin. I'm naught but a trainee."

Paladin Savage paused, but did not lower his weapon.

"Perhaps you know of my paladin? Tristan Lyons?" Braeden looked around at the other trainees, half-hoping one of them would support his story, but they either avoided his gaze or stared at him with revulsion. Not surprising, but annoying just the same.

He tried again. "I was originally assigned to Paladin Moreau. He's gone, as you may have heard."

Finally, comprehension dawned. "So you're the reason Moreau left." The paladin slid his sword back into its sheath. "They should've tossed you out instead."

Braeden inclined his head. "The High Commander does not share your opinion."

"That may be, demon," Paladin Savage said, "but in the practice yard, *I* am the law. And I will not teach you."

Braeden gritted his teeth. "Fine. Will you inform the High Commander or shall I?"

Paladin Savage didn't much like that. "I will permit you to observe the training as a spectator," he conceded.

And so here Braeden was, alone and a good ten yards away from the training yard. The black cloth of his robes soaked in the heat of the sun like a sponge, and the warmth made him drowsy. To keep himself awake, he began pricking the tips of his fingers with his dagger, watching the small dots of red form at the surface. *Wasteful,* his old master would have scolded. Braeden ignored the imaginary rebuke, digging deeper into his skin.

His grasp on consciousness continued to slip. He hadn't slept well; he'd spent the better part of the previous night trying to figure out what it was that bothered him about his new roommate. Braeden generally categorized people into one of two buckets: those who feared him and those who wanted him dead. Sam didn't fit neatly into either bucket, but that wasn't what set off Braeden's internal alarms. Something was off about him, in a way Braeden couldn't quite put his finger on.

"What are you doing?"

Braeden looked up to find Sam staring at him in horrified fascination. He followed Sam's gaze to his hand, where his dagger had pricked deep into the skin between his knuckles. Blood pooled in a dark red circle.

"Sorry," Braeden said, withdrawing the blade and wiping his hand clean on the grass. Letting his blood was as natural to him as breathing, but it wasn't a habit he liked to publicize.

"Doesn't that hurt?"

Braeden must be hearing things, because he could have sworn he heard concern in Sam's voice. He shook his head. "The pain is insignificant. And I heal quickly."

Sam reached over and grabbed his wrist, lifting it up to inspect his hand. "Amazing. The cut is already sealed over."

Now it was Braeden's turn to stare. No one ever touched him so casually, not even his old master. Who *was* this Sam of Haywood?

Sam flushed a brilliant shade of red, dropping his wrist. "S-sorry," the boy stammered. "I was curious."

Braeden shrugged, hiding his shock. His skin still tingled where Sam had touched him. "Why aren't you with Paladin Lyons?" he asked, rubbing his wrist.

"Training ended ages ago," Sam said, sitting down in the grass directly across from him. "You don't mind, do you?" Bewildered, Braeden shook his head.

"Thanks." Sam shoved a small wrapped bundle between them. "I didn't see you at the midday meal, so I came to find you. I thought you might be hungry so I nicked a few extra pastries from the kitchens."

Braeden had no idea what to make of Sam's thoughtful gesture. "Thank you," he said awkwardly. He unraveled the handkerchief, revealing three miniature fig pies and a half dozen crispels basted in honey. His mouth watered at the sweet, fruity smell, his stomach growling. He hadn't even realized he was hungry.

Sam laughed. It was a soft, husky sound that made Braeden's spine tingle. "You're drooling," Sam said.

Braeden responded by throwing a crispel at Sam and then wolfing down three himself.

Once Sam finished licking the last of the honey off his fingers, he asked, "Can I tell you something in confidence?"

Between bites, Braeden nodded, his curiosity piqued.

Sam looked down at his lap, his face slowly flaming to red. "I lost to Tristan today."

"You do that a lot," Braeden said.

"Do what?"

"Blush."

Sam moaned, slapping his hands to his cheeks. "I know, it's horrible. It's the curse of my Gods-forsaken skin. I take after my moth—" He stopped mid-sentence. "Never you mind."

"You do know Paladin Lyons is considered the best swordsman among the Paladins, if not the whole of Thule, do you not? It's no shame to lose to a man like that."

Sam slammed his fists on the ground. "The next time we fight, I'm going to win. I'll defeat him if it kills me." He heaved a deep sigh. "In the meantime, I shall have to live vicariously through you."

"Whatever would you want to do that for?" Braeden asked incredulously. He wouldn't wish his life on anyone.

Sam looked at him as though it were the most obvious thing in the world. "You're the strongest trainee here." He flung himself backward onto the grass. "Gods, what I would give to take Tristan down a notch."

Sam made quite the picture, one hand over his forehead and the other clutched over his heart. He looked ridiculous, Braeden thought, rubbing at his wrist again. "I have come to the conclusion," he drawled, "that you are an even stranger duck than I."

Sam sat up at that. "Oh no," he said, once he regained his composure. "No one would ever mistake you for a duck. A cat, maybe, with those eyes, but never a duck." He grinned, the pink of his tongue peeking out between his teeth.

Braeden was taken aback, at first, by Sam's blatant dig at his appearance. But before he could stop it, a low rumble grew in the pit of his stomach till it burst out of him, beyond his control. He threw his head back and laughed, the sound of his mirth carrying across the courtyard.

"I take it back. You *are* a strange duck," Sam said. "Absolutely quacking." He stood up, brushing remnants of crispel and grass from his breeches before offering Braeden a hand.

Braeden allowed Sam to pull him to his feet, ignoring the tingling sensation that traveled up his entire arm.

He wondered if he'd made a mistake coming here.

CHAPTER 5

It took Sam a week to gather the courage to join Braeden for breakfast. She wasn't afraid of his reception so much as the reaction of the other trainees. And sure enough, as soon as she sat down, the entire hall was gossiping about the trainee who dared sit at the half-demon's table.

"Faith in blood," Sam complained. "Don't they have anything better to talk about?"

Braeden paused, a spoon of oatmeal halfway to his mouth. "If their gossiping bothers you, you could sit elsewhere."

She glared at him. "Are you trying to get me to leave?"

He sighed, setting his spoon down. "I didn't say that."

"Because if you'd prefer to be alone—"

"Sam," he said sternly. "Thank you. I appreciate the company."

"Oh," she said in a small voice. "You're welcome, I suppose."

His lips twitched, the beginnings of a dimple indenting his left cheek. "Has anyone ever told you you're very combative?"

"Just about everyone I've ever met."

He broke out into a full grin, and for a moment, she was entranced. His smile was rusty, like his mouth didn't quite know what to do, but it warmed up his whole face. She stared at him for an inappropriate length of time before standing abruptly. "I'm going for second helpings."

Sam made her way to the center table, where breakfast was laid out buffet-style. As she reached for the ladle in the vat of porridge, she felt scalding hot liquid run down her back. She yelped, fruitlessly trying to pluck the plastered tunic from her skin.

She whirled around to find Fenric holding a half-empty bowl of oats. "Oops," he said. A smirk played across his lips. "It was an accident. My humble apologies."

"Humble apologies? You did that on purpose."

He leaned in close and said into her ear, "Perhaps." He gave her a big slap on the back, right on top of where he'd spilled his oats. His hand came away covered with muck. "Disgusting," Fenric said, wrinkling his nose. "You really ought to clean yourself up."

By the time she cleaned herself off and arrived at the practice yard, the trainees already held practice swords in hand.

Of course Tristan noticed. "The illustrious Sam of Haywood has decided to grace us with his presence," he said, looming over her. "By the way, you're wearing your breakfast on your chin."

Sam scowled, wiping at her mouth with the sleeve of her tunic. She'd barely had time to change shirts let alone wash her face.

"He'll come 'round one day," Will said from beside her. Will was a scrappy lad with ginger hair and an unfortunately freckled face. Sam gave him a pointed stare. He shrugged it off. "Or maybe not."

"William, Sam, stop your dawdling!" Tristan said sternly. "The two of you can practice dueling."

"Again?" Will groaned. "Sam always wins. A man's ego can only take so much abuse."

"Good thing you're still a half-grown pup, then," Tristan said.

Sam sniggered, and Will shot her a dirty look. She shrugged, smiling. "It's funny when it isn't aimed at me."

Sam and Will moved to the middle of the field where they could spread out. "Swords at the ready!" Tristan shouted. Sam stepped her right foot forward, bent her knees, and shifted her hilt to her left hip. Will copied her stance. "Begin!"

Sam indicated with her chin. *You first.* After a slight shake of his head, Will lunged forward with his blade. She parried his thrust easily.

"My turn," she said, catching the right side of his sword with her blade's edge. She swung again, and again, driving him backwards.

Will managed to regain his footing, slashing at her torso. She danced out of the way and then darted in close, rapping his knuckles with the flat of her blade. His sword fell out of his grasp. Sam fought off a grin as she pressed her sword point into the underside of his chin.

"I don't know why I even bother," Will said dejectedly. "Perhaps I'm meant to be a farmer after all."

"Don't be ridiculous," she said. "You'll make a fine paladin."

He sighed. "You're better than me, Sam. Better than all of us."

Finally, some acknowledgment of her skill. If only Tristan agreed. Shaking her head, Sam retrieved Will's discarded sword and handed it to him. "Again."

It was mid-afternoon by the time Tristan let them put down their practice blades. Sam wouldn't have minded continuing on longer, but Will's frustration was written plain on his face. He hadn't landed a single solid blow, and she'd disarmed him more times than she could count.

"Don't you ever get tired of winning?" Will asked her.

She grinned. "No."

"Well, I'm tired of losing. It gets depressing, you know." He looked at her sideways. "I suppose you don't know."

"You defeated Gavin just yesterday," Sam pointed out gently. "And I lost to Tristan."

Will rolled his eyes. "That hardly counts."

As soon as they finished training, Tristan pulled her aside. "You were late this morning."

Sam started to explain about Fenric, and then thought better of it. She doubted Tristan would be sympathetic to her excuses. "Aye, I was late," she said instead. "What's my punishment?"

"Chores," he said, folding his arms over his chest. "You know how to find the armoury on your own?"

She nodded.

"Ask for Paladin Locke. He'll show you how to properly clean and oil a sword."

"You want me to clean your sword?" she asked hopefully. That wasn't such a bad penance.

"Not my sword," said Tristan. "Ten swords of Paladin Locke's choosing."

Sam groaned. Cleaning ten swords would take forever, and she still had the afternoon's training ahead of her.

The Paladins' armoury was located on the opposite end of the fortress, so Sam cut through the courtyard to shorten the distance. She had assumed that Paladin Savage, like Tristan, would have already ended morning training—she'd learned early on he *hated* to be interrupted for any reason. To her surprise, his entire trainee group remained in the courtyard, standing in a tight circle. But where was Paladin Savage?

She squinted, spotting him at the circle's center. The paladin's sword was drawn, his pose threatening.

Braeden glided into the circle, as somber as ever in his stark black robes, his silver hair tied in a long braid down his back. As far as Sam could tell, he wore no armor, but . . . She gasped. Two twin blades were strapped across his back in an X. She had never seen anyone fight with two swords before.

Paladin Savage's mouth moved, but from where she stood, she couldn't overhear him. Braeden gave a terse nod in reply to whatever it was the paladin said, and the paladin returned with a condescending pat on the shoulder. She saw the half demon flinch.

Braeden stepped back and drew his two swords from their sheaths. He rolled his wrists, whipping the blades through the air in elliptical patterns. When he didn't let up, Sam realized that the movement was not a warm-up, but some sort of dynamic starting stance.

Braeden's swords whirred around faster and faster, till they were little more than a blur, but he did not attack. Paladin Savage smirked and said something to Braeden. He then gave a slight toss of his head and lunged, thrusting his sword.

And bounced off like he'd struck coiled spring.

The shock on the paladin's face was almost comical, a mirror of her own. What had just happened? Braeden hadn't blocked him; he'd *repelled* him. She'd never seen the like.

The paladin's astonishment faded fast into anger, and he leapt forward, slashing his sword in a downward arc. Steel clanged against steel, and his elbow shot backward at an awkward angle.

He swung his sword faster and harder, higher and lower, but it was no use. Nothing could get through the impenetrable wall of Braeden's whirling swords.

Paladin Savage brought his blade above his head, the look in his eye murderous. His expression made Sam nervous. Attack him already, she thought at Braeden. End this before he tries to kill you in earnest.

Braeden's swords stopped spinning. His wrists faced out, blades pointing in opposite directions. It left him wide open, his torso unguarded. What in the name of the Gods was he doing?

Paladin Savage charged, his sword crashing down. Sam squeezed her eyes shut, cracking one lid open in time to see the paladin's blade pass through nothing but air. She hadn't seen Braeden move.

Neither had Paladin Savage.

Braeden stood a yard behind him, pressing the tips of his swords into the back of the paladin's neck. "Yield," Braeden said clearly. He held his head high, his chin stubborn and proud.

Sam looked from Paladin Savage to Braeden and back again. Rage and humiliation darkened the paladin's swarthy complexion to purple.

For a moment, she thought he was going to refuse to withdraw. His chest puffed up and his shoulders rolled back, but he deflated in his next breath. "I yield. Well fought," he said, spitting out the words like poison. He retreated, and with a grimace, faced the rest of his trainees. "Dismissed." His eyes landed on Sam, who had done her best to remain unnoticed. "What are *you* looking at?" he snarled, his cheeks flushing a dull red.

"I—I . . ."

"That's enough out of you, Haywood. Go find Paladin Locke in the armoury and see that he finds you work to do. That's an order."

"But—" She hung her head. "Aye, Paladin."

Sam couldn't sleep. It wasn't for lack of exhaustion; eight hours of training and twenty polished swords later, her body ached in places that had never ached before. As she lay awake in the dark for that first hour, she blamed the excitement of the day for the quickness of her heart. Or maybe the reason was Braeden; she was not yet accustomed to sharing a room, let alone with a boy.

But now her heart raced in uncomfortably fast beats; she could feel her pulse leap against the base of her throat. Sweat matted her hair, trickling down her neck and back, and her hands were clammy. Something was wrong.

"Braeden," she whispered. "Braeden, are you awake?"

"Aye."

"Do you feel that? It feels . . . not right."

Braeden lit a candle by his bedside, the soft glow casting shadows across his face, highlighting the otherworldliness of his eyes. No part of him looked human.

She gulped. "Braeden?"

"Aye, I feel it, too." He was fully clothed in his Rhean black robes, two wickedly spiked knives in either hand. He gave her bedclothes a cursory glance. "Get dressed."

Sam didn't hesitate. She grabbed the closest pair of breeches and a tunic and ran into their private privy. She spent a moment ensuring that her chest binding was in place and then dressed hurriedly.

"Do you know how to use a knife?" Braeden asked.

"Well enough, I suppose," she said. "What's going on? Why do I need a knife?"

"No time to explain. Here, catch." Braeden retrieved another small dagger from the folds of his robes and tossed it across the room. The dagger sunk into the floor with a resounding thunk, missing Sam's toe by a scant inch.

"Are you mad?" she gasped.

Braeden shrugged. "I thought you would catch it." He crossed the room in three long strides and grabbed her by the wrist. "Come on, they're almost in the fortress."

"Who's almost in the fortress?"

Braeden's slit pupils spun counterclockwise till they ran horizontally, a black dash across the crimson of his irises. "Demons," he said. He shivered, his pupils elongating. "They're inside."

CHAPTER 6

SAM SHUT THE door to her room, wincing at the loud creak. The hallway was dark and empty, lit only by the paltry glow of a single candle. Trainees were not supposed to be out of bed at this hour. Tristan had never specified the punishment for breaking curfew, but she doubted she would enjoy it. "Maybe we should wake Tristan," she whispered. "He'd know what to do."

"We don't have time to convince him the threat is real," Braeden said. "He'll just try to stop us."

"Why wouldn't he believe you?"

"Why should he?"

Sam had no answer to that. "Braeden—" she started. He put his finger to his lips.

His warning came too late. Tristan wrenched his door open, wearing a dark scowl. "What do you two think you're doing?"

Braeden shot her a reproachful glance—she hadn't been *that* loud—and then swept a bow. "Please accept my apologies, Paladin Lyons, but you'll have to save our dressing-down for another time." He gripped her shoulder. "Are you coming?"

Sam opened her mouth to explain herself to Tristan, but her mind went blank.

Paladin Tristan Lyons had left his room dressed only in his smallclothes.

"What's with the red face, boy?" he asked.

"Y-y-your clothes," she stammered. "You aren't wearing any."

Tristan looked down at his bare, very male torso. "Surely you've seen a man in his smallclothes before?"

Of course she hadn't! She was a lady! "Y-yes, Tristan," she lied.

"Never mind what I'm wearing or not wearing. Why are you two out of bed after hours?" he demanded.

"Demons, Paladin," Braeden said. "They're inside the fortress."

"That's impossible," Tristan said flatly. "The fortress is warded from demons."

Sam's eyes widened. "You can ward against demons? Why don't we place wards everywhere?"

"It's a lost art. This fortress was built right after the Age of Shadows. The wards were cast then." Tristan crossed his arms over his chest. "Go back to bed."

"What about me?" Braeden asked quietly. "I'm here, aren't I?"

Tristan frowned. "Maybe you're not demon enough to set off the wards. I don't know."

Braeden's gaze flicked to Sam, as if to say I-told-you-so. She shrugged her shoulders helplessly. She'd followed him on a feeling. Tristan would need more than that.

Braeden pushed back his right sleeve, revealing a sinewy, well-muscled arm and the most intricate tattoo Sam had ever seen. A dark red pattern of glyphs wrapped itself around his skin from shoulder to wrist. But it wasn't the elaborate design of Braeden's tattoo that monopolized Sam's attention.

The circulation of his blood was a visible thing; the blue veins in his arms stood out, pulsating rhythmically, and as his blood ebbed and flowed, his skin rose and receded like the waves of the ocean. Sam stared, transfixed.

"I can sense their presence," Braeden said. "Their blood calls out to mine. When a demon is within range, my blood responds like this."

"Let's say you're right," Tristan said with frank disbelief, though his gaze was locked on Braeden's undulating skin. "Say demons somehow broke through the wards and are in the fortress. You thought to take them on yourselves? Two untested trainees with half a brain between them?"

Sam wanted to give a nasty retort, but Braeden silenced her with a slight jerk of his head. "We haven't the time to worry about protocol or niceties. You can join us or punish us on the morrow."

Tristan swore under his breath. "Fine," he grumbled. "Let me get dressed, and then I will escort you. And when there are no demons, I will escort you back to your room, where you will remain for the rest of the night. Are we agreed?"

"Aye," Braeden said.

"Aye, Tristan," Sam echoed.

The great hall was eerily quiet. A feeling of thick malevolence choked the air, ten times thicker than it had been in Sam and Braeden's chambers. The room lay in darkness but for the flame of their torch and the silver light of the moon glimmering through the cut glass of the gothic windows. Warped black shadows crawled across the room and scuttled over the walls, but that was all they were—shadows.

"I don't see anything," Sam whispered.

"They're here," Braeden said.

The skepticism faded from Tristan's face. "Be on guard, lads."

"Paladin, with your permission, I'll draw them out of hiding," Braeden said. Tristan nodded his assent.

Braeden ran the tip of his knife along the inside of his arm. Blood welled from the cut and trickled down to his fingers before splashing onto the pale cream of the tiled floor.

"They can't resist the lure of blood," Braeden explained. "Not even from one of their own." He let a few more drops of blood spill from his veins and then ripped a strip of cloth from his robes, wrapping it efficiently around his wound.

For a moment, nothing happened. Only their uneven breaths and the slight rustle of fabric interrupted the quiet of the night.

Two crimson spheres winked into existence at the rear of the hall, backlit by an infernal glow. Sam sucked in a gulp of air. She'd seen eyes like those once before.

"First demon?" Tristan asked her softly.

Sam shook her head. "My second."

He gave her a curious look before turning to Braeden. "It's only the one. I can handle it my—" He shut up as a second pair of crimson orbs joined the first, followed by a third. "All right, let's split. Sam, you take the one on the left, I'll go after the one in the middle, and Braeden, you take the right."

Braeden held up a hand. "Wait."

A fourth and a fifth set of eyes appeared, followed by a sixth and a seventh . . . Sam stopped counting as a sea of red swept across the hall. How many were there? Certainly more than one paladin and two trainees were meant to handle on their own. Her heart skipped a beat. She wasn't ready for this yet. Tristan had been right; she'd been a fool to think she could take on a demon herself.

"Sam, light the lamp to your left," Tristan ordered, pressing the torch into her hand. "Move!"

Startled out of her trance, she turned her attention to the ensconced fixture on the nearest wall. She lit it quickly and then set the torch aside. Light flooded the room. Sam blinked, grateful for the reprieve from darkness—till she caught a proper glimpse of the intruders.

Tristan swore under his breath. "Bloody hellhounds."

Even on all fours, the demon hounds were as tall as humans and so lean they were nearly skeletal. Their mighty jaws snapped open and shut, revealing rows of razor sharp teeth. Saliva dripped from their jowls. A terrible, fetid stench permeated the room, and Sam came close to retching.

"Not just hellhounds," Braeden said, pointing. "Look."

Sam and Tristan looked where Braeden was pointing. A giant serpent slithered across the floor, moving at a speed that belied its enormous size. Mottled green and brown with a pale yellow underbelly, the snake had three hooded heads, each with its own set of enlarged fangs and flicking tongue.

Tristan shuddered. "I *loathe* snakes."

Sam gaped at him. The almighty Tristan Lyons feared something? In spite of her own mounting fear, she broke out into a grin. Even heroes had their weaknesses.

"What do we do now?" she asked.

"We fight," Tristan said grimly. "And we pray." The demons edged closer, sniffing the air with their long snouts.

"There's no plan?"

"Don't die," Tristan said, and with a yell, sprinted into the throng of demons.

She watched with a mixture of awe and dread as Tristan carved his way through demon after demon. He was beautiful to watch, a whirlwind of man and sword, spraying blood in a never-ending spiral.

"What are you waiting for?" Braeden hissed. "Go!" He shoved her none-too-gently before leaping into action, knives streaming through the air.

Before Sam had time to think, one of the hellhounds charged her. Staring into its cruel crimson eyes and canine face, she was transported back two years ago, to the woods in Haywood where her mother had died. Her voice echoed in Sam's head.

"Run. For the love of Emese, run!"

Sam turned on her heel and bolted.

A large body slammed into her side, knocking her to the floor. As she struggled to right herself, massive jaws clamped around her waist and flung her into the air as if she were nothing more than a dog's chew toy. She plummeted towards a wide, gaping mouth framed by pointed teeth the length of her head. Sam closed her eyes, imagining her end in the pit of the hellhound's stomach.

Sam was submerged in liquid, wetness seeping through her clothes. But as she opened her eyes, she was not, as she had feared, soaked in digestive fluids. By sheer, dumb luck, she had landed blade first, the force of her landing driving her dagger deep into the hellhound's throat. She stood knee high in a pool of demon saliva and blood. Trying not to gag, she retrieved her dagger, using it as leverage to free her feet from the sticky substance.

"It won't die till you cut off its head!" called Tristan. He leapt neatly over the corpse of one demon then sliced clean through another's neck.

Sam followed Tristan's advice, hacking away at the demon till its head was completely severed from its body. Gods, how she wished she had a sword instead of this pathetic butter knife.

A glint of steel caught her eye, and Sam clapped her hand against her forehead. Why hadn't she thought of it earlier? She darted between the carcasses of two hellhounds, then pulled down one of the swords from the wall. Shoving her dagger into her boot, she tested the blade's edge, wincing as it cut through her skin. It would do.

Imbued with new confidence, Sam marched towards the thick of the fray, sword at the ready. Despite Tristan and Braeden's efforts, most of the demons still remained; it would not be an easy victory, if it were a victory at all.

Sam buried her new sword into the closest demon, ripping through its ribcage and into its heart. The creature sank onto its hind legs, letting out one last bay as she liberated its head from its body. Without pausing, she moved to her next target, ramming her sword through flesh and bone.

As she fought her way through the horde of demons, she found herself back-to-back with Tristan. Wordlessly, they acknowledged each other, striking the enemy in unison, felling demons left and right.

The three-headed snake rose up above them, balancing on its single tail. Its jaws hinged open at an obtuse angle as if to swallow them whole. Without warning, it struck. Sam and Tristan just barely managed to roll out of the way. Now, she was mad: that was the second time tonight something had tried to eat her.

Tristan mopped his sweaty face with the back of his hand, smearing blood across his cheeks. "We can beat this thing," he said, a hint of fatigue creeping into his voice. "You attack from behind; I'll distract it."

While Tristan engaged the demon in an elaborate game of cat and mouse, Sam ducked and dodged her way around to the serpent's tail. With a running start, she planted her sword and vaulted off the floor, propelling half way up the snake's vertebrae. The scales were rough and ridged, cutting into the palms of her hands, but she pushed aside the pain, climbing higher till she reached the serpent's hooded neck. Gripping onto the folds of its loose skin with one hand, she held her sword aloft with the other, jamming it deep into the skull of its leftmost head.

The problem with beheading a three-headed snake is that there are three heads to behead. Sure enough, the decapitation of one of its heads was not enough to kill the demon. Instead, the now two-headed serpent reared back, sending Sam sailing across the room. Her legs buckled beneath her as she crashed. She attempted to get to her feet, but the instant she put pressure on her right ankle, her eyes crossed at the pain. Hoping to use her sword as a crutch, Sam realized with dawning horror that the blade remained lodged inside the snake's one severed head.

Sensing injured prey, four hellhounds encircled Sam, gnashing their teeth and licking their chops. She was surrounded, with only a dagger for protection.

But this time, Tristan was in no position to play the hero. The snake demon had coiled itself around his legs, trapping him where he stood. Only his sword, which he rotated above his head in a quick, fanlike motion, shielded him from the serpent's venomous fangs.

Where was Braeden? Sam hadn't seen him since he had launched his first attack. Was he still alive? Tristan had been at her side, if only for a time; Braeden had been left to fend for himself.

"Braeden!" she shouted, praying to the Gods that somehow everything would be all right.

A deafening howl pierced through the din of battle, forcing Sam to her knees. Even the demons seemed startled by the sound.

From the remaining mass of demons, a lone, man-shaped figure emerged. Braeden.

But the figure wasn't Braeden. Or at least not the Braeden she remembered. The rust-colored eyes, pupils stretched so thin they were almost invisible, those were his. But there was a savagery to them she'd never seen before. The creature—for he was more demon than man—was bare to the waist, his previously lithe frame filled with bulging muscle and thick striations, bordering on deformity. The silver hair she'd grown accustomed to seeing tied in a braid or piled in a topknot fell in loose, wild waves to his hipbone. He spread his arms wide, and a wall of demons assembled behind him, pawing at the ground.

"Braeden?" she called again tentatively.

Braeden turned to her and smiled, a feral grin that spoke of cruelty to come.

Sam swallowed. She was as good as dead.

CHAPTER 7

BRAEDEN DIDN'T FEAR much in life. Why would he be afraid of monsters when he was one himself? He'd been told he was evil since he'd left his mother's womb, and after a time, he'd started to believe it true. His childhood had been marked by long days and nights he couldn't remember, and he'd wake to find his lips and teeth smeared with blood that wasn't his.

There wasn't much to fear when he was his own worst nightmare.

His master had taught him to harness the demon within him, till all that remained were his cursed eyes and the blood seal that wrapped around his arm like a vise. When his master had branded the tattoo into his skin, Braeden had wanted to howl at the pain. But such was the price of control.

Braeden soon learned that like any other seal, his could be breached. His demon had been bound with blood, and it could be freed just the same. He had only to cut into his own flesh, and blood and demon would seep out. His master had warned him that his blood was a potent weapon to be used sparingly; like a drug, the power flowing through his veins was addictive.

It wasn't the addiction that scared Braeden, but the loss of his humanity. The more of his blood he spilled, the less of his humanity remained. And when only the tiniest shred of his human consciousness was left, that was when he could connect with the demons. Not in any meaningful way—most demons lacked the rational thought patterns underpinning true communication. But they recognized Braeden as one of their own. More than that, they recognized him as their leader. These creatures that were so often agents of chaos bowed to him as though he were the alpha among wolves. Now *that* frightened him.

Braeden could count on one hand the number of times he'd intentionally reached such a state. Oh, he'd used his blood often enough—to boost his strength and stamina, among other fun tricks. But tonight he'd spilled too much from his veins, and he bordered on the point of no return.

He struggled not to lose himself to the mob mentality of the demons. Demons understood two emotions—hunger and fear—and intertwined with their minds, he was overwhelmed by their desire for death and destruction.

A remnant of rationality tugged at the back of his mind. As their thirst for violence infected him, Braeden became aware of a strangeness about his bloodlust, a singular focus at odds with the anarchic nature of a demon. The demons thought as one, driven towards a single target. Sam.

Braeden could smell Sam's blood from across the room, sweet and seductive. The desire to rip into his skin felt like a compulsion, as if his very survival were dependent on tasting the boy's flesh. Beside him, the hellhounds fought against their mental restraints, eager for a mouthful. He wouldn't be able to keep them obedient for much longer. He was having enough trouble controlling his own urges.

Braeden pushed through the fog in his mind. Preventing the demons from attacking required his full concentration, and he would have to release his mental hold on them in order to fight. Sam, by the smell of him, was hurt and in no shape for fighting off hellhounds. Braeden couldn't protect him, not from this many demons. He didn't want the boy to die.

Odd, Braeden didn't think he'd ever cared before about the fate of another human.

He needed to get to Sam before it was too late. Braeden lifted his nose to the air and inhaled, guided by the scent of Sam's blood. Teetering on the edge of control, he was caught between wanting to find Sam and wanting to satisfy his bloodlust. He reeled himself in, forcing his mind to focus.

He saw Sam's sword before he saw Sam. Nestled deep in the back of an enormous serpent skull, it stuck out straight in the air like a silver flagpole. The hilt was covered in Sam's blood.

Braeden tugged the sword free with both hands, wiping off the gore on his robes.

Then he heard his name.

"Braeden!" Sam cried, his voice high and desperate.

He moved swiftly towards the voice. Faith in blood. Sam was surrounded by four demons that had escaped Braeden's control. Braeden looked down at the sword in his hand. If he didn't act quickly, the hellhounds would tear Sam apart.

There was no other alternative. Drawing a dagger from his robes, Braeden closed his eyes and prayed to the Gods who had never heard from him before. With a keening cry, he plunged the dagger deep into his heart.

For what could have been seconds or hours, Braeden drifted in darkness. When he came to, he thought he'd lost himself to one of the violent blackout periods that had marred his youth. But Sam was still alive, and the only blood that soaked his hands belonged to his still-beating heart.

"Braeden?"

He saw himself reflected in Sam's eyes, a monstrous parody of his usual aspect. And he saw clearly that Sam feared him. Gone was whatever tentative trust they'd built between them.

For the first time since he'd stabbed himself, his heart began to hurt.

Move, he told the demons surrounding Sam. They bowed their heads to their paws and lowered their tails between their feet, backing away.

Trembling, Sam pointed a dagger at Braeden—the dagger Braeden had given him.

His mouth crooked up at the irony. "I believe this is mine." He wrenched the blade away from Sam, returning it to the folds of his robes. The color drained from Sam's face as he stared at his empty hands. Braeden could barely look at him. "Here," he said, thrusting forward the sword he'd retrieved from the serpent demon's skull. "Thought you'd prefer to use this."

Sam's face went from white to scarlet. "I am the world's biggest ass," he said quietly. "Thank you."

Braeden shrugged in reply.

Leaning on his sword for support, Sam asked, "Why aren't the demons attacking? Don't you think it's strange?"

He ignored the question. "You need to get out of here while you still can. You're hurt."

"I can't leave you and Tristan," Sam protested. "I want to help."

"You're of no use to us injured," Braeden said. "If you want to help, find reinforcements. Get out of here and warn the High Commander we've been infiltrated."

Sam looked as though he wanted to protest further, but with a curt nod he obeyed, hobbling towards the staircase at the rear of the great hall.

As soon as Sam was gone, Braeden let his grasp on the demons slip. He felt the last of his control over them snap. The demons moved sluggishly at first, as if waking from a daze. And then, of a single, vengeful mind, they converged on him.

Braeden slipped his knives into his hands and braced for the onslaught. The demons were ravenous now, and this time the blood they craved was his.

Snarling its rage, a hellhound leapt for his throat. Another dove at his ankles. Braeden sidestepped, slicing through the neck of the hound at his feet and twisting his knife into the belly of the other. He tore his knives from their flesh, striking again and again, till they both lay dead.

Then another demon attacked, sweeping a heavy clawed paw at his face. He dodged and then shot forward, embedding a knife in its throat. He pushed the blade all the way through, then ripped it free, taking the demon's head with it.

He lost himself to the fever of battle, killing without thought or hesitation. He was as violent and as merciless as the hounds who hunted him, but stronger and smarter. He was the predator and they the prey. They died like flies around him.

"Braeden. Braeden!"

Distantly, he heard his name. He shook the cobwebs from his mind, focusing on where and who he was.

A hand touched his shoulder. "It's over, lad," Paladin Lyons said. "They're all dead."

"Good," Braeden said, his throat dry. "Good." He looked

around the great hall, noticing that they were no longer alone. Paladins and trainees filled the room, armed with weapons but dressed as though they'd just rolled out of bed. They were staring at him.

Braeden shifted uncomfortably under their scrutiny. "How long have they been here?"

Tristan cleared his throat. "A while. You put on quite the performance. You didn't leave much for the rest of us to do."

One of the trainees stepped forward, the boy they called Fenric. He was a particularly unpleasant boy, with a high opinion of himself and never a nice word to say to anyone. Braeden tried to avoid him as much as possible. "You!" he cried out. "You brought the demons here."

Braeden gaped at him. "I beg your pardon?"

"We know it was you," Fenric said, his voice trembling with hatred. "Paladin Savage is dead."

CHAPTER 8

SAM TAPPED HER good foot nervously, waiting to be called into the High Commander's office. A summons from the leader of the Paladins was not something to be taken lightly in any circumstances.

The funeral pyre for Paladin Savage had still been burning when Lord Astley announced the High Commander was investigating the attack on the fortress. Sam could read between the lines—Braeden was under investigation. It's not fair! she had wanted to shout. He saved us all, you fools!

A pang of guilt coursed through her. Was she really any better than Braeden's accusers? She'd be lying if she said she'd never questioned his motives. For a moment there last night, she'd been convinced he had meant to kill her. She could have sworn she had seen her death in his crimson eyes.

"The High Commander is ready to see you," Lord Astley said, interrupting her thoughts.

She gulped and nodded, limping after the secretary. Lord Astley stopped outside the ornate double door to the High Commander's office and rapped his knuckles against the wood.

"Enter," a muffled voice called.

"Go on." Lord Astley pushed the door open and gestured for her to enter, then closed the door behind her.

Her steps faltered, overwhelmed by the sheer amount of *stuff* crammed into one little room. The office showed the signs of decades' worth of collecting, overflowing with fine antiques and odd artifacts and trinkets. There was no discernible rhyme or reason. Mismatched tables sported various baubles and bibelots: a porcelain teapot sat next to the bronzed figurine of a warrior from the Age of the First Men, and a gilded snuffbox rested atop an exquisitely crafted chessboard. On the walls, hung archaic weapons made of bone and wood. Beside them, draped giant scrolls with obscure symbols and ancient scratchings.

Sam was so engrossed in her surroundings that she almost didn't notice the High Commander. He sat behind his desk, an unremarkable man with unremarkable features. Vaguely, she recalled his face from the opening ceremony. He caught her eye and smiled slightly.

"Please, Sam, take a seat," he said in his enthralling tenor. Again, she was struck by the loveliness of his voice, hypnotic and smooth as velvet. Shaking off the spell, she obliged, pulling out a chair from underneath the desk.

"Sam of Haywood," he mused. He stared at her for an uncomfortably long time. She fidgeted under his gaze. "How did you come to join the Paladins, Sam?"

She blinked. "Excuse me?"

The High Commander tilted his head, studying her. "We so rarely have trainees from Haywood. I confess I'm curious to know more about you."

"There isn't much to know," she said cautiously. The last thing she needed was for the High Commander to pry into her background.

"You are Lord Hawkins' second son, my secretary tells me," he said, propping up his elbows on his desk. "I am unfamiliar with his name."

That's because he doesn't exist, she thought wryly to herself. "My father became a bit of a recluse after my mother died," she lied smoothly. "A broken heart, you understand."

"Did your father train you?"

"My father? He . . . well, he did, some," she fumbled. "My father is the one who first taught me the sword."

"He must be very proud."

Sam bit the inside of her cheek. Her father didn't know where she'd run off to, and if he did, he'd demand her return immediately and forbid her from ever holding a sword again. It wouldn't be the first time, either. "My father wanted me to follow a different path."

"And yet here you are."

She raised her chin. "Here I am."

He folded his hands together, cradling his jaw in his hands. "Why?" he asked, as if he were genuinely interested. "Why defy your father?"

"I thought we were here to talk about Braeden," she said sharply.

He raised an eyebrow. "Is there something about Braeden you feel I ought to know?"

"N-no," she stumbled. Why was she here if not to discuss Braeden?

"Then we need not discuss him."

"But what about Paladin Savage?" she burst out. Half the trainees were ready to condemn Braeden for his murder, and the High Commander wanted to discuss her relationship with her father?

His face turned to stone. "A tragic loss."

"And Braeden?"

"Saved the lives of hundreds of men."

She sagged against the back of her chair. "Aye, he did." Relief warred with confusion. "Why did you bring me here, then, if not to talk about him?"

The corner of his mouth twitched. "Tristan warned me you were impertinent."

She gasped. "He said that about me to *you*?" She'd kill him when she saw him next.

"He also said you were a fine swordsman and a quick study."

Her cheeks heated. "Tristan said that?" Sam had thought Tristan would bite off his own tongue before paying her a compliment.

The High Commander chuckled at her reaction. "Aye, he did, lad. He does not give praise lightly, our Paladin Lyons."

Sam bowed her head. "Thank you, High Commander."

His voice softened to just above a hush, his words a gentle caress. "I spoke with Tristan at length about the events of last evening, and I met with the coroner. If the fault must lie with someone, it is with me. I thought we were invulnerable."

"The wards," Sam said, "why did they fail? Why now, after all this time?"

The High Commander's eyes went wide, and then his face smoothed over. "Tristan mentioned the wards, did he?"

She nodded. Were they supposed to be kept a secret?

He sighed. "The last warders are long gone, and most of their knowledge is gone with them. But we do know that wards are mortal creations. And anything made by mortals erodes over time. Nothing human can last forever."

She mulled this over. "So you're saying that the wards' failure and the attack on the fortress was completely random?"

The High Commander shook his head. "Nothing is ever random, Sam. Not the attack on the fortress nor you being here today. It's just a question of putting the puzzle pieces together."

Now she was more confused than ever. "Why *am* I here?"

"Because," he said, his smile quizzical, "you're a piece of the puzzle I have yet to figure out."

Sam left the High Commander's office thoroughly shaken, feeling as though she'd been through an interrogation. The High Commander had asked her a number of deeply prying questions about Haywood and her family—most of which she'd had to lie about—and almost nothing of Braeden or the demons. It was all very strange.

While the High Commander had assured her he believed in Braeden's innocence, the vast majority of the trainees weren't so sure. Thus when Sam went down to breakfast, she was shocked to find Braeden in the company of others. The fire-haired Will and a wiry, thin boy with dark skin and spectacles sat across the table from him.

She slipped onto the bench beside Braeden. "Are these two bothering you?"

Will glared at her. "Really, Sam?"

Braeden didn't respond; he just rolled his crimson eyes toward the ceiling.

Sam shivered. "Don't do that. It's scary."

"You're Sam of Haywood, right?" the bespectacled boy said. His voice was high and thin. "I'm Quinn of Kashmar."

"Why are you sitting here?" she asked Will and Quinn bluntly.

Will scowled. "Not everyone thinks like Fenric does. He thinks he can say and do as he pleases just because his father is Andrel Vane."

"Besides," added Quinn, speaking directly to Braeden, "the High Commander says you had nothing to do with it. I think I'll listen to him over Fenric."

"Has he told *everyone* who his father is?" Sam asked.

"Yes, that's how he introduces himself," Will said. And then, in a pitch-perfect imitation of Fenric's aristocratic drawl, he said, "I'm Fenric of Icetower, son of Andrel Vane, greatest paladin who ever lived."

They all had a good chuckle at that, even Braeden.

"That's blasphemous, you know," Sam said, when they stopped laughing. "I don't think Andrel Vane could hold a candle to any of the first Twelve."

"True enough," Quinn acknowledged. "And Tristan Lyons is better than Vane ever was, or so they say."

Her mouth went dry. "Tristan is?"

Quinn nodded. "He's supposed to be some sort of prodigy. He's the youngest First in recorded history. Apparently the High Commander took him under his wing when he was little more than a boy. It's amazing, considering Lyons' past." He flushed under his dark skin. "Sorry, I'm rambling."

Will grinned. "Quinn's father is a scholar. It's rubbed off on him."

Quinn shot Will a sidelong glance. "Much to my father's dismay, the only area of history I was ever interested in studying was Hartwin the Brave and the Paladins. I can recite the name of every First of the Sword since the Twelve. In order. It's a fun party trick."

Sam stared at him. "How many have there been?"

"172," Quinn said.

Will nudged him with his elbow. "Remind me to never bring you to any parties."

Quinn scoffed. "Like you get invited to any, farmboy."

Sam thought Will might take offense, but he smiled

good-naturedly. "Farmers still throw parties, Quinn. We just dance in our barns alongside the cows."

She imagined twirling in one of her elegant court gowns, only to step in a pile of cow dung. "Really?"

Will and Quinn looked at each other and then burst out laughing. "No, not really," Will said, still laughing. He reached across the table and patted Sam on the shoulder with mock sympathy. "It's not your fault you were born a lord's son."

Ha! She wondered how they'd react if they knew she was a lord's *daughter*, and the daughter of a duke to boot.

Will's freckled face fell. "Now I've gone and offended you. I don't *dislike* all nobles."

"Just most of them," Quinn said, and Will threw him an annoyed glance.

She waved her hand dismissively. "I'm not offended. I'd rather be a paladin than a lord, anyway."

"And I a paladin instead of a stuffy old academic," Quinn said.

"I've got a black thumb," Will said ruefully. "Believe it or not, I'm a worse farmer than I am a swordsman."

They turned to Braeden expectantly. "Is it my turn to say something?" he asked.

"It would be in the spirit of things," Will said. He offered Braeden an encouraging smile.

"All right," Braeden said with a resigned shrug. "I want to repay my sins."

The smile slipped from Will's face, and Quinn looked down at the ground. What sins? Sam wanted to ask.

Braeden sighed. "I did it wrong, didn't I?"

"You're fine," Quinn assured him. Will recovered his smile and nodded in agreement.

Sam felt a grin tug at her lips. "Quinn, Will," she said, "you can sit with us anytime."

Braeden's eyes flicked to hers. "Us, is it?"

"Aye." She met his gaze, daring him to challenge her. "Us."

The next few days passed *mostly* without incident. While the High Commander had publicly declared Braeden's innocence, many of the trainees remained convinced otherwise, and Sam was considered guilty by association. Fenric and his cronies teased and tripped her at every opportunity. They played all sorts of practical jokes that were less than well-intentioned. Braeden, of course, had it far worse than she did.

Will and Quinn continued to join them for meals, commiserating about Fenric's repeated offenses and talking circles around Braeden, who didn't seem to know what to make of them. Sam, for one, was grateful for the company. She hadn't had people she could call friends in a long time, not since well before she'd left Haywood.

One week after the demon attack on the fortress, Lord Astley announced there would be a tournament. The trainees buzzed with excitement: finally, a chance to distinguish the strong from the weak and earn a little personal glory. Unless something went terribly wrong, Sam was confident she'd do well.

Will and Quinn were less certain.

"You'll do great," she told them over dinner. "A week from now we'll all be celebrating."

"Easy for you to say, Lord Invincible," Will said darkly.

Sam brightened. "Are they calling me that now?"

Will and Quinn exchanged glances. "No," they said in resounding unison.

Braeden covered a cough that sounded suspiciously like a strangled laugh.

Her glare encompassed all three of them. "I was trying to be supportive."

"Don't be," Quinn said.

"Fine." Sam made a show of turning up her nose while spooning soup into her mouth. A trickle leaked down her chin—not the desired effect. She wiped her mouth and took another slurp, grimacing. "Is it me or is the soup unusually salty tonight?"

"Mine tasted normal," Will said with a cheerful grin. "Your soup was probably Fenricked."

"We're using his name as a verb now?" Quinn asked, an eyebrow arching over his spectacles. "I'm not sure he deserves the honor."

"It's a curse word," Will said. "Fenricked. Like f—"

Will was interrupted by the loud clearing of a throat. "William," Tristan said stiffly. Will's face turned the same shade as his hair. Sam snickered into her soup.

"Sam, Braeden, I need to speak with you," Tristan said. "Privately." Taking their cue, Will and Quinn pushed back the bench and left their seats to Tristan.

He sat down across from Sam and Braeden, looking uncharacteristically uncomfortable. It was several long moments before he spoke. "I wanted to thank you," he said. "Both of you. A lot more paladins would have been dead if it weren't for your efforts." He scratched the back of his head. "I'm sorry it took me so long to say it."

Sam's mouth fell open. She wasn't sure which shocked her more—that the great Tristan Lyons had thanked them or that he'd apologized.

Tristan spoke again, this time with a quiet anger. "What you did, Braeden—those were the deeds of a paladin. You deserve to be acknowledged for it, not persecuted. I'm embarrassed for my brothers." Braeden ducked his head, his cheeks tinged with pink.

Tristan drew in a breath. "The High Commander feels that, given the unpleasantness of the situation with Paladin Savage, it would be in your best interest to leave Heartwine now."

"What?" cried Sam. "The High Commander is forcing Braeden out? How is that fair?"

Tristan glowered at Sam. "No, Braeden is *not* getting forced out. The three of us will just be leaving Heartwine earlier than I originally planned."

"The three of us? Leaving? Where to?" Sam demanded in a rush. "What about the tournament?"

Tristan rubbed his head in his hands. "You are exhausting, do you know that? We're headed for the West."

"And the tournament?"

"For you there will be no tournament. We leave at first dawn on the morrow."

CHAPTER 9

"WAS IT REALLY necessary to leave so Gods damned early?" Sam groused, hugging her horse's neck. The mare was a poor substitute for a pillow. "It's not even light out yet."

"Yes, it *was* necessary," Tristan said. "And we would have left earlier if I hadn't had to physically drag you out of bed like a spoiled babe."

"Four hours of sleep is not humane."

"If you were looking to be coddled, boy, you've come to the wrong place."

"Children, children," Braeden murmured with a hint of a smile.

"It's *your* fault we had to leave at this ungodly hour," Sam complained. "If it weren't for you—" she choked off her words as she realized what she'd said. "Gods, Braeden, I didn't mean it!"

Braeden wouldn't look at her. "It's fine." With a sharp "Hyah!" he spurred his horse into a gallop.

Tristan and Sam watched as Braeden slowed his horse to a trot, still in eyesight but far enough away that he wouldn't be able to converse with them. "You're an idiot," Tristan told her.

"I know," she replied miserably.

Dawn broke over the horizon, the orange of the sun painting stripes of pink and purple against the fading indigo of the night sky. The dirt road they traveled was deserted; the nearest village was still miles away and the high walls of the Paladins' fortress were now a tiny speck in the distance. Sam had passed through this land before as she made her way from Haywood to Heartwine, but in the shadowed glow of dawn, it was unrecognizable.

They traveled in silence for several more hours, interrupted only by the thud of hooves against packed ground and the rustling of leaves as the wind whistled through the trees. Braeden still plodded on ahead, and Tristan seemed too disgusted with her to make conversation. So with no one but her horse to keep her company, Sam was hit by a wave of loneliness. She missed Will's and Quinn's constant jabber. She hadn't even gotten a chance to say goodbye.

Sam almost cried for joy when she saw the top of a picket fence and thatched roofs in the distance. People, she thought happily. People who *talked*.

Braeden drew his horse to a stop when the village was in clear sight, waiting for Sam and Tristan to catch up to him. He'd donned a conical straw hat, the brim pulled low over his eyes. With only the bottom of his lower lashes visible, he looked like a young foreign lord come to visit the countryside.

"We're just passing through, lads," Tristan warned as they neared the village gate. "We've got miles to go before nightfall."

Though it was only a few hours past dawn, the small village of Gwent was already bustling with activity. The local merchants stood behind their stalls in the market square, hawking their wares to any and every passerby within earshot. The smell of fresh gingerbread wafted in the air from the bakery, and the steady pounding of mallet against cowhide resonated from the tannery. Women in their long woolen gowns and wimples clustered around the village well, trading gossip while they waited their turn to draw water, and the children played games at their mothers' feet.

"Paladin Lyons!" a voice cried in greeting. A round little man waddled over to their horses, a wide smile plastered on his sweaty face.

"Master Collop," Tristan acknowledged.

"Dare I hope that you will spend the night? It's good for business when I can claim a paladin among my patrons."

Tristan shook his head. "Not tonight. But I wouldn't say no to a bite of breakfast before we continue on our way."

"Of course, of course," the innkeeper said. "Will your companions want to breakfast as well?"

Sam's stomach rumbled in anticipation. Master Collop chuckled. "I'll take that as a yes. Right this way."

The Laughing Bear came rightfully by its name. Even at this early hour, the inn drew a crowd, and the sounds of laughter and merriment were infectious. A group of young men hooted and hollered at a kitchen maid, a pretty slip of a girl with the voice of an angel, who was singing atop a table. Sam tapped her good foot in time to the music—till she got a better listen at the bawdy lyrics.

As they wound their way around the inn to the nearest empty table, they were stopped a dozen times. Everyone seemed to have something to say to Tristan, whether it was to tell him about the birth of a new foal or the latest village scandal. A few of the men were bent on introducing Tristan to their daughters, but he politely declined their entreaties. Braeden kept his eyes downcast and did not remove his hat.

"I thought we would never eat," Sam said as the innkeeper's wife set down plates of kippered herring and mugs of watered wine in front of them. "Who knew you were so popular?"

Tristan shrugged. "I've come through here before. Master Collop has been a good friend to the Paladins."

When they were about halfway through their breakfast, the innkeeper paid them another visit. "If you have a moment, Paladin Lyons, I need to speak with you in private. I have news that may be of interest to you."

Tristan pulled a gold coin from his belt pouch and slid it across the table. "Braeden and Sam are my trainees. They are to hear your news as well."

"Very well." Master Collop swept up the gold coin and deposited it into his apron. "I hear rumors, Paladin."

"You know I don't put much stock in rumors," Tristan admonished.

"Aye, that I do, Paladin. But I think these rumors are worthy of your attention." The innkeeper's eyes darted right and left. "I hear you're headed west."

Tristan's expression didn't change. "Go on."

Master Collop coughed into his hand. "I have an innkeeper friend at The Stag and Bull in Pirama. Business has been tough lately, and he asked to borrow a few sovereigns, just to stay afloat. 'Business is that bad?' I asked him. Now, John Byrd—that's his name—is as loyal to the Paladins as they come. He understands what you do for Thule, same as me. But things are bad out west. Terrible, John tells me."

"How do you mean?"

"The locals think there has been a new breach in the Afterlight into our world. Ridiculous, I know. But the demons are appearing in greater numbers than ever before, demons that haven't been seen in thousands of years. People are saying and believing crazy things."

"Isn't Paladin Reynard stationed in Pirama?" Tristan asked. "I would think he'd have called for help if the situation were truly dire."

The innkeeper wrinkled his brow. "I assumed he had. I thought that was why the High Commander was sending you west."

Tristan shifted in his seat. "Is that all?"

Master Collop shook his head. "No, Paladin." He leaned in closer. "Have you heard of the Uriel?"

Tristan's eyes widened for the barest second. "The Uriel?" he repeated.

"The Uriel," Master Collop whispered. "I don't know much about them, but John says they're causing a real stir out west. They say they can protect the West from demons better than the Paladins. And they've already amassed a decent sized following. John thinks a rebellion is coming; he's heard rumbles about it. And folks are already refusing to stay at The Stag & Bull since John has the Paladins' emblem carved on his door. That's why he needed to borrow the money."

Tristan rubbed the blond stubble at his chin. "It's grim news you share, Master Collop. I'll have to write of this to the High Commander." He slid another two sovereigns across the table. "Can I trust you to deliver the letter? And to keep quiet about these rumors till I return?"

The two coins vanished into Master Collop's apron. "You can put your faith in me, Paladin."

Half an hour later, Master Collop walked them to the stables, a slight jingle to his step. "You be careful, now," the innkeeper cautioned as he brought out their horses.

"I always am," Tristan said.

"You too, Master Sam and Master Braeden. And you listen to Paladin Lyons. He's a good man, he is." The innkeeper bowed as low as his rounded body would allow. The sock cap he wore slipped off his head, revealing his shiny bald pate.

Once Master Collop was no longer in sight, a helpless giggle escaped Sam's lips. Tristan brought his horse close enough to hers so that the back of her head was in range. "Idiot," he scoffed, smacking her across the nape of her neck.

"Oy," she protested, rubbing at the tender skin. "I couldn't help it. That man is just so silly."

"Aye, Master Collop is quite silly," Tristan admitted. "But we'd do well to heed his words. He may be a bothersome old gossip, but his information is seldom wrong."

"What did he mean about another breach in the Afterlight?" she asked.

"Now that's blather, if you ask me," Tristan said. "No one has breached the Afterlight, not since the Age of Shadows. It's warded."

"Didn't you say that about the wards in the fortress?" Braeden asked dryly.

Tristan opened his mouth and then closed it. "Point taken."

They continued on the road again, now with far more amiability than the frosty silence of the morning. Tristan took the lead, setting a pace that was as fast as they could reasonably push the horses. Sam's right ankle still ached, but she pushed it out of her mind.

The road was not nearly as desolate as it had been between Heartwine and Gwent; the villages were not spread so far apart here, and merchants with their goods in tow traversed the dirt path between one village and the next. But Tristan wanted to reach the city of Cordoba before they closed the gates at nightfall, so he did not allow them stop again, and they ate their midday meal in the saddle. It was a good thing, too, for by the time they reached the city, it was already dusk.

"I hate Cordoba," Braeden muttered darkly as they neared the city gates.

Sam turned to Braeden in surprise. "Why?" She hadn't spent more than an hour in Cordoba, and had only passed through, so she knew little about the city or its people.

It was Tristan who answered. "Given its proximity to Heartwine, Cordoba is a Paladin bastion, and the city is very impassioned about our cause. You might say that their passion borders on fanaticism." Tristan twisted in his saddle towards Braeden. "I take it your, ah, unique heritage may have raised a few eyebrows?"

Braeden grimaced, tugging his straw hat lower over his eyes. "Something like that."

CHAPTER 10

$\mathcal{T}$RISTAN WAS GROWING impatient. If The Laughing Bear had been full, The Twelve Peers inn was overflowing. Even the foyer was crowded with people, and he had to shove and elbow his way to the front desk. A woman in a too-tight dress and far too much makeup stood behind the counter, thumbing through the guest book.

"Excuse me, Mistress . . ." Tristan started.

"Rosamund," she supplied, focused on her bookkeeping. "What can I do for you?"

"I need three rooms, please. For me and the lads," Tristan said, nodding towards Sam and Braeden.

Mistress Rosamund guffawed. "Three rooms? 'Ave you seen the place? You'll be lucky if you don't 'ave to sleep in the stables."

Tristan clutched her hand and pressed a light kiss to her knuckles. "My lady, isn't there anything you can do?" He lowered his voice. "For a paladin and his trainees?"

Mistress Rosamund finally looked at him, a blush staining her cheeks. "Well now, let me see 'ere," she murmured. "Per'aps the three of you would be willin' to share a room?" She lowered her eyes, then peeked at Tristan through her spidery lashes. "Though I would be 'appy to share me own chambers wiv *you*, love."

"Ah, madam, you are too kind, but I think the three of us will have to share a room. We've an early start to the morning, and I've a feeling if I stayed with you, we wouldn't be doing much sleeping," Tristan said with a wink. Behind him, Sam made a gagging noise.

Mistress Rosamund cackled delightedly. "Too bad. Meg!" she barked. A young maid scurried to the front desk and bobbed a curtsy. "Meg, I need you to show the misters 'ere to their room.

Room 317, it'll be." She leaned against the counter, showing her ample cleavage to its best advantage. "An' if you change your mind, love, you just let me know."

The room Mistress Rosamund rented out to them was a tight squeeze, but it would do. Meg promised to have a footman bring up extra pallets, so they wouldn't have to share a bed. Tristan knew well that they wouldn't always be so lucky; he'd spent most of the past decade on the road, and he took his comforts where he could.

"I'm going to grab a drink or two downstairs," he announced, feeling sociable. "Either of you care to join me?"

"I'll pass," Braeden said.

"Sam?" Tristan asked.

Sam shrugged. "Why not?"

Evenings at The Twelve Peers were a raucous affair, and Tristan couldn't help but laugh at the shocked expression on Sam's face. His eyes grew wider and wider as the inn's patrons pushed the boundaries of propriety to their limits and beyond. Men and women whirled around the floor in a mockery of a waltz, their bodies pressed so close together that not even an inch separated them. Several fillies sat perched on the knees of their misters, tittering and whispering sweet nothings into their lovers' ears. Tristan thought Sam might faint when a roguish fellow planted a kiss right on his lady's lips.

"I didn't know you were such an innocent," Tristan teased.

"It's improper," Sam hissed. "Don't these people have any decency?"

Tristan clapped his trainee on the shoulder. "Welcome to city life, lad." He steered the boy towards the sole empty table. "Let's get you a drink."

Tristan beckoned the nearest serving wench and watched appreciatively as she sashayed her way over to their table. "What can I get for you?" she asked.

"Your finest red wine will do. And there's an extra gold coin in it for you if you care to join us," Tristan said, waggling his eyebrows in an exaggerated fashion.

The serving wench grinned, displaying crooked white teeth

that somehow made her all the more appealing. "I'll be back with wine in a shake."

Tristan watched her walk away, letting out a low whistle. "That's a fine looking woman."

"If you say so," Sam said dubiously.

Ironically, when the serving wench—Alice, she told them—returned with three tankards and a pitcher of wine, the lass only had eyes for Sam. She slid her chair as close to him as was physically possible and touched his arm at frequent intervals. Sam seemed oblivious to her overtures and chatted with her as though they were bosom friends. Tristan was unused to getting passed over for another, but he supposed Sam was attractive in his own way, if a woman liked her man to be pretty.

Feeling like a voyeur, Tristan excused himself from their table. He figured he might as well rout out the local gossip to see if he could learn anything else of the Uriel.

After an hour of flirting and flattering, Tristan came away with a single name—Denya, a priestess of Cathair, the Night Lord. He'd been told that if anyone in Cordoba knew anything of the situation out west, it would be she. Tristan was quite pleased with himself; he'd even managed to ferret out the priestess's location, and it only cost him a silver penny.

When he returned his attention to where he had left Sam, he had to fight back a groan. The fool boy was stewed to the gills, swaying back and forth on his stool. It seemed only Alice's firm grip on his forearm kept him from tipping over. It was no wonder how he'd gotten himself in such a state; with her free hand, Alice discreetly poured the last of the wine into Sam's tankard.

Tristan considered allowing the serving wench to have her way with his drunk imbecile of a trainee, as that was clearly her intention, but decided to take pity on the boy. "Come on, lad," he said, gripping Sam by the elbow. "I'll take you up to bed." He dipped his head in apology to Alice, who pouted good-naturedly as Tristan dragged Sam away.

They had just made it to the stairs when Tristan felt Sam's full weight slump against him. "Sam?"

The boy said nothing, continuing to lean against him.

"Sam?" he repeated, a good deal louder. Sam stayed silent.

Tristan gripped him by the shoulders and shook. "Sam!" he shouted. No response.

Tristan would have been concerned if he didn't see the rise and fall of Sam's chest. Sam wasn't dead; his idiot trainee had passed out from overindulgence. "Why me?" he asked the Gods, though of course they didn't answer. Cursing under his breath, he scooped Sam into his arms and began trudging up the stairs. Sam, still asleep, sighed softly and wrapped his hands around Tristan's neck.

"You need to eat more," Tristan told his sleeping bundle. In response, Sam snored and nuzzled his nose against Tristan's sternum. "You stop that!" he snapped.

The climb up the stairs seemed inordinately long. Though Sam was hardly a heavy burden, Tristan was hot and out of breath by the time they reached their room. Shifting Sam against him so he could hold him with one arm, he rummaged around in his belt pouch for the room key and pushed the door open with a foot.

Braeden looked up from the book he was reading. "All right then?"

Tristan dumped Sam unceremoniously on the empty bed pallet. The boy snorted, grabbed at a nearby pillow, and curled his body around it.

Tristan nodded at Sam. "He had too much to drink." Sam punctuated the statement with an earth shattering snore.

Braeden's lips threatened a smile. "I can see that."

Tristan studied Sam's corpselike form. "He's going to hate himself in the morning."

"Aye."

"Unfortunate, really, that we have to wake up early."

"Indeed."

Tristan met Braeden's eyes, which crinkled at the corners. He felt his lips twitch once, twice, before the two of them doubled over with laughter.

Sam continued to sleep, undisturbed.

CHAPTER 11

Sam woke up with the worst headache of her life. It felt like she'd been bludgeoned with a mace. When she tried to sit up, her vision crossed and her stomach roiled with nausea. "I'm going to be sick," she managed before retching into a strategically placed chamber pot.

Tristan thumped her on the back. "Get it all out, lad. That's it."

"Why are you shouting?" she gasped in between heaves.

"I'm barely whispering," Tristan said, smirking. "You're sick from too much drink."

"Impossible. I just had one drink . . . two drinks"—she counted on her fingers—"I—I don't remember."

"I'll remind you. You had a few drinks too many," Tristan said. "I had to carry you up to bed."

Her face flamed to red. "You did not."

"He did," confirmed Braeden, leaning against the doorpost of their inn room.

Traitor, she mouthed, and then emptied the remainder of her stomach contents into the chamber pot.

"Clean yourself up and get ready to leave," Tristan said once she'd finished gagging. "We haven't a moment to waste."

As soon as Sam was dressed and capable, Tristan shuffled them out of the Laughing Bear and on the road to some private temple. The temple was hidden away on a small parcel of land that the rest of the city seemed to have forgotten. A solitary dirt path led to a small chapel and outdoor shrine, and then it forked off to a little stone cottage with a thatched roof and a single round window. A strange green smoke rose from its chimney.

Tristan tried knocking on the front door, but no one answered. He twisted the brass knob and pushed, and the door gave easily.

With a shrug, he stepped inside, ushering Sam and Braeden to follow him in.

They stepped into a rudimentary kitchen area. A tiny figure stooped over the stone hearth, stirring a pot with a bone-thin arm that had the knobbiest elbow Sam had ever seen. Stark white hair in a waist-length braid swayed as the old woman grabbed ingredients from various drawers and cabinets and added them to the simmering brew. Ominous green vapors rose from the pot. After a dash of something, they settled into a silver mist.

"I wondered when you would come."

They all jumped, even Braeden. "How did you know we were here?" Sam asked.

Still bent over her pot, the old woman flicked the lobe of her left ear. "I do not need eyes to see you, child."

"Who told you we were coming?" Tristan asked sharply.

She straightened and turned to face him, her craggy features splitting into a smile. "Why, you did, Paladin Lyons." She snorted at his perplexed expression. "There are no secrets in Cordoba. And you, Paladin, are as discreet as the town crier."

Tristan's mouth flapped open and closed a few times. Sam had to restrain an errant giggle; Tristan was clearly unused to being spoken to with such candor. "You are Denya, Priestess of Cathair, are you not?" he finally got out.

The old woman nodded. "I am she."

"I heard you might be able to help us," Tristan said. "We're in need of information of a somewhat delicate nature."

Denya fluttered bare eyelids, a wicked, girlish smile on her colorless lips. "Of course I am able to help you." Her grin widened. "The question is if I am willing."

Tristan gritted his teeth. "I can pay for information. Name your price, and the High Commander will see that you are paid."

The old woman drew herself back in umbrage. "I am a priestess of Cathair, not some common strumpet. If I choose to aid you, it is because the Night Father wills it so."

"And how do you determine that?" Tristan asked, crossing his arms in front of his chest.

"Simple," Denya said. "I will ask."

Tristan rolled his eyes heavenward. "And what, will he answer?"

Sam drew in a sharp breath of air at his rudeness. He hadn't blasphemed the Night Lord, but he walked a thin line. What had happened to Tristan to make him such a skeptic?

The old woman placed her hands on her hips, glaring up at him. "I see you have little respect for the Gods, and even less for their messengers."

"I learned long ago to put my faith in myself, not the Gods," Tristan said, returning her glare. "I respect them, but I don't rely on them. Now will you help us or not?"

Denya sighed, and then waved her hand toward a small table and chairs. "Sit," she said. "I will hear your questions. Perhaps I will answer them if you answer my questions in return."

They settled themselves around the table in awkward silence. The spark of humor vanished from Denya's rheumy eyes. Her gaze landed on Braeden, and she started, as if noticing him for the first time. Braeden ducked his head, staring fixedly at the surface of the table. With what appeared to be a great force of effort, the priestess returned her attention to Tristan. "Speak, Paladin. What secrets do you want to know?"

Tristan leaned forward in his seat. "What can you tell me of the Uriel?"

The old woman tilted her head to the side, reminding Sam of a crow. "I will not answer that question, Paladin, not yet. Tell me first why you wish to know."

Tristan let out a huff of air. "But you have heard of the Uriel, yes?"

A cryptic smile played across the old woman's mouth. "Aye, Paladin, I have. It won't be long till all of Thule has heard their name."

"You sound like you admire them," Sam accused. Tristan scowled at her as though she'd spoken out of turn. She ignored him, awaiting Denya's response.

Denya wrapped her fingers along her long white braid, tugging on its ends as she considered Sam's question. "What was it Paladin Lyons said of the Gods? I respect them, as one should any powerful force." She shook her head, pursing her thin lips.

"You've managed to divert me. What do you want from the Uriel, Paladin Lyons?"

Tristan ground his jaw. "The inquiry comes from the High Commander. That is all you need to know."

"The High Commander's spies extend throughout the West, do they not? What could you possibly hope to learn from me that the Sub Rosa cannot tell you?"

Tristan took his time before answering. "The Sub Rosa can find out who the Uriel are, and some of what they're doing. I want to know the why."

A white eyebrow rose. "Does why really matter?"

"Aye," Tristan said. "Why is always the most important part."

Denya gave Tristan a long speculative look. "Your view is unique, Paladin Lyons, especially for a man of your position."

"A man of my position?"

"Aye, Paladin. You are the High Commander's muscle. Muscle acts and does not question."

Tristan gripped the edge of the table. "I am more than my sword, priestess."

"Does your High Commander know that?"

Sam thought steam would come out of Tristan's ears. "Watch your tongue, old woman," he growled. "Your words border on treason."

Denya smiled faintly. "You're as hot tempered as they say, Paladin Lyons." She sat back in her chair. "I have heard enough."

Any effort Tristan had been making to remain composed went by the wayside. "You've told us nothing!"

The priestess rose to her feet, black eyes flashing. "I will tell you this, Paladin. The High Commander is right to fear the Uriel."

"Why?" he asked. "Have they named us their enemy?"

Denya snorted. "Who would be fool enough to do that?" She shook her head. "No, Paladin, the Uriel challenge you in deeds, not words. In the West, people turn to them for protection before they do you. You can rely on the Uriel, they say."

"And you cannot rely on us?" Tristan asked, obviously affronted.

The priestess shrugged her bony shoulders. "Go west, Paladin. See what you find." She studied Tristan, and then her gaze raked over Sam and Braeden. "I will give you a name," she said finally. "Sander Branimir. You won't soon forget it."

Tristan's expression was guarded. "I've never heard of this Sander."

"But you will," Denya promised. "Out West, they hold him in as much regard as Cordoba holds the High Commander. Rumor has it Branimir grew up poor, the son of a farmer from a small hamlet. Humble beginnings or not, the man runs the Uriel like he's held a scepter from the cradle." Just above a whisper, she added, "He's the sort a man would die for."

"So is the High Commander," Tristan said.

"Aye, Paladin, that he is," Denya said with the faintest of smiles. "Let us hope it never comes to that."

CHAPTER 12

$\mathcal{B}$ACK AT THE Twelve Peers, they spoke no more of the Uriel or of the strange priestess. Sam would have liked to ask more questions of Tristan—what did he know of the Uriel, and why did they make the High Commander so nervous?—but he was clearly in no mood for it. Instead, he gave her and Braeden the rest of the day to themselves, with a firm warning to stay out of trouble.

So Sam spent some time exploring the city of Cordoba on her own, grateful for the small freedom. It was a vibrant place, full of all manner of people: burghers in ordinary gowns and tunics, peddlers in garish colors, men with the ear to nose chains of the sea folk. Sam imagined you could find anything you ever needed or wanted here—spices from the East, silks from Westergo, fruit from the tropical lands in the South, medicines and herbs alleged to cure every ailment.

But the long nights and longer days of the past week soon caught up to her. She returned to the inn before the sun even set, made her excuses, and retired early to bed.

And yet, despite her exhaustion, sleep didn't come easily. Only after hours of lying restlessly in her pallet did she finally fall asleep, and then into a dream.

The first thing Sam saw was the woman. She was, without question, the most beautiful woman Sam had ever seen. Her face was inhuman in its perfection, as though her delicate features had been hewn from marble. Her eyes were closed, lashes fanning her cheeks, and her sensuous lips were parted as though she were in ecstasy. She leaned against a tree that bloomed pale pink cherry blossoms.

The Goddess Tree. Where was she? Had she somehow returned to Haywood?

The woman smiled, her eyes still shut. "Sam," she crooned, the name on her lips an invitation. She undulated her hips against the trunk of the tree.

Sam turned away, embarrassed. Any man would die a hundred deaths or confess to a thousand sins to be in Sam's place. But underneath her men's clothes, Sam's heart would never beat fast for a woman.

"Sam," the woman said again, pushing herself away from the tree. Now, she was demure, her eyes downcast as she approached.

Sam took a step back. "What do you want?"

The woman smiled sweetly, reaching out to cup Sam's cheek. "Who are you, Sam of Haywood?"

Sam shivered at her touch, and a warning sounded in the back of her brain. Don't trust her. "I-I'm nobody," she stuttered.

The woman's smile grew over-bright. "Will you not tell me who you are?"

Sam pressed her lips firmly together. Her instincts were seldom wrong, and they were screaming at her now. Do not trust her!

The woman's perfect features shifted into ugly fury. "Tell me," she snarled. "You will tell me who you are." She dug clawed nails into Sam's cheek, piercing the skin she'd just caressed.

Faith in blood, it hurt—but Sam clenched her jaw, ignoring the pain. "I'm nobody," she repeated.

"You lie!" the woman shouted. She backhanded Sam across the face, and then drove her nails in deep, gouging her to the bone.

Sam awoke in her bed writhing in agony, clutching her face with both hands. When she pulled her hands away, her fingers were dry; she had half expected to find them wet with blood. Just a dream.

Out of the corner of her eye she saw a dark shadow silhouetted by moonlight streaming through the window. The shadow was human in shape—or mostly human, for out of its back unfurled monstrous wings that spanned the width and length of its body. Its glittering crimson stare burned into her.

A beam of moonlight struck its face. Sam let out a shocked breath. The demon's visage was a mirror image of the woman's from her dream—but as though the reflection in the mirror had been warped. What had been beautiful perfection on the woman was a twisted mess, its features put together like mismatched puzzle pieces.

Sam looked wildly around for Tristan and Braeden. Both men were still fast asleep.

She didn't have a moment to waste. "Wake up!" she shouted, reaching for the dagger from the night table beside her pallet.

The demon gave a flap of its mighty wings and lunged for her. Sharp claws narrowly missed her head as she rolled off the bed and out of harm's way. She staggered to her feet, readying for the demon's next attack.

"Faith in blood," Tristan said in a hushed voice, suddenly standing behind her. "What is that thing?"

Thank the Gods, he was awake. "I saw it," Sam said. "I saw it in my dreams."

Tristan's jaw fell slack. "Dreamwalker," he whispered. "It can't be."

"Dreamwalker?" she asked, but Tristan shook his head and ignored her.

"Look out!" cried Braeden, crouching on top of his mattress, a knife in either hand. The demon was airborne again, circling them like a hawk. He threw his knives toward the pale underside of its wings, into the joint where wing met skin.

The demon howled, a terrible, inhuman sound, flapping its wings frantically. It gave one final flap, screeched, then touched its toes to the floor, folding its wings behind it.

Hissing through its teeth, the creature held up its long dangerous-looking talons.

Its crimson eyes were still locked on Sam. It edged forward, step by step, preparing to spring.

Tristan darted forward and plunged his sword deep into its gut. He drew the sword up and twisted, exposing its ribcage and pumping heart.

His blade still buried in the demon's chest, his gaze found Sam's. "Finish it," he said.

His voice echoed inside her head. It won't die till you cut off its head!

Crossing the floor to Tristan, she thrust her dagger into the demon's throat till it pierced through the other side. With all her strength, she wrenched the dagger sideways. Its head rolled to the floor, mouth frozen in a scream.

Sam stared at the head. Separated from its winged body, it appeared all too human. She swallowed down a lump of bile. "The demon—it spoke to me. In my dream it wanted me to talk."

Tristan ran his fingers through his hair. "To live in such times," he muttered. "It should be impossible."

"What should be impossible?"

"In the stories of old, there are demons that can manipulate dreams," Tristan said. "Dreamwalkers, they were called. It was said they made the realm of dreams their domain, that they could use it as a means of travel. But they haven't been seen in thousands of years, not since they were imprisoned in the Afterlight with the worst of the demons. They were supposed to be gone forever."

"You think that was one of them?" Sam asked.

Tristan shook his head. "I don't know what to believe."

"For whatever my opinion is worth," Braeden said, bending over to retrieve his knives from the demon's corpse, "I can tell you this demon is different from any I've ever encountered before."

"How so?" Tristan asked.

Braeden wiped his knives clean on his robes. "It was intelligent. It had complex thoughts, like you or me."

Tristan swore. "I must write of this to the High Commander. But first we have to leave Cordoba. Immediately."

"Why?" Sam asked, covering a yawn. "It's not even close to morning."

Tristan glanced sidelong at Braeden. "A demon in Cordoba is not exactly a common occurrence, and this"—he gestured at the demon's corpse—"will incite some unnecessary misunderstandings."

"They'll blame me for it," Braeden said without any obvious emotion, "just like they did at the fortress."

Sam made a face. "That's stupid." Where was the logic in that?

"It's Cordoba," Braeden said, as though that explained everything.

Tristan frowned at them both. "Less talking, more packing."

Getting rid of the demon in secret was a gruesome affair. They hacked up the body, wrapped the pieces in bed sheets, and once outside, Tristan took out his tinderbox and set it afire. They left The Twelve Peers when the last of the demon's corpse had been burned to ashes. The streets of Cordoba, so boisterous just hours earlier, were dead quiet. With the moon as their only source of light, they kept the horses at a slow walk, careful to avoid any missteps. The gatekeeper was asleep at his post, and they had to rouse him from his slumber in order to get him to raise the city gates. He would have refused, too, had Tristan not revealed himself as a paladin.

As the excitement from the demon attack tapered off, Sam began to feel the effects of lack of sleep. "Are we riding for much longer?"

"I want to get at least two hours' distance away before we rest," Tristan said. "Why?"

"I'm practically falling asleep on my horse, that's all," she replied with a hint of a whine.

"You're beginning to annoy me," Tristan told her. "You knew full well when you joined the Paladins what you signed on for. I've gone days without sleep when I've had to."

"Fine," she grumbled, shutting her mouth.

After several minutes had passed, Tristan spoke again. "Braeden, can I ask you something?"

Braeden grunted in the affirmative.

"There's no easy way to ask this," Tristan said with an apologetic laugh. "We've had two demon attacks in the past week. We rarely see them with such frequency, especially in such close proximity to warded territory." He dragged in an audible breath. "Does your presence have anything to do with it? I'm not suggesting you're drawing them on purpose, of course. I don't blame you for Paladin Savage's death."

"It's fine," Braeden said. "I'd wonder, too, if I were you. But the answer is no. I've always had to seek demons out, if I wanted to fight them. I cannot control where and when they show." Sam felt Braeden's eyes on her back. "I'm not sure why we've seen so many demons of late. But there must be a reason."

A long silence followed his reply. Sam concentrated on keeping her eyes open; several times her forehead collided with her horse's neck as she nodded in and out of sleep, and once she nearly fell out of her saddle. To her frustration, neither Tristan nor Braeden seemed to be having any trouble. She stuck out her tongue at their backs.

By the time Tristan motioned for them to dismount, Sam was all but ready to collapse. They walked their horses off the main dirt road to a hidden enclave in the surrounding woods and tethered them to a tree. Tristan erected a small wedge tent, just large enough to squeeze three bodies side by side.

"I'll take the first watch," he said. "Braeden, I'll wake you for the second watch, and Sam, you'll take the third. Get sleep while you can."

Sam didn't need to be told twice. She rolled out her bedding and crawled beneath her blanket. The ground was uncomfortably hard, but at least her ankle no longer bothered her so much. Only the occasional twinge reminded her that she'd injured it just a few days before.

She felt Braeden crawl in next to her. "Sam?" he whispered.

"Yes?"

"Did you feel anything strange earlier tonight? Before the demon appeared?"

"I had a bad dream," she replied sleepily. "Why do you ask?"

He hesitated before responding. "I can sense the presence of demons, well before they're in range to attack. But this one . . . this one I didn't sense till you shouted for us to wake."

"What do you think it means?"

"I don't know."

"Maybe you should say something to Tristan," she suggested.

He shifted again, flipping over onto his back. "I'd rather not. Not yet anyway," he said. "It could have been a fluke. I'll tell him about it if it happens again."

"Tristan can be an arrogant ass," Sam said, "but I think we can trust him."

"You're more trusting than I am." He said nothing more, and Sam wondered if he'd fallen asleep.

"Braeden?"

"Yes, Sam?"

"Thanks for trusting me."

CHAPTER 13

THE NEXT FEW days left Sam exhausted. As soon as Tristan felt they had made enough distance from Cordoba, he had begun daily training sessions. If Sam had thought training at the Paladin fortress had been hard, drilling two-on-one with Tristan was brutal. It wouldn't have been so bad if he allowed them to use weapons, but Tristan made them perform callisthenic exercises that Sam swore he'd invented just to torment them. She knew that Braeden was half a demon, but she was beginning to think that Tristan wasn't entirely human either. The man never tired, and—good Gods, was he *whistling* now?

"You're off tune," she accused.

Tristan twisted around in his saddle to glare at her. "You don't know the song. How could you possibly judge whether I'm off tune?'

"I don't need to know the song to know your rendition is terrible."

His frown deepened. "What's got you in such a foul mood?"

She *was* in a foul mood—she hadn't had a bath or a proper night's sleep in ages and she felt vile. She was too tired and cross to pretend otherwise. "Why must you torture us with your whistling? You have no reason to be so cheery."

"I wasn't aware I needed a reason to be in good spirits," Tristan said. "Besides, Braeden doesn't mind my whistling. Right, Braeden?"

Braeden let out a loud cough and cantered his horse up ahead of them.

"It's not that bad!" Tristan called after him, reserving his scowl for Sam. "If you must know, I'm looking forward to our arrival in Haywood. We'll be there in half a day's ride."

Her heart sped up. "We're stopping in Haywood?"

"Aye," Tristan said. "I have business with the duke. You'll have time to visit with your family, if you'd like."

"Great," she muttered. No need to tell Tristan that the duke was her family. She would have to make sure she stayed out of sight for the duration of their stay. There were too many people who might recognize her, and too few she could trust to hold their tongue. If she had her druthers, she would never come back to Haywood. There was nothing for her there anymore.

As they closed the final distance between Cordoba and Haywood, the scenery began to change. Rolling dunes flattened and the occasional pockets of thicket spread till the land was green as far as the eye could see. The air thickened with humidity and the clouds gathered in the sky, blocking the sun's rays but not their warmth.

Once the all-too-familiar turrets of Castle Haywood came into view—the only home she'd ever known—Sam retrieved a cloak from her pack, hiding her face beneath its hood.

"Are you mad?" Tristan asked incredulously. "It's boiling hot out."

"I'm cold," Sam lied, hoping he couldn't see the perspiration on her upper lip. When he wasn't looking, she dabbed at her damp face with her sleeve. Braeden, however, caught her at it, shooting her a quizzical look. *Later,* she mouthed, though she wasn't sure what tale she'd spin.

It was nearing dusk when they reached the murky waters of the castle moat. The moat was a relatively new addition to Haywood; the duke had grown increasingly paranoid in the years since his wife's death and spared no expense when it came to the city's security. Hundreds of sentries were stationed on top of the city wall. But, as Sam knew well, the duke's security was not infallible: for years, she had bribed the guards to keep her training a secret from her father. After her mother had died, not only had he stopped training her, he had also demanded she stop training altogether.

To Sam's surprise, the sentries lowered the drawbridge without any delay or questions. They must have recognized Tristan— which was odd, because there were few people the guards knew on sight besides the city folk who lived in Haywood year round. Tristan did say he had business with the duke, so perhaps they had been waiting for his arrival.

They rode their horses across the wooden deck and down the main boulevard into the heart of Haywood. The hustle and bustle of the city was at its peak this time of year as Haywood prepared for the annual grand fair, held during the last week of every summer. Shop windows were crowded with the latest wares, and it seemed new stalls had cropped up on every street corner. Caravans of traveling merchants were squeezed in between, carrying spices and silks and all manner of exotic goods.

Sam felt like a stranger in her own skin as they passed the sights and sounds and smells of her former home. Nothing much appeared to have changed since she'd left, but she could hardly expect Master Dwyer to slip her a tartlet when she passed his bakeshop, nor would Master Wayland, the blacksmith, usher her inside his forge for her to admire his latest creation. He'd made Sam her first sword when she was just a little girl, upon her mother's request and her father's reluctant approval.

It was an odd sort of homecoming. There were no friendly faces for Sam to greet, only people to hide from. She hunched over in her saddle, hood pulled low over her eyes, avoiding the gazes of anyone but her traveling companions.

Tristan led them straight to The Courtier, the finest inn in Haywood. Nestled between a row of red and blue houses, the inn was a five-storied affair with its own private stables. Its owner, Master Ibarra, doubled as one of the city's most prominent moneylenders, and he used his extra profits to lavish the inn with every conceivable amenity. Only the very wealthy could afford The Courtier's exorbitant rates.

After a footman stabled their horses, Master Ibarra came to greet them and escorted them inside. Sam pretended fascination with a spot on the floor, studiously observing her feet. She'd never before made the innkeeper's acquaintance, but all of Haywood knew her face.

"Paladin Lyons," he said, smoothing his oiled mustache. "It's good to see you again."

Tristan inclined his head. "And you, Master Ibarra. I trust business has been good."

Master Ibarra sighed. "Never good enough, I'm afraid. But enough of business. Tonight I am at your disposal. Name anything you need, and I will see that it is yours."

"Thank you, Master Ibarra," Tristan said. "I must confess I'm surprised to see you. I thought you'd have a servant attend to us instead, what with all the preparations for the fair."

"His Grace told me you were coming, so I wanted to see to you myself," the innkeeper said with a flourish of his hand.

Sam's ears perked up at the mention of 'His Grace.' The duke had informed Master Ibarra of Tristan's arrival? He only gave advance notice for the most important of dignitaries.

"Ah, yes," Tristan said, "I wrote to the duke before we left Heartwine to let him know I'd be passing through."

Master Ibarra smoothed his mustache again before speaking. "About His Grace—" the innkeeper paused, a pained expression on his face. "Actually, it's probably best if he tells you himself." He reached into his belt pouch and removed a sealed letter that had been folded into quarters. "From the duke." He handed the letter to Tristan.

Tristan broke the seal of the letter and quickly scanned its contents, his face growing perplexed. With great precision, he refolded the letter and tucked it into the top of his trousers. "We'll be needing three rooms for the next few nights," he said to Master Ibarra.

The innkeeper bowed. "Very well. If you'll follow me."

Master Ibarra guided them up four flights of stairs to the best rooms in the inn. It wasn't till she'd reached the third flight that Sam realized she would have an entire room to herself. It was the most privacy she'd had in weeks. Despite the stress of being in the world's most dangerous place to her identity, she felt positively giddy.

Once they were settled, Master Ibarra bowed and excused himself, informing them he'd be in the mead hall should they need him.

"Okay, lads," Tristan said. "We need to talk." He sagged onto a nearby settee and began removing his boots.

"Is everything all right, Tristan?" Sam asked, feeling much warmer towards him than she had earlier in the day.

"Everything is fine," he replied, pulling off another boot. "I think it is, anyway."

"What did the duke want?" Sam asked, forcing nonchalance into her voice.

"That's what I wanted to talk to both of you about," Tristan said, straightening. "We've received a summons. The duke wants us to dine with him tomorrow evening."

"Us?" Sam and Braeden exclaimed in horrified unison.

"It's a tremendous honor," he continued, oblivious to his trainees' dismayed reactions. "His Grace is one of the most powerful men in all of Thule. Tomorrow night, you must acquit yourself with the dignity befitting a Paladin trainee. *My* trainees. The duke is rather fond of me. Don't embarrass me."

Sam gaped at Tristan. The Duke of Haywood was *fond* of him? The duke wasn't fond of his own daughter!

"Are you certain you want me to come?" Braeden asked with a hint of defiance. "I wouldn't want to cause you embarrassment."

"Don't be ridiculous," Tristan said. Sam liked him better for it. "You're my trainee, same as Sam. The duke would expect no less. He's eager to meet both of you."

"Why?" Sam asked. The Duke of Haywood she knew had little interest outside of politics and no time for anyone who didn't figure into his machinations. Why would he waste his breath conversing with a paladin's trainees?

"I don't know," Tristan admitted. "His letter said he had news to share with me alone, but he insisted on meeting the two of you. Idle curiosity, I suppose."

Sam shook her head. Her father never did anything without deep thought and careful calculation.

"Listen," Tristan said, rising to his feet. "The duke is a very important man, so try not to do anything foolish. And remember, you two are a reflection on me."

"I think we can manage," Braeden said dryly.

Sam was not so certain. For all his faults, no one would call the duke stupid. Her short hair and men's clothes would never fool him. If her father saw her, he'd know it was her in an instant. He wouldn't even have to drag her back to Haywood; she was already there. She needed to get out of dinner, at whatever cost.

When they went their separate ways to bed, Sam was still without any ideas. She could run away again, but that would defeat the whole purpose. What she needed was an excuse—or a disguise so good her own father wouldn't recognize her.

After an hour of tossing and turning, brilliance finally struck. Brilliance, or extreme stupidity, but she was too desperate to care which.

She knocked on the door between her room and Braeden's. He unlocked the door a moment later.

"Thank the Gods you're still awake."

"What's wrong?" Braeden asked, allowing Sam to slip past him into his chamber. "You've been acting strangely all day." He closed the door behind her and took a seat on the edge of his bed.

"It's complicated," she said, wincing at the understatement. Complicated didn't begin to cover it.

Braeden arched an eyebrow. "I can do complicated."

"I'll explain it all to you someday, I promise," she said. She hoped she'd be able to keep that promise, and that he wouldn't hate her when she told him. "But for now, I need a favor."

Braeden nodded for her to go on.

She just had to come right out and say it. "I need you to punch me."

Braeden nearly fell off the edge of the bed. "What?"

She tried again, more slowly, "I need you to punch me. In the face. Hard."

Braeden abruptly stood up and closed the distance between them, cupping her face in both hands. A scant inch separated their noses—and mouths, but Sam willed that thought away—and up this close, Sam could see that Braeden's eyes were beautiful, the irises shimmering shades of red with tiny flecks of gold. In spite of herself, she shivered.

"Sorry," Braeden said, dropping his hands and backing away. A dark red warmed the ochre of his cheeks.

"What was that for?" she asked indignantly.

"I was searching for signs of illness. Clearly, you've gone mad."

"It's not madness, it's—" she stopped. "I've got some money saved up. I'll pay you to do it. How about three gold sovereigns?"

"I wouldn't do it for five hundred." He plopped back down on the bed, folding his arms over his chest. "Sam, why don't you tell me what's really going on?"

Sam had once been told that the best lies were distortions of the truth. So she'd try to come close to the truth. Still, she felt guilty about lying to Braeden.

"What I'm about to tell you, you can't tell anyone," she said, her voice just above a whisper. "Especially not Tristan. Do you swear on the Gods?"

Braeden looked nonplussed, but he agreed. "Aye, I swear."

She drew in a steadying breath. "I lied about my lineage to the Paladins. Lord Hawkins is not my father. There *is* no Lord Hawkins."

His brow knitted into a frown. "I don't understand. Why lie? And what does that have to do with anything?"

She couldn't meet his gaze. "The Duke of Haywood is my father."

Braeden was silent for several beats. "Are you lying to me now?"

"No," she said hoarsely. "I swear it on the Gods and on my mother's grave."

"Are you his heir?"

She crossed her fingers behind her back. I'm sorry, Mother. "No, Braeden. I'm his ill-gotten bastard."

She could see the wheels in his mind turning as he processed her lie. "This is . . . unexpected. I don't know the right thing to say."

She offered him a tentative smile, burying her guilt. "Say nothing. Just help me. I can't see my father tomorrow, not looking like this."

"Would it be so bad?" he asked. "Seeing your father?"

"Yes, it would," she retorted. "My father thinks I have no business fighting demons just because I'm a g—" She swallowed her words.

"Because you're a what?" Braeden prompted.

Faith in blood, she'd almost betrayed herself. She needed to watch her tongue. "Because I'm a bastard. My father would never have allowed me to join the Paladins. If he finds out I'm here, he'll force me to come home."

"That's tricky," he acknowledged. "But how will a punch in the face solve anything?"

She pinched the skin on the inside of her arm hard, show- ing the new purple-blue spot to Braeden. "I bruise easily. If you blacken my eyes and bloody my lip, the duke won't know it's me."

"Would you like me to break your nose as well?"

Sam thought it over. "I'd rather you didn't. I'd prefer not to do any permanent damage to my face, if I can avoid it."

Braeden gave her a long, searching look, and then buried his face in his hands. His shoulders began to shake.

"Will you do it?" she prodded.

"You're mad," Braeden gasped between laughs. "Absolutely stark raving mad."

"So you won't do it then?"

"Not for all the gold in the king's treasury," he replied, still laughing.

"Fine," she snapped. "If you won't do it, I'll find someone who will."

CHAPTER 14

S AM HAD FAR more experience skulking about the city streets at night than any young lady had a right to. She owed her skills to the duke: no sooner had her mother's grave cooled than her father had taken her aside and informed her that her days of swordplay were over. Tempers flared, and they'd both said terrible things to the other that they could never take back. The duke, naturally, was the victor, and Sam wound up without a sword. In place of her sword lessons, she'd been given a governess to teach her all the things a well-bred lady ought to know.

It was no wonder she'd run away.

The governess was a dragon of a woman, fond of pointless drills and endless lectures, but she also kept society hours. She seldom woke before noon, and, enamored of the vibrant nightlife at court, stayed out well into the evening, leaving her charge to her own devices. Sam had taken advantage of these lapses of supervision, practicing training drills in the early mornings before any of the court was awake and escaping into the heart of the city at night to learn what else she could of combat.

So Sam was something of an expert at sneaking out undiscovered, and she knew the city streets of Haywood like the backs of her hands. She knew all the seediest pubs and gambling houses, the best fencing clubs, and the toughest underground pugilism rings.

By the time she stepped through the front door of the Wanderer's Tavern, it was well past the hour for anyone respectable to be out of bed. The common room had emptied out, and the remaining patrons were a motley, unsavory bunch. Men leaned against the walls, wiping the ale from their beards and making lip claps at anything female that crossed their vision. At the tables, they played at cards or dice, drinking all the while. Others sagged in their chairs, heads down on the bar, snoring with abandon.

It didn't take her long to pick her target. The man stood by himself in the corner of the room, wavering on his feet, holding onto the wall for balance. He had a mean, blotchy face and the glassy eyed look of inebriation. He wasn't a big man—perhaps half a head taller than she, and two stone heavier—but that suited her purposes perfectly.

Sam sidled up to him and made a show of looking him up and down. "You, sir," she said, loud enough for the entire room to hear, "are a drunk."

The common room fell silent, waiting for the man's reaction. Unsteadily, the man pushed himself from the wall. "What did you call me?" he asked, slurring his words.

"A drunk," she repeated. "You're so drunk I bet you couldn't hit me if you tried. Not with my hands tied behind my back."

"Ish 'at right?"

"That's right," she sneered, clasping her hands behind her. "Just you try it."

The man wound back his arm and swung his fist at her face. And missed.

Sam started laughing. "You missed. I can't believe you missed." With a growl, the man swung at her again.

This time he didn't miss.

When Sam looked at her reflection in the mirror the next morning, she didn't know whether to laugh or cry. Her nose—while she was almost certain it wasn't broken—was red and twice its normal size. Bruised purple-black and puffy, her left eye was so swollen that only the tiniest sliver of eyeball peeked through the lids. Her bottom lip was split, and her entire face was bumpy from multiple contusions. She didn't recognize herself.

Well, that had been the goal, hadn't it?

Tristan exploded the instant she walked down to breakfast. His butter knife dropped to the table with a clatter. "Gods' teeth, boy, what did you do to your face?"

Sam cringed at his tone, scrunching up her eyes and forehead, and then immediately regretted it. Good Gods, her face hurt.

Tristan shoved back from the table, jumping to his feet. "What part of 'the duke wants us to dine with him' did you not understand? You were supposed to look *respectable*. How did you even get your eye to turn that shade of purple?"

"I'm sorry," Sam said contritely, schooling her face into a meek expression. She hoped she at least *sounded* apologetic.

"Sorry isn't good enough." Tristan pinched the bridge of his nose and breathed deeply, twice. "The duke is a very important man to the Paladins, Sam. And he's a very important man to me."

"Why?" Sam blurted. Her father had always seemed more self-important than important to her, though she had to admit, he had kept her somewhat sheltered.

"My reasons don't affect you. Needless to say, I wanted—I *want* to impress him. And I told you, did I not, that you are a reflection on me. Sam, have you seen *your* reflection? I swear, it's like you mistook your face for your shield." He jabbed his finger at Braeden, who was already several bites into his oats. "What do you know about this?"

Braeden registered her injuries with a stony face. Great, now he was angry with her, too. "I assure you I had no involvement."

Tristan let out a heavy sigh. "You certainly can't meet the duke looking as you do."

A seed of hope took root in her chest. "Really?" she said with feigned disappointment. "What a shame."

Braeden's spoon paused halfway to his mouth. A small snort escaped his nose.

"What?" she snapped, still annoyed he hadn't agreed to help her. Braeden shrugged, pointedly avoiding her gaze.

Tristan sighed again, plopping back down in his seat. "Well, what's done is done. I shall find a way to fix this."

"How?" she asked suspiciously.

"I don't know yet," he said, "but I'll figure something out. I always do." He buttered another piece of bread, pausing to glance over at her. "Stop making that face. It hurts to look at."

"I'm not making any face," she protested, then noticed he was grinning. "You lout."

Four hours later, Sam stared dubiously at the dozens of small pots and jars. *This* was Tristan's solution?

"Now, don't you furrow your brow, Master Haywood. You'll create wrinkles in your pretty skin."

Sam scoffed. "Are you blind? Now is hardly the time to be worrying about wrinkles in my 'pretty skin'."

"Nonsense," Leona said, her impressive bosom all but falling out of her dress as she bent over to pat cream across Sam's abused cheeks. "I can tell you're right handsome under them bruises. Almost as pretty as a girl."

Sam found herself blushing. "You probably say that to all your . . . clients." Sam hadn't the faintest idea of how to talk to a courtesan; Leona was the first she'd ever met. She seemed nice enough, but Sam had a hard time getting past her choice of trade.

Leona glared at her, and then glanced back at Tristan. "This one needs to learn how to accept a compliment." She turned back to Sam. "And you aren't a *client*. I'm doing this as a favor to Paladin Lyons."

"You *are* the best, Leo," Tristan said, patting the courtesan's knee affectionately. Sam wrinkled her nose.

Leona placed her hands on her generous hips. "Don't think very highly of me or mine, do you, Master Haywood?"

Now Sam felt guilty. Leona had done nothing to deserve her censure. "It's not that. It's . . ." she floundered, searching for an excuse. "It's all these cosmetics. Wearing makeup doesn't seem very . . . masculine."

Leona seemed to accept that response and resumed applying various ointments and powders to Sam's face. "You'd be surprised how many men use a little o' this and that now and again."

"Really?" Sam asked, fascinated.

Leona nodded. "Usually it's to hide a love bite from the missus, but sometimes a man just wants to pretty himself up a bit."

Sam leaned forward and asked in a low voice. "Have you ever made up Tristan?"

Leona gave a husky laugh. "Some men don't need any help looking pretty."

"You're talking about me," Tristan declared. "I can tell."

"You are as vain as ever, Paladin Lyons," Leona said. "It's a good thing you're handsome."

"A high compliment from the loveliest lady in Haywood," Tristan said with a wink. Leona tittered into her hand. Sam fought not to roll her eyes.

"Am I as handsome as Paladin Lyons yet?" Sam asked, interrupting their flirtation.

Leona chuckled. "Just about." She took a fine paintbrush and dipped it in a thick green paste. "Helps with the redness," she explained when she saw Sam's skeptical gaze. She pressed a horsetail brush into a white crystallized powder, and then mixed the substance into a small dish of rosewater. Carefully, she painted Sam's skin, her touch quick and gentle.

"All done," Leona said finally. "Couldn't do nothing about the swelling, but at least your face is all one color."

Sam turned to face the mirror, and turned her head this way and that. Leona had done wonders with the magic of cosmetics. Her skin was a uniform shade of beige, and Leona had even managed to hide her split lip. Her eyes were still two different sizes, her jaw line swollen and her nose unusually bulbous, but that was good—necessary—to fool her father. She looked uninjured, but best of all, she didn't look like herself.

"You're a genius, Leona," she said, hugging her impulsively. Leona seemed taken aback at first, but returned the hug after a moment's hesitation.

"You're a strange one," the courtesan told Sam. "Good luck with the duke."

She was going to need it.

CHAPTER 15

WAITING IN THE entrance hall of Castle Haywood, Sam was amazed by how little had changed since she'd run away. It hadn't been that long, really—not even two months—yet she'd expected her home to show the signs of her absence. But the room looked as though time had frozen: at first glance, everything was the same, down to the wax-coated chandelier that was still missing two candles and the splotch of burgundy on the carpet where a guest had spilled his wine.

"Have you been inside Castle Haywood before, Sam?" Tristan asked, intruding on her reverie.

"Aye, once or twice," she said vaguely, pretending to be fascinated with a nearby painting. She blinked in surprise as the painting came into focus. It was a watercolor of a lilac, one she'd painted herself five years ago. The duke must have moved it from her bedroom after she left. She swallowed down a lump that had formed at the back of her throat. Now was not the time to get sentimental.

Sam felt a warm hand on her shoulder. "Are you all right?" Braeden asked in a low voice.

"I'm fine," she said with more certainty than she felt, turning around to face him. She tried to smile, but smiling stretched the scabs on her lips, and her attempt became more of a grimace.

"You still look like you, you know," Braeden said, his expression unreadable beneath the low brim of his hat.

"He won't recognize me, I'm sure of it." Her eyes darted back to the lilac watercolor. Why had the duke moved it there? If she didn't know better, she would call it sentimental.

"I've heard he's clever, the Duke of Haywood," Braeden said.

"He *is* clever. Just not . . . observant." She was counting on that. With a shake of her head, she tugged on Braeden's sleeve. "Come on, Tristan's going to think we're conspiring against him if we keep to the corner like this."

Braeden grabbed her wrist before she could leave. "I can help you, if you'll let me. If something happens."

Sam laughed mirthlessly. "If the duke recognizes me, it's all over. Trust me on that."

"I can help," Braeden insisted, his grip on her wrist tightening. "I can make him forget you're even in the room."

Sam raised her free hand to touch Braeden's shoulder, but stopped halfway when she caught Tristan watching them. "You're a good friend, Braeden," she said, letting her hand drop to her side.

Two circles of red bloomed beneath his high cheekbones. "We're friends?"

"Aren't we?"

Braeden's lips curved into a rare smile. "Friends," he agreed.

Sam felt something shift between them, but a new voice, once she hadn't heard in months, interrupted her thoughts before she had the chance to think too deeply on it.

"Paladin Lyons, Masters Braeden and Sam," the voice called with an affected accent—the Lady Jocelyn Colton, her former governess. Now there was one person Sam hadn't missed, and no doubt the feeling was mutual. Frankly, she was shocked Lady Colton had retained a position with the duke after her charge had run away. She had not been well-liked by any of the staff, and it was clear as day to anyone who paid attention that she was angling to be the duke's next wife. Sam had always been entertained by the woman's efforts to win over her father; the governess had yet to learn that the Duke of Ice didn't give a whit about anyone. He wasn't about to start with her.

"His Grace will see you now. If you'll follow me," Lady Colton said with a curtsy. Sam flinched as her former governess's eyes met hers, and for a horrible second, she thought the horrible woman had seen through the pounds of cosmetics and swollen features. But the governess stared far longer at Braeden than she did at Sam, and apart from the pinched disapproval of her mouth, she had no obvious reaction.

As Sam followed Lady Colton, she felt the tangle of nerves at the pit of her stomach crawl up around her throat, threatening to strangle her. In mere moments, she would see the duke, her father, her only remaining parent. But would he see Sam of Haywood, Paladin trainee, or Lady Samantha?

Lady Colton brought them to the great hall, and then, much to Sam's relief, excused herself. She didn't need the governess lurking when she came face to face with her father.

The Duke of Haywood sat at the high table on a dais at the end of the great hall, sipping a goblet of wine. Though the vast room was full of courtiers, he sat alone. Most men of power liked to surround themselves with advisors and sycophants, but the duke preferred his privacy. He'd once told Sam the only judgment he could trust was his own.

Tristan led them up to the dais, stopping just before the stone steps. "Your Grace," Tristan said, bowing low. Sam almost dipped into a curtsy out of sheer habit, but managed a clumsy head bob. Braeden swept into a bow with much more aplomb.

"Tristan, my boy, it has been far too long," the duke said genially. Sam gawked at the familiarity—and warmth—in the duke's greeting. Where was the Duke of Ice? In her eighteen years, she couldn't recall a time her father had spoken to her with such affection. "We have much to discuss, you and I. But first, bring your companions to the dais. I look forward to making your trainees' acquaintance."

Reeling over her father's change in demeanor, Sam's feet stayed frozen to the ground. Tristan put a firm hand on the small of her back. "Introduce yourself to the duke, you idiot," he hissed into her ear, giving her a shove.

"S-sorry," she stammered, stumbling up the steps to dais. She bowed till her nose nearly touched the ground. "Sam, Your Grace."

The duke chuckled. "Get up, lad. You do me too much honor."

She knew she couldn't hide her face from him forever. Slowly, she straightened, meeting the yellow-green eyes that matched her own.

Her body tensed as she waited for those intelligent eyes to fill with recognition, for the anger that coursed through him like a river to bubble up and crash down on her in waves. She waited for him to tell her she was ten kinds of foolish, that she had brought dishonor to him, and more importantly, to Haywood. She waited for him to reveal her as the woman that even heavy bruising, men's garb, and years of training couldn't hide. He would expose her as the most heinous of liars. The worst part was that all of it would be true.

But the words never came.

"Tristan tells me you are from Haywood," the duke said.

You could have knocked her over with a feather.

"A-aye, Your Grace," she stuttered, struggling to hide her shock. He hadn't recognized her. Unbelievable.

"Lord Hawkins' son—I do not remember the Hawkins name. I thought I knew all the aristocracy."

"My father does not get out much, Your Grace," she said, repeating the lie she told the High Commander. "He hasn't been much for society since my mother passed."

The duke's face softened. "I see," he said. "Would that I could have done the same."

Sam stared at him. For a moment there, he sounded almost human.

"Sam of Haywood, it is my pleasure," the duke said formally. "May you bring honor to your family and to Haywood."

And with that, her introduction to the duke was over. Sam shuffled off the dais, and then watched stupidly as the duke greeted Braeden in kind.

That was it? She'd dreaded this meeting all night, and he was done with her in mere minutes? A feeling suspiciously like rage boiled up inside her. He was her father, Gods damn it! Mentally, she scolded herself for her illogic. She should be celebrating; if he'd recognized her, everything she'd worked so hard for over the last few years would be over. But she just couldn't countenance that he had stared directly into her eyes and saw nothing of his own daughter. She'd always questioned their relationship; here was the damning proof that she was nothing more to him than an afterthought.

"Let's eat, shall we?" the duke said after all the pleasantries had been exchanged. He gestured for Tristan to sit at the seat of honor beside him.

She and Braeden were relegated to dine on the benches with the lesser nobles and knights, a novel experience for Sam. As Lady Samantha, she'd had a permanent place of residency by her father's side on the dais. Even when he didn't join his people for meals—which was more often than not—Sam would sit at the raised platform, eating by herself, or occasionally with the visiting lord or lady she was meant to entertain. It had been a lonely existence, being the daughter of a duke.

Sam and Braeden sat shoulder-to-shoulder across from a young knight, who looked to be about Tristan's age, and a portly noble Sam didn't know. They nodded at Sam and Braeden, staring a little longer than necessary at Braeden. He yanked his hat down over his eyes self-consciously.

Sam elbowed him gently. "Stop worrying. They know you have my fa—the duke's approval."

Braeden pushed back the brim so he could look at her. "You were right. He didn't recognize you."

Sam felt a sharp pang in her chest. "I know. I told you he wouldn't."

He nudged her shoulder with his. "I'm sorry."

Her heart constricted. Somehow, Braeden had seen through her mask of indifference to her hurt. "Thank you," she said, willing her voice not to shake. Stupid emotions.

Her gaze wandered over to her father and Tristan at the dais. The duke gripped Tristan by the elbows, talking in low, intent tones. Every now and again, Tristan pinched the bridge of his nose like he tended to do whenever he was frustrated or upset. The mood between them had taken a sharp turn from their initial exchange.

"What do you think Tristan's talking about with the duke?" Sam asked. "They look so serious."

Braeden shrugged. "If it involves us, I'm sure he'll tell us."

"Aren't you at all curious?"

"Not really, no."

She sighed. "You're no fun."

"I just mind my own business."

"And I repeat, no fun."

Braeden glared at her. "Why don't you ask him? Look, he's headed over our way now."

Sure enough, Tristan strode towards them in long, angry steps. "On your feet. We're leaving." Without bothering to wait for them, he did a turnabout and marched out of the great hall. Braeden and Sam looked at each other and then hastily pushed back from their bench, running out after him.

They found Tristan in the courtyard outside the castle keep, staring off into the distance. His handsome face looked haunted, his blue eyes bleak.

"Tristan," Sam asked softly, "Is everything okay?"

"No," Tristan said, after a long pause. "No, it's not."

Sam didn't know what to say. How did men comfort each other? Women hugged, they soothed, they cried—not that she'd ever been much good at any of those things either. Instead, she asked, "Do you want to talk about it?"

His face still turned away, he answered, "A woman of great importance to me is dead."

Sam felt her mouth go dry. "Who was she?"

His clouded gaze met hers and then shifted away. "Lady Samantha, the daughter of the Duke of Haywood," he said. "And if she were still alive, she would have been my bride."

CHAPTER 16

$\mathcal{I}$F SAM WERE the sort of girl prone to fainting, she would have fainted right there on the spot. But as things currently stood, she wasn't supposed to be a girl, so fainting wasn't even an option.

"You're *engaged*? To *her?*" she got out. She simply couldn't make sense of it. Since when was she engaged to be married? This was the first she'd ever heard of it. And why had the duke told Tristan she was dead? True, she'd left home without warning or a note, but that didn't make her *dead*. Missing, perhaps, but not dead. Dead was so final.

"*Was* engaged," Tristan corrected. "She was the reason I first came to Haywood. The duke wanted to see if we would suit."

Her mind flashed back to that terrible day in the woods, when the demon had killed her mother, and then Tristan had showed up like a hero out of a fairytale. "The day you saved Lady Samantha. You were in Haywood because my f—because the duke wanted to discuss your betrothal?"

Tristan nodded. "A lucky coincidence." His eyes narrowed. "How do you know that tale?"

She ducked her head. "Stories have wings, Tristan. Everyone in Haywood knows of your heroics that day."

Tristan waved his hand. "It was nothing."

"Was it?" she said between gritted teeth. It had been everything to her. And now the memory seemed sullied. It wasn't fate that had led Paladin Lyons to her in the woods that day, but her father's attempts to sell her off like chattel.

He sighed and massaged his temples. "We would have been good together, she and I."

"Did you l-l-love her?" she stammered. Gods, she was going to be sick to her stomach.

Tristan shot her an incredulous look. "I barely knew her. How could I possibly have loved her?"

His straightforward answer knocked the air out of her. "Why do you care then?"

Tristan scowled. "The woman was to be my wife. Have you no heart, man?"

"Have *you*?" Sam wasn't sure she could wrap her mind around the idea of Tristan with, well, *feelings.*

Tristan looked down, dragging the toe of his boot across the ground. "I've been with the Paladins for a decade now, mostly on the road, and more often alone than not. My family is dead. Maybe I just want someone to come home to. Someone to mourn for me if I don't come home." He blew out a breath. "It's silly, but I imagined Lady Samantha to be that person for me. I wanted her to be."

For a moment, Tristan looked so forlorn and vulnerable, Sam thought her heart would break. Guilt gnawed away at her insides. "For what it's worth, I'm sorry." The words sounded hollow, even to her own ears.

"No need to apologize. You couldn't have done anything."

"Right," she said weakly. Except it *was* all her fault, not that she could ever tell him that. "Did the duke say what happened to his daughter?"

"No, he refused to talk about it."

"But I'm not—" She bit down on her tongue. "The duke—is he grieving?"

Tristan glowered at her. "She was his only daughter. What do you think?"

"I don't know," she said honestly. Her father had always been distant, even when her mother had been alive—too busy keeping the castle and duchy in order, she supposed. His daughter was a convenience; her existence ensured the continuity of his line. But she'd embarrassed him, his daughter who refused to follow the dictates of society, always with an errant smudge of dirt across her cheek and a sharp tongue that was more inappropriate than not. And he'd given her hand away without the courtesy of telling her. She couldn't imagine him grieving, not for her. He'd used up all his grieving for her mother.

But there was the watercolor painting. And despite the years of bad blood between them, that single painting made her hope.

Braeden put a hand on her shoulder, and she blinked up at him in surprise. She'd almost forgotten he was there. "You lost someone, too," he said into her ear. Oh Gods, that stupid lie she'd told him. Braeden thought she'd lost her half-sister. She gave him a quick, awkward smile.

"It's strange," Tristan said, "thinking your life is going to turn out one way, then finding yourself headed in an entirely different direction. Perhaps I was never meant to have a wife or family."

For an instant, she was overtaken by a vision of what could have been: she sat at the dais in the great hall of Castle Haywood, her hand clasped around Tristan's steely bicep. Two children flanked their sides, golden-locked like their father. Sam shook her head, banishing the vision to the furthest recesses of her mind where it belonged. She'd chosen another future.

Tristan rubbed his eyes and shook himself, shrugging off his melancholy like an over-warm coat. "All right, lads. Here's what we're going to do now."

"What's that?" Sam asked.

Tristan swung an arm around her shoulder. "Let's get rip-roaringly drunk."

CHAPTER 17

$\mathcal{T}$HERE WERE CERTAIN advantages—or disadvantages, depending on how you looked at it—to being half a demon. No matter how much Braeden drank, he never felt the effects of alcohol. And though they'd been drinking at the tavern for hours, he was sober as a Sun Sister.

Tristan and Sam, on the other hand, were absolutely tap-shackled.

The first time they broke out into song, Braeden had been amused. By their third go-round of "Dancing with Demons in the Night," he was grinding his teeth. By their seventh rendition, Braeden began contemplating death, and he couldn't be sure if their demise or his own was preferable.

After finishing the last verse—for the final time, he hoped—Sam stumbled over to Braeden's seat by the bar. "Why aren't you drinking?" he slurred.

He lifted his tankard of ale. "I *am* drinking."

"Clearly not enough," Tristan said, coming to stand beside him. "Barmaid!" he shouted, snapping his fingers. "Another three pints."

The barmaid scrunched her nose in disapproval. " 'Aven't you boys 'ad enough to drink? I'm thinkin' I ought to cut you off."

Tristan slid a copper coin across the bar and offered the barmaid a lopsided smile, waggling his eyebrows in an exaggerated fashion.

The barmaid put her hands on her hips. "Two hours back, your smile might o' seduced me. Now you just look like a sloppy fool, same as the rest o' these drunkards." She slid the coin back towards Tristan. "You keep your copper."

Tristan's face fell into a pout. "Fine, we'll take our business elsewhere. Sam, Braeden, let's go." He staggered towards the exit, dragging Sam behind him.

"Thank you," Braeden murmured to the barmaid, sliding across a few extra coins for her trouble. She gave him a pitying look.

"Good luck to you, mister!" she called as he chased after his wayward companions.

Braeden trotted out into the night, spotting them just as they turned off the main road. Breaking into a sprint, he easily caught up with them.

"Where are we going?" Sam asked, panting. The boy had to jog to keep pace with Tristan's long legs.

"You'll see," Tristan said with a wicked grin, ducking into a narrow side street. He stopped in front of an unassuming building at the very end of the street. The half-timbered house was indistinguishable from any other, apart from the painted emblem of a fig tree above the door.

"You can't be serious," Braeden muttered, instantly recognizing the emblem.

"Behold, our final stop of the evening," Tristan said, with an exaggerated flourish of his arms.

Sam scratched at his head, squinting. "I don't know this place."

"That's because you have morals," Braeden said. And Tristan seemed hell-bent on corrupting them.

Sam looked at him blankly. "What do you mean?"

Braeden just shook his head. He would let Tristan handle this one.

"You're too good for a demon," Tristan said, jabbing an accusatory finger into Braeden's sternum.

He barked a laugh. "Half-demon, if we're splitting hairs. And it's not that I'm good—I'm not interested."

Tristan clicked his tongue. "You need to learn to live a little. Embrace your wild side. Tonight we're celebrating. Or mourning. I forget which." He pointed at his trainees. "That's an order from your Paladin."

Sam stamped his foot impatiently. "What are you two talking about?"

Tristan clapped him on the back. "Tonight, my boy, we're going to make you a man."

Braeden groaned and dropped his forehead into his hand.

"I'm confused," Sam said, beginning to look wary. "Aren't we all men here?"

"*I* am a man," Tristan said, puffing up his chest. "*You* are a boy. This will remedy your woman problem."

Sam's eyes rounded. "My woman problem? I wasn't aware I had one." He narrowed his gaze. "Why do I have a woman problem and Braeden doesn't?"

"I suspect Braeden has already taken this particular rite of passage," Tristan said, chortling to himself. He nudged Braeden with his elbow. "Am I wrong?"

Embarrassment heated his cheeks as an unwanted memory flitted through his mind. "No, you are not wrong."

"That bad, eh?"

"None of your damned business."

"What are you two nattering on about? What rite of passage?" Sam demanded.

"Your virginity, Sam," Tristan said bluntly.

Sam tripped over his own two feet, his sluggish reflexes kicking in just before his face hit pavement. "W-what makes you think I'm a virgin?" He could barely even get out the words.

Tristan guffawed. "Your face is the color of a tomato. I'd stake my life that the only sword you've ever wielded is the one beside your hip."

"So crude," Braeden murmured.

Ignoring Sam's sputtering, Tristan continued, "Worry not, trainee, we'll rid you of that encumbrance this eve."

"H-how?" Sam said, a hint of alarm in his voice. "I'm not much good with women."

"I assure you, these, ah, *girls* are a guarantee."

"What do you mean?"

Braeden rolled his eyes. "Gods, Sam, you *are* an innocent. Our dear Paladin has brought us to a whorehouse."

Tristan sniffed. "I prefer the word *brothel*. It sounds more refined."

Sam inhaled a sharp breath and tried to cover it with a yawn, stretching out his arms as wide as they would go. "You go on without me. I think I'm too tired. My face hurts a bit, too. Besides, I'm out of coin. I'll just turn in—"

"Nonsense," Tristan said. "It's my treat. Consider it a reward."

"I'd rather not—"

"Don't be ungrateful, boy," Tristan said, gripping the collar of Sam's tunic. "Are you coming, Braeden?"

Sam all but dug his heels into the ground as Tristan dragged him towards the brothel. Braeden didn't understand why Sam was so reluctant. The whores wouldn't fear his touch, not like they would Braeden's. Perhaps Sam, in his innocence, had equated sex with love. He snorted at the idea. Love was a woman's fantasy, and certainly not for the likes of him. "I'm coming," he said, tugging down on his hat.

Despite the late hour, it took only a single knock before a servant greeted them at the door. The servant was a hulking brute of a man, his broad shoulders filling the entire doorway. "The madam'll be wiv you in a moment," he said after a cursory inspection, angling his large body so they could enter the building.

Braeden had to hand it to Tristan—for a "brothel," the interior was quite elegant. The owner obviously had an upper crust clientele in mind, and the décor straddled the line between tasteful opulence and tawdry. The furnishings in the foyer were clearly of an expensive make, but the red and black color scheme belonged no place other than a whorehouse. A smattering of candles cast the room in a dim light, meant to seduce the senses. Incense mingled with the smells of perfume, cologne, and sex.

A statuesque woman emerged through velvet curtains at the back, the no-nonsense gait of her walk and conservative neckline of her dress indicating that *her* wares, at least, were not for sale. "Evening, gentlemen," she said, weighing and measuring their worth with intelligent, beady eyes. "I am Mistress Rowena. What's your pleasure?"

Tristan fished out a handful of gold sovereigns from the pouch at his belt. "I have coin to spend and three men in need of a warm bed."

The madam arched a dark, penciled brow. "It's a warm bed you seek or a woman to warm it?"

Tristan grinned. "I think you know my meaning." He jingled the coins in his palm for emphasis.

Mistress Rowena eyed the money hungrily. "Aye, I think I do. Any preferences? Special requests? Will you be together or separate?"

"Separate, definitely separate," Tristan said quickly. "As for special requests, do you have a girl who's good with, ah, inexperience?"

Mistress Rowena raised both eyebrows. "Inexperience? You, milord?"

"No, no, not me." Tristan moved a few steps closer to Mistress Rowena, and leaned over conspiratorially. "The short lad. It's his first time."

She tilted her head to better look at Sam. "Is there something wrong with him?"

"I can hear you, you know!" Sam said, glaring at the Mistress Rowena. "And there's nothing wrong with me."

"Of course there's not," Mistress Rowena said soothingly. "I have just the girl. Are you partial to blondes?"

"N-no preference," Sam said, his face pale and glistening with sweat.

"And for you, milord?"

"Brunette. Petite. Someone with a bit of fire to her," Tristan said, frowning a little. "You're up, Braeden."

Braeden sighed, and removed his hat. "I'm not particular," he said softly. "Someone who isn't skittish, I suppose." He turned the full force of his gaze on Mistress Rowena.

She shuddered with revulsion and took a faltering step back. "What are—" she halted, glancing sideways at Tristan. "As you wish. I'll see who I can find. I'll have to charge you extra given your . . . affliction. And if there are any injuries—"

"There won't be."

"So you say," she said, sniffing. "All right, then. I'll be back in a moment with your girls."

Braeden closed his eyes and willed himself elsewhere. Despite what Tristan had said earlier, Braeden wasn't a saint. He had urges, like any other man, and he had acted upon them, sometimes in ways he wasn't proud of. He wished he were more like Sam, innocent and not yet jaded by the fairer sex. Perhaps Sam would be spared from the cruelty of women. *Sam's* whore wouldn't cry like the girl Braeden's master had brought to him for his first. Braeden had been fifteen, and the whore nearly ten years his senior. He had been shy, nervous; he knew his master had paid her well, but in his boyish pride, he had wanted nothing more than to please her. She fulfilled her duty in silence, tears streaming down her face. And when they'd finished, she had vomited, proving that none of her disgust had been feigned. He'd tried to help her, to hold her hair back as she emptied the contents of her stomach, but she'd shoved him away. "Don't touch me," she had said. "I'd rather die than be touched by you again."

A light touch on his chest shook him free from his memories. "Mistress says I'm to be wiv you for the evenin', love."

Braeden opened his eyes and waited for the whore's reaction. Her skin fell ashen beneath her rouge, and she let out a little frightened squeak. She wanted to run; he could hear it in the frantic beating of her heart and see it in the twitch of her muscles.

He sighed. Some things never changed.

CHAPTER 18

THE COLD SPLASH of reality was enough to sober Sam up. Faith in blood, now she was obligated to spend the entire night in bed with a whore.

The girl Mistress Rowena had brought her was pretty in the conventional way, with delicate features, pale blonde hair, and a willowy, almost frail, form. She wore an ethereal white gown that Sam supposed was intended to be virginal, but the thin fabric revealed more than it hid. No proper lady would ever be caught in such a dress.

She bobbed a curtsy, her lips curving into a demure smile. "Follow me, master." She glanced up at Sam through lowered lashes, a seductive tease. Underneath her lashes, her eyes were cold and dead. Sam shuddered.

Sam followed the girl up the stairs towards the private rooms, her hands slick with sweat. The prostitute's white dress floated in front of Sam like a flag of surrender. There were no two ways about it: Sam was buggered. How would she explain to the girl why she wasn't interested in her affections? Or explain to Tristan in the morning how her night had been?

Dread warred with hope that she would somehow avert disaster. It was foolish, unfounded hope, but she clung desperately to it nonetheless.

The whore pulled a key from her bodice and pressed her ear against one of the doors. "This one's ours," she said after a moment, unlocking the heavy bolt with practiced ease. "Right this way, master. Or is it milord?"

"Just Sam is fine." Remembering her manners, she asked in a strained voice, "And by what name should I call you?"

She tossed Sam a flirtatious smile. "You can call me whatever you like, love."

Sam cringed inwardly. This was not going to end well. "What's your given name? I'd like to call you by that, if I may."

The prostitute scowled, but hid her reaction quickly. "Lucy."

"Lucy's a fine name."

"It's boring," she retorted with a spark of anger. She pushed the door open, ushering Sam inside.

Soft candlelight bathed the chamber in a romantic glow. Rose petals were strewn on the floor and covered the quilt of the massive, canopied bed, the real centerpiece of the room. And though the nights had yet to turn cold, the hearth crackled with an inviting fire.

Despite the precariousness of her situation, Sam was tempted to laugh. Tristan must have paid good money to see her brought properly to "manhood." She was almost sorry to disappoint him.

Lucy sashayed across the room to the canopied bed, arranging herself to her best advantage. She patted the mattress beside her. "Take a seat, Sam."

Sam sat down on the opposite end of the bed.

Lucy patted the mattress again. "I won't bite. Not unless you want me to."

Heat rushed to her cheeks at the whore's bawdy proposition. "I think I'm fine for now," she squeaked.

Lucy sighed, scooting closer to Sam. "There's no reason to be nervous. I already know you're a virgin, so you don't have to pretend otherwise. Just tell me what you like, and we'll make your first time a memorable one."

If it were possible to die of embarrassment, Sam would have dropped dead on the spot. She flushed scarlet from the base of her neck to her hairline. "Would it be all right if we just talked?" she asked desperately.

Lucy swept her blonde hair over her shoulder and smiled archly. "Talk? Whatever you desire, Sam. Would you like to hear about what I'm going to do with your—"

"No! No, I meant, just *talk*," Sam said in a strangled voice. "Like—" she searched the room frantically for an idea. Her gaze landed on a wooden bookshelf. "What do you like to read?"

The prostitute folded her arms beneath her breasts. "I can't read."

"Oh," Sam said, biting her lip. "Well, what do you do when you're not . . . working?"

Lucy snorted. "You really don't know how to talk to a woman, do you? No wonder you're still a virgin."

Sam ought to have taken offense, but Lucy was right. She didn't know the first thing about talking to a woman, not as a man. She'd never paid much attention when she'd been on the receiving end. "What about your family? Are they well?" she asked, grasping at straws.

Lucy rolled her eyes. "I'm a whore, not some noblewoman you met at the fair. You and me, we don't talk about family." She stood up from the bed, her hands skimming over her curves. "*This* is what we talk about. You like what you see?"

"Errr," Sam said, completely at a loss. "You look lovely?"

"Compliments, that's the way to a girl's heart," Lucy said, nodding with approval. "Or into her skirts, as may be."

Funny, Sam had always felt uncomfortable when the men at court had given her compliments. They'd always seemed so contrived, like they'd expected something from her in return. Looking at Lucy, Sam was inclined to believe that most men did have expectations.

"You are very beautiful," Sam said stiffly. "Your hair is . . . long and silky." She'd wax poetic about Lucy's toes so long as it kept them talking and out of bed.

Lucy fanned herself with her hand. "You're a regular poet." Reaching behind her, she undid the buttons of her gown till she stood in nothing but her chemise. If the gown had been indecent, the chemise was downright scandalous, leaving little to the imagination. "Your turn," she said to Sam.

"I'd really rather not."

Before Sam could register what she was doing, Lucy crossed in front of her and knelt between her knees, caressing her jawline. Sam winced; the skin was still tender. "You're a right pretty one," Lucy said in low, seductive tones. "I bet the rest of you is as pretty." She reached for the top of Sam's tunic, deftly unfastening the top two buttons.

Sam slapped away her hands in horror. "Stop that!" she hissed, jumping to her feet. Her heart was beating so hard she thought it might burst right through her shirt.

Lucy's face grew pink with frustration. "Your master says I'm to see to you no matter what. And he's already paid Mistress Rowena on your behalf." She rose from her knees and slid up Sam's body. "So I ought to do what he says, don't you think?"

Sam held her at an arm's length. "I just want to talk!"

"Sure you do, love. But we can talk with fewer clothes, no?"

"I'd like to keep mine on, thank you," Sam said firmly.

"No matter, you can keep your clothes on if you'd like," said Lucy with a sigh, and for the briefest of moments Sam thought she'd won.

The whore gave her a coy smile, running her fingers across Sam's exposed collar bone and trailing them down her chest. "Let's undo a few more of those buttons of yours. It's only fair."

Sam took hold of Lucy's wrist, praying that her binding had done its job. "Stop it. I mean it."

Lucy ignored her, her free hand wandering lower, massaging between Sam's legs. "You're big for a small lad, I can tell," she murmured. Her hand snaked under Sam's tunic and dipped beneath the waistband of her trousers.

Sam grabbed for her errant hand, but too late. Lucy's forehead wrinkled with confusion. "There's naught but air in your codpiece," she said slowly.

"You're mistaken," Sam said flatly. What else was she to say?

"I felt what I felt." Lucy's eyes rounded. "You're a woman."

Gods damn it. Sam hadn't been sure if Lucy would be able to put two and two together. "That's an insult. I'm—"

"Don't bother denying it. I may be a whore, but I'm not stupid." Her eyes narrowed in speculation. "Where are your breasts?"

"I'm telling you, I'm a—"

With the ferocity of a wildcat, Lucy tore open the buttons of Sam's tunic, exposing the linen bandage underneath. Her eyes gleamed with triumph. "There they are." She walked a circle around her, regarding her with careful interest. "So you're a woman."

There was no more point in denying it. "Aye."

"Who else knows?"

Sam looked down at her feet. "No one," she whispered. "No one but you."

"What about the men you came with?"

"They know nothing."

Lucy tapped her lower lip with a manicured nail. Her cold eyes were bright with calculation. "What's it worth to you to keep me quiet?"

Anything and everything.

CHAPTER 19

*B*RAEDEN WASN'T SURE who was more relieved when a knock came at his door, he or his whore. He hadn't touched her, the terror in her eyes as repulsive to him as his crimson stare was to her. When she'd reached for the tie at his waist with unsteady fingers, he'd enveloped her hands with his own, stopping her. He'd meant to reassure her, to tell her she needn't bother continuing, but even this small amount of physical contact frightened her. He'd known men who got off on fear, but he wasn't one of them.

He and the prostitute both went to answer the door, nearly colliding, but she recoiled immediately. Braeden ground his teeth. He wasn't a fragile fifteen-year old boy anymore, and he had no patience for the prostitute's antics.

"What?" he snarled, swinging the door open.

Sam blinked up at him. "Am I interrupting?"

Braeden glanced back at the cowering girl. "Trust me, you weren't interrupting anything." He took in Sam's appearance. His short hair was mussed, and his right cheek sported a raw scratch. He had thrown on his cloak over his clothes in spite of the warm air. The ripped collar of his tunic peeked out of the top of the cloak. "What happened to you?"

Sam hugged his cloak closer. "I'm in trouble, Braeden."

"Of what nature?"

Sam's gaze darted to the trembling prostitute behind Braeden. "I promise I'll explain, but not here. Will you help me?"

"Do you even need to ask?"

Sam nodded. "I do. And let me say in advance, I'm sorry for getting you involved. I didn't know what else to do."

Braeden shuffled his feet. "You're my friend, Sam. I haven't had many."

Sam's eyes shone with unshed tears. "I hope you still will be, after." He brushed his cheekbones with the back of his hands and gestured for Braeden to follow him. Braeden followed Sam to a room a little ways down the corridor. "I'm sorry," Sam said again and pushed the door open.

Braeden was seldom surprised by anything, but the sight that greeted him on the other side of the door was fairly shocking. Sam's whore sat on her knees in the middle of the bed, her hands and ankles bound behind her, her mouth gagged. She wore only her chemise; her bindings and gag appeared to have been fashioned from the white fabric of what used to be her dress.

"Gods, Sam."

"It's not what you think!" Sam said quickly.

"What is it you believe I think?"

Sam's cheeks burned red. "That I'm some sort of pervert."

Braeden felt a smile tug at his lips, in spite of the oddness of the situation. "That actually hadn't crossed my mind, but there's a thought. Is that what this is?"

Sam started. "No! Gods, no." He covered his face with his hands. "She found out something. A secret. A secret no one can know."

Braeden folded his arms over his chest. "You're going to have to give me more than that."

Sam walked over to the bed and loosened the whore's gag. "You tell him. I can't bear to."

She spat the cloth out of her mouth. "Bitch," she sneered. She turned cold, hate-filled eyes to his. "You're traveling with a bitch."

"Watch your mouth, whore," Braeden said icily.

The prostitute laughed, the sound high and brittle. "I may be a whore but at least I'm honest about what I am. I don't think you understand me." She leaned forward, her hands straining against her bindings. "Your companion is a woman."

Now it was Braeden's turn to laugh. "Don't be ridiculous."

"Braeden." Sam's voice was pleading. He unbuttoned the fastenings at his neck, his heavy cloak sliding to the floor. Now, Braeden could see the extent of damage to Sam's tunic, which was torn to his navel. Pale skin peeked through the gaping fabric, along with . . . linen bandages?

"I don't understand. Are you hurt?"

The prostitute looked heavenward. "She bound her chest, you idiot."

"It's true," Sam said sadly. "Lucy found out and was going to tell Tristan, and . . . and you, and I don't know who else. I panicked." His voice—no, *her* voice—cracked. "I just wanted to be a Paladin."

A thousand chaotic thoughts ran through his head, threatening to overwhelm him. Sam—*his* Sam, his friend—was a woman? A woman and a Paladin trainee? How much had she seen that she shouldn't have these past few weeks? What had he told her that he shouldn't have? How could she have so blatantly lied to him?

"Braeden, I'm—"

He didn't have time for an existential crisis, not right now. Tucking away the magnitude of this revelation for later, Braeden held up a hand, silencing her. He turned to the prostitute. "Lucy, is it?"

"Aye. You believe me now, I take it," the prostitute said, smirking.

"So I do. Are you planning to talk?"

Lucy lowered her lids to half-mast. "What's it to you if I do?"

"Answer the question."

Lucy ran her tongue over her lips. "Interesting." Her face lit with avarice. "I'll repeat myself then. What's it worth to you—to both of you—to hold my tongue?"

"Wrong answer," Braeden said. He pulled a dagger from the folds of his robes, brandishing it menacingly.

Lucy sneered. "You think I'm frightened by a butter knife and those funny eyes of yours? You're little more than a boy. You don't have the guts to carry out your threat."

Foolish woman. If she had any sense, she'd be terrified. He'd seen far bigger and stronger men tremble at just the sight of him. He wondered if it were greed or a complete disregard for her own life that made her fearless.

But every human had their limits; it was only a matter of finding hers.

"Turn around," he growled at Sam. He didn't want her to watch him do this. Bracing himself for the pain, he impaled himself through the heart.

Someone screamed—Lucy, he thought, or maybe Sam—but Braeden was too absorbed in the changes overtaking his body to care. Red crossed his vision as his muscles swelled, his spine curved and reformed, and his nails lengthened into claws. His jaw elongated, fangs springing forth from his gums. He needed no mirror to know he'd become a living nightmare. He saw it in Lucy's face.

And Sam's, but that was an unavoidable consequence.

"Demon!" Lucy shrieked, her body shaking with fright. She'd finally reached her limits.

And he'd almost reached his. A thirst for violence surged through his veins as his human side warred with his demon instincts. For once, Braeden was grateful for the fear his abilities incited. "Aye," he growled, allowing his bloodlust to show in his face. "Demon."

He moved to her side with inhuman speed, raising his dagger, still dripping with his heart's blood. A pathetic mewl escaped Lucy's lips. Braeden brought the blade down, tearing through the fabric that bound her wrists.

He pointed at her freed hands with his blade. "Untie your feet."

"W-why?" she stuttered. "Why are you letting me go?"

He fixed her with his most terrifying glare. "Because you won't tell anyone what you saw this evening. *Right?*"

Lucy jerked her head up and down.

"Good," he said. "Because if you do, I'll kill you and everyone you care about." The threat tasted vile on his tongue, but he'd done far worse before and for less reason.

"I won't say anything. I swear it," she babbled.

He nodded once. "Here's what's going to happen now. I want you to go to the room four doors down from here. It's unlocked. There's a girl in the room called Minnie. You're to spend the night in the room, and you can tell her I told you to do so. Do we understand each other?"

Lucy nodded frantically.

"Then go."

She scrambled to untie her feet and fled from the room, slamming the door behind her.

Braeden inhaled a long breath, allowing his boiling blood to cool to a simmer. His fangs and claws retracted, and his body returned to its normal state. Then, taking a moment to collect himself, he turned to face Sam. "So you're a woman."

"Aye."

"Sam—is that even your real name?"

"It's Sam. Samantha, really."

"You told me you were the bastard son of the Duke of Haywood." His voice sharpened. "You lied to me."

Sam sunk down onto the edge of the bed. "I'm sorry, Braeden. You don't know how sorry I am. But what should I have said?"

"The truth, damn it!" he shouted. He massaged his temples. Gods, he never lost his temper. "I don't even know you. Who are you, Sam of Haywood?"

CHAPTER 20

"WHO ARE YOU, Sam of Haywood?"

Sam opened her mouth to weave another lie. She could tell Braeden that she was just another girl, perhaps a servant to a high born lady, or maybe the daughter of a knight. Yes, she could convince him of that latter fiction, she was certain. She was a more than proficient liar; in the years since her mother died, she had honed it into an art form. She'd been lying for so long—what was one more falsehood added to her already black slate? He knew that she was a woman. Wasn't that enough?

But as she looked at Braeden—Braeden, who had rallied to her defense on the flimsiest of explanations, Braeden, who had saved her without expecting anything in return, Braeden, who was her friend, or had been—she couldn't say the words. He might hate her for who she was, but the unmistakable hurt in his eyes was her doing, and she'd be damned if she put it there again.

She closed her eyes and braced for the fallout. "Lady Samantha Haywood, daughter of His Grace, the seventeenth Duke of Haywood."

Braeden dropped to the floor in a crouch and buried his head in his arms. "Gods damn it, Sam. Samantha. *Lady* Samantha. I don't even know what to call you anymore."

"I'm just Sam," she said in a small voice.

Braeden lifted his head to glare at her. "You were never 'just Sam.' Your father is one of the most powerful men in the kingdom. And you're Tristan's—" He paused, shaking his head. "Faith in blood, this is messy."

"I didn't know," Sam said. "About Tristan, I didn't know."

"Does it matter?"

"Of course it matters!" she cried. "I'm not a bad person,

Braeden. I didn't intentionally set out to hurt Tristan, or you, or anyone! I just wanted to be a Paladin more than anything."

Braeden swore under his breath. "You're a woman, Sam."

"And you're a demon!" she shot back.

Emotion flashed across Braeden's face, but he hid it quickly. "What of it?"

"I'm not trying to be cruel, Braeden. I don't care who your father was. But you and I both know that there are people who would deny you the right to fight with the Paladins because of some accident of birth. Well, by some accident of birth I was born a woman. I can't change that any more than you can change your parentage."

"It's not the same. *We're* not the same," Braeden said, his nostrils flaring. "You were born with a purpose."

"A purpose decided by my father! You haven't allowed your father to dictate how you live your life. Why should I let mine?"

"My father is a demon!" Braeden shouted, rising from his crouched position. "Your father is a duke who wanted to see his daughter married. How can you even make a comparison?"

Braeden's chest expanded and contracted in quick, uneven breaths, his fists clenched by his sides. Sam had never seen him so enraged. Somehow, she had to make him understand her side. She'd done what she'd done because she'd had no other choice.

She closed the distance between them till a scant inch separated their bodies and placed a hand over his heart. "Our hearts beat to the same drum," Sam said fiercely. "We hear the same calling, you and I."

Braeden stared silently at the spot where her palm met his chest. She removed her hand self-consciously. "Why do you want to be a Paladin, Braeden?"

Braeden shook his head as though waking from a daze. "It's complicated," he said finally. "In part in penance, I suppose. I owe humanity a debt, for what I am and what I've done."

It wasn't the answer she'd expected, nor the one she'd been looking for. "I joined the Paladins because I'm meant to fight for the people of Thule. Just as you are. *That's* my Gods-given purpose." She raised her chin. "I'm sorry for many things, but I won't apologize for following my heart. I don't feel I should have to ask for permission, though I find myself begging for yours."

"You're asking me to lie to Tristan. To let him continue grieving for a betrothed who isn't dead."

She flinched, but pressed on. "I'm asking a lot of you, I know."

Braeden turned his back to her, hiding his thoughts. An eternity passed before he spoke again. "I'll do it."

A tentative hope blossomed within her. "Are you certain?"

He nodded once. "Aye."

On impulse, Sam threw her arms around his neck. "Thank you," she whispered.

"Don't do that in public," Braeden said gruffly. "People will suspect."

Sam dropped her arms immediately, her cheeks heating. "Sorry." She returned to the canopied bed and flopped backward onto the mattress, shielding her face with her hand. Gods help her, she was on the brink of tears.

Braeden hovered over her from the foot of the bed. "In retrospect, I should have guessed that you were a woman. I knew there was something off about you from the start."

She removed her hand from her face. "Something off about me? What a flattering turn of phrase."

Braeden shrugged. "My skin tingles whenever I touch you. And you smell funny."

"I *smell* funny?"

The right corner of his mouth quirked upwards, releasing some of the tension between them. "You smell a good deal better than Tristan, I'll tell you that much."

"A high compliment," Sam said wryly.

Braeden sat down on the bed beside her. "I hope you're prepared with a story to tell Tristan in the morning. He had very specific expectations as to how you were going to spend the night."

"I'll invent something when the time comes."

"Should be easy enough for you."

Sam winced at the bite in his tone. "I really am sorry for lying to you. I want to regain your trust. Will you forgive me some day?"

Braeden propped himself on his elbows and looked at her. "I

need some time," he said after a pause. "But I'd like for us to be friends again."

"Me too," Sam said. "I'd like that very much."

Sam woke in the morning with a terrible headache and a mouth so parched she tasted sand. Groggily, she forced herself upright, stumbling as the floor lurched beneath her. Once the contents of her stomach no longer threatened upheaval, she sought out Braeden, who still slept in an armchair, his neck bent at an unnatural angle. If he was uncomfortable, the fault was entirely his own. Sam had offered to share the bed—which could have easily accommodated four people, let alone two—but Braeden had adamantly refused.

Dark circles shadowed the skin beneath his sooty lashes, and she was reluctant to rouse him. But they needed to be dressed and coherent before Tristan emerged from wherever he had disappeared to. Gods knew what he would think if he caught the two of them coming from the same room.

She tapped on his collarbone with her knuckles. "Braeden, time to wake up." He jerked awake, flailing his arms as his hips skated forward out of the seat. "You should have slept in the bed," she scolded.

He blinked at her blearily. "It wouldn't have been proper."

Sam sighed in frustration. "Confound proper. If you start treating me like a woman, I'm done for."

"I promised I'd help you hide your secret, didn't I?" he said, retying the bow at his waist before attacking the laces on his boots. "What does it matter how I treat you when we're alone?"

"You're bound to slip up, eventually. I'm still the same person—deal with me as you always have. Forget that I'm a woman."

Braeden snorted. "Unlikely." He gave his bootlaces a final tug and straightened. "I'll leave first."

"Understood."

When she rejoined Braeden outside the brothel's front door, Tristan had yet to make an appearance. "Where is he?" Sam asked irritably.

Braeden pointed to a hunched-over figure on the opposite side of the dirt road. The man retched violently into the pale pink hydrangea before withdrawing his head from the foliage. He wiped his mouth with the back of his hand and sank against a nearby tree. "That would be our esteemed Paladin," Braeden said.

"He's going to be unusually pleasant today, isn't he?"

Braeden's lips twitched. "Undoubtedly. Let's go greet your betrothed, shall we?"

"Not funny, Braeden."

He ignored her, crossing the street in long, confident strides. Sam started after him at a jog but slowed her gait as trepidation took hold. She didn't like trusting her secret to another person, even if that person was Braeden. And she still hadn't fully worked out what to tell Tristan about the events of the previous evening.

But as she neared Tristan, she could see that he was in no state to listen to stories, true or not. His face was gray and drawn, blond hair damp against his forehead, and his eyes were fixated on his flaring nostrils in a cross-eyed stare, as though he were channeling all his powers of concentration into breathing.

"Are you all right?" she asked.

Tristan held up a finger and then bolted into the hydrangea bushes, clutching his stomach as he heaved into the flowers. This last bout of vomiting must have done a little more good; when he returned, his face had lost its sickly grayish cast, though he remained unusually pale. "That's better," he croaked, and grimaced. "Remind me never to get that drunk ever again."

Sam's gaze traveled over his wrinkled tunic and grass-stained breeches. "What happened to you? Did you end up sleeping out here last night?"

"I don't want to talk about it," Tristan grumbled. "In fact, I don't want to talk at all. My tongue feels like it's three sizes too big."

"I'm sorry to hear—"

"No, don't speak," Tristan interrupted. "I don't want to hear you talk either." He leaned against a tree for support. "Here's what we're going to do. I'm going to rest my eyes for a quarter hour."

Sam smirked. "Rest your eyes?"

"Aye. Hush. I suggest you two do the same."

"And then what?"

Tristan closed his eyes and slid his back down the tree trunk. "And then let's get the hell out of Haywood."

A quarter hour turned into an hour and an hour turned into two. By the time they remounted their horses, the sun was already high in the sky. Tristan was none too pleased at the late start to the day, but he was to blame for their late start, and he knew it.

They left Haywood with little fanfare. The duke, in typical fashion, did not bother to see them off; now that Tristan was no longer to wed his daughter, he likely had lost interest. Haywood, swept up in the madness of the Grand Fair, just two days hence, barely acknowledged their departure. It made for a quick exit.

Tristan set a breakneck speed in an effort to make up for lost time, riding their horses at a near gallop. Haywood was soon only a speck in the distance, the curved road wide and open with nary a soul in sight. Sam wondered if she would ever see her home again.

When the horses began to flag, Tristan led them to a nearby stream and told his trainees to dismount. "We'll rest here," he said.

"For the evening?" Sam asked. "We still have a few hours of daylight."

Tristan patted his horse's flank, encouraging it to drink from the stream. "The horses are already fatigued," he said. "Besides, you and Braeden have hardly trained since we arrived in Haywood. Now is as good a time as any."

Sam bit back a groan. Nothing like training after half a day's hard riding, and on top of a night of drinking too. "More calisthenics? Or will you let us hold actual weapons?"

"I was planning on the latter, but in light of your impertinence, I've changed my mind," Tristan said archly.

"Wonderful. Calisthenics are *so* practical for killing demons."

"Someone will cut out that sharp tongue of yours one day, and when I say I told you so, you won't be able to reply. And to be clear, I said no weapons; I didn't say no fighting. Some hand-to-hand grappling is in order, I think."

"Okay," Sam said, feeling more optimistic. She'd enjoyed the few grappling lessons she'd had.

"Now that I have your hard won approval," Tristan said, "let's begin. We're going to start by practicing the three basic tie-in positions, so you'll need to face each other. Braeden, move closer. Closer. There, that's good."

Braeden and Sam stood a little over a yard apart, their nearness emphasizing Braeden's significant height advantage. He stared straight ahead at a spot above Sam's head, avoiding eye contact.

"Now, step your right foot forward—no, Sam, that's your left—so that your legs cross at the knees. Burn this foot position into your memory. It's the same for all three starting stances. Okay, now, Sam, I want you to grip Braeden's upper arms around the outside, and Braeden, you grip Sam's upper arms from the inside."

To Sam's embarrassment, Braeden's hands easily encircled her upper arms while her own fingers couldn't even touch. She squeezed a little, surprised at the hardness of Braeden's triceps and a little unnerved. Though Braeden still refused to meet her eyes, he wasn't as apathetic as he pretended; a faint blush stained the ochre of his skin.

"Excellent," Tristan said. "Both of you, drop your right hands and shift your left hands to each other's elbows. Good. This is the single arm tie-up." After they executed the starting stance to his satisfaction, he continued, "The next and final starting position is the double-waist tie-up. Braeden, reach around Sam's waist and grab your wrist with the opposite hand. Sam, you do the same to Braeden."

Braeden and Sam now stood in an embrace, their arms around each other's waist. The only air separating their bodies was in the small space between their hips. Their knees rubbed against one another as they shifted, and the back of Sam's head rested on Braeden's shoulder. Their embrace was that of lovers, not fighters.

Braeden broke off their embrace and stormed off into the surrounding woods.

Tristan scratched his head. "What's wrong with him?"

Sam shrugged helplessly and focused on calming her racing heart. She neither wanted nor appreciated this new awareness of

Braeden. Had touching him always felt so strange or was it the result of the new dynamic of their relationship?

Braeden reappeared moments later. "Sorry. I had to deal with something."

"Verbose in your explanations as always," Tristan said. "If there are no more interruptions?" Braeden shook his head. "Splendid. As you were."

Expressionless, Braeden wrapped his arms around Sam's waist once more, and she trembled, damn her traitorous body. "I won't tell," he whispered into her ear, his breath tickling the sensitive skin. He must have mistaken her reaction for fear, not . . . whatever this new sensation was.

"Sam, don't interlock your fingers," Tristan instructed. "We're going to practice the lift and throw next."

They practiced the lift and throw till Sam grew sick of thumping her skull against the earth. She'd learned how to fall properly long ago, but that didn't mean she enjoyed it. Moreover, she was convinced Braeden was going easy on her, tipping her over like a teapot instead of throwing her to the ground like he should. When it came to her turn to practice on him, she made a point to drop him unceremoniously on his head.

As dusk drew near, Tristan allowed them to spend the last few minutes of their training grappling. "Let's make this quick," Tristan said. "First one on the ground is the loser and has the fine privilege of digging the latrine."

They began in the first tie-in position, gripping each other's upper arms as they spun around. After a moment of inaction, Braeden removed his hands from Sam's arms and grabbed her behind the neck with a clasped grip, dragging her head forward and down till she butted his chest. She struggled against his firm hold and shoved hard at his elbow till it was high enough that she could duck underneath it.

He was too quick, though, locking her in a one-armed chokehold. Wheezing, she swung her arm backwards and pushed against his body with as much force as she could muster. He stumbled back a few inches and she wormed her way out of his grasp.

Sam circled Braeden, her competitive instincts now fully

engaged. A bead of perspiration rolled down her forehead and off the tip of her nose, landing on the rim of her mouth. She tasted salt as she ran her tongue over her upper lip.

Braeden's eyes zeroed in on her mouth. Seizing the opportunity, she crouched down and shot forward, streaking across the grass. The crown of her head connected with Braeden's solar plexus, sending him sprawling. She'd won.

It was too easy.

Braeden came up onto his elbows. Before he could rise to his feet, Sam jumped on top of him, shoving his chest hard. "You wretch!" she snarled. She shoved him one more time for good measure and then stalked off, muttering to herself.

"First you, now Sam. Am I missing something here?" she heard Tristan say.

Braeden's reply was lost to her as she stormed off into the trees. He had *let* her win. For the Gods' sakes. Was there anything more humiliating? Or more insulting?

After venting her frustration on a rotten tree stump, she went and helped Tristan set up camp, ignoring his efforts to make small talk. Then she set off in search of Braeden to have some words.

She found him deep in the woods, bare to the waist, muscles rippling as he shoveled dirt. When he saw her approach, he dropped the trowel and hastily stuck his arms into the sleeves of his robes.

"Stop it!" she snapped. "I've seen your bare chest a hundred times before. Don't be modest on my account."

Braeden ignored her and continued dressing. "It was different then."

"That's just it," she said. "It's *not* different. Not to me, and not to Tristan. Stop treating me like I'm a woman."

"We're alone now," Braeden said, knotting the tie of his robe into a bow.

"I'm not talking about when we're alone! Today, at training—what do you call that?"

Braeden blushed—not exactly the response Sam was anticipating. "You mean when I walked off?" he asked. "That was . . ." he floundered.

"Not that, you idiot! Our fight, at the end. Did you think I wouldn't be able to tell?"

Now Braeden looked well and truly confused. "Be able to tell what?"

Sam searched for something to throw at his head—a medium-sized rock would do nicely. "That you let me win!"

His face darkened. "That's complete shite, Sam."

"It's not *shite* and you know it. You could have easily evaded my lift and throw. Why didn't you? Because I'm a woman? Because I couldn't possibly handle a real fight?"

"Gods, Sam, give me some credit," Braeden said, scowling. "I may have just learned you're a woman, but I've known for far longer that you can fight. I'm not trying to take that away from you."

"Then why did you let me win?"

Braeden let out a huff of frustration. "I didn't let you win. I was caught off guard."

"By what?"

"Nothing of import," Braeden said evasively. "It was a momentary distraction and it won't happen again."

"Hmph."

"Harrumph away. I didn't intentionally allow you to win. Satisfied?"

Sam nodded begrudgingly, though she remained skeptical.

"Then let me go back to digging the latrine. And give me some more time to adjust. It hasn't even been a full day."

Sam's face grew hot. She had been unconscionably selfish and self-centered. "Sorry. I'll leave you be." She turned and headed for the camp, the wind carrying Braeden's quiet sigh to her ears.

CHAPTER 21

$\mathcal{I}$T TOOK A week of near constant travel before they again reached anything that resembled real civilization. The land between Haywood and Catania—the nearest city—was sparsely populated. Just the wagon road, endless woods, and the occasional small farm.

Though a week's journey was not overlong by most standards, Sam had never made it out to Catania before. The Duke of Catania, and his much younger duchess, had visited Haywood a few times when Sam was a child, but whether they would remember her face, even if it were fully healed, was dubious.

Considering their relative proximity, Sam was surprised by how different the two cities were. Perhaps the contrast was heightened by the excitement for Haywood's Grand Fair, but Catania seemed downright miserable in comparison. At this time of year, when the weather was still warm and the marketplace was full of new wares, the city was supposed to be at its brightest. The business district of Catania, however, was a somber place. The merchants and shopkeepers were alternately harried or sour-faced, and their customers stared at their feet rather than their companions. And it was so *quiet*. There was no shouting, no loud arguments, no excited haggling. Everyone spoke in hushed whispers and kept their exchanges short and succinct.

"Will we be staying in Catania long?" Sam asked Tristan, eager to be elsewhere.

"Just for the night. We'll leave at first light tomorrow," Tristan said, stopping to admire a pair of leather boots.

"Good," she said, hugging her cloak tighter despite the heat.

Tristan arched a brow. "Don't think much of Catania, do you?"

She shook her head. "It's depressing."

Tristan looked around as if seeing the city for the first time. "You know, it is rather dreary. I hadn't noticed."

"Is the whole city like this?" she asked.

Tristan stroked the blond stubble on his chin. "I can't say for certain. I know a few of the paladins posted here, and they're a raucous lot. I'd hardly characterize them as gloomy. We might run into them while we're here—they frequent the Hog in Armor, where we'll be staying the night."

━━━━━━━━━━

They arrived at the Hog in Armor a little past sundown, after they'd finished replenishing their supplies at the market. Inside, the inn was a far cry from the muted tones of the city. Servants bearing food and drink traipsed back and forth across the entrance hall, and even when the door was shut, they could hear laughter and music spilling out of the common room.

Behind a desk in the lobby sat the innkeeper, a tiny man with delicate spectacles perched low on his nose. "Can I help you?"

"Aye," Tristan said. "We need a place to sleep for the night. Three rooms, if you have them, but three pallets would do as well."

The innkeeper took in their disheveled appearance, dusty and grimy from the road—and then his gaze fell on Braeden. His eyes bulged behind his glasses. "We're full."

He hadn't even bothered to check his books. Tristan frowned at him. "Why don't you take another look?"

The innkeeper sniffed and adjusted his spectacles. "I'm afraid we can't accommodate you and your men at this time, but there is another inn on the main thoroughfare that I'm sure would be more than happy to take your business."

Tristan leaned against the innkeeper's desk, towering over him. "I have stayed at this inn before, and I intend to stay here again tonight. Check your books."

The innkeeper was unruffled. "You must have procured a room from my predecessor. The Hog in Armor is for men with refined tastes, and to be blunt, we don't serve men of your ilk."

"Men of my ilk? You listen to me, little man— "

"Lyons! That you?"

The innkeeper turned to the source of the new voice and blanched. "I-I did not see you there, Paladin. You know this man?"

The newcomer was a broad-shouldered, stocky fellow with hair and beard a fiery shade of red that would rival Will's. "Know him? This here's the finest swordsman in the kingdom, except for maybe the High Commander himself. And even I wouldn't place any bets on that fight. You ever spar with the High Commander, Lyons?"

Tristan nodded in greeting. "Good to see you, Sagar. And I can't say I have."

"Shame, that. Would love to know who'd come out on top." He jerked his thumb at the innkeeper. "Is Crompton here treating you right?"

"Actually, he was just telling us that all the rooms were full," Tristan said, his displeasure obvious.

The innkeeper, Crompton, dabbed at his forehead with a lace handkerchief. "My deepest regrets, Paladin Lyons. Had I known who you were— "

"Spare me the false apology. Do you have rooms available or not?"

Crompton opened his bound ledger and flipped through the pages. "I have two rooms on the third floor. Will that suit the needs of you and your men?"

"My trainees. Paladin trainees," Tristan clarified. "That will suit just fine."

"Begging your pardon. I'll take you to your rooms myself whenever you are ready." Crompton looked back and forth between the two paladins. "Will you be attending the party this evening?"

"Of course he's going," Paladin Sagar said, clapping Tristan on the back. "Lyons, bring your trainees, too." Heading for the common room, he lowered his voice to a stage whisper. "Don't mind old Crompton, boys. He warms right up once he knows you're with us."

"Hold up, Sagar," Tristan said, before the other Paladin could exit. "What is this about a party?"

Sagar grinned. "You came to the Hog in Armor on a good night, my friend. The Paladins have all but taken over the inn—best lodgings you'll find west of Heartwine, after all—so Crompton's been so kind as to host monthly gatherings on our behalf. It's good fun, I promise."

"Perhaps," Tristan said noncommittally. "Who will be there?"

"Oh, only everybody who's somebody in Catania. Paladins, nobles, the wealthier merchants, and the like." He made a mock-pouting face. "Come on, Lyons, I'll be bereft if you don't show. Besides, your trainees deserve a break for putting up with your sorry hide. Terrible traveling companion, our Tristan." He winked at Sam and Braeden.

Tristan sighed. "I suppose we could stop by."

Beside Sam, Braeden flinched.

"Excellent," Sagar said. "I'll tell the others you're coming. They'll be thrilled to have a legend in their midst." He clapped Tristan on the shoulder. "Now if you'll excuse me, I have errands to run before the night gets going. Crompton will take good care of you in the meantime." He pointed at Tristan. "I'll see *you* later, and your trainees, too. What are your lads' names again?"

"We didn't say," Sam said. "It's Sam of Haywood, Paladin."

Sagar chuckled. "A trainee just like his paladin. Got a bit of a mouth on you, don't you, boy?"

Sam had no idea how to respond to that, politely or otherwise.

"And you, boy?"

Braeden kept his gaze trained on the ground, his crimson eyes barely visible. "Braeden of Rhea."

Sagar tipped his head. "Pleasure to make your acquaintance, Sam, Braeden. I'll see the lot of you in an hour's time."

After Paladin Sagar took his leave, Crompton led them to their rooms as he'd promised, apologizing a hundred times for his hostile welcome. Naturally, Tristan had a room to himself while Braeden and Sam were given the adjacent room. With a final apology, the innkeeper made an obsequious bow and scurried away.

"Are we really going to this party?" Sam asked.

"Aye, once we no longer smell like horse manure," Tristan replied. "From what Sagar said, it sounds like half the city will be there tonight. You never know what you might overhear."

"*All* of us?" Braeden asked, fingering the brim of his hat.

"You'll be with me, so you'll be fine," Tristan said. He looked

Braeden up and down. "Though I think you ought to wear some-thing more conventional. You and I are of a height if you want to borrow clothes."

Braeden took a moment to consider it. "All right," he agreed, much to Sam's surprise. She'd never seen him in anything but his black Rhean robes.

Sam and Braeden's room had a private bath, so the two of them took turns bathing. A servant had filled the tub with hot water, but by the time Sam stepped into the water, it was barely lukewarm. But, as she reminded herself, a lukewarm bath was better than no bath at all.

When she emerged from the bath, clean and fully dressed, Braeden was buttoning the top of a brocade doublet that accented his broad shoulders and tapered waist. Tight, tan breeches clung to the well-shaped muscles of his thighs and calves. Sam reminded herself that such clothes were the height of fashion and concentrated on forcing her eyes above his waist.

Braeden grimaced. "I look ridiculous, I know."

"No! You look . . . nice. Truly," Sam said, watching Braeden struggle with the final button. "Here, let me." Standing on her toes, she slipped the silver button through its thread loop, her fingers grazing Braeden's neck. A strange frisson of energy shot up her arm, and they both jumped at the contact. "Sorry," she said, coloring furiously.

A knock came at the door that separated their room from Tristan's, ending the weird interlude. "Let's go," Tristan said through the door.

The party was already in full swing by the time they arrived in the large, private tavern at the back of the inn. The common room was lined with people, pushing and shoving as they waited to be admitted. Crompton stood by the tavern door, granting and denying entry like a king passing judgment on his subjects.

Inside the tavern was a cacophony of sound. Men shouted over the gambling tables as cards traded hands and dice tumbled. Leathered feet stomped in tune to a minstrel's bagpipe, and men and women whirled with wild abandon around what little open space remained.

It was hard to ignore the women in the room. Every female in attendance, from guest to server, wore a black partial mask that covered the forehead and nose but left the lower half of the face exposed.

"Why are the women wearing masks?" Sam asked Paladin Sagar after he'd greeted them.

Sagar pinched the bottom of a nearby barmaid, who hopped and let out a little squeal. He watched appreciatively as she flounced away. "Some fine women in here tonight," he said, more to himself than anyone in particular. "What was it you were saying, boy? Oh yes, the masks. They afford the women a bit of privacy for our little gatherings."

"Privacy? Why do they need privacy?"

"Why, privacy from their brothers and husbands, of course. This isn't the sort of party a lady should be seen attending."

"Then why do the women come?" Sam asked.

Paladin Sagar elbowed Sam in the ribs, hard enough to make her grunt. "Because this isn't the sort of party a lady should be seen attending."

"I see," Sam said, not seeing at all. She watched as a woman in a hooded black dress flirted with two men at once, stroking one's cheek while caressing the forearm of the other. Now she'd really seen everything.

Paladin Sagar slapped his knee. "By the Gods, lad, if you could see yourself. Your face is as red as my hair." He shook his fist at Tristan. "Lyons, you need to do your duty by your trainees, man. The boy's as innocent as my own sister."

Sam and Braeden traded uneasy glances. Tristan had never asked her about what happened in the brothel, and she hoped he didn't start now, in front of Sagar. "Not so," she said, thinking quickly. "How about a drink and a game of Hazard?"

"There's a lad," Paladin Sagar said, thumping her on the back.

As the night wore on and the general level of inebriation grew, so did the impropriety of the revelers. The men playing dice had their wagers piled high in front of them, shouting and cursing as they argued over their bets. A fair number of the partygoers had paired off and were in varying stages of intimacy throughout the tavern. The black masks only hid so much.

Three drinks and four rounds of dice later, Sam somehow found herself at a table alone with Sagar. His face had grown markedly redder over the course of the past few drinks, and his words were beginning to slur together. Still, he was a Paladin, and that meant affording him the proper respect he deserved.

"You're lucky, boy, you know that?" Sagar was saying. "Not a one of us is better than Lyons. Not a better man in the kingdom." He smiled faintly. "I remember when he was just a boy himself. Almost a man, but not quite. Wouldn't talk to anyone when he first came to Heartwine except the High Commander. But I got him to talk to me eventually."

"Why?" Sam asked. "Why didn't he talk?"

Sagar stared at her with feverish eyes, and then shrugged off her question. "He's the best, Tristan Lyons. I'm his oldest friend, did he tell you that?"

Her tongue caught in her mouth. She didn't know whether to lie or tell the truth—or whether he'd remember either way.

Sagar smiled with all his teeth. " 'Course he didn't. That's Lyons for you. Never has much time for anything but killing demons."

"What else should he be doing?" Sam asked, genuinely curious.

"Ah, to be young again." Sagar raised his half-empty glass. "Life is for living. For drinking. For tupping." He snorted. "Boy, your face has gone purple. You are far too innocent to be in my presence."

Sam, grateful for the excuse to leave his company, left Sagar to finish his drink alone. She searched the room for Braeden and found him skulking in the corner nearest the exit.

At some point during the night, she'd also lost track of Tristan. He had disappeared into a crowd of paladins when they'd first arrived, all of whom had wanted to be regaled with the stories of his latest triumphs and updates from the fortress.

"Let's stroll around the room," she said to Braeden. He agreed to join her, abandoning his solitary corner.

It didn't take Sam long to spot Tristan. He leaned against the tavern wall, a hooded woman in a black dress pressed against him.

She threw back her head with a husky laugh, allowing strawberry blonde locks to escape the confines of her hood.

"Who is that woman with Tristan?" Sam asked.

"Why, jealous?" Braeden asked.

"What? No! No, I think I recognize her." She squinted, studying the woman's pert mouth and the classic lines of her face. "I do recognize her!"

"Oh?"

"She's the Duchess of Catania!" Sam hissed. "I'm sure of it."

"Forgive me if this is an ignorant question, but so what? Will she recognize you?"

"No, I don't think so. She hasn't seen me since I was a child, and I was too far beneath her notice, anyway." She tugged on his sleeve. "Braeden, she's married. To the duke!"

Braeden sighed. "Tristan's a grown man. He can make his own decisions. And besides, she's hardly the only married woman here tonight."

"It's not about Tristan, Braeden, truly. I don't care what Paladin Sagar said about the masks—if I can recognize her, so can everybody else!" Sam shook her head, appalled. "Since my mother died, my father has taken his pleasures outside the marriage bed, but he would never flout it in public like this. And consorting with the Paladins no less! It reflects badly on both her and us."

Braeden halted in his tracks, pausing to look at her. "You know, *Lady* Sam, you can be a little condescending sometimes."

"Don't call me that!" she snapped. "And what do you mean?"

"Your father loves his women in secret, beyond the scrutiny of the public eye. Why? Because he's ashamed of them? Or because they can say no to him in public?" Braeden shrugged. "And yet you feel his behavior is less shameful than fraternizing with the high and mighty Paladins. Seems a bit arrogant to me."

Sam flushed. "You'll be a Paladin one day, Braeden, so you better not let them hear you speak that way. And say what you will about my father, but I think there's something to be said for discretion."

"Why doesn't that surprise me?"

"Oh, give it a rest, Braeden! Look, it's not just about Tristan and the duchess. This whole party—" Sam said, spreading her arms. "It's dishonorable!"

At her last word, *dishonorable*, Tristan dislodged his hand from the duchess's right hip and gently pushed her away. Though Sam stood across the tavern, and there was no way he could hear her over the din, his gaze somehow found hers.

"You know, Sam, he thinks you're dead."

"I know," she said quietly, turning away. She didn't want to watch him anymore. "Braeden?"

"Yes, Sam?"

"Let's get out of here."

CHAPTER 22

TRISTAN HAD NEVER had any trouble finding women. And they'd never had any trouble finding him. It wasn't because he was particularly suave or clever, but because he had a fair face and a hard body that turned heads. He'd always used his looks to his advantage—more often for pleasure than for not—and tonight would be no different.

The woman in the hooded black dress had made clear her intentions, sliding her foot up and down his shin. She was a beautiful woman, with a lovely hourglass of a shape, but Tristan had little interest in a romantic liaison.

"My lady—" he began, unsure of how best to put her off without obstructing his designs.

She trailed her fingers along his forearm. "Call me Lilah."

"Your Grace, we both know that's not your real name."

The Duchess of Catania pouted prettily. "It is for tonight."

Tristan groaned inwardly, but kept his smile on his face. He had to play this just right. "My lady, there is no denying you are a beautiful woman—"

"Thank you, Paladin," she purred, attempting to entwine herself around him.

"—but I am certain His Grace would not approve of our entanglement." He put his arms on her shoulders to hold her at bay.

The duchess snorted indelicately. "His Grace and I have an understanding. He does what he wants, and I do the same."

His smile strained at the edges. Infidelity was more common than not among the higher ranks, but he'd seldom heard it put so bluntly. "Though you are lovelier than the stars, I did not approach you for an assignation, but for the pleasure of your company."

She turned a fetching shade of pink. He would have to be blind not to notice she was attractive, but she did little to heat his blood. Besides, he was here for a different game.

Tristan steered her towards a private corner. "My lady, you are the toast of Catania. You must talk to everyone and hear everything. Tell me, have you heard the name Sander Branimir?"

"The name sounds familiar," she said slowly, tapping a finger against her lips. "Why do you ask?"

He went for a combination of truth and flattery. "The High Commander was asking after him. I thought since you were so well-connected his name might have passed your ear."

"I'm afraid I haven't heard anything," she said, "but I did see something."

Tristan couldn't believe his luck. "You *saw* something?"

She nodded. "A letter, on my husband's desk. It was signed Sander Branimir."

"Did you read the correspondence?"

She shook her head. "I only caught a few words, and the name. I don't interfere in my husband's business, and he doesn't interfere in mine."

A loveless marriage, then. "You have no idea what it said?"

Again, she shook her head. "Only that it was addressed to my husband and signed by your Branimir."

What could the leader of the Uriel want from the Duke of Catania? Did he hope to ingratiate himself with the duke? Tristan was left with more questions than answers.

After another few minutes of halfhearted flirting, Tristan determined his conversation with the Duchess of Catania had no more fruit to bear. He skimmed the room, searching for Sam and Braeden, and found Sagar instead. With a quick bow to the duchess, he made his escape. "Excuse me, but I think I see an old friend."

Sagar was well in his cups, and when Tristan could endure no more of his incoherent babbling, he decided it was time to leave. "Have you seen my trainees?" he asked. He thought he'd caught a glimpse of Sam while he'd been talking to the duchess, but he hadn't seen him since.

"Who? Oh, the lad with the funny eyes and the short one with the mouth?" Sagar scratched his beard, an intense look of con-centration on his face. "Think I saw 'em leave together."

"Nice of them to tell me," Tristan grumbled.

"Can't blame 'em. You didn't look like you wanted interrupting."

He sighed. "I better go after them and make sure they don't get into any trouble."

"There was a time you were the one causing trouble, not the one cleaning it up. You remember those days, Lyons?"

Tristan gave the other paladin a steady look. "Aye, Sagar. You were the one leading me into it. And then I grew up."

Sagar took a long swallow of his drink. "It's a sad day for the Paladins to have lost the great Tristan Lyons to respectability. Think I might need another drink to toast his passing."

Tristan bit his tongue to avoid saying something he'd regret. "Have a good night, Sagar."

It was well past midnight by the time Tristan finally escaped the party, which despite the late hour showed no signs of abating. He made his way upstairs and to his room without disruption, hesitating behind the door that separated his room from Sam and Braeden's. It was late but, damn it, they should have told him they were leaving. Squaring his shoulders, he knocked.

Sam answered the door, rubbing his eyes and blinking.

A long silence passed between them. A flicker of something passed behind Sam's eyes—hurt or disappointment, Tristan wasn't sure which. He resisted the urge to smooth out the wrinkles in his shirt. He'd done nothing to be ashamed of—if anything, he'd been unusually well-behaved. He'd turned down a damn duchess, for the Gods' sakes, not that he had to explain himself to his own trainee.

"Well?" Sam asked, breaking the silence. "It's not morning, is it?"

"No, not yet. We have a few hours till dawn."

"Then why are you here?"

Tristan cleared his throat. "I was . . . concerned."

Sam's brows rose into his hairline. "For me?"

"Yes, for you. And Braeden, too. I couldn't find either of you at the party."

"Well, we're here, sleeping," Sam said, giving him a flat stare. "If there's nothing else?"

Tristan was a little taken aback at the boy's coldness. Normally Sam was all fire and spirit. "No, that was it."

"Then goodnight, Paladin." Sam shut the door between them. Tristan had been summarily dismissed.

He stood staring at the closed door for a while longer, wondering what he'd done to deserve his trainee's censure and why it bothered him so much.

━━━━━━━━━━━━━

Dawn came just seconds after he had drifted off to sleep, or so it seemed to Tristan. It was a strange thing, fostering trainees—when he'd traveled on his own, he would have allowed himself to doze for another hour. He'd been beholden to no one. But now that he had his trainees—or his *lads,* as he now thought of them—he did what he said he would and he did it with a smile. Or at least without a frown. Most of the time.

Once he'd dressed, he burst into Braeden and Sam's room without pausing to knock. "Wake up, you lazy slugabeds!"

Sam and Braeden were already wide awake, clothed and packed, sitting on the edge of their respective pallets as though they'd been waiting for him forever. "Well," Tristan said, a little dismayed that he wouldn't get to lecture them, "I'll finish packing then."

They departed from the inn's stables shortly thereafter, the sun still partially hidden by the horizon. Tristan kept the horses to a brisk pace, but not so brisk that they couldn't manage conversation. But apart from answering his occasional questions with monosyllabic responses, Braeden and Sam were silent—not just with him but with each other, too.

Their unusual silence persisted over the next few days. Each day was much the same: they rode their horses till the animals tired, trained till nightfall, and then made camp only to rise and repeat on the morrow. Such a pattern wasn't out of the ordinary for travel, but without Sam's regular banter and Braeden's pithy remarks, even the most trivial of activities seemed off.

Tristan didn't know what to make of it. He'd thought Braeden and Sam had developed a camaraderie of sorts—he'd even begun to envy their closeness, at times—but something had disturbed their easy friendship. They moved skittishly around each other, retreating whenever one of them drew too near. Yet as soon as they drifted apart, their eyes invariably sought out the other.

Except for when Sam's eyes sought out Tristan. Tristan caught Sam staring at him on more than one occasion, his expression shifting between doleful and guilty. Sam's lingering stares agitated him, eliciting a thickness in his chest that felt suspiciously like *feelings*. Tristan didn't do feelings.

On the evening of the fifth day of this nonsense, Tristan attempted to reach out to Sam the only way he knew how. After an hour of practicing their archery—one of the few fighting arts in which Tristan didn't have natural talent—he offered to spar with Sam. "Wouldn't want you to get rusty," he said, handing the boy a longsword.

Sam's face lit up, but still, he said nothing. Tristan wondered if he ought to have lent Sam his Paladin's blade, just to hear him sing its praises.

While Sam may have repressed his enthusiasm for fine weaponry, he couldn't stifle his competitive instincts. Once he altered his stance into ready position, pommel at his right hip and sword point aimed at Tristan's heart, the hangdog expression he'd worn all week was replaced by one of concentration.

Tristan struck first, his blade sliding along steel as Sam parried his attack. He smacked the trainee's sword, hard, from the opposite side, and followed it up with an immediate remise. He launched a quick riposte, and then another, but Sam's sword was there to meet each successive attack.

There were a few reasons Tristan was considered an unmatched swordsman—his strength, his speed, and an inexplicable gift for anticipating his opponent's next move. But Sam's sword work had an unpredictability to it that kept Tristan quite literally on his toes.

Unaccustomed to practicing with an opponent who was worth his salt, Tristan swung his sword out in a wild, diagonal cut, a powerful but sloppy blow that left him wide open to attack. His blade whistled through air as Sam dodged out of the way, the momentum of his swing carrying him well within striking range. He shifted his feet to regain his balance, but not before Sam whipped the foible of his blade across the side of his neck.

Tristan touched his raw skin, and drew back fingers coated in blood. "You won the bout," he said, staring at his red fingers in disbelief.

Sam's face fell. "You're bleeding like a stuck pig. I'm so sorry, Tristan."

Tristan heard a roaring in his ears. "Are you *apologizing*?"

"Errr. Yes?"

"Dare I ask why?"

"Because I hurt you."

Something inside Tristan snapped. "We were sword fighting, you clotpole! You're supposed to hurt me!" He dropped his sword and marched so close to Sam that the boy had to crane his head backwards in order to meet his angry glare. "A fortnight ago you would have crowed victory and heaped insults upon my head. What's going on, Sam?"

Sam looked at his feet. "Nothing, Tristan."

"What a crock of shite! You've had this pathetic look on your face and you've barely said a word all week. I can't stand it anymore. Have I wronged you in some way?"

"Have *you* wronged *me*?" Sam asked, shaking his head fiercely.

"Then why are you looking at me like I'm your favorite horse who went lame?"

"I am doing no such thing!"

Tristan heartened at the outrage in Sam's tone. He was beginning to worry that he'd done something to kill the boy's spirit, though he couldn't imagine what. "I beg to differ."

"Well, you're wrong," Sam said defensively. "And my face isn't pathetic either."

"You can't see your own face," Tristan pointed out. Sam bared his teeth in response.

Tristan slapped him heartily on the back. "There's the Sam I know and love!" Sam's cheeks turned pink at his words. "Oh, come off it, Sam. It's healthy to express affection for your fellow man." He took in a fortifying breath. "I want you to know that you can come to me. If something's bothering you, I mean." He ran his fingers through his hair. "I'm not very good at these things, but I'll try. We have a long road ahead of us, and I haven't much enjoyed the last week."

Sam kicked at a tuft of grass. "You can talk to me, too, if you want," he offered tentatively.

Something caught in the back of Tristan's throat. "Don't you worry about me," he said, reaching out to tug a lock of the boy's hair.

Sam swatted at his hand. "I really hate it when you do that."

Tristan tugged the lock of hair again, harder this time. "Too bad." He bent over to pick up his discarded sword. "Let's help Braeden make camp, shall we?" Sam flinched at Braeden's name, but nodded his agreement. "What's going on between you? You've been acting strange around each other all week."

Sam's face reddened again. "I'm fine. If anyone's acting strange, it's him."

Tristan rolled his eyes. "This is ridiculous," he said. "Braeden, come here, boy!"

Braeden, who had been hammering stakes into the ground a short distance away, ambled over. "Yes, Paladin?" He carefully avoided looking at Sam.

Tristan's glower encompassed both Sam and Braeden. "I won't pretend I know what's happened between you two. But whatever *this* is," he said, gesturing at the space that separated the two of them, "it stops now. Are we clear?"

The trainees looked at each other, and then their feet. "Yes, Paladin," they said in unison.

"Good. It's settled then," he said, clapping his hands together. That had been easy enough. "Now let's finish making camp before it gets any darker, or we'll be sleeping out in the open."

"Gods, I would kill for a proper bed right about now," Sam groaned.

"You might have to," Tristan said. "Tomorrow we'll be in Westergo."

If a line were drawn down the kingdom's middle, Catania would fall squarely on the left. But it wasn't till a traveler reached the borders of Westergo that he could consider himself truly in the West. The West was not like the East, its weather was colder and its people harder, more willful and less tethered to the influence of the Center. And for the first fifteen years of his life, the West was what Tristan had called home.

Tristan had grown up in a village far smaller and further west than the city of Westergo, but he knew enough to tie his coin pouch about his neck and to hide a spare knife in his boot for easy access. He'd been to Westergo just once before, and the memory wasn't a fond one.

If Catania had been unfriendly, the city of Westergo was unequivocally hostile. Sinister eyes followed the three travelers as they made their way down the wide throughway, and greedy hands pawed at their clothes and horses. Tall, rickety buildings loomed over the street on either side, casting dark shadows across the cobbled road.

The city folk were an odd amalgamation of the very poor and the very rich, although the former significantly outnumbered the latter. A fine lady in a surcoat of blue damask strolled by at a leisurely pace, but as she paused to examine a silk veil at a nearby street vendor, her sleeve fell back, revealing a bejeweled dagger strapped to her forearm. Hidden in the shadows, a young street urchin in tattered rags eyed the woman hungrily as she pulled a silver coin from her purse and paid the merchant for the veil. Tristan hoped the boy noticed the two large, hired guards who trailed the lady at a close distance, and that he wouldn't try anything foolish.

The street urchin darted out from his hiding place, weaving in and out of the crowd, his eyes never leaving the lady in blue. "Shite," Tristan muttered under his breath. The fool boy was going to get himself killed.

Tristan dismounted and grabbed the whelp by the scruff of his neck just as he passed by their horses. "Ger'off!" the boy yelped, struggling in Tristan's firm grip. "I ain't done nothin'!"

Tristan spun the boy around to face him. "You were about to," he said, jerking his head towards the young pickpocket's intended victim.

"Wot's it matter to you, gaffer? She's the mark, not you."

Tristan bent close so that his mouth was level with the boy's ear. "Do you see the two men to your left, near the stall selling cutlery? Big fellow, and the one with the shifty eyes?" The boy hesitated, and then nodded. "Good," Tristan said. "They're hired guards, son, for the lady's protection. You get anywhere near her and they'll gut you like a fish."

The boy shook his head. "I's fast," he said. "And I's needin' the money."

Tristan squeezed the boy's bony shoulders, hard enough to make the boy wince. "If you're so fast, how'd I catch you?"

The boy glared at him mutinously. "I wasna payin' attention to you, gaffer."

"And were you paying attention to the lady's men, before I pointed them out to you?"

"No," the boy admitted, scrunching his nose. "But I'da been fine."

Tristan looked to the heavens. "May the Gods save me from stupid boys." He drew the leather cord out from underneath his tunic, pulling his coin pouch free. "Here," he said, pressing a coin into the boy's palm. "Don't spend it all at once."

The boy's eyes boggled when he saw the coin was gold. "Thankee, milord," he said solemnly, closing his fingers tightly around his bounty. He bobbed his head in a small bow, and then he scampered away.

"What'd you do that for?" Sam asked, once the boy had disappeared and Tristan remounted his horse. "The boy's a thief."

Tristan turned in his saddle to look at him. "Did you see the way his clothes hung off him? I'd bet my last copper he hasn't eaten a proper meal this month."

"But you didn't even discourage him from stealing again," Sam said.

Tristan dug his knees into his horse's sides and clucked, urging the mare forward. "No, I discouraged him from getting caught."

"Tristan!" Sam exclaimed.

"You must have never gone hungry before," Tristan said. His stomach almost rumbled in remembrance. There was a time when he, too, would have done just about anything for a loaf of bread. "Hunger makes thieves of most men."

Sam chewed on his lower lip, mulling it over. "I still say stealing is wrong."

"Not everything's so black and white, Sam," Braeden said suddenly, bringing his horse level with Tristan's. "You of all people should know that."

Sam looked as though he wanted to say something, but settled for sticking out his tongue. Braeden's mouth quirked up reluctantly. Good, thought Tristan. He would have throttled the both of them if they had returned to the weird behavior of the previous week.

Their horses clopped through the crowded street, the heavy foot traffic constraining their gait to a slow walk. The city stank of animal dung, refuse, and human sewage, the putrid odor only growing stronger as they rode deeper into the heart of Westergo.

Up ahead was a strangely discordant sight. On their left, a hundred or so small dilapidated shanties leaned precariously against one another, not all of them entirely intact. A cluster of crude workshops and factories spit out smoke and heat, which lay over the crumbling tenements in a thick blanket. Men and women with an air of desperation and children with wide, hungry stares poured out of every nook and cranny.

On their right was a sprawling palace that rivaled Castle Haywood in its size and grandeur. The marble exterior formed a large U-shape around lush gardens and two long, rectangular pools. Elegantly dressed couples meandered arm-in-arm through the maze of hedges and orange blossoms.

"Gods," Sam swore, wrinkling his face in disgust. Even Braeden's inscrutable features registered distaste. "Is that monstrosity where we're headed?"

"Aye," Tristan said, taking in the overwrought architecture. Seeing the lavish display of wealth side by side with such extreme poverty was a shock to the system. He'd seen the palace from afar the first time he had traveled through Westergo, but he'd hardly been in a position to step inside its gilded doors. "I'm told the entire Westergoan aristocracy resides here. And a few paladins, as well."

"Friends of yours?" Braeden asked archly.

Tristan shook his head. "None I've met. The High Commander stationed the men out here shortly after I became a trainee."

"And they've been here ever since?" Sam asked. "That seems an awfully long time to stay in one place."

"The Westergoans have always been a little unruly," Tristan said. "There were the beginnings of an uprising when the Paladins were first sent out here, and they had to diffuse any insubordination. Now they're here for insurance."

Out of nowhere, Tristan felt a small hand wrap around his left ankle. "Hold up," he said to Sam and Braeden, yanking on his reins till his horse drew to a complete stop. He peered down at a tiny slip of a girl, her dirt-smudged face streaked with tears. Gods damn it, he hated tears. Especially little girls' tears. The little beggar girl was going to play him like a fiddle, and he would very likely give her everything she asked for. "What is it, child?" he asked, trying to sound stern.

The little girl's face crumpled. " 'Tis me brother, milord," she sobbed. "They's beatin' him somethin' fierce and I's afraid they's gonna kill him." She hiccupped and blew her nose into her threadbare frock. "He—he said to find you, milord. He said you'd help us."

Tristan grimaced as the girl dissolved into a fresh bout of sobs. "I think you have me mistaken for someone else. My companions and I are just passing through Westergo. I'm afraid I don't know your brother."

"Please, milord," the girl pleaded. "He's me only brother. 'T'aint fair what they's doin' to him. They's gonna whip him till he's dead. I seen it happen before." She sniffled, water leaking from her eyes and nose like a fountain. "I's sure he meant for me to go and find you, milord. Couldna been anyone else."

Tristan swung his legs off the horse and crouched down beside the girl. "I really don't know your brother, miss, but mayhap I can help anyway. Who is this 'they' you keep referring to? And why do they have your brother?"

" 'Tis the Paladins, milord," she said. "They's sayin' he's a thief."

Tristan's blood ran cold. "A thief?"

"Aye, milord." She twisted her hands in the material of her dress. " 'Tis me birthday today, and Charlie—that's me brother—wanted to buy me one of them fancy cakes at the baker's shop. I told him not to do it! I says to him them cakes are awful expensive. But he told me he had the money, that he'd buy it for me proper. And he showed me this gold coin—"

Tristan's heart dropped to his stomach. "Gold coin, you say?" he asked hoarsely.

The girl nodded. "I bit it and everything to make sure it was real. And first I thought he stole it, but he promised me he got it fair and square." Her eyes swept over Tristan. "He says he got it from a tall gaffer with gold hair and a mean scowl. He mentioned your friends, too," she added, pointing at Sam and Braeden. They exchanged twin looks of horror.

Tristan cursed under his breath. "So what happened?"

"He tried to pay for the cake with the gold coin. The baker—he's a nice gaffer—he woulda accepted it, too. But one of them Paladins happened ta be passing by, and he says me brother stole the coin. Charlie says that no, he was given the coin honest. But the Paladin, he just laughs, and says me brother's now a thief *and* a liar. And that thieves and liars hafta be punished." Her chin quivered. "Now they's gonna flog him in the city square."

"Shite," Tristan swore, and then mumbled a brief apology for his coarseness. He rose from his haunches to his feet.

"What are you going to do?" Sam asked.

Tristan glared at the trainee. "What do you think?" He held out his hand to the little girl, and she tentatively placed her small hand in his. "All right, girl, just where is this brother of yours?"

The girl tightened her grasp around Tristan's waist, sharp ribs poking into his back as they rode towards the public square. "Please hurry, milord," she said. "We don't have much time."

Tristan nudged his horse into a cantor, plowing into the

crowded street. "Move!" he bellowed, nearly trampling several bystanders. He could hear Sam and Braeden cursing behind him as they struggled to keep up.

The city square was really more of a rectangle, surrounded by stone and brick buildings on three of its four sides. The fourth side opened up to the street, but it was damned near impenetrable with so many people. It seemed as though the entire city had come out to witness the boy's punishment, though it was hard to say whether they had been summoned or had come of their own volition. Whatever their reason for being there, they were in Tristan's way and blocking his view of the proceedings.

He dismounted his horse at the edge of the square and lifted the little girl from the saddle. "Here," he said, passing the reins to Sam. "You and Braeden stay with the horses."

"But—" Sam protested.

"No buts. This is my doing. I'll handle it." Tristan kneeled in front of the little girl. "I need you to be my eyes. Can you do that?" The little girl nodded emphatically, and he swept her onto his shoulders. "Do you see your brother?"

She twisted, her knobby knees knocking Tristan painfully in the chin. "He's up there, milord!" the little girl cried, pointing towards the platform in the middle of the square.

He restored her to the ground. "Thank you, milady," he said gravely.

She giggled at his formality, her cheeks dimpling. But her merriment quickly faded at the steady beat of a drum. "They's startin'," she said, her eyes wide with dread.

"I'll fetch your brother, I swear it," Tristan promised her. "In the meantime, I need you to stay here with Sam and Braeden. Will you hold Braeden's hand for me while you're waiting?"

Braeden paled. "I don't think that's a good idea, Tristan."

Tristan leaned in towards her ear. "I think he's afraid of you," he whispered. "Are you afraid of him?"

She scowled. "I's afraid of no one, 'cept maybe the Paladins and me mam." She made a show of inspecting Braeden, staring at him openly. "You gots funny eyes and funny clothes, milord, but me mam would make you piss in your boots."

"Your mam?" Braeden asked, fiddling with his hat.

"Aye, milord. Well, me gran. Lost her eye and half her face in a fire, but 'tis her remaining eye you need to be afraid of." She pulled on Braeden's sleeve. "I's not scary though, if you want to hold me hand like milord says."

Braeden reluctantly unfurled his hand, and she laced her tiny fingers through his. Tristan almost laughed at the wild panic in his eyes. "Be safe," he told them, and then began muscling his way through the crowd.

As Tristan drew closer, he could see a long line of men in binds of rope around the perimeter of the platform. There were men in the prime of their lives and white-haired men old enough to be grandfathers. And—faith in blood, there he was—the boy from the street, Tristan's failed pickpocket. Charlie. The poor boy looked terrified, and worse for the wear since Tristan had seen him last. What had they done to him?

Two men stood in the middle of the platform, wearing the formal red regalia that marked them as Paladins. One of the men, a large blond man with a braided beard, held a long-tailed whip in his right hand. The man beside him, a thin, gray-haired man of middling years, had a familiar look, but Tristan was almost certain he'd never met him.

The blond paladin untangled the tails of his whip and knotted each of the cords three times. "Gods," Tristan swore aloud, shouldering past a cluster of onlookers.

"People of Westergo!" the blond man boomed. "We have here before us criminals of the worst kind. Do they deserve to be punished?" Uneasily, the crowd gave its assent. He moved behind the first convict in the line, stroking the whip handle with his thumb. "This man stands accused of arson." He gave the convict an experimental tap across his shoulders. The man flinched at the contact, but did not cry out.

The Paladin moved onto the next convict, an ancient man so stooped over with age he could hardly stand. "And this man played truant on his taxes. A man of your advanced age surely knows better than to shirk his responsibilities." He shook his head, clicking his tongue against his teeth. Then, without warning, he lashed out with his whip, striking the old man along the backs of his ankles. With a startled cry, the old man crumpled, groaning in agony.

Tristan clenched his fists, his temper rising. He needed to get to them before they got to Charlie. Gods help the boy if he arrived too late.

Tristan was nearly at the foot of the platform when the blond Paladin came upon the little boy. His heart stuttered in his chest.

The blond Paladin clutched his hand to his breast. "Ah, corrupted youth. There is nothing more tragic." He exhaled in an exaggerated sigh. "But youth does not exempt you from justice. We can only hope that a sound beating can cure you of your evil. This boy"—he turned towards the crowd, raising his voice—"stole a full gold sovereign, and when confronted by the law, he tried to pass it off as his own. He *lied*. And so he must be doubly punished." His piece said, he gave the boy a vicious kick in the back of the legs. Charlie squealed, sagging onto his knees.

Tristan struggled to maintain his composure—who were these men to think they could take justice into their own hands? They were paladins, not kings! He wanted to punch them right in their smug, self-righteous faces. But that would not help save Charlie.

The gray-haired man crossed to his companion. "Again," he said. "Hit the boy again."

The whip struck Charlie across the chest. "It hurts," the little boy sobbed. "It hurts!"

The whip drew back, to strike again. Before the blow could land, Tristan vaulted onto the platform, catching the down-stroke in his hand. He ignored the burning sting, rubbing his palm against his breeches. "What in the name of the Gods is going on here?"

The two paladins exchanged shocked glances, and then returned their attention to Tristan. The blond man pulled the ends of his whip from Tristan's grasp, glaring at him. "I could ask the same of you. How dare you interrupt?"

"You've made a mockery of justice. Where are these men's defenders? Where is their trial?"

The blond man scoffed. "These men have no defenders. Who would come forward for the likes of them?"

Tristan took a step forward. "I would." He pointed at Charlie.

"I gave him a gold coin just this morning. The coin was rightfully his."

"You lie."

"I speak the truth, as does the boy. But even if he lied, a public flogging is hardly a fitting punishment for such a petty crime."

The blond man snapped his whip. "Perhaps we ought to whip *you*, my lord."

Tristan raised a brow. "I wouldn't advise it."

"And why is that?"

Tristan looked at him unflinchingly. "You couldn't lay a finger on me if you tried."

The gray-haired man guffawed. "You must be from out of town. You're speaking to the Paladins, boy."

Tristan's lip curled in disgust. These men might be paladins in name, but they certainly weren't in deed. "As are you, *old man*."

A muscle ticked in the older paladin's jaw. "I am Paladin Parsall, and this is Paladin Boyle. We have been tasked with watching over this city by the High Commander himself."

Tristan rolled his eyes. "And a *fine* job you're doing of it." He retrieved his knife from his boot and placed a comforting hand on Charlie's shoulder. "You'll be all right, boy." Kneeling beside him, he slashed through the ropes that bound the boy's wrists. Charlie rose shakily to his feet and then darted around Tristan, cowering behind his legs.

"What do you think you're doing?" Paladin Boyle demanded. "What right do you have to interfere?"

Tristan rested his knuckles on the boy's head. "I told you, I gave this boy a gold coin. You would have him unfairly punished for my generosity."

"You might be a paladin, and that is dubious," Paladin Parsall said with a sneer, "but we have been defending the people of Westergo for nigh on six years now. You don't know these people like we do. If we didn't use a firm hand, the city would dissolve into chaos. What are you, a year out of your apprenticeship? You're young, Paladin, but you will learn the ways of the world soon enough."

Tristan gnashed his teeth. "I may be young, but even among the Paladins, my name commands some respect." He swept them a mocking bow. "Paladin Tristan Lyons, at your service. And I swore the same oaths as you: to serve and protect Thule. You've overstepped your bounds."

Paladin Boyle spat at his feet. "Paladin Lyons? Prove it."

Tristan sighed, and removed his coin pouch from underneath his shirt, pulling out a neatly folded piece of parchment paper from the leather sack. "Here," he said, unfolding the document. "See the Seal of the High Commander for yourself."

Paladin Boyle ripped the paper from Tristan's hands. "It's addressed to a Paladin Tristan Lyons," he admitted. "But it says nothing of our business."

"Your business, as you call it," Tristan said, spreading his arms to encompass the stage, "is not the business of the Paladins. I suggest you take another look at your vows." He gripped Charlie's hand reassuringly. "I'm taking the boy with me when I leave this stage. The others, too."

Paladin Boyle's jaw tightened. "Perhaps the boy is innocent, but the others are guilty."

"Consider it a day of amnesty," Tristan said. He began freeing the convicts from their binds, one by one. "I am not so naïve as to believe that a few harsh words from me will put a stop to your puerile justice system. The High Commander will be hearing of this."

"The more fool you, then, if you think he'll condemn our behavior."

Tristan felt his blood boiling in his veins. "How dare you cast aspersions on the High Commander's character," he said, his voice low with fury. "Your antics may not be his top priority, but he won't turn a blind eye to this." He leaned closer. "In the meantime, if I find out you've touched a hair on the boy's head, I'll deal with you myself. Do I make myself clear?"

Paladin Parsall swallowed. "Aye, understood."

"Now return the boy's gold to him."

Paladin Parsall's neck was red with humiliation, but he did as he was bade, chucking the gold coin at the boy's feet. Charlie hesitated, and then snatched up the coin, depositing it into his breeches.

"We'll be off, then," Tristan said, reclaiming Charlie's hand.

Paladin Boyle's eyes narrowed. "You'll get your comeuppance one day, Paladin Lyons."

Tristan faced the Paladin with a smile that could freeze fire. "That well may be," he said. "But it won't come from the likes of you."

CHAPTER 23

$\mathcal{T}$HE REUNION BETWEEN brother and sister was a joyous one. The little boy and girl spoke too quickly in their broken tongue for Sam to follow the conversation, but she could pick out their fervently whispered I-love-yous. The girl kept calling the boy something that sounded like, "Ee-jut", but she said it with such affection that Sam couldn't be sure of its meaning.

Tristan insisted on buying the children two of the fancy cakes that had led to Charlie's arrest. Charlie ate his pastry in two large bites, his cheeks bulging as he chewed and swallowed. "It took you all of thirty seconds to eat that thing," Tristan remarked. "What a waste of your gold coin that would've been."

The little boy licked his frosting coated fingers. "I'da bought it for me sister. Wouldna been a waste."

His sister, at least, knew how to savor a rare treat. She split her cake into two, and nibbled daintily on one half. Shyly, she offered the other half to Braeden.

Tristan pressed his hand to his heart with mock indignation. "You wound me, my lady. I rescue your brother, yet you offer your cake to Braeden? What does a man have to do to earn himself a sliver?"

"Buy one for yourself," the girl said tartly, her cheeks turning rosy.

Sam grabbed Tristan's elbow, pulling him aside. "Stop it, you're embarrassing her. Braeden is likely her first infatuation."

"What do you know of a little girl's infatuation?"

Sam had firsthand experience, but she wasn't about to tell him that. "Enough to know she fancies herself in love with Braeden. She's been mooning over him ever since you made him hold her hand."

Tristan chuckled. "I would never have thought of Braeden as a heartbreaker."

Sam glared at him. "So women should only fall in love with a pretty face like yours, then."

Tristan grinned. "Don't worry, you and Braeden can have my leftovers."

Sam punched him hard in the shoulder.

"I was only jesting!" Tristan squawked.

After the cakes were eaten, Tristan, Sam, and Braeden bid the children farewell.

"Thankee, milord. We won't forget you, not never," Charlie promised, his back straight and proud.

"Take care of your sister, Charlie," Tristan said, mounting his horse. "And if the Paladins try to give either of you trouble again, remind them of my name."

"What *is* your name, milord?" the little girl asked.

Tristan inclined his head. "Paladin Tristan Lyons, First of the sword."

═══════════════

They didn't stay in Westergo much longer, though Sam knew that Tristan had originally planned for them to spend the night. "I don't want to stay in this city any longer than I have to," he said. Sam couldn't agree more. They paused only to water and feed their horses before continuing on down the main through-way, past the opulent palace and the slums, then out of Westergo through its westernmost gates.

"Where to next, Tristan?" Sam shouted over the sound of their horses' hoofbeats.

Tristan slowed down so that the necks of their horses were aligned. "Pirama will be our next stop. I'll need to send a report back to the High Commander."

"Pirama? Didn't the innkeeper in Gwent say something about Uriel sympathies?"

"Aye, he did. The Paladins may no longer be welcome in Pirama. We'll need to be on our guard."

"You think we may not be *welcome*?" Sam asked. The Paladins were always treated as honored guests, wherever they went. "The Uriel have that much power?"

Tristan's lips flattened into a grim line. "I don't know," he said. "The High Commander believes they pose a dire threat. I'm not yet convinced."

"And if they do?"

"I don't concern myself with hypotheticals. I'll follow the directive of the High Commander, as I always do." He urged his horse ahead once more, signaling that the conversation was over.

They only managed a couple of hours of solid riding before a thunderstorm forced them to seek shelter off road. The sky was an inky purple, topped by billowing clouds so dark they were nearly black. Crisscrossed branches of lightning streaked down from the heavens with a sharp crack. It was all Sam could do to keep her frightened horse from bolting.

By the time they set up camp and secured the horses, it was too wet to start a fire. Sam's clothes were soaked through and she was chilled to the bone. "We sh-should have s-stayed in Westergo," she managed to get out, her teeth chattering.

Tristan rummaged through their bags in search of a dry shirt and swore when he found none. "You two didn't want to be there any more than I did. That place made me sick."

He was right, Sam conceded. Till she had left Haywood, she had wanted for nothing, and even now, on the road, she never went hungry. The poverty-stricken people of Westergo, with their quiet desperation and hopeless stares, had opened her eyes. And worse—they were mistreated at the hands of the Paladins. The uneasy feeling at the pit of her stomach was guilt. "You're r-right," she acknowledged. "But I'm still f-f-freezing."

"We all are, but there's nothing we can do about it till the storm breaks. I suspect we'll have to hunker down here for the night." Tristan pulled off his leather boots and turned them upside down, dumping out a small puddle of water. His tunic and breeches quickly followed suit, till he stood in nothing but his smallclothes.

"What are you doing?" Sam squeaked.

Tristan gave her a hard look. "My clothes are sopping wet. I suggest you do the same unless you want to catch your death of cold."

Braeden, too, removed his outer garments, his black robes sloshing to his feet. Sam stared. The two men stood under the fractured cover of the trees, rainwater sluicing down their well-honed chests. Where Tristan was big and brawny, Braeden was lean and powerful, handsome in the dark of the storm.

"Well?" Tristan asked.

Sam put her hands up defensively. "I'm f-fine. M-my c-clothes aren't that wet." She pointedly ignored the ghost of a smile that flitted across Braeden's lips.

"Suit yourself," Tristan said and crawled into the tent.

Braeden sauntered toward her and reached out to touch the sodden fabric of her tunic. "Stay warm, Lady Sam," he said, and then entered into the tent after Tristan. Sam stuck her tongue out at his back before following him inside.

It was one of the most uncomfortable nights of Sam's life. As Tristan had predicted, the rain did not let up. It battered the leather roof of their shelter all through the night. They lay close together—for body heat, Tristan had said. And because Sam was the smallest, she had to lie in the middle, wedged between Braeden and Tristan. Braeden looked slightly scandalized, but true to form, he said nothing and turned his back to her.

Tristan soon drifted off to sleep, his chest moving up and down in even breaths. Sam closed her eyes, but she was unbearably cold. She shuddered as chills raked her from head to toe.

"Can't sleep?" Braeden asked softly.

She shook her head, locking her jaw to keep it from rattling.

Braeden touched her hand. "Gods, your skin is like ice."

Sam flipped onto her side, facing him. "I w-wasn't aware," she whispered acidly. Another shudder rocked her.

Hesitantly, Braeden wrapped his arms around her torso, hugging her to him. "Just for a little while," he said.

Sam was too cold to think beyond snuggling into his warm chest. The heat of his body was like a furnace against hers, soothing away her shivers, and she soon fell asleep to the steady beat of his heart.

Sam jolted awake to a cold nose nudging her shoulder. Faith in blood! Braeden's arms were still wrapped around her waist, her body fitted snugly against his. She could feel him pressing against her. Tristan, meanwhile, must have shifted during the night. He'd buried his face in her hair, and his long, bare leg draped over her hip.

She was effectively pinned between the two men.

"Braeden," she hissed. "Braeden!" He tightened his embrace and nuzzled her neck, letting out a light snore.

Sam panicked silently. Maybe if she pretended to be asleep, she could avoid any awkwardness when Tristan and Braeden awoke. She was all too aware of Braeden's hands, spanned high across her ribcage, and Tristan's mouth, which now rested against her forehead.

After what felt like hours, Braeden finally stirred. She could feel the instant he became fully cognizant of his surroundings—and the compromising position they'd slept in. He froze against her body, his breath short and hot on her neck. He dragged his arm out from under her and rolled to the opposite side of the tent. "Gods damn it," he muttered.

Sam maintained her false slumber for a few more minutes, but grew impatient waiting for Tristan to wake up. Tristan's lips had a mind of their own, drawing ever-closer to her mouth. Unsettled, she turned her head and tried to wriggle out from under his leg.

The tip of Tristan's tongue traced the rim of her ear. Sam sat up with a start, shoving at Tristan's leg. "Get off me, you big lug!"

Tristan's lids popped open. His gaze turned lucid after a few quick blinks. "Sorry," he said with a sheepish smile. "I must've mistaken you for a woman in my sleep. You're as slight as a girl, anyway." He lifted his leg from her hips and kicked her lightly in the stomach. "And I was having such a lovely dream, too."

Braeden cleared his throat. "I think the rain has stopped."

Tristan pushed himself up onto his knees. "Excellent. Let's see if we can locate some dry clothes. I want to be on the road in ten minutes."

They arrived in Pirama just before nightfall. The city was built at the foot of the Elurra Mountains, the longest mountain range in Thule. Half the city was tunneled into the mountainside while the remaining half stood underneath the sky, surrounded by a high wall made of great gray stones carved from the mountain.

The gates to the city were already closed, but after some wheedling from Tristan, the gatekeeper let them in through a small postern door, just tall enough to fit a man on horseback.

"Be careful, milord," the gatekeeper said, securing the door behind them. "I'd seek lodgings quickly if I were you. You don't want to be outdoors after dark if you can avoid it. It's dangerous."

"Dangerous? How so?" Tristan asked.

"Demons, milord. We've had attacks near nightly for more than a month now."

Sam scanned the empty street, searching for signs of trouble. "What about the Paladins?" she asked. She ignored Tristan's dirty look. "Haven't they helped?"

The gatekeeper scratched his chin. "The Paladins? I haven't seen hide nor hare of them, not since Paladin Reynard left. He was all right, Reynard, but he was called back east four months ago. The paladins who replaced him—they've kept to themselves these past few months."

Tristan glanced up at the gatekeeper's tower, frowning. "What about you? Are you safe up there, alone?"

The gatekeeper shrugged. "It's my job, milord," he said. "You be safe now." With a parting salute, he climbed the ladder to return to his post.

They drove their horses deeper into the city of Pirama. In the fading light of dusk, not a single soul stirred. Only the clip-clop of their horses' hooves and the occasional nervous whinny cut into the silence. "I don't like this," Tristan said. "Braeden, do you sense anything unusual?"

Braeden's mouth crooked into a sardonic grin. "Demonic, you mean?" He shook his head. "Not now, though I can sense a lingering presence. The city was attacked recently. Maybe last night."

"Stay alert, both of you. Demons aren't the only threat in this city. And keep your eyes peeled for The Stag and Bull."

After a few wrong turns, they found the inn in the labyrinth of tunnels drilled into the mountainside. The Paladins' sigil was carved into the wood of the inn's door, but half of the circle and pentagram had been scratched off.

Tristan hopped off his horse and tried to turn the knob on the door, but it was locked. He rapped sharply on the wooden frame.

The small window at the top of the door slid open. Narrowed eyes peered down at them. "Who goes there?"

Tristan dipped his head in a slight bow. "Are you John Byrd?"

"Who's asking?"

"Paladin Tristan Lyons, good sir," Tristan said. He gestured at Sam and Braeden behind him. "These are my trainees. Though I'd appreciate it if you kept our titles quiet."

The voice behind the door harrumphed. "What do you want, Paladin?"

"Two rooms and a bit of food and drink, if you have it."

"You'll pay for your stay?"

"Aye, of course."

Several locks rattled and unlatched, and then the door swung open, revealing a squat, grizzled man with a long, unkempt beard down to his chest. He scowled up at them. "Come in, come in, you're letting in the cold air. I'll see to your horses." The man ushered them inside and then let himself out. "Wait right here and I'll come back for you in just a moment."

The hollowed-out area where they waited looked more like the opening to a cave than the entrance hall to an inn. The gray rock of the mountain formed a natural ceiling and walls that, were it not for the glow of the sconce torch, would have enclosed them in total darkness. Even with the torch, it took a moment for Sam's eyes to adjust to the shadowy light.

The innkeeper returned, opening and closing the door behind him, relatching all the locks. "Follow me," he said, leading them into the tavern. The tavern was wide and spacious, lit by small clusters of black and white candles placed on the center of tables throughout the room. In the back was a crude stone stairway to the lodging above. "Kitchen's closed, but there's fresh bread and jam. Find a free seat and I'll serve you." He came around the bar and began pouring himself a drink.

Sam eyed the mostly empty inn suspiciously. "Does anyone else work here besides you?"

He snorted in disgust. "I lost all my hired help two weeks ago. Thank the Gods for my wife, or I'd be cooking too. I don't know a compote from a custard, so be grateful for that small favor."

"John Byrd," Tristan said, getting right down to business, "Glenn Collop of Gwent gave us your name."

"Aye," the innkeeper said, crossing his arms. "What of it?"

"He said you were a true friend of the Paladins." Tristan tilted his head to the side. "Perhaps he was wrong?"

"I won't lie to you, Paladin Lyons. Times change. Pirama's not the city it once was. People are dying by the day. It's hard to remain loyal when you cry out for help and no one comes to your aid. I *want* to believe in the Paladins, I do. And I'm no fan of the Uriel either."

Tristan lowered his voice. "What do you know of the Uriel, Master Byrd?"

The innkeeper jerked his head towards two men drinking in the far right corner of the tavern. "There's a table of Uriel men over there, Paladin, if you'd like to find out for yourself."

"You serve the Uriel?" Sam asked, aghast. The innkeeper really had no loyalties.

"These days, I serve whoever pays my bills. I can't afford to be choosey. So don't go making trouble, now."

Tristan shot Sam a quelling glare. "Fair enough," he said. "We'll take that bread and jam now." The innkeeper nodded and left them to themselves.

"I can hear them," Braeden said softly. "They knew we were going to be here."

"Who?" Tristan asked.

"The Uriel." Braeden inclined his head slightly at the two men the innkeeper had indicated.

Tristan raised an inquisitive eyebrow. "How did they know we were coming?"

Braeden shook his head. "I don't know. But they've been waiting here for us."

"Do you think it's a trap?" Sam asked.

"Only one way to find out," Tristan said, heading straight for their table. Trading shrugs, Sam and Braeden rushed after him.

The two Uriel watched them approach, their expressions unreadable in the muted light. Sam stared at them in return. One of the men was so badly scarred that his face would turn as many heads as Braeden's. The other Uriel was a hulking brute, with hands that looked as though they could crush stone to dust.

Tristan draped his arm across the back of an empty chair. "Good evening, gentleman."

The Uriel rose from their seats and assessed them with cool reservation. Tension hung between them, and then the scarred man smiled a slow, amused smile that stretched the ugly white welts along his cheeks. Sam tried not to cringe.

Tristan reached his hand across the table. "Tristan."

The scarred Uriel returned his grip. "Paladin Tristan Lyons. The pleasure is ours."

Tristan started at the sound of his full name. "How did you—"

The scarred Uriel laughed, a harsh, rattling sound. "Golden hair, large sword, arrogant swagger. Your reputation precedes you." He turned his head, his eyes boring into Sam then shifting to Braeden. "And you must be Tristan's trainees. Sam and Braeden, is that right?"

Sam looked to Tristan, unsure of what to say. How did they know her name? Tristan was famous, but she wasn't anybody, not anymore.

"You have us at a disadvantage," Tristan admitted. "You know our names, yet we do not know yours."

"Adelard," the Uriel with the scarred face said, sinking back into his chair. He flicked his companion's elbow. "And this is Donnelly."

"Hullo," Donnelly said, his high, soft voice at odds with his beefy build. Sam was almost startled into laughing.

"Sit," Adelard said, gesturing at the empty chairs. "The road from Heartwine to Pirama is a long one. You must be tired."

"Not so tired," Tristan said, giving him a grin full of shark's teeth. He pulled out a chair and sat. "Tell me, Adelard, why are you here, at The Stag and Bull?"

"I could ask the same of you."

"You knew we would be here," Tristan said sharply. "How?"

A long look passed between Adelard and Donnelly. Donnelly's head dipped to his drink, and he stared at the frothing liquid as though it held all the world's secrets. "You know who we are, Paladin, don't you?" Adelard asked. "Just as we know you."

"Uriel," Tristan said grimly. "You are Uriel."

They did not try to deny it. "We are on equal footing, then," Adelard said. "I should like to continue to be forthright. The Paladins have their spies, and we have ours. You've been asking around about us, and we wanted to know why."

"The priestess in Cordoba," Sam said. "Denya. She spies for you, doesn't she?"

Adelard's gaze swept over her. "Very good," he said. "Denya is a priestess first, but yes, she is our informant. One of many."

"That is not very godlike behavior," Sam retorted.

Adelard arched a black eyebrow, contorting his scarred face. "It is if she believes her god is on our side. Then she is doing God's work."

"Why are you telling us this?" Tristan asked. "Why give yourself away?"

"We've nothing to hide, Donnelly or I or any of the Uriel. We're not interested in playing your High Commander's power games."

Tristan's jaw tightened. "What *are* you interested in, then?"

The Uriel's dark eyes gleamed, and he leaned forward in his chair. "Protecting the people of Thule. Our goals are not so different, Paladin."

"Thule doesn't need you," Sam said, scowling. "They have us."

Beside her, Tristan groaned softly. "Ignore him. He speaks before he thinks."

Adelard chuckled, waving his hand in dismissal. "He is young. And he only said what you are thinking. Spend some time in the West, Paladin Lyons, and see if you still feel the same." He sat back in his chair. "I will do you one better. Come by our encampment in West Pirama tomorrow morning. There, you can ask all the questions of the Uriel that you'd like."

"You would open your doors to a paladin?" Tristan asked incredulously.

"We close our doors to no one except demons, Paladin Lyons."

Braeden lifted his head, the faint glow of candlelight accentuating the contrast of his slit black pupils against the crimson of his irises. "And to me?"

Adelard gave him a considering look. "You're no demon. I've fought and killed enough to know." He drained his cup of wine and pushed back his chair. "Should we expect you on the morrow?"

"We'll be there," Tristan said.

Adelard helped Donnelly to his feet and offered Tristan his hand once more. "Till tomorrow, Paladin."

CHAPTER 24

BRAEDEN JERKED AWAKE to the sound of Sam's soft breathing. The inn room was dark as a tomb, but with *his* eyes, he had no trouble seeing.

He and Sam were alone in their room, he was sure of it. Nothing else moved or made a sound. And yet he knew, as sure as he was breathing, they wouldn't be alone for long. *They* were coming. Demons.

He pushed back his sleeves, watching the tides of his blood swell underneath the skin on his arm. The familiar, seductive pull was a potent one, pushing him to the edge of his control. His hands twitched at his side, his fingers curling into claws, eager to rip away the flesh that contained his inner monster.

For an instant, the walls of the inn room fell away as Braeden was consumed by an insatiable hunger. But Sam's sleeping form filled his vision, and the bloodlust faded into something else, something he didn't dare name.

The fog in his brain cleared, and he acted before he could think too long on the torrent of emotions that flooded him every time he looked at Sam. He shook her awake.

Sam opened her eyes with a gasp. "Gods, Braeden, I was having the *worst* dream—"

He cut her off. "There are demons coming." He shivered, and not from cold. "I can feel them."

"Are you certain?" she asked. Braeden twisted his arm so that his rippling skin was on full display.

Sam needed no more proof than that. With a grim nod, she threw aside her covers and shoved off the bed. "Let's go get Tristan."

Fortunately, Master Byrd had put Tristan in a room just down the hall from theirs, and they found it with little trouble. Sam reached out to knock on the door and then paused. "Do you think he's still sleeping?"

"I would think so."

Sam stepped back from the door. "You do it."

Braeden rolled his eyes. "Really, Sam?"

She scuffed her foot against the carpet. "He's scary right after he wakes up."

"Fine," he said, more amused than he let on. Sam would charge into battle without a second thought, but Tristan had her running. Shaking his head, he knocked, hard enough to rattle the frame. Rumpled from sleep, Tristan opened the door and looked at him expectantly. "Demons," Braeden said. He need say no more.

"Hold that thought," Tristan said, disappearing back into his room. He returned seconds later, water dripping down his hair and face, but looking considerably more alert. "Can you pinpoint where they are?"

Braeden was a little taken aback that Tristan accepted his warning at his word. It was a strange, new thing to him, being trusted. "They're not inside the city, not yet. The bulk of them are maybe just under a mile away, due north."

"The bulk of them?" Sam asked. "They're not all together?"

"Demons are like wolves," Braeden explained. "When there are more than a couple in the vicinity, they operate in packs because they're stronger that way. But there are lone demons just as there are lone wolves. It's harder for me to sense a demon when it's by itself."

"Can they sense you?" Tristan asked. "Does it go both ways?"

Braeden's heart twisted. There were some things best left unsaid, some secrets best left buried. He gave Tristan a cool look. "Not till it's too late."

Tristan held his gaze for a moment, and then pulled his eyes away, ushering them inside his room. "Grab weapons from the chest by the bed. And before you ask, Sam, no, you can't have my Paladin's sword."

Sam's face fell in disappointment while Tristan chuckled to himself.

Outside the inn, Pirama was as silent as when they had first arrived, but the air seemed thicker, as if a storm were brewing. The sharp-ridged peaks of the mountain cloaked the city in a dark, uneven pall. A winged creature flew overhead, too far above to make out. Tristan shot it down with the bow he had slung over his shoulder. It fell to the ground in a small back clump. Braeden prodded the creature with his boot. Just a bat. They were all too tense, even he.

Shutting his eyes, Braeden released the first mental shield that kept the demons out of his mind. He felt their tug at the edges. "They're close," he said, ignoring the rush of blood in his ears. "Less than a quarter mile."

"No point waiting around to be ambushed," Tristan said. "You lead, and we'll follow."

Braeden drew a knife and sliced into his skin, letting the thrall of the demons carry him. Their savagery lured him in like a fish, and he took the bait, following the line back to the source. He walked with eyes closed, as if under a compulsion, but he held on to the part of him that was human and kept it safe.

"Where are we?" Sam asked when Braeden's feet came to a halt.

Braeden opened his eyes. He had led them into the mountains, to the top of a narrow pass between two near-vertical rocky faces. The ground was covered with layers of stones and pebbles, and the chalky path beneath them was worn and well-traversed. The pass glimmered with flecks of silver and gold under the light of the half-moon.

In the distance, a bell rang, its peel spelling out a warning. "They're here," Braeden said.

"Shite," Tristan cursed, his head swinging from right to left. "Where are they?"

Braeden put his finger to his lips. "Listen, and you'll hear them." Claws scuttled and scraped on rock, close enough now that anyone could register the sound. Something rattled and buzzed, and he could pick up a faint humming.

"I hear them, but I can't see a thing," Tristan said between clenched teeth. "If we stay here, we're doomed. We won't be able to attack till they're too close for comfort."

"How many of them are there? Can you tell, Braeden?" Sam asked, squinting into the dark.

"More than ten and less than a hundred, but more exact than that I can't say. The first of them are a short distance away now."

"You can see in this light?" Tristan asked.

Braeden tapped the corner of his eye. "One of their few benefits."

"Convenient for you," Tristan said, "but Sam and I are handicapped in the dark. We'll need to draw them out of the pass if we're to stand any chance of winning."

"That might be problematic," Braeden said. "They're coming in from both sides."

"How is that possible?" Sam asked with a hint of nervousness. "How could they have gotten behind us?"

Braeden pointed up. Three oversized worms, with spiked tails and shovel-shaped heads, slinked down the sides of the mountain from above, leaving behind a slimy secretion that glowed a faint green in the dark. When the worm demons reached the bottom of the mountain side, hundreds of skinny, segmented legs descended from holes in their body walls, and they scuttled on the ground like centipedes. "That's how."

Tristan shuddered. "Absolutely vile. I loathe worms more than anything else."

"I thought you hated snakes," Sam said.

"I hate anything that moves without legs. It isn't natural, I tell you."

"Those creatures look like they have legs to me. Several hundred of them."

"Sam?"

"Yes, Tristan?"

"Shut up."

Ignoring their banter, Braeden pulled his swords free from the scabbards strapped to his back, two in either hand. The front ranks of the demons, advancing from the north side of the pass, were ten yards or less away. "They're almost upon us."

"Stay alert," Tristan said. Directing his attention to Sam, he added, "Remember, you can't rely on your eyes in this light."

As he spoke, a large hellhound darted out from its pack, rushing toward them on its long, powerful legs.

"Tristan, watch out!" Braeden shouted.

It was easy to forget when there was no fighting to be done that Tristan was a master swordsman, but he took only seconds to remind them. The demon had no sooner reached his feet than Tristan had sent its head rolling to the ground. A fountain of red spurted from its neck, splattering Tristan's breeches.

The stench of demon blood wafted through the air, sending the other demons into a frenzy. Braeden smiled. His swords were thirsty, too.

Braeden ran, launching himself at the nearest demon. With the blade in his right hand, he sliced through its forelegs, and with the left, he carved through its neck. Leaping over its furry body, he drove his sword into the next.

He kept one eye on Sam as he fought. She was contending with one of the worm demons, riding astride it as it squirmed to shake her off. She plunged her sword deep into its flat head. It let out a bone-chilling scream as it died. Satisfied, she pulled the blade from its carcass and moved towards her next target, not noticing the hellhound creeping up behind her.

Braeden sprinted towards her, throwing one of his swords like a spear at her stealthy attacker. Pierced through the flank, the hound let out a high whine, stumbling backward. Sam whirled around to face him, scowling. "I had that," she said. "I can handle myself. Go find your own demons to kill."

It wasn't like there was a shortage. No matter how many demons he felled, more demons replaced them. He ripped through them mindlessly, stealing backward glances at Sam when he could. He couldn't help himself, though he knew she could hold her own.

"Gods, they're never ending," Tristan grumbled in between panting breaths. "A little help would be nice."

"We *are* helping!" Sam said indignantly.

"I meant help from the Paladins. Where in the Gods' names are they? I heard the warning bell ring ages ago."

To Tristan's point, though the ground was awash with blood

and viscera, they had barely made a dent in the demons' numbers. Even Braeden was beginning to feel strained by the long fighting. He would need to access his extra reservoirs of power if this kept up.

Two large flames lit the south side of the pass. "Look! I think someone's coming!" Sam shouted. Long, humanoid shadows flitted across the mountain walls, shrinking in size as they drew nearer.

"Paladins," Tristan said. "Certainly took them long enough to get here."

"No," Braeden said slowly, his pupils constricting as the flames flooded the pass with light. "It's the Uriel."

A thick ring of demons separated Braeden, Sam, and Tristan from the fast approaching men, but Braeden was close enough to see that the shadows belonged to Adelard and Donnelly. The two Uriel were joined by several other men he didn't recognize.

Adelard carried a burning torch in one hand and a maul in the other. The haft of the maul was no longer than his arm from shoulder to wrist, and the heavy hammer head bore a spike on the back end, sharp enough to pierce the toughest armor or the thickest hide. Donnelly held a torch of his own in one hand and a scimitar in his other.

"Halt!" Adelard commanded his men. The demons halted, too, distracted by the smell of fresh prey. "Who goes there?" he called into the passage.

"It's Paladin Tristan Lyons, with my trainees," Tristan shouted back. "Where are the Paladins?"

Before Adelard could respond, a worm demon swung its barbed tail at Sam. She stepped aside at the last possible moment and chopped off its tail, exposing its swollen innards like a hock of ham. Sam yelped as the severed tail flailed on the ground, narrowly missing her feet, till Tristan cut it into so many pieces that it resembled minced meat. "Pay attention, Sam!" he snapped.

"I *am* paying attention," she said. "I just wasn't expecting that thing to move!"

"I don't care what you expected. Stay vigilant. Now, finish off the damn thing."

With a parting glower, Sam marched towards the worm,

which wriggled about drunkenly without its tail. "Stupid worm," she muttered, and then chopped its head clean off.

Braeden lost sight of Sam and Tristan as four demons converged on him at once. He raised his swords and spun, cleaving through tendon and bone. He crouched low to the ground, readying for their next attack. As he swung out his right arm, sharp teeth bit into his left shoulder, tearing through muscle and tissue. He snarled at the searing pain. A green, fluorescent fluid leaked from the wound, burning holes in his clothes. Venom from one of the worm demons.

Shoving the pain aside, he sunk his sword into the worm's rubbery skin, hacking off a segment. He slashed again, cutting through the fleshy projection over its mouth, and then drove his second sword into the new opening, splitting it in half. His next blow went through a hellhound's gullet.

Though the wound was already healing over, streaks of fiery pain shot through his shoulder, like nothing he'd ever felt. His breaths came in short, shallow gasps, and his vision wavered, threatening to fade to black. He staggered forward, leaning on his swords for balance.

Through drooping lids, Braeden saw Adelard crash into a circle of demons with a roar. The Uriel swung his heavy hammer, bashing its blunt head into demon skulls and impaling their necks with its spike. He followed through with his torch, wielding it like a weapon. The air reeked of scorched skin and fur.

Fighting to stay conscious, Braeden searched through the carnage for Sam, hoping she was faring better than he. Where in the Gods' names was she? He could only see Tristan and the Uriel, their voices echoing loudly through the narrow pass.

"I know I said we'd see each other on the morrow—" Adelard paused to bat at a demon with his maul. "—but I was hoping to meet at least after dawn."

"I couldn't think of a better time to renew our acquaintance," Tristan said drolly. "In fact, I wouldn't have complained had you arrived even earlier."

"We were delayed. There were a few one-off attacks in the heart of the city."

"No matter. I'm glad for the help, though I was expecting it to come in the form of the Paladins."

"Pirama learned not to rely on the Paladins months ago."

On unsteady feet, Braeden moved toward the two men. "Have you seen Sam?"

Tristan froze. "I thought he was with you."

"No," Braeden said grimly. He brought the tip of his curved blade to his breastbone.

"What are you doing?" Tristan cried out.

The world went crimson as his blade burrowed into his heart. "Finding Sam."

CHAPTER 25

S AM LOVED THE feel of a sword in her hands. With a sword, she could *do* anything, *be* anything. She felt lethal, empowered, as strong as any man. She could fight forever, it seemed.

But despite her boundless enthusiasm, her body grew weary. Her swings came slower and slower, and her sweaty palms began to chafe against the shark skin of her grip.

She paused to catch her breath, leaning against her sword. A fierce wind shrieked around her, drowning out the sounds of battle. It was close to pitch black, too—the light of the Uriel's torches didn't carry to the part of the pass where she was fighting. She swore under her breath. Sam couldn't see the others—she could hardly see at all. She must have gotten separated. Drat Tristan for being right, she should have paid better attention. Now she was alone in the dark with only her sword for company.

Not totally alone, she amended. In the darkness, she could make out the shapes of hellhounds, flews pulled back to show their sharp, salivating smiles. Their eyes glowed like crimson beacons. Massive, steel-toed paws scraping over rock and stone, the demons closed in around her. Sam counted ten of them.

Before she could panic—or even think about panicking—a long, preternatural howl rent the air. Claw and sword whirled into the wall of demons that surrounded her, sending bits and pieces of fur and flesh in every direction. Sam wiped off a stray intestine that had landed in the crook of her elbow. It shriveled into twine at her feet. She stared at the desiccated tube, wondering if her own bowels were ripped from her stomach would they deteriorate so easily.

Half of the hellhounds were dead or dying, but it was the surviving demons that captivated her attention. What in the Gods' names had happened to them? In a matter of seconds, they'd gone from violent creatures of chaos to little more than tame puppies. They sat on their hind legs, so still they seemed almost frozen. She raised her sword, bracing for an attack that never came.

And then she saw Braeden, shouldering past the demons as though he had nothing to fear. His gaze locked on hers, eyes as red as she'd ever seen them, glimmering in the moonlight. What remained of his robes was in tatters, exposing his bare and battered body. The muscles in his arms were swollen like overripe melons, and blood dripped down his stomach from a gaping wound in his chest.

He lurched towards her, closing the distance between them with inhuman speed. He stood inches away, watching her.

Sam's pulse sped up—he wasn't himself, that much was obvious. "Braeden?" She searched his face for some sign of emotion or recognition—anything. He said nothing, silent and unblinking under her scrutiny.

"Braeden," she said again, putting some grit into her voice. She tapped him on the breastbone with the hilt of her sword. "Anybody home in there?"

He growled, low in his throat. Sam instinctively took a few steps back.

Braeden lunged for her. "Mine!" he snarled. He clamped her torso to his and bent his head to her neck, scraping his tongue along the base of her throat.

Sam gasped and pushed at his muscle-bound body. "Braeden!" She trusted him—really, she did—but he was looking at her like she was a tasty morsel. She reminded herself that they were friends, or something of the sort. Friends didn't eat friends, even if they were a little deranged.

Braeden's body swayed and his eyes shuttered closed. When he opened them again, their crimson glow had dimmed and a modicum of intelligence had returned. "Sam."

Relief flooded her. "Idiot." She shoved him again. "What was that?"

"Had to find you. Worked." Braeden rubbed at the inflamed skin around the hole in his chest. "Worked too well."

Sam stared as blood leaked from the wound in a slow, steady

stream. "I can see through to your heart. Did you do that to yourself?"

Braeden nodded. "Direct to the heart is more effective. Sometimes too effective. I'm sorry if I scared you."

Sam waved her hand dismissively. "I wasn't scared," she said, though she had been, just a little bit. She peered over at the demons, who remained stock-still. "Why aren't they attacking us anymore?"

Braeden grimaced. "When I'm like this—" He gestured at his grotesquely muscular form, "I can feel what they're feeling, and they can feel what I'm feeling. But my will is stronger."

"So you're controlling them?"

"Not exactly. My will is overpowering theirs, for now, but they want you very badly, Sam."

"Me?" she squeaked. "You mean because I'm human?"

"It's more than that. There's something about you that draws them to you. This isn't the first time I've noticed."

Sam swallowed down bile. "Why?" she asked. "Why me?"

Braeden shrugged his bulky shoulders. "I wish I knew. I worry that they want you like my father wanted my mother. I couldn't live with myself if I let that happen to you."

Sam squashed the cold fear that his words evoked in the pit of her stomach. "*I* won't let that happen to me. I don't need to be rescued, by you or anyone."

Braeden's tightly controlled mask slipped and he gripped her upper arms. "You don't understand. I'm a monster, Sam. I hang on to my humanity by the barest thread. What happens if I let go? What happens if there are so many demons that their will subjugates mine? What if it's my teeth that rip into your throat? I almost lost control just now."

Sam placed her hands over his. "But you didn't. And you won't. I know you, Braeden." With a forced smile, she pushed him away. "Besides, what makes you think I'd ever let you bite me?"

He gave her a look. "Funny."

"I try." She adjusted her sword into position. "Come on, let's end this."

Braeden nodded curtly, raising his blade. "Together," he said.

She returned his nod. "Together."

CHAPTER 26

$\mathcal{T}$RISTAN STARED AT the Uriel encampment illuminated by the dawnlight creeping over the mountains. It lay within a hanging valley at the far side of the pass, high above the main dale and the river far below. A stream cut diagonally across the valley, flowing past the encampment to a waterfall at the valley's mouth. The fort itself was crudely formed, surrounded by a deep outer ditch and a turf rampart topped by a palisade of heavy timber stakes, with gated entrances at the midpoint of each of its four walls. Roofed sheds and buildings of varying size were strategically arranged throughout.

The main Uriel base, according to the Sub Rosa, was in the city of Luca, on the western side of the Elurra Mountains. But he'd heard nothing of their operations in Pirama. The Sub Rosa were the best spies in Thule—how could they possibly be ignorant of it? The more he learned about the Uriel, the more he felt like he'd been purposefully left in the dark.

Adelard led Tristan, Sam, and Braeden to the door of one of the largest buildings. "This is the infirmary," the Uriel said. "Do you mind if I check on my men?" A few of the Uriel had been wounded fighting off the demons in the pass.

"Go ahead," Tristan said. He would have wanted to do the same if any of his men were injured. Braeden and Sam nodded, and the three of them followed Adelard in.

Once inside, Tristan was shocked not only by the modernity and size of the infirmary but also by the number of people it supported. Most of the sickbeds were filled, and not just by the Uriel. The patients included the elderly, several women and children, as well as a few men who looked as though they had never so much as touched a weapon.

Tristan plucked what he assumed to be a surgical tool from a nearby table, examining the ironwork. It looked more like a torture device than an instrument of medicine.

A surly man in a white linen hat and bloodstained clothes grabbed the tool from Tristan's hands. "Don't touch that!" he snapped, stomping off down the aisle.

"Don't mind the good surgeon," Adelard said. "He's no doubt had a busy night."

"What is this place?" Sam asked, a bit green in the face.

"An improvised hospital for victims of demon attacks. It's only been up and running for a month now, and we're short on medical supplies. But we try to help as many as we can, regardless."

"What's wrong with the local doctors?" Tristan asked.

"They're either dead or long gone, I'm afraid," Adelard said. "There's one doctor who stayed in East Pirama, but his prices are out of reach for most."

"And what do you charge for medical treatment?"

"We encourage our patients to pay what they can. Usually, they wind up paying close to nothing, if anything at all," Adelard said ruefully. "But at least if they come to us, they're safe from a second attack while they're at their most vulnerable."

It was a good idea, Tristan hated to admit. Briefly, he wondered why the Paladins hadn't thought to set up something similar. Although, in all fairness, most of the cities east of Pirama had their own hospitals and doctors and had no need of their interference. Besides, resources only extended so far, and the Paladins were warriors, not healers. Surely the Uriel knew that offering any service for free was not sustainable. He questioned their motives—no one did anything out of pure altruism. "What's in it for the Uriel?" he asked, not expecting an honest answer.

"We saw a need and we filled it. It's what we do."

A man's scream erupted from the back of the infirmary. "Quiet!" the surgeon barked. He inserted a wooden, screw-shaped gag into the man's mouth. "Bite!" The man did as instructed, his breath coming out in wheezes.

The surgeon retrieved a wicked-looking bow-frame saw. The patient's eyes went wild with fear, and he thrashed against the bed. "Hold still, damn it!" The surgeon threw himself on top of the flailing man. "Adelard, you with the sticky fingers"—he pointed at Tristan—"the rest of you lot! I need your help!"

Adelard turned to Tristan and raised an eyebrow in an unspoken challenge. Tristan nodded resolutely, and he, his trainees, and Adelard rushed to the surgeon's side.

"How can we help?" Adelard asked, pushing back the sleeves of his tunic.

"Hold him or this amputation will go poorly."

Sam gulped audibly. "Amputation? His leg doesn't look so bad to me." The patient bobbed his head up and down in agreement.

The surgeon fixed Sam with a frosty stare. "Are you a practitioner of medicine? No? Then keep your opinions to yourself." He pulled out a small pair of scissors from his pocket and cut off the man's breeches at his left knee. "The original wound site is here," he said, pointing to a missing chunk of leg that was still weeping blood. The skin around the wound was black and filmy, and dark red lines fanned out from the swelling, patterning his limb like a spiderweb. "The wound is infected. It's spread all the way to here." The surgeon brought his scissors to the man's kneecap and pricked the skin with their tip. A yellow, foul smelling discharge trickled down the man's leg.

Sam made a retching noise, and Tristan ignored his own heaving stomach.

The surgeon returned the scissors to his pocket. "Adelard, grab his arms and hold them above his head. "Sticky Fingers, I want you to hold down his right leg. If he kicks me while I'm working, it could kill him. You two"—he pointed at Sam and Braeden—"stand on opposite sides of the bed. You, I need you to put light pressure on his pelvis. You, lie across his chest." Once he was satisfied with their positioning, he picked up the bone saw again. "Look away if you're squeamish."

The next hour was a gruesome one. The surgeon worked quickly and efficiently, rotating the saw against the top of the patient's knee with the ease of practice. Master Evans bucked against Tristan's grip on his right leg, and by the time the lower left limb was removed, Tristan was covered in sweat. Disposing of the amputated limb, the surgeon then heated an iron cauter in a fireplace. He applied the white-hot end of the metal to the bleeding stump, searing the wound closed. The patient shrieked and then passed out.

Tristan released his grip on the man's leg, and the surgeon handed him a bucket. "What's this?" Tristan asked.

"It's for you, if you need to be sick. Do your business and then pass it around." When Tristan hesitated, the surgeon added, "There's no shame in it. I've done it myself a time or two."

Tristan leaned over and emptied a week's worth of food into the bucket. He wiped his mouth, surprised at his violent response. He hadn't even realized that he was nauseated.

Tristan was embarrassed at his weakness for just a moment, before Sam and Adelard quickly followed suit. Only the surgeon and Braeden abstained. "I've seen worse," Braeden said with a shrug.

"Thank you all for your help," the surgeon said. "Now get out of my sight." He returned his attentions to the patient, slathering his leg with a foul smelling concoction of the Gods knew what. Adelard and Tristan exchanged twin looks of horror and then glanced away.

"He's prickly," Sam said once they'd walked a short distance.

"Aye, but he's the best surgeon in the West, short of our doctor in Luca," Adelard said. The Uriel beckoned at a woman wearing a starched white wimple and carrying a pile of fresh linens. "Elspeth, where are Raj and Kelly?"

The woman adjusted the bundle of linens to her hip. "They went home to their wives while you were assisting His Royal Grumpiness. They'll be fine, don't you worry. Well, excepting Raj's pinky, but there's not much Asa could do with the missing bit somewhere at the bottom of a demon's belly."

"Thank you, Elspeth," Adelard said. She dipped into a curtsy and then strode purposefully down the aisle, her long black skirts whisking about her ankles.

"Your men—Raj and Kelly—they don't stay here at the encampment?" Tristan asked.

Adelard shook his head. "No, they live with their families in East Pirama. And they're not my men, not really."

Tristan wrinkled his forehead. "What do you mean?"

"I think it's easier if I show you. Come, follow me." Adelard led them out of the infirmary and towards an expansive fenced off area at the rear of the encampment.

Behind the fence, hundreds of men practiced with weapons, running through basic drills. The enclosure was evidently a training yard of sorts—but to Tristan's eye, none of the men looked worth training. Most of them were painfully green and many were severely out of shape.

As for their weapons, well, they wouldn't be found in the Paladins' armory. A few men held wooden practice swords, but the vast majority were armed with peasants' weapons—cudgels, staves, pitchforks, and the occasional hunter's bow.

If these men were the future of the Uriel, then the High Commander had nothing to worry about.

"Are these your latest recruits?" he asked, trying to hide his derision.

Adelard snorted, leaning against the fence. "Them? Gods, no. Our standards may not be as high as yours, Paladin, but they're pretty damn close. This training program is our newest initiative, and one of our proudest accomplishments."

"So if they aren't recruits, who are they?"

"Folk from Pirama and some of the neighboring towns. You see, Paladin, what we realized when we came to this city is that the Paladins can't defend everyone, and neither can we. The demon attacks have become too frequent and their numbers too great. This is our solution."

Tristan watched as one of the men from Pirama attempted to dodge an attack and tripped over his own feet. "You're putting them up for slaughter."

"They're up for slaughter either way. This way they at least have a fighting chance," Adelard said. "And they're not all so rough around the edges. Raj and Kelly are probably our finest examples of what this program could amount to."

That revelation caught Tristan off guard. He'd seen them fight—they hadn't the skill or finesse of the Paladins, nor of Adelard or Donnelly, but their contributions on the battlefield had been most welcome. "They're not Uriel?"

"Just citizens of Pirama who want to fight for their home." Adelard rested his chin against the fence post. "Can you imagine if every one of these men in here could fight like Raj and Kelly? Or even half of them? This city would be a different place."

"And what are the Paladins supposed to do?" Sam asked, crossing his arms over his chest. "Kick back our heels and watch?"

Adelard whirled around. "No, Sam. So long as there are demons, the people will always need a champion. What we're offering to teach them is self-defense. Freedom from constant fear. To keep our knowledge and our skills to ourselves"—Adelard frowned, his scars twisting downward—"that's selfish and cruel."

"I think it's brilliant," Braeden said, his face flushed. "What you're doing here, that is."

Tristan looked sharply at Braeden. The trainee was rarely so outspoken, and his color deepened under Tristan's scrutiny. "Why did you bring us here?" Tristan asked the Uriel. "Why are you showing us this?"

A small smile touched the Uriel's lips. "You don't know much about us, do you, Paladin Lyons? Well, know this—we're not fools, whatever else you might think. We're fully aware that whatever you've seen here today, you'll report back to your High Commander. We not only expect it, we encourage it."

"Why?" Tristan asked. "Why would you risk revealing so much to your enemy commander?"

"If you think the High Commander doesn't already know we're here, then more fool you. But he's not our enemy, and he doesn't have to be. Tell him what you've seen here, Paladin. Tell him that the Uriel and Paladins are not at counter-purposes."

"What makes you think I believe that?"

Adelard stared at him hard. "You don't, Paladin, not yet. But you will."

CHAPTER 27

S AM WASN'T MUCH for conversation on the long walk back to The Stag and Bull. Her interactions with the Uriel had left her confused and off-balance. She'd expected to hate them—*wanted* to hate them—but struggled to find a concrete reason. She'd fought with them side-by-side, and they'd slain demons as well as she.

Still, the High Commander had warned them that the Uriel were a threat, not just to the Paladins but to all of Thule. Sam could not help but feel as though she'd been cleverly manipulated, shown a version of the Uriel that they wanted her to see. And besides, if they truly wanted to protect Thule from demons, as they claimed, why hadn't they simply joined the Paladins, like she had? Why start their own organization?

She was so lost in thought that she didn't notice they had made it back to the inn till Tristan flicked his fingers against her shoulder. "Are you planning to come inside sometime this century?"

Sam slapped his hand away. "Aye, I'm coming. I wasn't paying attention."

"That seems to be a running theme with you of late."

Before she could reply, Braeden leapt to her defense. "Leave it alone already. You've been harping on Sam all day."

Sam and Tristan both turned to gawp at him. Braeden *never* talked back to Tristan; that was her role. "Are you all right?" Tristan asked him. He didn't even sound angry.

"I'm fine. Why wouldn't I be?" Braeden rubbed at his shoulder and then caught Sam staring. "I'm fine," he insisted. He narrowed his eyes at her and gave a slight jerk of his head. She knew what that meant—say nothing of his shoulder to Tristan. Why was

Braeden allowed to worry about her, and not vice-versa? It hardly seemed fair.

"I don't know about you two, but I'm famished," Tristan said, heading for the front door of the inn.

After watching the surgeon amputate poor Master Evans' leg, Sam had been convinced she'd never want to eat again. But her rumbling stomach had other ideas. "I could eat," she said. "But shouldn't we freshen up first?" They had yet to change out of their battle clothes, and judging by Tristan and Braeden's disheveled appearance, Sam was sure she looked a frightful mess.

Tristan shook his head. "No, we need to remind Pirama that the Paladins are still invested in their city," he said. "Our clothes are proof we haven't forgotten our duty, and nor should they."

They earned quite a few curious stares when they walked into The Stag and Bull bedecked in all their bloody battle glory. Master Byrd took one look at them and grunted in gruff approval. He led them to a free table in the tavern, setting warm drinks and bread in front of them. "Try not to get blood on everywhere if you can avoid it. It's bloody difficult to scrub out, you know."

"We'll try," Tristan said. "What have you got in the kitchen?"

"Some roast mutton, potatoes, and barley soup," Master Byrd said. "There's some cold bacon too, if mutton's not to your taste."

"The mutton will do just fine," Tristan said. Master Byrd dipped his head in acknowledgement and ducked into the kitchens, returning a moment later with three bowls of soup, soon followed by three plates of steaming mutton and three halved potatoes.

Tristan reached into his coin purse for payment, but the innkeeper stopped him. "It's on the house," he said. "You more than paid for your meals last night."

"Thank you," Tristan said. "I hope in time your faith in the Paladins will be restored."

"Mayhap it will be. Will you be staying in Pirama much longer?"

Tristan shook his head. "Just another day or two."

"Too bad," the innkeeper said, sounding genuinely disappointed. "Tell your High Commander to send a few men like you our way. Pirama needs you."

"I will," Tristan promised. "Thank you again for the food." The innkeeper bowed and left to attend to another patron.

"I still can't believe the other paladins never showed," Sam said, sawing into her meat.

Tristan put his finger to his lips. "Keep your voice down," he ordered. "But I agree, it's inexcusable. I plan to mention their absence in my next letter to the High Commander. It's no wonder the Uriel have been able to make inroads."

Sam paused with a bite of mutton halfway to her mouth. "You're writing to the High Commander? You're not writing anything about me, are you?"

Tristan snorted through his nose. "After everything that has happened over the past week, you think I'd waste words on you? I need to update him on the Uriel and Pirama. You might warrant a passing mention, if you're lucky."

"I wonder how they got the idea," Braeden mused, swirling his pinky in his ale. He didn't seem to be addressing anyone in particular.

Sam couldn't follow his train of thought. "Who got what idea?"

His gaze met Sam's, his strange eyes unfocused and glazed over. "Hmm? Oh, the Uriel. I think their civilian training program is brilliant."

"So you've said. Three times."

"Did I?" Braeden offered her a loopy grin.

Normally, Sam had to pry a smile out of Braeden. He looked . . . silly. As long as she'd known him, he'd never been that. Something was not right with him.

"Did he hit his head during the battle last night?" Tristan asked her out of the corner of his mouth.

"Not that I'm aware of," Sam said. His shoulder, on the other hand . . .

"I'm not deaf," Braeden said, loud enough to draw outside attention. "My hearing is fine, as is the rest of me."

Sam clenched her jaw, fighting for patience. Who did Braeden think he was fooling? He wasn't himself, and he was doing a piss-poor job of hiding it. Sam started to say as much, but Tristan cut her off. "We believe you," he placated. "Isn't that right, Sam?"

"But—"

"*Right*, Sam?"

She glared at him, but followed his lead. "Right, Tristan." She didn't understand why she couldn't point out the plainly obvious—if Braeden couldn't *pretend* to be fine, then he was far from it. Gods help her, she was worried for him.

"Let's finish our food, and then I think we would all benefit from a midday repose," Tristan said. Braeden nodded distractedly and picked at his mutton. Juice dribbled down his chin.

It was difficult to watch him eat. Each time a piece of meat traveled down his throat, his whole body trembled with the effort. Sam alternated between sneaking worried glances at Braeden and staring daggers at Tristan. Stupid, stubborn men.

Braeden pushed away from the table, sending his chair tottering on its legs. "I'm done," he announced, swaying on his feet. "I think I'll to bed, now." With a parting nod, he staggered towards the stone stairway at the back.

"Braeden," Tristan called after him, "you need a key!"

Braeden twisted around to look at him, flapped his hand in dismissal, and continued on his way.

Tristan grabbed Sam's wrist from across the table. "Follow him upstairs, and don't let him leave your sight. Something's wrong."

Sam yanked her hand free from his grip. "You think I didn't notice?"

Tristan didn't rise to the bait. "Sam," he said sternly, "Braeden is not the sort to ask for help, no matter if he needs it. If he's hurt or sick, you'll need to tread carefully. He won't want your interference."

"Then he's a fool." She understood stubborn pride better than anyone, but Braeden had no reason to refuse her help. He didn't have to prove anything.

"Men are all fools, you and I included," Tristan said. "Watch after him, and come fetch me if it's serious." He held out the room key to her. Sam snatched the key and bolted after Braeden.

Sam took the stairs two steps at a time. On the third floor, she found Braeden sprawled against the wall next to their room, panting as though he'd just run for miles. Stepping over his legs, she unlocked the door and pushed it open. She extended her hand to him, but Braeden batted it away.

"I told you, I'm fine," he said, struggling to his feet. He stumbled into the room and then pitched face-forward onto his pallet.

Sam folded her arms over her chest. "Aye, you're *fine*."

Braeden's head moved up and down against the mattress. "Fine," he said, his voice muffled. "Just ti—" He gasped as his body spasmed and jerked. "Tired," he finished lamely.

"You're being an arse," Sam informed him. She kneeled on the pallet beside him. "Turn over."

"Pushy," he mumbled, but did as she bade, flipping onto his back.

Sam brushed the hair from his temple. Braeden's eyes went wide at her touch, and he tried to lift his head from the pallet. "Be still," she said, pressing him back down. She lay the back of her hand against his forehead then drew it away with a yelp. "Faith in blood, Braeden. You're burning up."

He turned his face to the side. "I don't get sick."

"Braeden, if you're not sick, then I'm a man."

His lips kicked up into a semblance of a smile. "That's not so farfetched," he said. "I've never been sick in my life. Another rare gift from my father."

"Well, your humanity is showing. You're sick." Sam pointed a finger at him. "Untie your robes."

Braeden's silver eyebrows almost disappeared into his hairline. Sam blushed. "I want to see your shoulder, you idiot!"

Braeden hugged his injured shoulder protectively. "No."

Sam glowered at him. "If you're concerned about offending my delicate sensibilities, don't be."

Braeden's watery eyes found hers. "Don't worry, I get it. You're neither delicate nor sensible."

"Apparently a side effect of your illness is an unfortunate sense of humor."

"I'm not ill, and I've always had an unfortunate sense of humor."

"So show me your shoulder, then. What's the harm?"

"No," Braeden repeated stubbornly.

Sam sighed. "I didn't want to have to resort to this." She leaned over his torso and grasped the fabric of his tattered black robes near his wounded shoulder. She tore it apart the seams. Falling back onto her heels, she covered her mouth with both hands. "Gods, Braeden."

Bull's eye rashes covered the entire length of Braeden's arm and the design of his tattoo was distorted by crusted, pustular lesions that peppered his skin from the midpoint of his limb and above. The pent-up fluid in his upper arm had leaked out and dried in yellow slabs, giving his skin a deflated, rubbery appearance. Two deep puncture marks speared through the intricate glyph on his shoulder, breaking the line of the inner and outer circles. Around the puncture marks, the skin was black.

"Is it that bad?" Braeden asked.

Sam slapped her palm to her forehead. "You can't see your shoulder properly, can you? I'm no doctor, but I'd wager my right hand your wound is infected." She touched his brow again and hissed. His skin was so hot he had actually scalded the back of her hand. "Braeden, you need a doctor."

Braeden gingerly sat up, using his good arm to shift his weight. "Sam, I appreciate your concern, but you need to stop treating me like I'm human. I'm not, and I never have been. This—illness—or whatever it is will pass on its own accord."

Sam bit her lip. "Will you at least let me help you wash it? It can't be good to leave dirt in an open wound, even for you."

He shrugged his shoulders, and then winced. She gave him a knowing look. "If you must," he conceded.

"Thank you," she said, rolling off the bed. "I'll be back with supplies in a minute. Don't move from this spot."

Sam filled a small basin with water in the privy and retrieved a spare tunic and salve from her pack. She soaked the tunic in the water and then returned to Braeden's side. She lay his hand in her lap, gently wiping away the dried blood and debris on his forearm. "Does this feel okay?"

Braeden nodded, his lids heavy. "Feels good."

Sam edged her ministrations higher, closer to the site of the wound. "Still okay?" she asked.

"Fine," Braeden said, gritting his teeth. Beads of sweat formed on his upper lip.

"I'm going to clean your shoulder now," she told him. He nodded, squeezing his eyes shut.

Sam held the wet cloth just above the bite marks. "Here goes," she said, and pressed the fabric directly to the wound. The instant she touched his skin, Braeden's eyes rolled up into his head and he fell backward against the bed.

"Braeden!" she cried out, thinking for a panicked moment that he was dead. But she saw the ragged rise and fall of his chest, his breathing labored. Still, he was breathing. She almost sobbed in relief. "Idiot man," she said to his passed-out form. "I'm getting Tristan. If you die while I'm gone, I swear I'll bring you back from the grave and kill you myself."

With a last, backward look at Braeden, Sam dashed down the hall and pounded on Tristan's door. He answered almost immediately. "He's bad, Tristan," she said, swallowing down the lump in her throat. "He's out cold, and I think his wound might be infected."

"What wound?" Tristan asked sharply.

"H-his shoulder," Sam said, looking down at her feet. "He was bitten during last night's battle. He didn't want me to tell you."

Tristan made a visible effort to contain his anger. "We'll discuss your lack of judgment later," he said. "For now, take me to him."

Though he'd been slow to act before, Tristan now moved as though he were keenly aware of the urgency of the situation, shoving Sam aside and marching over to Braeden's prone body straightaway. He checked Braeden's pulse, listened to his heart, and inspected his wounded arm, careful to not touch the wound itself. "It's bad," Tristan confirmed.

Sam threw up her hands. "I told you! Now what? If he dies, I'll—"

Tristan eased off the pallet and came to stand in front of her, placing his large hand on the top of her head. "Let's not worry till we have to. His vitals are still very strong."

"But his skin is so hot. I've never felt the like."

"Sam, we can't judge Braeden by the same standards we would ourselves."

"He's still human!"

Tristan dropped his hand from her head, stepping back to look at her. "He's human where it matters, Sam. I want you to know I believe that. But you can't deny the demon's blood that flows through his veins. I don't think Braeden himself fully understands how it affects him."

"So what do we do? Sit around and pray to the Gods he doesn't die?"

"Of course not. I don't believe in leaving a man's life up to fate. I'll find a doctor, one who is used to dealing with the unusual." He headed for the door. "I'll leave now."

"And me?" Sam called after him. "What do I do while you're gone?"

"Pray to the Gods he doesn't die." Tristan sniffed the air and wrinkled his nose. "And bathe. For all our sakes."

Bathing seemed so self-indulgent, but Tristan was right that there wasn't much Sam could do for Braeden. She knew how to clean and bandage a basic wound, but she knew nothing of treating an infection, and she didn't dare touch his shoulder again, not after the last time. She had no choice but to wait for Tristan to come back with a doctor.

To her great displeasure, Tristan didn't return till dusk, with none other than the Uriel surgeon in tow. "You brought *him?*" she asked incredulously. "But he's with the Uriel!"

"Lovely to see you again, too," the surgeon said. He set down a large physician's bag by Braeden's pallet. "For the record, I'm not 'with' the Uriel—I *work* with the Uriel."

"There's a distinction?" Sam asked, eying him skeptically.

"Aye, it means they pay my bills, but the only loyalties I owe are to my oaths of medicine."

"Don't rush to conclusions," Tristan said. "I assure you, he's the best man for the job."

The surgeon began unpacking his bag, dumping out the conical mouth gag and three long needles. "It's true," he said. "The only other doctor in Pirama is barely fit to treat a sick dog." He withdrew a magnifying lens, hooked retractors, a bottle of leeches and a hand fan. "Besides, I studied demon anatomy. Your Paladin thought that might come in handy."

Sam ignored the smug look on Tristan's face and said, "I wasn't aware that demon anatomy was a study."

"It isn't officially. But when more and more of my patients started coming in with injuries from demons, my curiosity was piqued. I've conducted quite a few autopsies on demon corpses over the course of the last year."

Sam scowled. "Braeden's not a corpse yet, in case you haven't noticed."

The surgeon returned her scowl with his own. "I've yet to mistake a live patient for a dead one. Now, move aside." He sat down on the edge of the pallet and grabbed Braeden's wrist, feeling for his pulse. "He's severely overheated, but his pulse is steady. How long has he been out?"

Tristan looked to her. "Sam?"

"A few hours now," she said. "I touched his shoulder, there, where the skin's all black, and he collapsed."

"Did you try to rouse him?" the surgeon asked.

She'd been too nervous to touch Braeden again after he'd lost consciousness—she hadn't wanted to make things worse. "No, should I have?"

"No harm done," the surgeon said. "I'll try now." He slipped his arm underneath the armpit of Braeden's good shoulder and wrapped another arm around his lower back, carefully moving him into a seated position. The surgeon snapped his fingers at Sam. "Grab that paper fan. He needs cool air."

Sam jumped to obey him. "Like this?"

"Good." He tapped on Braeden's chest with his knuckles, eliciting a hollow sound. "Braeden," he called softly. "Braeden, can you hear me?"

Braeden's eyes fluttered open. Sam exhaled a breath she hadn't realized she'd been holding. "What happened?" he croaked. His gaze swung to the surgeon. "What are *you* doing here?"

"According to Sam, here, you passed out," the surgeon said. "You're quite ill, lad."

"Impossible. I don't get sick."

"On a scale of one to ten, where one is no pain and ten is excruciating, how would you say you feel?"

"Three," Braeden said.

The surgeon lifted an eyebrow.

"Maybe four."

"So we can agree, then, that your body is out of balance with its normal state?"

Braeden huffed. "I suppose."

"Then I would characterize you as ill, and I'm considered somewhat of an expert on the matter." The surgeon rubbed his chin, as though an interesting thought had just occurred to him. "Why do you say you don't get sick?"

"I've never been sick. Never."

Sam stopped her fanning. "But Braeden, your wound was inflicted by a demon."

Braeden scoffed. "You think that matters for someone like me?"

"Explain your shoulder, then."

"What of it?"

Tristan held up his hands. "Stop, you two. Sam, you should know better than to rile up a sick patient."

"Sorry," she muttered. She hated quarreling with Braeden, but his obstinacy was enough to make her scream.

The surgeon ignored them both. "I'll take a look at that shoulder now." He grasped Braeden by the ankles and shifted him so that his legs hung over the side of the pallet. Braeden's face darkened; Sam could tell he didn't appreciate the indignity of being manhandled.

The surgeon held up the magnifying lens to Braeden's shoulder, peering through the glass for several minutes. "The tissue around the wound is dead or dying," he said, drawing back. "I'll need to remove it surgically."

"His whole arm?" Sam asked, her heart in her throat. She flashed back to the Uriel infirmary, the horrible crunch of metal sawing through bone still fresh in her mind.

"Don't get overexcited," the surgeon said, retrieving a razor-thin scalpel and placing it on the bedside table. "I just need to excise the topmost layer of skin around the shoulder area. It's a relatively minor surgery."

Braeden's crimson eyes went wide. "You mean to remove my tattoo?"

The surgeon blinked. "It will be necessary to remove part of it, aye."

"You can't."

The surgeon crossed his arms. "The tissue death will spread to the rest of your arm if I don't. So unless you prefer I amputate the entire limb—"

Braeden gripped the surgeon by the wrists, hard enough to make him flinch. "Keep your knives away from my tattoo, surgeon."

The surgeon let out a puff of air through his nose, rubbing his bruised wrists. "Do you want to die, boy?"

Braeden's mouth tightened. "If you remove my tattoo, you'll wish me dead. Trust me on that." He ran the tips of his fingers along the complicated glyphs that curled around his bicep. "I can't be allowed to live without it."

Sam and Tristan looked at each other with silent questions. What did Braeden mean? He'd never said anything about his tattoo before. And to think he knew all her secrets.

Tristan glanced at the surgeon. "Asa, would you leave us for a moment?"

He gave a terse nod. "I'll wait outside."

Once the door was shut behind him, Tristan took the surgeon's place by Braeden's side. "This better not be some nascent fit of vanity. A bit of pretty ink isn't worth your life."

Braeden's lip curled into a sneer. "What use have I for vanity?"

Sam winced at the rancor in his voice. She would never have accused Braeden of vanity, even in jest—he wore his self-loathing on his sleeve—though she still hoped his opposition to surgery was unfounded. "Help us understand," she pleaded with him. "Why would you risk dying for a tattoo?"

"It's more than a tattoo," Braeden said heavily. "It's a seal. This 'pretty ink,' as you call it, is the only barrier that keeps my demonic side in check. It's what allows me to function as human—or maintain a semblance of humanity, as the case may be. Without it, I'm no better than any other demon." He smiled without humor. "I'd rather risk infection as a human, than die with a Paladin sword through my neck, and the Gods only know how many more deaths to my name."

Tristan angled his head to better view the tattoo. "Have you always had it?"

Braeden shook his head. "Not always, no, though I was little more than a child when I was marked."

"And before?"

Braeden squeezed his lids shut, as though the memory pained him. "I was a monster," he whispered. "I had no control, no way to repress my violent tendencies. I have no idea how many innocents died at my hand—it could have been tens or hundreds or thousands. I would lose myself for hours, days, weeks, and wake from my madness with no recollection of what I did."

Tristan compressed his lips into a thin line. "And a design on your skin is what holds this violence at bay?"

Braeden lifted his chin. "It's no mere design. It's a ward."

Sam let out a small gasp, and Tristan was silent for several moments. "Who alive knows warding?" he asked in an awed voice.

"The man who raised me," Braeden said, his crimson eyes gone distant. "He took me from an orphanage across the Rheic Ocean, in a city called Yemara. I called him Master."

Sam pictured Braeden as a small child, his strange, crimson eyes overlarge in his thin face. He must have been so lonely, so afraid. "Your master, why did he come for you?" she asked.

Braeden hesitated before answering. "He came for me because he knew he could help me, in a manner of speaking. And that I could help him in return."

"Was he good to you?" Sam asked, because she had to know.

Again, Braeden hesitated. "In his own way, yes. If he was not kind, he was never cruel, not to me." His fingers danced over his tattooed skin. "And whatever else he did, my master saved me from myself. I could forgive him everything for that."

She drew in a long, shaky breath. "You won't part with your tattoo, will you?"

Braeden held her gaze. "Not for anything."

Sam pulled her gaze from his, focusing on a spot on the carpet. Tears welled up behind her eyes, but she refused to let them fall. Damn Braeden for making her tear up in front of Tristan. She didn't cry on principle.

"Your mind is made up?" Tristan asked.

Braeden nodded. "If I'm going to die, I want to die as myself."

"Understood," Tristan said, rising from the bed. "I'll inform Asa."

A moment after Tristan stepped outside, the surgeon reentered the room, muttering under his breath about foolish boys and their foolish pride. "Boy!" he barked. "Let me make it clear that I don't agree with your decision."

"If I drop dead, no one will blame you," Braeden said dryly.

The surgeon grunted his displeasure. "I'll do what I can without touching your tattoo. Your Paladin says it's off limits to my scalpel."

"Thank you," Braeden said, twisting his torso to give better access to his injured arm. He sat there stoically as the surgeon poked and prodded. The surgeon pinched a large abscess near Braeden's elbow and squeezed till a thick green discharge squirted from the head of the swelling. Feeling sick to her stomach, Sam had to look away while the surgeon drained several more abscesses.

After an hour or so of these ministrations, the surgeon stood and wiped his hands with a small towel. "I've done all I can. We'll just have to hope that the necrotic tissue will heal itself. Drink plenty of water and stay abed for the next few days. If you aren't improved by then, we'll broach the topic of your tattoo again." He began repacking his medical bag.

Tristan rummaged through his coin purse and extracted two gold sovereigns. "For your time."

"Generous of you," the surgeon said, dropping the coins into the front pouch of his bag. "Oh, before I go, Adelard asked me to give this to you." He withdrew a sealed enveloped from the front pouch and handed it to Tristan. "I'll be on my way, then." Slinging his bag over his shoulder, he tipped his head and exited the room.

As soon as he was gone, Tristan tore open the envelope and scanned the contents of the letter. His mouth dropped open. "Well, I'll be."

"What is it?" Sam asked.

Tristan folded and unfolded the letter, reading it again. "It's an invitation to dinner," he said. "From Sander Branimir himself."

Sam gaped at him. None of the Uriel behaved like they were supposed to. "Let me see the letter," she demanded. He handed it over wordlessly.

Sam stared at the words, written in a neat, flowing script. She read aloud, for Braeden's benefit.

Paladin Lyons,

I have been informed that you are traveling through the west to find us. Welcome back.

"Welcome back?" she asked. "What does that mean?"

"I was born out West," Tristan said. "Though how he knows that I haven't the faintest idea. Keep reading."

As it so happens, I am also interested in finding you. If your travels take you through Luca, it would be my pleasure to host you for dinner at our encampment. Your trainees are invited as well, should you wish to bring them.

I know of you, Paladin Lyons, but you likely know little of me. Know this: though perhaps you think us at odds, I am a man of my word, and a man of honor. No harm by my hand or my men's will befall you in Luca. I give you my solemn promise.

It is high time we meet, don't you think?

Awaiting your response,

Sander Branimir

Braeden gave a low whistle which turned into a racking cough. "Sorry," he said between gasps of air. When his coughing eased, he asked, "Will you accept the invitation?"

"Accept?" Sam sputtered. "You can't be serious."

Tristan leaned against the wall by the door. "I might. It's a good opportunity."

"But we could be walking straight into a trap!"

"I don't think so," Tristan said, stroking the stubble on his chin. "I don't know this Sander's motives, nor do I know the Uriel's. The High Commander believes they intend to supplant us, but we have no proof of that yet. Without having met the man, it's hard to assess how much of a threat Sander and his Uriel present. Regardless, if any of the Uriel threaten or attack us, they might as well declare war on all the Paladins. No sane man would do that lightly."

"That's assuming the Uriel are sane," Sam grumbled. "So you'll accept?"

"I didn't say that. I'll have to think about it. We need to visit Luca anyway." Tristan kneaded his temples, his face troubled. "Yet another thing to include in my note to the High Commander."

"What of Braeden?" she asked. "How can we go to Luca with him in his current condition?"

Braeden glared at her, struggling to sit upright. "I'm not an invalid."

Tristan groaned, thunking his head against the wall. "I beg of you, let's not start this up again. Braeden, you will do as the surgeon ordered and rest for the next few days. If, by some miracle, your wound heals sufficiently, you can come with Sam and me to Luca."

Braeden's lips tightened at the edges. "And if it doesn't?"

"We'll reevaluate." Tristan reached for the doorknob. "I need to write to the High Commander before it gets any later. I'm likely to fall asleep in my ink pot as is. Sam, look after Braeden tonight."

Sam rolled her eyes. "Like you need to tell me."

Braeden snarled, although it was difficult to tell whether his frustration was directed at her or Tristan.

Tristan chuckled, unoffended. "See you on the morrow." He opened and shut the door behind him, leaving the room in an uncomfortable silence.

They broke the awkward silence in unison. "I'm sorry."

"Why are *you* sorry?" Braeden asked.

Sam sat down on her pallet, hugging her knees to her chest. "Because you're angry with me." Fighting with Braeden wasn't like fighting with Tristan—she and Tristan were always at each other's throats, and half the time she enjoyed their bickering, not that she'd ever admit to that aloud. But Braeden was her rock; she didn't want his anger.

He sighed wearily and lay down on his pallet, facing the ceiling. "I'm not angry with you, Sam. I just don't need to be coddled."

Sam closed her eyes and gave voice to the feeling she'd been denying. "Braeden, I'm scared for you." The prospect of his death was far scarier than any demon she'd ever faced. Her breath hitched. When had he come to mean so much to her?

A faint blush stained Braeden's too-pale cheeks. "Don't be. If you had any sense, you'd be scared *of* me, not for me."

"You don't scare me. Your wound does."

Braeden craned his neck to peer down at his injured shoulder. "I have a theory about this wound."

She snorted lightly. "A theory?"

Braeden slanted a glance at her. "I have theories sometimes." He returned his gaze to his wound. "The demon bite obscured one of the glyphs in my tattoo. I think that is what is causing all of this."

Sam creased her forehead, not understanding. "How is that any different than what the surgeon told you? He said the wound is the source of your illness."

"I'm telling you, I don't get ill. Not in the way you're thinking of illness. I think my body may be reacting to the damage to the glyph. Like the part of me that's locked away senses a hole in the ward and is fighting to get out. I feel . . . restless."

"Braeden, you can barely move."

He grimaced. "I'm aware of that, thank you, but it doesn't change how I feel. Let's just hope the damage isn't permanent. And if it is—"

"If it is, we'll find a way to fix it," Sam said firmly. "But I have a theory, too."

Braeden's mouth curved up. "And what's that?"

"I don't think you need your tattoo."

"Sam—" he said warningly.

"Hear me out. I'm not saying you never needed it. Maybe you really did as a child, before you learned control. But now, I think it's little more than a crutch. I think you have enough willpower to control your demon all on your own."

Braeden rasped a dark laugh. "Are you willing to test that theory? Because I'm not." His lashes dipped to diamond-cut cheekbones. "You don't know what I was like, before."

"You're right, I don't," she said. "But I know what you're like now. And I think in a few days, if your wound hasn't healed, you should let the surgeon remove the infected skin." Braeden started to protest, but she cut him short. "I won't hound you about it again till it's imminent. Just promise me one thing."

"What, Sam?"

"Don't you dare die on me and leave me alone with Tristan."

He smiled. "It's a promise."

CHAPTER 28

SLEEP ELUDED BRAEDEN, in spite of the bone-weary fatigue that claimed him. His lids were shut, yet he was conscious of his heart rattling against his ribcage and the pulsating fire in his shoulder. His skin felt stretched to its brink, strained and ill-fitting over his trembling body.

Braeden turned his neck to face Sam's pallet, careful not to move his shoulder in the process. She was curled towards him, one arm pillowing her head and the other reaching halfway across the distance between their beds. She was asleep, but her sleep was troubled, worry lines wrinkling her brow and her mouth set in a frown. For a brief moment, Braeden wondered if her worry for him was what disturbed her sleep, but he quickly banished the arrogant thought. No doubt she was just having an ordinary nightmare. He should wake her, spare her from her bad dream.

"Sam," he said softly. She stirred, raised her head and murmured his name, and then collapsed in a heap, asleep again. A small smile touched his lips. He ran his fingers over the upturned corners of his mouth. He must have smiled more in the short time he'd known Sam than he had in his entire lifetime before. He'd never met anyone like her, and it wasn't only because she donned men's clothing, or wielded a sword almost as well as Tristan. Sam was—

Braeden's muscles went rigid, and then jerked spasmodically as a jolt of fiery pain coursed down his spine. The acrid taste of metal filled his mouth, and he dimly thought that he must have bitten his tongue hard enough to bleed.

His back arched off the pallet and his eyes rolled into his head. He could feel the rush of blood through his veins as his muscles swelled, his skin rippling to accommodate his engorged body.

A powerful thirst consumed him, and his tongue slurped at the pooling blood at the back of his throat. He was vaguely aware that he had felt like this before, when he plunged his knife into his heart to loosen the chains that bound his demon instincts, but he held no knife now. Something had triggered the release of his beast, and he didn't hold the trigger.

Panic cut through the fogginess of his mind. His wound! Had it managed to break his master's seal? If he was no longer restrained . . . and Gods, Sam was in the pallet next to him! A howl of rage and sorrow escaped him as his body seized once more and finished its transformation into the wretched monster he'd held at bay for more than a decade. His vision blurred, and then faded to black.

CHAPTER 29

CAUGHT IN THE purgatory between dream and waking, Sam's mind was awake, but her body was paralyzed. Try as she might, she couldn't pry her eyelids open. Logic whispered in her ear that her paralysis was fleeting, nothing but the fading remnants of a stubborn bad dream. But while logic whispered, panic roared. Sam fought like a madwoman to move one tiny muscle.

After what could have been minutes or hours, Sam's eyes opened to darkness. If she squinted, she could make out vague shapes. The night was silent but for the quiet thump of her heartbeat and the sound of her uneven breathing.

It was then that she realized that the only breathing she heard was her own.

Oh Gods. Braeden.

She whipped her head towards his pallet, half-expecting to find him dead. But she couldn't find him at all. His bed was empty.

She cursed under her breath. Where could he have possibly gone? Just hours before, he'd barely been able to move. He was deathly ill, for the Gods' sakes. He was supposed to *rest*.

Grumbling to herself, Sam swung her legs over the side of her pallet, intending to search for Braeden. She lit a candle by the bedside, filling the room with a faint glow. Satisfied, she turned around and took a step forward, tripping over something solid at her feet. She heard a low, menacing rumble.

Sam struggled to regain her balance and grasped onto biceps as large as watermelons. Two unblinking red eyes stared at her.

Sam swallowed. "Braeden?" Crouched on all fours, he was more demon than human, bone-like spikes protruding from his rounded back. He was massive, his arms and neck as thick as tree trunks.

She tried smiling at him. "Thank the Gods you're all right. You scared me for a moment." He scared her now, but she shoved that traitorous thought aside.

Braeden said nothing, his body vibrating with tension. A strip of white flashed across his jaw as his lips peeled back into a parody of a smile, revealing gleaming fangs. He rumbled again, the gravelly sound vicious in his throat.

This is not good, thought Sam. She searched his face for a hint of the man she knew, and came up short. All she saw in his eyes was death. "Braeden?" she whispered again, hating that she was afraid of her friend.

Braeden shuddered violently and then leapt for her, tackling her to the ground. He snapped his teeth at her neck, narrowly missing as she shoved his heavy body off her, flipping him onto his back. He yowled, clawing to get out from under her. Clamoring back onto his hands and knees, he leapt for her again. She rolled out of the way, and he crashed full force into her pallet. The bed slammed into the wall, splintering into pieces.

With horrifying certainty, Sam realized that Braeden meant to kill her. He was bigger than her and faster than her, and he could see better than her—but in the end, all those things didn't matter. His greatest advantage was that she didn't want him dead.

The Gods had granted her one small favor: Braeden had no weapon. He was lethal with a knife and sword, and quick as a demon. But tonight he fought her only with his body. Which meant she maybe stood a chance.

With single-minded determination, Sam sprinted over to Braeden's undisturbed pallet. She tore off the pillows and blankets, hunting for one of his daggers. Gods knew he hid the things everywhere.

She found a knife tucked beneath the straw mattress and pulled it out by the handle. Putting the bed between them, she held out the knife in front of her. "I'm armed now," she warned him, her hand shaking.

Her warning—if he could even comprehend it—did little to daunt him. He charged, his claws outstretched as he jumped over the pallet that separated them. Sam hopped sideways, and he sailed past her, snarling. His attacks weren't hard to dodge; this beast lacked the subtlety and unpredictability—and most significantly—the intelligence that made Braeden such a deadly fighter.

Sam could win this fight. The problem was she didn't want to.

She didn't want to know what would have to happen after she won.

Braeden lunged for her again, but this time she met him head on. He clamped her by the waist, sharp nails digging into her flesh. Before he could move in for the kill, Sam wrapped her arms around his thick torso, and squeezed, holding him upright. "Double-waist tie up," Sam murmured, her face buried into his chest. His still-human heartbeat drummed against her ear. "Braeden, do you remember? We practiced this once, you and I."

He gnashed his teeth together, straining his neck for a bite of her flesh. He remembered nothing. Braeden was gone.

She slithered her knife in between them, pressing the tip into the base of his throat. "I'll do it," she whispered. "I'll do it if I have to." She pushed the point in, parting the topmost layers of skin, blood trickling down his throat in a slow river. Braeden growled and tightened his grip on her waist in response. "Don't make me do it, Braeden." Her voice choked up. "Please, Gods, don't make me do it."

Could she even do it? Could she kill the man who had risked his life for hers, who had kept her most closely guarded secret, who liked her in spite of it? She could have been a woman alone in a man's world, but she wasn't. She had Braeden, her ally, her friend. Her maybe something more. The last was a thought she'd never allowed herself, but who cared now, when his life was a knife tip away from ending by her hand?

Fat, angry tears trickled down her cheeks. "You stupid idiot, you promised you wouldn't leave me!" She beat her free hand against the solid wall of his chest, not caring if it made her vulnerable, not with her knife in his neck. "I know you're in there somewhere!" she yelled. "Stop being so Gods damned stubborn and snap out of it. This isn't you! You're better than this, Braeden." A sob caught in her throat, but she swallowed it down. Sam didn't cry, not for anything. The water leaking from her eyes and dripping off her chin didn't count. That was . . . that was . . .

She beat his chest harder, now slick with the wetness of her tears and his blood. Rage, wild and ragged, filled her, tearing her carefully erected barriers asunder, her thoughts chaotic and unrestrained. She had seen Braeden teeter on the edge of madness before, and he had come back from it every time. Yet now that he had stepped over the line, there was no turning back? All because of a tattoo? It was ridiculous, it was outrageous, it was unfair—

"Gods damn it!" Her voice exploded with the swell of emotion in her breast. She was going to lose him. They would never again train together, fight together, talk together. She would never again see his strange, beautiful eyes or his mouth turn upwards into his rare, lopsided grin. She treasured those rare smiles, those even rarer moments when he let down his guard and laughed with her.

Sam wasn't sure how long they stood like that, his arms crushing her waist and the tip of her knife sticking into his neck. She waited and waited for any excuse to let up, for the Gods themselves to intervene. But Braeden left her with no choice. His claws dug into her sides till she gasped with pain, and he angled his head, swooping down like a bird of prey.

Sam caught him by the jaw, his bared teeth inches from her face. She squeezed the hilt of her knife. "Goodbye, Braeden," she said, and kissed him.

It was meant to be a farewell kiss. Tearfully, Sam pressed her mouth to Braeden's maw. He growled low in his throat, his mouth stretched open wide as though he wanted to devour her whole. As he ground his jaw against hers, she cut her lip on his incisors, her blood trickling into their joined mouths. Braeden's tongue snuck out to swipe at her bottom lip, lapping up the coppery liquid. Sam gasped in shock at the touch of his tongue, her mouth opening under his.

And then he was kissing her back, violently, his lips molding over hers, his tongue thrusting inside her mouth. His hands left her waist and tangled in her hair, pulling her closer till she stood flush against him. He nipped at her lips, his nibbles just shy of painful, and then he cupped her face in his clawed hands and kissed her deeply.

Sam's eyes drifted closed. When she opened her eyes again, she knew what she would have to do, but till then, she would allow herself to get lost in the moment, to be with Braeden as a woman with a man, without the complications of the Paladins, secrets, or ruined tattoos. She flattened a hand against his chest, and she leaned into him, deepening their kiss.

Braeden growled again, tasting her everywhere—her lips, her tongue, her teeth. Sam felt an answering hunger low in her belly, and her tongue entwined with his till all she could see and feel and think was Braeden. Sam had never felt like this before, the sensations overwhelming. Her breath merged with his, and they breathed as one, in short, desperate gasps. The wildness that infected Braeden spread into her, and together, they were savage beasts, clawing to get closer to one another. Braeden's nails bit into her cheeks, and her knife sunk deeper into his neck as she dragged that hand from his chest to around his neck and then scratched down his broad back. This *thing* between them didn't smolder, it burned like fallen leaves set aflame.

"Sam."

The sigh of her name was so quiet that at first Sam thought she'd imagined it. But it was enough to bring her back down to earth, to remind her what needed to be done when this kiss ended. She squeezed her eyes tighter, unwilling to open them to the inevitable.

The kiss between them gentled, still urgent, but soft, almost reverent. Their lips lingered, and then pulled apart. Sam opened her eyes, ignoring the wetness that rolled down her cheeks. "Goodbye, Braeden," she whispered again, and re-angled the knife, readying to drive it home.

Braeden's hand wrapped around hers. "I believe this is mine," he said. A small, crooked smile curved his lips, and his eyes were bright with some foreign emotion.

The knife dropped from her hands, clattering to the floor. Sam launched herself at Braeden with so much force that he stumbled backwards, taking her with him as they fell into a graceless clump.

She grasped his face with both hands. "Braeden? Can you understand me? Are you really okay?"

"Aye."

The single word was like a balm to her soul, and she gave him a quick, bruising kiss. "Thank the Gods," she said, and then she punched him hard in the stomach. "Don't you *ever* do that to me again, do you hear me? The next time, I'll kill you, I swear it."

Braeden nodded towards the discarded knife. "You almost killed me just now."

Sam's face crumpled, and she had to grit her teeth to fight back the tears, Gods damn her stupid emotions. "Do you think I wanted to do it? I thought you were gone. I thought you had slipped over the precipice and weren't coming back. What should I have done?"

"You should have killed me," Braeden said matter-of-factly, rolling onto his side. He brushed his thumb against her cheek. "But I'm glad that you didn't."

Now that she was no longer swept up in the moment, his tender gesture caught her off guard, and she flinched against his touch. Braeden dropped his hand immediately. "You kissed me," he accused.

Sam looked away, embarrassed. "You kissed me back."

"Why? Did you think it would save me?"

Sam snorted. "I'm not some romantic fool who believes in the restorative power of a kiss. I thought I was saying goodbye."

Braeden arched a brow. "Do you always say goodbye like that?"

Her cheeks heated, and she punched him again. "Can't you just forget about it?"

Braeden's mouth flattened, and he pushed himself unsteadily to his feet. He held his hand out to her. "You want to pretend it never happened?"

She nodded, taking his hand and letting him pull her to her feet.

"Fine," he said, his tone inscrutable. "Then I'll forget this, too." He jerked her roughly to him, tilted her chin up, and brushed his mouth against hers. He pulled back from the kiss. "It's forgotten," he breathed into her mouth, and then released her, stalking to the other end of the room.

And that was how Tristan found them, Sam on one side of the room and Braeden on the other, with one pallet between them, the other scattered in ruins across the floor. "What in the name of the Gods is going on in here?" he bellowed, barging through the door.

Sam and Braeden jumped like guilty conspirators. "N-nothing, Tristan," Sam stammered, hoping that the shadowy light was poor enough to hide her blush. Her mind was still awhirl and her heart beat like a drum in her chest. Gods, she was a hypocrite, she'd told Braeden to forget they ever kissed, yet his last kiss replayed over and over again in her head, her toes curling involuntarily at the memory.

Tristan's voice snapped her out of her reverie. "Braeden, why are you out of bed? Where *is* your bed?"

Braeden kicked at a piece of straw that had sprung free from his former mattress. "We had an incident."

Tristan crossed his arms. "I can see that. You promised the surgeon you would rest."

"It wasn't his fault," Sam blurted. "Well, not entirely. You see, his tattoo . . ." she trailed off. It wasn't her story to tell. Besides, she didn't know what happened to him, not really.

Braeden sighed, sinking against the wall. "It was as I fore-warned you. My tattoo serves as a ward against the demon within me. The ward has been . . . tampered with."

Tristan stepped further into the room, stopping in front of Sam. He touched his index finger to the side of her jaw. "You're bleeding," he said. He turned to Braeden. "Did you do this?"

"Aye," Braeden said, his voice little above a whisper. "I lost control. I could have killed Sam. My demon wanted Sam very, very badly, and I couldn't fight it."

"But you did," Sam said. "You didn't kill me. You fought it and you won."

Braeden barked a short laugh. "I didn't fight it. We found common ground." His gaze held hers intently. "We both wanted the same thing."

Tristan looked between the two of them, his brow furrowing. Sam shuddered to think what his reaction would have been had he walked in on them just a few minutes earlier. She wondered if he would have killed Braeden if he were in her position. He certainly wouldn't have kissed him.

"You appear to be in control now," Tristan said slowly. "What of your wound? Does it still hurt?"

"Perhaps a little," Braeden admitted. He weaved through the room towards them, twisting his arm so they could more easily see his wound. The infected surface area had shrunk significantly, which surprised Sam—the way Braeden's body had expanded and distorted should have stretched the wound wider.

Tristan grasped Braeden's elbow gently and peered at his shoulder. "It looks better, I'll give you that. But your skin is hot to the touch and you still look feverish." He tilted his head, considering. "Braeden, do you think what happened between you and Sam will happen again?"

Sam choked and pretended to cough to hide her embarrassment. "Sorry," she wheezed. "Caught a bug in my throat." Idiot, she berated herself. Tristan hadn't meant their kiss.

"No, I don't think so," Braeden said, his eyes fixed on hers. Was he talking about kissing her or trying to kill her? Not that it mattered, his answer should have been "no" either way.

"Then let me ask you this one more time, and I promise it's the last I'll ask it of you," Tristan said. "Will you reconsider removing part of your tattoo?"

Braeden took a long time to reply. "If I haven't healed by morning, I'll do it."

Sam released a breath she hadn't known she'd been holding. It had taken him nearly killing her and her nearly killing him, but Braeden had finally decided to be sensible. Maybe he had started to believe in himself, or maybe he just assumed the damage had already been done. Whatever his reason, Sam got what she wanted—Braeden alive.

"Fair," Tristan said. "The night, or what's left of it, is yours. I suggest you stay in bed." He picked up a piece of the straw that was strewn about the room. "Guess you'll have to share one." And on that parting note, Tristan exited the room, oblivious to the distress he left them in.

CHAPTER 30

SHARING A BED was not in the cards for Sam and Braeden, not this night. Neither of them could forget they kissed, no matter what they pretended. After a brief argument, Sam took the floor, and Braeden the bed. He was the wounded one, after all, and needed rest far more than she. She wouldn't take no for an answer.

The floor was hard and cold beneath her, and every time she shifted, a new piece of straw tickled her nose or feet or back. She wrapped a thin sheet around her, but it provided little comfort. It shouldn't have mattered—with the marathon of events they'd had over the past few days, she should have been able to sleep standing up.

But she was too rattled to sleep. Ever since Braeden discovered who she was, she'd been off balance, unsure of how to act now that her two worlds had collided. She didn't know how to be Paladin trainee Sam and Lady Samantha simultaneously. Sam had thought she'd left Lady Samantha behind for good when she had joined the Paladins. She didn't want to be a lady, she wanted to be a Paladin. And paladins had no business going around kissing other paladins. Not for any reason.

Braeden's voice echoed inside her head. *Why?* Why did she kiss him? Even when Lady Samantha was her only identity, she hadn't been much of a romantic. She'd harbored a tendre or two over the years, but never had she acted on it. She hadn't been the sort to pine over men or flirt or gossip with her friends about the fine turn of a man's calves.

Till Braeden.

At the thought of his name, a fresh pang shot through her chest. When she'd touched her lips to his, she'd crossed some murky line, trespassing into new territory that she wasn't ready for, now or maybe ever. Their kiss had been wonderful and frightening and seductive, but it changed things between them irrevocably. Could a friendship survive such a kiss? They couldn't do it again, that much was certain. For the sake of their friendship and Sam's future with the Paladins. She'd made a choice when she'd discarded her life at Haywood for the Paladins. Lady Samantha might have loved a man, but Paladin Sam never could.

Sleep did come eventually, or it must have, for she closed her eyes in darkness and opened them again in candlelight. She blinked, pupils adjusting. Tristan's face blurred above hers and then sharpened. "Morning," he said.

"Urgh," she grunted, not yet able to form coherent words. She arched her back against the hard floor, stretching, and then forced herself upright. Her eyes shifted right, to Braeden's empty pallet. "Where is Braeden?"

"With Asa, in surgery, I suspect."

Sam bolted to her feet. "Why didn't anyone wake me?" She moved for the door.

Tristan grabbed her arm, halting her in her tracks. "Braeden wanted to let you sleep. He said this was something he needed to do on his own."

"Oh," she said, feeling a little hurt. It felt like a personal blow, especially after last night.

"He'll be fine," Tristan said, mistaking her somber expression for concern over Braeden's wellbeing. She *should* be concerned about his health, not fretting over some perceived slight. "It's a quick, easy surgery. Asa said Braeden would be patched up in time for breakfast."

"Good," Sam said absently, surveying the destruction they had wrought to the small room. She couldn't wait to get out of there, to put the evening behind her.

"Impressive, isn't it?" Tristan said dryly. "I've already remunerated Master Byrd for the damages. Cost me a pretty penny."

Sam reddened. "Last night was . . . not intentional."

Tristan's face softened. "I know." Then he grinned. "To be honest, I was far more reckless when I was a trainee, and for less reason. Most of the time there wasn't a reason, other than my own amusement."

"I'm not much for rule-breaking," Sam said. It was true, if you didn't count pretending to be a man.

Tristan snorted. "I'd hardly call you obedient. Have you ever accepted an order without protest?"

Sam sniffed. "I don't disobey your orders. I just vocalize my grievances."

Tristan's laughed. "Come on, let's head to breakfast. Surely you can find no grievance with that."

"Only that I have to share it with you," Sam said with syrupy sweetness.

Breakfast was an elaborate affair: the usual bread and cheese accompanied by a rich, creamy butter, salted fish, and a chine of beef. It was a meal Sam would expect to see on her father's dining table, not in some backwater inn. She bit into a piece of heavily buttered bread, her eyes fluttering closed as the golden, flaky crust melted in her mouth. Pure heaven.

Tristan was staring at her. "What?" she asked.

"Your expression . . ." he said, pink tingeing his cheeks. "Never mind. Ah, here's Braeden."

Braeden stood at the entrance to the tavern, light and shadow playing across his face, accenting the sharp angles. He searched the room, his eyes landing on Sam's. After a tension-filled moment, Sam looked away, her gaze falling to his shoulders. His left hand was wrapped around his upper right arm, holding it gingerly. So he had done it, then.

Tristan waved Braeden over. "How did it go?" he asked as Braeden pulled out a chair from their table.

"Fine," Braeden said. "The surgeon said that with the way my body heals, my arm should be fully mobile by tomorrow."

Tristan whistled. "Gods, that's incredible. You're a lucky man, Braeden." Braeden gave him a flat look, and Tristan coughed awkwardly. "Well, I do envy your healing ability. The last time I was seriously injured, I was bedridden for a fortnight."

"What about your tattoo?" Sam asked, willing her voice to sound normal.

"Damaged beyond repair," Braeden said, pushing back his

right sleeve to reveal thick white bandages. His eyes met hers again, drinking her in. "I'll learn to live without it."

Sam wasn't sure if he was talking about his tattoo or something else, but she nodded anyway. "That's good."

"Can you ride?" Tristan asked. "I was hoping to leave Pirama today, but we can delay our departure till tomorrow if necessary."

"I should be fine to ride, so long as I'm careful with my arm."

"And if a demon attacks?" Sam asked sharply.

A dagger appeared in Braeden's left hand, twirling around his fingertips. "I have another arm."

Sam shook her head, but Tristan seemed pleased enough by his answer. "Let's finish our meals and pack quickly, then. I'm eager to put Pirama behind us. Too little sunlight."

Indeed, the inn was buried so deep into the mountains that it was next to impossible to tell day from night. When they finally departed The Stag and Bull a short while later, the sun was almost too bright. Sam felt raw and exposed beneath the sun's penetrating rays.

Tristan kicked his horse into a gallop, and Sam and Braeden kept apace. Braeden guided his horse expertly with his thighs, his reins sitting unused in his lap. "Now he's just showing off," Sam whispered into her horse's ear. The piebald whinnied in agreement.

Tristan pulled his mare to a stop at the bottom of the mountain pass where they had fought alongside the Uriel. He dismounted and retrieved a shortsword and scabbard from his pack. He handed them to Sam. "Just in case," he said. "I'm not sure what sort of reception we'll get in Luca."

Sam looked up at the distant, snow covered peaks. "Luca is through here?"

"Aye," Tristan said. "Where Pirama was built into the mountains, Luca was built atop them. Only the most stalwart of men travel to and from the city."

"Why did the Uriel set up their encampment there, if traveling is so difficult?" Sam asked.

Braeden brought his horse beside hers. "It sends a message."

"It sounds like cutting off the nose to spite the face to me," Sam said, wrinkling her own nose. Those snowy peaks looked *cold*.

Tristan shrugged. "Who knows why the Uriel do anything? Perhaps our trip to Luca will enlighten us."

"Have you decided whether you'll accept Sander's invitation?" Sam asked.

"Still to be determined," Tristan replied. "I sent off a letter to the High Commander last night. We'll see what he says."

"How will he reach us in Luca?"

Tristan frowned at her, as though it were obvious. "He's the High Commander."

As Tristan had warned, the road to Luca was not an easy one. The mountain was impossibly steep in parts, and their horses tired quickly, so they had to break at regular intervals to allow the animals to recover. The terrain varied greatly, too—a meadow of brilliantly colored wildflowers would be followed by a field of snow. The snow fields were dangerous, according to Tristan, because rivers flowed beneath them, and it was hard to tell whether the snow had solidified enough to support their weight. He made them cross by foot, afraid that the combined weight of horse and man would send them plunging into the icy waters below. Sam skidded and slid her way through the snow, falling more times than she cared to admit.

The undulating crests and dips of the mountain path made it difficult to gauge their progress. They'd climb uphill for what seemed like forever, only to descend the same distance after they reached the summit. The trail was narrow and slippery—from melted snow or rain, Sam didn't know—and her heart stopped every time the horses' hooves slipped in the loose gravel.

But it was beautiful in the mountains, too. There were delicate flowers so blue they seemed artificial, and the uninterrupted vistas of lofty, gray bluffs against sky must have been painted by the Gods themselves. At one point, they paused just to watch an avalanche roll down the mountain slope. The avalanche was more than a mile away, but it was close enough that they could

see and hear the ice separate from the glacier and fall in crystallized shards to the ground below. It was both awe-inspiring and
terrifying.

When the sky turned orange as the sun ducked below the
mountaintops, Sam resigned herself to a cold night beneath the
stars. Tristan, however, had other ideas. "Just a little bit farther,"
he urged, stroking his horse's mane.

He led them off-trail through untamed brush and uneven
earth till at last an opening appeared in the narrowly packed
trees. A small wood hut stood in the clearing, unsophisticated but
well-kept. "We'll stay here for the night," Tristan said, leaping off
his horse.

Braeden and Sam followed Tristan into the small hut. It was
surprisingly spacious and warm, though Sam could hear the wind
beating against the roof. "How did you know about this place?"
she asked.

Tristan spread out a blanket onto the musty floor and lay on
top of it. "I stayed here once before, many years ago. I wasn't sure
it would still be here."

Sam pulled out another blanket and claimed the space at the
back wall, as far from Tristan and Braeden as possible. "What
were you doing in the Elurra Mountains?"

A muscle in his jaw ticked. "Running away," he answered after
a long pause.

From what? she wanted to ask but sensed that Tristan didn't
want to be pushed, not about this. So instead she asked, "You're
from the West, you said? Did you grow up near Luca?"

His jaw tightened. "Nay, further west. In Finchold."

That took Sam by surprise. Finchold was supposedly a ghost
town. It hadn't been inhabited in ten years, not since demons
overran the city. "That's, errr . . ." She struggled to find adequate
words. "How long did you live there?"

"Fifteen years," Tristan said through gritted teeth, his face a
dark cloud.

She opened her mouth to ask another question, but Braeden
caught her eyes and shook his head. "Sorry I asked," she muttered.

Tristan sighed. "Don't apologize. I shouldn't have snapped. I don't like talking about the past, that's all. I'd rather focus on the present."

Sam bit back her curiosity. Tristan was the one of them without secrets, the unflappable one, the one without a chink in his armor. What kind of sordid past could he possibly want to hide?

The conversation turned to more innocuous topics for the remainder of the evening, and they went to bed as soon as the sky faded to black. "We'll be in Luca tomorrow," Tristan told them with a yawn. "Sleep well. You're going to need it."

━━━━━━━━━━━━━━━━

Despite the harsh night winds, the wood hut proved sturdy, and Sam slept undisturbed till Tristan woke them at first dawn. She scarcely had time to process that she was awake before she was on her horse and on her way to Luca.

They drove their horses deeper into the mountain, pausing only to remove a small stone from one of the horse's hooves. After a few hours of riding, the gray, crystalline granite gave way to an orange-reddish sandstone, peppered with tiny holes like a honeycomb. Vertical columns of rock rose from the ground, twisting upwards into the heavens.

Their path narrowed and the steep sides of the mountains drew together, forming a winding canyon with smooth walls rounded by the wear of water. "Luca is through here," Tristan said.

The canyon ended, exposing a long, flat ridge that extended as far as the eye could see. Human hands had carved cylindrical columns, topped with acanthus leaves and an ornately designed lintel, into the face of the cliff, framing a large rectangular opening.

"How did they build that?" Sam asked wonderingly.

Tristan shrugged. "Nobody knows. It's been here since the Age of the First Men." He nudged his horse forward, disappearing into the opening. Sam and Braeden followed him, and they were plunged into total darkness till they emerged on the other side, where they found themselves on a high ledge overlooking a chasm so deep they couldn't see the bottom, only a hazy carpet of white where cloud met sky. A simple suspension bridge decked with wooden planks was anchored on either side of the chasm, swaying in the wind.

Sam swallowed a lump in her throat. She wasn't particularly afraid of heights, but this was pushing it. "Are we crossing over that?"

"I'm afraid so," Tristan said. "You can see why the Uriel established their camp here. It's damned near impossible to attack, at least by human means."

Sam eyed the rickety bridge warily. "If I lived in Luca, I'd never leave. I can't imagine crossing that thing regularly."

"You get used to it," Tristan said. "Besides, there are other ways in and out of Luca."

Sam glared at Tristan. "Then why in the name of the Gods are we going this way?"

"It's fastest," Tristan said. "Stop dallying, and let's cross already."

They made their way across the bridge slowly and carefully, Sam's heart in her mouth every time her horse took a slight misstep. But they made it over without coming to harm.

On the other side of the bridge stood a tall, manmade wall of brick and rose-red stone. Green vines hung against the wall in gnarled ropes, almost completely hiding the open archway into the city. "Welcome to Luca," Tristan said.

Though the sound was muffled outside the city walls, once they stepped through the archway, the city was as loud and bustling as Haywood during the Grand Fair. People brushed past them, a lightness in their step and laughter in their throats. Some were on horses, plodding along slowly but purposefully, while others huddled together in conversation. A few men on horseback patrolled the edges of the crowd, unhurried but watchful. Only they seemed to take note of Tristan, Sam, and Braeden. Sam assumed they were Uriel.

Luca had been built to accommodate the sloping incline of the mountain beneath it, with square, turreted buildings stacked together unevenly like a giant staircase. At the center of the city stood a gleaming white octagonal structure capped with an onion-shaped dome and a tall spire. It was unlike any castle Sam had ever seen.

"Tristan Lyons," a rough, male voice said, startling Sam from her observations. He was a thin, nondescript man in a dark cloak and hat, the brim shadowing his face. He curled his index and middle fingers to his thumb, and showed his hand deliberately to Tristan.

Tristan nodded curtly to the man, and turned to Sam and Braeden. "Stay here. I'll be back shortly." He leapt off his horse, handed the reins to Braeden, and followed the man into the crowd.

"What was that about?" Sam asked.

Braeden shrugged. "He'll tell us if he wants us to know."

"Aren't you curious?"

"Not really."

So he was going to play it that way, was he? "Fine, I'll ask him myself."

Tristan returned a moment later, wearing a ferocious scowl. He strode to his horse and swung into the saddle. He sat unmoving, gripping the reins till his knuckles turned white.

"Tristan?" Sam ventured. "Who was that?"

"Hush," Tristan hissed. "We can't talk about it here. We need to find an inn, somewhere private."

The first three inns they tried were so full they would have wound up sleeping in the stables with their horses. It was hard to believe that so many travelers visited Luca when it was so difficult to get there, but for whatever reason, people must have thought it worth the journey. The fourth inn, however, had a single spare room for them.

The innkeeper of the Mountain's Respite was a large, jovial man, with a thick mustache that wiggled madly whenever he smiled, which was often. He shook hands and accepted payment from several patrons before wiggling his mustache at Tristan, Sam, and Braeden. "Welcome to The Mountain's Respite. The name's Ewan Michaels. What can I do you gentlemen for?"

"One room, three pallets," Tristan said. "We'll be needing it for the next seven nights."

"We're staying in Luca for a week?" Sam asked, surprised. The longest they'd spent in any one place was three days, in Pirama, and that had been because of Braeden's injury.

Tristan narrowed his eyes at her in warning, and then faced the innkeeper. "We've got business in town, Master Michaels," he said, his tone barely civil.

"Not a problem, Master . . ." The innkeeper cleared his throat when Tristan didn't offer his name. He scribbled into his ledger and handed Tristan a set of keys. "Second floor, fourth room on your left. Three silver coins a night, two coppers extra for each additional pallet. You can pay me after your stay or upfront."

Tristan removed his coin purse from underneath his tunic. "We'll pay now," he said, withdrawing the appropriate amount.

Master Michaels swept the coins into his palm. "Enjoy, gentlemen. If there's anything else you need, don't hesitate to ask."

Tristan muttered a brief thanks and marched straight upstairs to their room, while Braeden and Sam scurried to keep up. He slammed the door behind them. "Sit!" he barked, gesturing at the small table and chairs in the middle of the room.

Sam and Braeden sat. "Are you going to sit, too?" Sam asked.

"No," Tristan said, pacing. "I need to pace."

"Are you going to tell us what's going on?" Braeden asked, quirking an eyebrow.

Hah! So he had been curious after all. "That's my line," Sam told Braeden. "Who was that man you were talking to?"

Tristan stopped his pacing. "What I say here cannot leave this room. Are we clear?" Sam and Braeden nodded. He continued, "That man was sent by the High Commander to meet us in Luca."

"A Paladin?" Sam asked.

"That depends on who you ask. Stealth is his trade, not mastery of weapons." He dropped his voice. "We call men like him Sub Rosa."

"He's a spy," Braeden said.

"He is whatever the High Commander needs him to be," Tristan said, drawing something from the folds of his cloak. "And today he brought me a letter. A missive from the High Commander."

"Does it say whether we are to join Sander Branimir for dinner?" Sam asked.

Tristan opened his palm to reveal a folded-up document, stamped with the High Commander's seal. "Read it."

Sam and Braeden reached for it at the same time, their fingers brushing. Sam felt Braeden's touch move through her, and then his hand was gone, leaving her feeling oddly bereft. "Go ahead," Braeden said calmly, as though he were completely unaffected. Damn him.

"Thank you," she said, struggling to keep her voice even. She unfolded the letter and began to read.

> *Tristan, I thank you for your thorough update. It pleases me to hear that your trainees are excelling*

"Excelling? You told the High Commander we're excelling?"

"Don't let it get to your head," Tristan growled. Sam smirked and resumed reading.

> *As much as I would like to comment on your trainees' progress in more detail, I must focus on more pressing matters. The Uriel are no idle threat, Tristan. The Sub Rosa now have concrete proof that they are conspiring to attempt a coup. They want the respect the Paladins command and the power that comes along with it, and they will take it from us by any means necessary.*

> *I should have warned you about them, told you what I had uncovered, but I had dismissed them as an idle threat. I can only hope that it is not too late to put a stop to them.*

> *Tristan, the time to act against the Uriel is <u>now</u> before they can undermine everything we have worked towards over the past hundred years. The future of the Paladins is at stake, and I am putting all my trust in you to save us.*

> *You wrote that the Uriel leader has invited you to dinner. I believe the Gods have gifted us this chance, and we must seize the opportunity. Do not let Sander Branimir fool you. Sander is a man of unspeakable evil, a bigger threat to our kingdom than a thousand demons. You are the Paladins'*

greatest hope, Tristan, and so it is with a heavy heart that I leave this task to you.

Capture Sander, at whatever cost, and bring him to me. That is an order.

Together, you and I will bring the Uriel to their knees. Together, we will uphold our legacy.

I will await you at the Diamond Coast. Godspeed.

Sam and Braeden stared at Tristan in confusion as they processed the letter. Tristan had trouble meeting their gaze. "I have never before been asked to mete out justice on a man," he said quietly.

"What will you do?" Braeden asked, like he thought there was a real choice.

Tristan closed his eyes and breathed deep through his nose. "I will obey my High Commander, as I always have."

"You're really going to take Sander as prisoner?" Sam asked. She hadn't trusted the Uriel from the start, but something about the High Commander's order made her uneasy.

"Aye," Tristan said. "And you're going to help."

CHAPTER 31

TRISTAN WAS A doer, not a plotter. He knew over a hundred different ways to behead a demon, but not the first thing about how to go about kidnapping a man from his own stronghold. Where did he even begin?

As for his own reservations, he'd have to set those aside.

For over a decade, Tristan had followed the High Commander's every command without question. He'd never had any reason to doubt the man who had pulled him from the ashes. The High Commander had given him purpose when he'd thought life wasn't worth living. Tristan owed him everything.

It wasn't far from Luca that the High Commander found him, nearly eleven years ago. Tristan had been walking aimlessly for days, maybe weeks. He was cold and alone and so hungry that he'd taken to gnawing on bare bones for the marrow.

Tristan had hidden behind a boulder when he'd heard the pounding of hooves and the baying of hounds. He hadn't seen another human being since he'd left Finchold—how was he to have known whether the sounds had belonged to man or demon? He'd closed his eyes and waited for teeth or claws or talons to tear his body to shreds. His soul already lay in tatters.

And then that voice, that impossibly beautiful voice, had called out to him. "You can't give up on life just yet, boy, not when the dead still need avenging." The High Commander had extended a hand to him, and Tristan had never looked back.

Tristan swore many oaths on the day he was anointed as a full Paladin, and among them he swore to obey the High Commander in all things. And so he would obey these orders, even if they unsettled him.

He just needed to figure out how to actually execute them.

"So what's the plan?" Sam asked, resting his elbows on the table.

"Accept Sander's dinner invitation," Tristan replied promptly. He could do this planning thing.

"Okay," Sam said. "And then what?"

"We go to the dinner," Tristan declared.

Sam's eyebrows pinched together. "And then?"

"We capture Sander."

Sam was speechless for a full thirty seconds. "How?"

Tristan drew his shoulders back and did his best to look assured. "I'm still working out those details."

Sam rolled his eyes. "In other words, you haven't the faintest idea."

Tristan glowered at him. So what if Sam was right? The boy should know better than to make light of his superior's shortcomings. He'd come up with a proper plan, once he'd had some time to think it over. He hoped.

"I have an idea," Braeden said slowly. "It's a little bit unconventional, but I think it could work."

"In light of the circumstances, I think unconventional is called for," Tristan said.

"I'm still thinking it through," Braeden said, "but what we need to do is draw Sander out, isolate him from his men. There are only three of us, and the Gods know how many Uriel. And if they all fight like Adelard and Donnelly—"

"Then we'll wind up their captives," finished Sam. "Or worse."

Tristan nodded impatiently. "Understood. Isolate Sander."

"How do you propose we do that?" Sam asked.

Braeden scratched under the bandage on his shoulder. "Assuming dinner will be held at the Uriel base, we'll need to find a reason to lure him away to somewhere we can make a quick exit. Here's where the unconventional part comes in." He looked directly at Sam. "One of us would need to dress as a girl."

Sam made a choking noise and started to cough. Tristan pounded him on the back. "Are you okay?"

"I'm fine," Sam gasped, though his skin had gone alarmingly white.

Braeden gave his fellow trainee a measuring look. "It'll have to be Sam. My features are too distinct to pull off a disguise."

Sam's hands curled into fists. "I won't do it."

Tristan frowned at him. "We all have to do what's necessary. You'll do your part."

Braeden told them the rest of his plan, and Tristan agreed it was sound. Sam, however, was less than enthusiastic. "Do I really have to do this?" he asked, his voice cracking.

"I'm sorry," Braeden said, looking down. "I don't see any other way."

Tristan didn't understand why Sam was so upset about donning a female disguise. Yes, it was embarrassing, but what were a few hours of mortification in the grand scheme of things? "Let's do it," he said with resolve. "I'll arrange for dinner with Sander tomorrow night. That gives us a day and a half to prepare." He dug out a few sovereigns and handed them over to Sam. "Buy yourself some feminine things."

"I'll help," Braeden said quickly. Sam pinned him with a glare that could cut through glass.

Tristan looked back and forth between the two of them, sensing he was missing something critical. "I'll leave you two to it." He walked towards the door and turned the knob. "I've got a dinner to arrange. I'll meet you back here at nightfall."

As soon as Tristan walked out of the room, Sam exploded out of her seat. "I could kill you! Your brilliant plan just ended any chance I had of ever becoming a Paladin. Do you hate me that much?" Tears sprang to her eyes, and she scrubbed furiously at her wet cheeks.

"I don't hate you, Sam." A stricken expression flashed across Braeden's face. "Gods, don't cry."

"I'm not crying," she said, ignoring the tears that called her a liar. "And if I were crying, it certainly wouldn't be because I thought you hated me." *Liar*.

"Fine," Braeden said neutrally. "Your cheeks are irrigating." The pads of his fingers hovered near her jawline, and then he dropped his hand to his side. He turned away from her. "We swore to serve the Paladins to the best of our abilities. Can you think of a better plan?"

"Your plan isn't going to work! I can't disguise myself as a girl when I actually am one!"

"That's exactly why it *will* work. Do you think Sander Branimir would be fooled by a man in a pretty dress?"

Sam shoved at Braeden's chest. "What about Tristan? You think he's going to see your idiotic plan through when the ghost of his betrothed reappears?"

"Lady Samantha is *not* making an appearance, Sam. I'd never ask that of you."

Sam laughed, a bitter, mocking laugh. "Shall I get my face beat in again so he doesn't recognize me?"

Braeden expelled an exasperated huff. "People see what they expect to see. We'll create a disguise that fools Tristan, too, without resorting to bruises and contusions. As long as the girl you pretend to be tomorrow isn't Lady Samantha, he'll never suspect otherwise."

"You're willing to risk my future on that assumption?"

"You're willing to risk the future of the Paladins on the assumption that I'm wrong?" Braeden returned. "You and I read the same letter—you know what's at stake. Think beyond yourself."

His last words stung, even as they rang with truth. She sighed heavily. "I have no choice in this, do I? I just hope you're right."

"I will be," Braeden said. "The day won't be tomorrow, but someday I think you should tell Tristan the truth. He might be more understanding than you think."

"He'll hate me."

"He might be angry with you for lying, like I was, but he won't hate you. You're a hard person to hate."

"It's too risky." Sam bit her lip. "You really don't hate me?"

"Never," Braeden said solemnly.

And just like that, some of the awkwardness between them dissipated. Sam let out a quivering breath and forced a smile. "Okay. Let's go buy my disguise."

Wearing women's clothes again felt like slipping into a stranger's skin. The gown Sam bought with Tristan's gold was modestly cut, made of a coarse green wool that itched terribly. Lady Samantha had never worn any cloth less fine than linen—most of her dresses had been silk—but the girl Sam was pretending to be was not the daughter of a duke.

Her chest was blessedly unbound, and in fact she had added padding. The long-sleeved gown was tightly laced, accentuating her enhanced curves, but the high neckline didn't hint at any cleavage. Cleavage couldn't be faked, after all, if one were really a man.

With white-gloved hands, she adjusted her wig in the mirror. The black horsehair was braided and confined in a crespine of knitted mesh, a style long out of fashion in Haywood but still fairly common in the West. She'd painted her face white with blaunchet, heavily rouged her cheeks, and rubbed lemon juice into her lips till they burned bright red.

The girl staring back at her in the mirror didn't look a thing like Lady Samantha.

She exited the privy and entered the inn room, where Tristan and Braeden awaited her. Nervously arranging her skirts, she asked, "How do I look?"

A stunned silence greeted her, and she feared the worst. Tristan spoke first, his voice husky, "You make a very pretty girl."

Sam blushed in spite of herself, not that it would show through all her war paint. "I can't decide whether I should be flattered or offended." It was the expected thing to say, if she were truly a man dressed as a woman.

Tristan stared at her as if dazed. "You remind me of someone, but I can't place who."

Sam shifted on her feet uneasily. "I've been told I have a familiar face." She prayed he didn't press the issue.

"That must be it," Tristan said. He rubbed at his eyes and blinked. "Are you ready for tonight?"

Thank the Gods, he didn't recognize her. Braeden answered, "Aye, we're ready."

Tristan adjusted the sword at his hip and fastened the brooch of his cloak. "Sam, I'll see you in an hour, and Braeden, make sure the horses are saddled." He turned to leave, his hand on the door.

She couldn't shake a nagging doubt. "Tristan," she called, and he spun around. "What happens if the plan doesn't work?"

"The High Commander told us at whatever cost." Tristan's cobalt blue eyes raked her over from head to toe. "You best have a dagger hidden underneath those skirts."

Sam patted the small lump on the right side of her hip, the bulge on her left, and then felt for a long ridge by her ankles.

She had three.

CHAPTER 32

*A*FTER MAKING A few inquiries, Tristan arranged to meet with Sander Branimir over dinner in the singular marble castle overlooking the city. The Beyaz Kale—translated as "the white castle" in the modern tongue—was an amazing feat of architecture, as old as Luca itself. In the early days of Thule, the castle was home to the King and Queen of Thule, till they were forced east by the first and only recorded breach of the Afterlight and the subsequent onset of demons. Now the Beyaz Kale belonged to the Uriel.

Tristan rode his horse up the steep ascent to the ancient castle. Up close, the Beyaz Kale glowed in the fading evening light, and gemstones inlaid in the white marble walls twinkled like stars. A groom awaited him at the top of the path, and Tristan reluctantly handed him the reins. The stables were in a small, separate building, making a quick escape difficult.

The arched doorway to the main building was open, and Tristan let himself in, though not without trepidation. The vestibule was lit by soft torchlight, empty apart from a solitary man of above average height, his face half hidden in shadow. The man closed in on Tristan slowly, as if he were approaching a skittish cat.

Shadows shifted, and Tristan could see white teeth in a crooked grin and a misshapen nose that had been broken several times over. They belonged to a rough, handsome face, etched with the deep lines of a man who laughed regularly and often. Strands of silver and gray threaded through hair that was once dark red, tufts of white curling around his ears and temples. He wore simple but finely tailored clothes, elegant enough for polite company but not so elaborate that he couldn't jump into action if the need arose.

The man extended a callused hand. "Sander Branimir." His voice was low and gravelly, but not unpleasant.

Tristan blinked back his surprise and returned the man's grip. He had expected to first meet with a servant or a lieutenant, not Sander straightaway. "Tristan Lyons."

Hazel eyes searched the room. "Your trainees, they did not come?"

"No," Tristan said, giving him no more than he had to. He'd never been a good liar.

"You distrust me." It was a statement, not a question.

Tristan lifted his chin. "So I do." That was no lie, not by half.

Sander chuckled. "Honesty is always appreciated." And damn if Tristan didn't feel a pang of guilt at that. Still smiling, Sander said, "Dinner awaits us in the tower, if you'll believe my promise that the food isn't poisoned. It's a long way up, so we can chat while we walk."

Together, they climbed the timber treads of the staircase to the upper levels of the castle. Sander had not exaggerated when he said the climb was lengthy; there must have been more than a thousand steps to the top.

While his leg muscles throbbed with a dull ache, Tristan had ample time to absorb his surroundings. He paused to look over the balustrade at the many floors below. "When I had heard last, the earl of Luca resided in this building." A nastier man there had never been, too.

"The previous earl passed on eight years ago."

"He had no heir?" Tristan asked, wanting to know how the Beyaz Kale had fallen into Uriel hands.

Sander's eyes took on a faraway look. "He had a daughter."

"Ah yes, I remember her." Tristan had met the earl's daughter only once, many years ago, when he was still a boy in Finchold. He recalled she was quite lovely and very kind. Nothing like her father. "A good woman."

"Aye, it's why I married her."

Tristan froze against the railing. Sander was married to an earl's daughter? He had been under the impression that the Uriel was peasant-born. "I wasn't aware you were of the aristocracy."

Sander barked a mirthless laugh, in sharp contrast to his previous good humor. "I'm not, not originally. Something her father never let us forget, not till the day she died."

"I'm sorry," Tristan said. "How did she die?"

Sander's open face shuttered. "It was a long time ago." He sighed, rubbing his temples. "You may as well know—she died in a demon attack, not long after we married."

Tristan reeled at the revelation of their shared pasts. He did not want to feel sympathy for this man, not for any reason. "I also lost my family to demons," he said stiffly.

Sander halted on the stairs. "I did not know that. You have my condolences."

Tristan suspected there was little the Uriel didn't know. He shrugged. "As you said, it was a long time ago."

Sander resumed his climb. "Let us speak of happier things. We have much to discuss, you and I."

Tristan followed Sander into the domed tower at the top of the stairway. A few men lingered just inside the entryway, including a familiar, scarred face. "Adelard."

Adelard greeted him with a hearty backslap. "You came! Good to see you under less dire circumstances."

"And you," Tristan said politely, a little taken aback by the Uriel's warm familiarity. "Will you be joining us for dinner?"

"Afraid I can't. The wife will have my hide. I think she suspects I prefer Cook's cooking to hers."

The gruff, battle-hardened man was married? Tristan had difficulty picturing Adelard as a domesticated husband. "Another time." Although if all went as planned tonight, the Uriel wouldn't be so hospitable.

Adelard shook Tristan's hand and headed for the stairs. "Stop by if you have a chance. Our rooms are on the third floor." He gave Sander a shallow bow and waved his goodbye.

Tristan turned to Sander. "Adelard lives here, with you?"

"Aye, many of the men do. This castle is too damned big to live here by myself." He led Tristan to the back of the circular room, where a small banquet awaited them. A beef roast, a stuffed piglet, and some veal sausages were laid out across an oak refectory table, along with quince bread and several types of fruit tart.

"Isn't this excessive for two people?" Tristan asked.

"I thought your trainees might be joining us." Sander grinned. "And this is a special occasion, is it not? I've never before hosted a Paladin."

"Why does that not surprise me?" Tristan muttered.

"Sit, sit," Sander said, as he did the same. He poured them both a glass of red wine and gestured at the banquet. "Eat."

Tristan scooped a few helpings onto his plate, but did not move to eat. "Why did you invite me here?"

"You don't mince your words, do you?" Sander remarked, with a small, amused smile.

"Nor do you," he countered.

Sander dipped his head in acknowledgment. "It has been said that I am blunt. But I won't apologize for it. I would begin our relationship on honest terms."

Tristan's eyebrows crept up. "Our relationship?"

Sander took a sip of his wine. "I'm interested in an alliance."

He quickly hid his astonishment. "With me?" he asked. "Or with all the Paladins?"

Sander tilted his head and gave another enigmatic smile. "You command a lot of respect, Tristan, and you are formidable with a sword, of that there is no doubt. But a war is not won on the shoulders of a single man." His lips flattened into a self-deprecating line. "I promised you my candor. You have the High Commander's ear, and I want him to hear me. I've tried to correspond with him directly, and he has yet to respond to any of my letters. But he did send me you."

Sander had written to the High Commander? Had the messages never been received, or had the High Commander chosen to ignore them? Either way, it didn't sit well with Tristan, and he suddenly felt ill-prepared for this encounter. "I'm sure the High Commander had his reasons," he said icily. "Why should we ally ourselves with you? Who granted you permission to raise an army?"

Sander put down his wine glass. "May I continue to speak candidly?"

"Don't let me stop you."

"The West is dying, Tristan. Little by little, we're being eaten away. Finchold and Valfort are gone, and you saw Pirama—the rest of the countryside is as bad or worse. I've been a Western man my whole life, and I refuse to abandon my home. But I'm an old man with my best years behind me—whether I live or die is inconsequential. There are others like me, stubborn and proud, and they'll defend their land to their death. And they *will* die, hundreds of thousands of men, women, and children, like lambs to the slaughter." He leaned forward, a dark gleam in his light eyes. "The demons are changing, Tristan, both in number and kind. There haven't been attacks of this enormity since the Age of Shadows."

Tristan wanted to protest, but the Uriel's words rang true. He'd seen for himself what had happened to Finchold, and it had been less than a month ago that they'd had a run in with a Dreamwalker.

"Here in the West we know what you in the East only guess at. But it's only a matter of time till you recognize the truth. And if we don't band together, then the another Age of Shadows will be upon us."

His warning ran exactly counter to what the High Commander had said. "And what truth is that?"

"The barrier to the Afterlight has been breached for a second time. The demons' prison no longer stands. They're free to come and go as they please. All of them."

Tristan snorted. "Blather. No one can break those seals."

Sander took another draught of his wine. "You had an attack on your fortress in Heartwine, did you not?"

"How do you know about that?"

Sander waved his hand. "Never mind that. How do you explain how the demons got past the wards?"

Tristan opened his mouth and shut it. "I can't."

"If those wards failed, is it so hard to believe that others might be failing too?"

Tristan shook his head. "I learned my history lessons same as anybody else. The breach that set demons loose upon the world was an accident of magic. That magic is long forgotten. Heartwine's seals will hold."

"Magic can be forgotten," Sander said, "but it can never be

stamped out. The wards didn't fail because we forgot how we made them. They failed because someone remembered."

"There hasn't been a warder in over a thousand years," Tristan said. "Where is your proof?"

The corner of Sander's mouth twitched. "Pirama doesn't stand as proof enough?"

Tristan folded his arms under his chest and gave him a non-committal look.

"There have been sightings of demons that haven't been seen since the time of the first breach. Nightmares that bleed into reality. Dreamwalkers roam the earth again, and if they're free, Teivel's provosts are not far behind." Sander ran a finger along the rim of his glass. "I do not blame you for your doubts, Tristan, you or your High Commander. What I'm suggesting is hard to swallow. But the Uriel have found something, Tristan, something important. Something I mentioned to the High Commander in my letters."

"What's that?"

"We found one of the seals to the Afterlight, buried in the rubble at the Diamond Coast." Sander's voice trembled with excitement. "Tristan, it's cracked."

"Impossible," Tristan said flatly.

Sander sighed. "I wish it were so. But you can't deny the truth when it's staring you in the face." He speared a piece of meat with his knife. "Something—or someone—is behind all this. We're going to find out what."

Tristan started to ask how, but he was interrupted by the clearing of a throat. A young man, a servant by his clothes, stood at the center of the dome, awaiting Sander's attention. He bobbed in an awkward bow. "Excuse me, sir, but there's a young lady here to see you. She claims it's urgent." The servant shifted his feet uncomfortably. "She did seem rather frantic."

Gods, Tristan had nearly forgotten the real reason he had joined Sander for dinner. The servant's message meant Sam was here, performing his part of the plan. "Shall we see to her together?" he asked Sander, forcing himself to remain calm.

"Sure, I'd appreciate the company." Sander asked the servant, "Where is she?"

"I told her to wait in the vestibule," the servant said. "Be fore-warned, sir, the lady was crying hysterically when I left her to find you."

In spite of the delicacy of the situation, Tristan felt a grin tug at his lips. Sam, in hysterics? This he would have to see.

It took Sander and Tristan half as long to descend the stairs as it had taken them to climb them. They did not converse on the way down, Sander driven by determined urgency and Tristan too edgy to pretend otherwise. Tristan's heart beat like the tattoo of a drum, and his clammy palms slid easily along the balustrade, slick with his cold sweat. He couldn't recall ever being so nervous or reluctant to follow the High Commander's orders.

What if the High Commander was wrong? Could he have made a mistake in his judgment of Sander?

Appalled at the traitorous direction of his thoughts, Tristan shoved them aside and focused on the feminine figure in the vestibule of the Beyaz Kale. A hand lay flat against the chalk-white walls and dragged down, accompanied by a horrible wailing sound like that of a drowning cat. Delicate shoulders—funny how delicate they seemed when encased in women's frippery—shook with apparent grief, and great, gulping sobs racked the gently curved frame.

Tristan rushed to the figure at once. "My lady, what is the cause of your distress?" He grabbed the hand on the wall and brought its fingers to his mouth, as if he were going to impart a kiss. In between the knuckles, he hissed, "Sam, you're overdoing it. You're supposed to be frightened, not mourning the dead."

Wide green eyes glowered back at him, tears glistening on the edge of artificially-darkened lashes. "Oh, you're good," Tristan breathed, releasing his trainee's hand. While the crying noises Sam made were out of a bad play, the tears at least looked real.

Sander moved by his side, and Sam resumed his ridiculous caterwauling. "My lady," Sander said gently. "Can you tell us what the trouble is? I will help you if it is within my power."

Sam made a show of sniveling, dabbing at his eyes with his dress sleeve. "I don't mean to be any trouble," he hiccuped, his voice pitched higher than Tristan was accustomed to. Sam sounded remarkably like a woman. "I'm traveling by myself, you see. I have no husband or brother, and I didn't know where else to turn. I heard tell of the Uriel, that you might be able to help, and I saw this great big castle at the center of the city, and, well, here I am." Sam sniffed loudly and blew his nose like a trumpet. Tristan shot him a covert glare—*that* was not feminine in the slightest.

Sander said, "You've managed to find the Uriel, my lady. But why have you sought us out?"

Sam let out a moan of despair. " 'Tis a demon, milord. A terrible creature, with sharp teeth and great claws and glowing red eyes." He shuddered, quite believably. "It almost killed me, but I got away, just barely."

Sander put his hand on Sam's shoulder. "You're all right now, my lady. The danger has passed."

Sam shook his head wildly, his black braid whipping behind him. "Nay, milord, the danger is still there! I'm staying at an inn, you see, and in my haste to get away, I locked the demon in the room behind me. What if it is still inside? And worse, if it escaped, I fear what it will do. I was so anxious to leave that I did not think to warn others in the inn." Sam looked down at the floor, the picture of dismay.

"You did right to come to us," Sander said. "A demon on the loose is a serious problem. I'll take a few of my men and—"

"My lady, was it just the one demon?" Tristan cut in. Sam nodded tearfully. Tristan faced Sander. "Surely a single demon does not require more than two men. Why don't you and I go together? We can resume our talk of"—he gritted his teeth—"an *alliance* after this matter has been dealt with."

Sander beamed at him and said, "It would be my honor, Paladin." He seemed genuinely pleased at the prospect.

Guilt settled over Tristan like a heavy blanket, but he forced a smile. "It's settled, then. My lady, I assume you traveled here by horse?"

Sam mopped at his cheeks. "Aye, milord. I left him with the groom." He dropped into a flawless curtsey, and Tristan was suitably impressed. Where had the boy learned to curtsey like a duchess? "I'm ever so grateful to you both," Sam said, fluttering his eyelashes.

Tristan fought back an eye roll. "Sander, will you lead us to the stables?"

"Follow me."

Tristan placed his hand firmly against the small of Sam's back and guided his trainee out of the front archway. Underneath his hand, Tristan could feel the bones of the corset that cinched Sam's waist to feminine proportions. Sam felt so much like a woman that Tristan's mind began to play tricks on him, even though he knew the truth of it. He needed to clear his head and concentrate. "Is Braeden prepared?" he murmured against the boy's wig.

"He'll be ready," Sam said, barely moving his lips.

The groom brought out their horses: Sam's piebald, Tristan's chestnut mare, and a handsome black stallion for Sander. "I need to fetch my weapon and let my men know I'm leaving," Sander said. "Will you help the lady with her horse?"

"Of course," Tristan said. He kneeled beside the piebald and cupped his hands. "Your foot, madam."

Sam sent him a look of pure venom, but permitted Tristan to boost him up onto the horse. Sam leaned over to adjust his gown so he could ride astride modestly, and a round, purple and white object fell from the folds of his skirts. Tristan scooped it up from the ground. "An onion?"

"Braeden said my crying lacked conviction," Sam whispered. "Get rid of it before Sander sees!"

That explained the tears. Tristan smashed the onion beneath his boot. "You have no future as an actor," he told Sam. He stood up, dusted off the dirt from his knees, and mounted his own horse.

Sander returned with a quarterstaff in hand and expertly swung himself onto the stallion's saddle. "Where to, my lady?"

"The Mountain's Respite," Sam said. "Do you know it?"

"I know every inn in this city," Sander said. "Paladin Lyons is staying there, too."

It didn't surprise Tristan that Sander knew where he was lodging, but he hoped the Uriel would dismiss it as mere coincidence. Sander didn't seem to harbor any suspicions, but the man hadn't become the leader of thousands of men by being a fool. Sam's ruse was damned convincing, though; no one would guess that the raven haired beauty was Tristan's trainee. He hardly believed it himself. "Let's ride," he said, spurring his horse into a run.

They galloped down the curving declivity of the mountain

road, a blustering wind pressing at their backs. Their pace was inhibited by Sam, who had enough sense to curtail his horse's gait to an acceptable level for a lady.

When they arrived at the inn, it was no longer dusk, but well and truly night. The frenetic beat of the city had slowed, and the once-packed streets were near to empty. Milky moonlight cast an eerie sheen across the urban landscape.

Sander offered Sam a hand down from his horse, and Sam accepted it without hesitation. He dipped into a quick curtsey as thanks, and Tristan thought, not for the first time, that Sam affected the carriage of a woman too easily.

The stablehand was nowhere to be found, so they tied up their horses themselves and crossed to the front door of the inn. Tristan felt ill with anticipation, and he could see in Sam's eyes that he felt it also. Sweat formed on Tristan's brow, but he ignored it. "Will you show us to your room, my lady?"

Sam ducked his head. "Y-yes, milord. It's on the second floor." He glanced back at Tristan, biting his lip. Tristan gave him the slightest of nods in encouragement.

The innkeeper was gone, too, and Tristan idly wondered where Braeden had stowed him. He hoped that duty was worth the many sins he had committed and had yet to commit this night.

"Where is Ewan?" Sander asked, a hint of sharpness creeping into his voice.

They needed to act now and quickly, before suspicion pointed their way. "Perhaps his disappearance is related to the demon," Tristan said, thinking on his feet. "We shouldn't tarry any longer. My lady, please lead us upstairs."

Sam made a shallow curtsey and headed straight towards their rented room. He put his ear to the door and made a pathetic attempt at a whimper. "The demon's still there, milords! I can hear it growling." A deep, menacing growl echoed into the hall-way, lending credibility to his words.

"Hand me the key," Tristan said. He fitted it to the lock. "Stay back, my lady, I would not want you to get hurt." To Sander, he said, "Shall we?"

Sander gripped the shaft of his quarterstaff with both hands. "After you."

Tristan twisted the door open and stepped inside. He held onto the doorknob till both Sander and Sam had entered the dark room, and then he shut the door behind them.

Sander twisted his neck, looking at Sam. "My lady, you shouldn't be in here. It's not safe for a—"

Before he could finish, a blur of black and silver hurtled across the room, the demon come to life. "Shite," Sander swore, narrowly sidestepping the attack. Braeden leapt at him again. Sander threw up his quarterstaff just in time to prevent Braeden's elongated claws from piercing his skin, but the force of their collision sent them both tumbling to the floor.

Sander rolled on top of him and lifted his quarterstaff into the air, prepared to deliver a skull-crushing blow to Braeden's head. He froze at the kiss of steel at his neck.

"Drop your weapon," Sam snarled into his ear.

The quarterstaff clattered to the floor. "Ah. I thought it might be something like this," Sander said with a half-smile.

"Hold out your wrists," Tristan said tonelessly, and he tied Sander's hands together with rope.

"My ankles too?" Sander asked, who still straddled Braeden.

"No," Tristan said. "I need you to be able to ride." He brought Sander to his feet, and Braeden moved out from underneath him, his eyes ablaze with red from his previous efforts.

"I'll ready the horses," Braeden rumbled. He rubbed at his bare chest, where his knife had punctured his breastbone. The wound was already knitting itself together.

Sander looked at him appreciatively. "You must be Braeden. Nice trick."

Did nothing ruffle this man? Even in the face of abduction, the Uriel seemed faintly amused. Tristan said to Braeden, "Put on some proper clothes first. We don't want to draw any unnecessary attention."

Braeden stepped into his robes, which he'd discarded in a black pool of fabric at the far corner of the room. "Can I change?" Sam asked.

"No time," Tristan said. "I need you to walk in front of Sander so no one can see his wrists till we're on horseback."

"This dress itches," Sam complained. "You owe me for this."

Finally, Sander's face registered astonishment. "You wouldn't be Sam of Haywood, would you?"

Sam swept into a mocking curtsey. "In the flesh."

Sander began to laugh. "Gods, that's good," he hooted. "I never would have guessed."

Tristan scowled. "You do realize the implications of your situation, do you not?"

Sander sobered, his laughs subsiding. "Better to laugh than to cry, no?" And then, shockingly, he winked. "Besides, I haven't given up on you yet, Tristan."

Damn the man for pricking his guilt. "Let's go," he said gruffly.

They maneuvered Sander through the hallway and downstairs, and miraculously did not bump into a single patron. Before leaving the inn, Tristan tucked a handful of sovereigns into the binding of Master Ewan's ledger. Tomorrow, the innkeeper would wake up with a nightmare of a headache, but at least he would be well-compensated. Guilt slightly assuaged, Tristan steered Sander towards the stables.

With Braeden's help, Tristan lifted Sander up onto his stallion and then tethered the horse to his own chestnut with rope. It was an inconvenient way to ride and would slow them down, but Sander was an accomplished equestrian and did not need the use of his hands to spur his horse to escape. They would sacrifice speed for the assurance of his capture.

Braeden had already packed the horses with their loads, so they were off as soon as they all were saddled. Under the cover of night, they rode hard and fast till the western gates of Luca were in sight. Sander did not raise protest, clinging silently to the pommel of his saddle with his bound hands.

In seconds, they would be underneath the west arch and through it into Swyndale, where the Uriel's hold would not be quite as strong. They couldn't rest in Swyndale—Tristan hadn't mapped out how far loyalty to the Uriel extended—but they would be out from under the shadow of the Beyaz Kale. A laugh burbled up from deep inside Tristan. They'd done it. Their insane plan had actually worked.

Tristan celebrated too soon. An arrow swooped down, whistling past his ear as his horse skittered sideways. The archer stood atop the west gates, another arrow notched in his bow. Four men clambered down the knotted vines covering the gates, barring their path, and another five men joined them below, armed to the teeth.

One of the men stepped forward, the glint of the moon highlighting his disfigured face. He held his spiked mace at the ready. "Paladin Lyons," Adelard said, his voice cutting through the night like a whip. "You've interrupted my dinner."

Never let it be said that Sam didn't come prepared to do battle. As soon as the Uriel archer had loosed an arrow, the boy ripped his gown to his knees and withdrew three daggers from his garters—good Gods, the boy was actually wearing garters—frilly scraps of white fabric peeking out from beneath his petticoat.

A girl ought to be ashamed of exposing so much leg, and the Uriel men, those who did not know her to be a he, gaped at the sight of pale white calves and ankles. The legs were deceptively feminine, slender, with only the finest coating of hair, so Tristan could understand their mistake.

"What do we do now?" Sam asked Tristan, clearly itching for a fight. He clutched two daggers in each hand and holstered the third in the tight lacing of his bodice.

"We have no choice. We must fight," Tristan said grimly, dismounting from the saddle. He couldn't fight on horseback, not with Sander's horse tied to his.

Adelard spat on the ground. "You disgust me. You would use an innocent woman to further the Paladins' ambitions?" He wiped his mouth with the back of his hand. "And to think I actually liked you."

"Innocent woman?" Sam said. He shook his daggers at Adelard meaningfully. "Do I look innocent to you? And besides, I'm not a—"

"Sam, shut up," Tristan ordered. Like always, the boy's irrepressible mouth betrayed too much.

As Sander had done, Adelard began to laugh, but his laughter lacked real mirth. "Sam of Haywood? Oh, that's rich."

Sam edged his horse closer. "Laugh all you want, Uriel, while you still have breath for laughter."

Adelard took a step forward and held his mace straight out

in front of him. "There are ten of us, and three of you. This is a fight you cannot win." He dropped his mace to his side. "Release Sander and it will be as if this never happened. You'll go your way, and we'll go ours."

"I can't accept that bargain," Tristan said, with a touch of regret. He would have happily divorced himself from this Uriel business, but he knew his duty.

"There are two paths you can take to get to the same conclusion," Adelard said harshly, "but only one way to leave Luca with your lives and dignity intact."

"I have yet to be bested in combat, by man or beast," Tristan said. "Perhaps it is your men who should consider turning tail." He unsheathed his sword, the jet black obsidian of the scimitar's blade nearly invisible against the dark sky. "Sam, Braeden, weapons at the ready."

Braeden's eyes flared with red for the second time that night, the telltale splotch of crimson wetness radiating out from his breast where his knife had found its mark. He jumped down from his horse and stood by Sam's, one hand on the piebald's flank and the other hanging down by his hip, a monstrous combination of claw and manmade steel. They were as ready as they'd ever be.

"On my mark!" Adelard shouted. "Charge!"

Time slowed, the battleground stretching out before Tristan like a game of chess. He and Adelard careened from opposite corners down the same unobstructed path while the Uriel pawns advanced towards Sam and Braeden. Braeden tore at his clothes and howled in murderous rage. A dagger, cast from Sam's hand, parted the air in a graceful arc, seeking its fleshy target.

"Stop!"

The power in Sander's voice could not be ignored, and both the Uriel and paladins drew to a halt, daggers and arrows falling harmlessly to the ground. Gone was the composed, insouciant man who had smirked and joked throughout his own kidnapping. Even hunched over his horse with his hands imprisoned, Sander exuded such authority that no doubt remained that this man could command five thousand men, and more.

Straightening as best he could given his restraints, Sander

said, "That will be all, Adelard. Return without me to the Beyaz Kale and let these men go in peace."

"Sir!" Adelard exclaimed in protest, his mace still raised above his head.

"I made a promise to these men," Sander continued, as if Adelard had never spoken. "I promised that neither I nor my men would harm them while they stood on Lucan soil."

"The circumstances have changed. They *assaulted* you," Adelard said. "Surely that releases you from your promise."

Sander's mouth hardened. "I will not be made a liar." He spoke loud enough for all the Uriel to hear. "Nor will I condone human blood shed on my behalf. That is not what we do. That is not who we are. We must remember our purpose always, even when others forget theirs."

Despite his unwavering loyalty to the Paladins, in that moment, Tristan could not help but believe that this was a man of honor, and that Sander shamed them with his speech. He looked at Sam and Braeden, reading confusion on their faces, and he wondered if they felt as ashamed as he.

With a shout of frustration, Adelard threw his mace to the ground. "So we should do nothing? We should just let them take you Gods know where to do Gods know what? That is folly, Sander! I can't allow it."

Tristan stared at the angry Uriel in disbelief. No one would have spoken to the High Commander with such freedom; no one would dare, not even he.

"Do you still follow my orders, Adelard?" Sander asked, his tone mild.

Adelard bowed his head. "Till the death, be it yours or mine."

"Then you will do nothing. You will let them take me," Sander said. "And you will lead the Uriel in my stead till my return."

"*If* you return," Adelard said bitterly.

"You must have faith in your fellow man. On that you and I have always agreed." Sander looked to Tristan. "Will you release me, Paladin?"

The Uriel leader's gaze held a world of expectations, and so Tristan averted his eyes. "I cannot say."

Sander nodded. "Not yet, then."

Arrogant man. Tristan owed him nothing and would promise him nothing. "I will do as my High Commander tells me, no more and no less." He sheathed his sword and returned to the saddle. "By your leave."

"By *his* leave, not *mine*," Adelard said. He turned his back to their horses. "Get out of my sight."

CHAPTER 33

SAM BURNED HER dress that night in silent contemplation. Everything about the evening had been too close for comfort, from the fit of her dress to the near-battle with the Uriel to the way Tristan's eyes wandered over her small but still-present curves. She was sick of it all: the hiding, the lying, the constant guilt churning in her gut. She'd run away from home to gain control over her life, and yet somehow she'd lost it.

Sam observed Sander, who leaned back against the tree he was tied to. In some ways, he was freer than her; the rope that bound him could be cut. Not Sam, the chains of her sex would hold her back forever. She wanted to be a warrior and a woman, but she wasn't allowed to be both. So she'd made her decision, and if given a second chance she would make it again. She just hadn't expected it to chafe.

After the small fire consumed the last of the green cloth, Sam shifted closer to Sander. She'd been assigned the first watch of the night—they were to take turns making sure the Uriel leader didn't escape. Sander was wily, Tristan warned, and she needed to be careful.

"Don't engage him in conversation," Tristan had said. "The man has a silver tongue, and before you know it, he'll have convinced you to undo his binds and run away with him, too."

With his torso wrapped in rope and his head drooping into his chest, Sander didn't appear to pose much of a threat. He was old enough to be her father, with an attractive but unremarkable face, apart from his very crooked nose. If his tongue were his only weapon, Sam wasn't too concerned. Whether he spewed venom or poetry, nothing he could say would persuade her to his side.

She crept closer still, a twig snapping under her feet. Sander's head shot up and his eyes pierced through her. He smiled at her and said nothing, turning his gaze to the stars. He began to hum softly—an old, familiar song—the notes rising and falling in his rough, compelling voice.

"Stop that!" she snapped.

His humming ceased. "Singing is good for the soul."

"Perhaps you should have become a bard, then."

Sander's smile widened. "I should have liked to be a bard, but life had other plans for me. You know a thing or two about that."

Sam furrowed her brow. "About what?"

"Duty and capability. Isn't that why you joined the Paladins?"

Sam had no answer for that; her reasons for joining the Paladins were intertwined and complex. One duty had been allotted to her at birth, but she cast it aside for another. She had natural talent with a sword—that was no boast but simple truth—but did that give her the right to follow the path she'd chosen?

Sander searched her, his eyes amber like a wolf's in the glow of firelight. "How long has Tristan known?"

"Known what?" she asked.

"Known that you're a girl."

Sam froze as her world crashed down around her. "I'm not a girl."

"Beg pardon. How long has Tristan known that you're a woman?"

Fear made her stomach heave. "Tristan doesn't know I'm a woman because *I'm not one.*"

He didn't believe her; she could see it in his face. "So he doesn't know."

"I'm a boy, a man, a male," Sam lied with conviction. "How else would I have become a Paladin trainee?" She drew the short sword from the scabbard at her hip. "Shall I demonstrate I am worthy of the name?"

Sander eyed the sword warily. "Are you going to kill me now that I know your secret?"

Horrified, Sam dropped the point of the blade to the ground. "Of course not! And-and there's no secret to know. I was just going to show you a few sword forms, to prove my point."

"I already know you're good with a sword, Sam of Haywood. Adelard lauded your skill in Pirama."

Adelard had spoken well of her? He was unlikely to praise her again. But she had bigger worries at hand than the loss of the scarred Uriel's favor. "So then why would you think me a girl? I fight as well as any man."

"From what I hear, you fight better," Sander said, eyes crinkling at the corners. "But swordplay and boys' clothes does not a man make."

"I'm not a girl," Sam repeated, clinging desperately to the lie. And to think she'd thought Sander had no real weapon. He could destroy her with his words, armed as they were with truth.

Sander flicked his gaze over her. "Any man who sees you in a dress would have to be a fool to believe you anything but a girl. You moved in that gown like it was second nature and you curtsied like a dream. You wouldn't have pulled off tonight's charade unless you'd been playing the part your whole life. You can deny it all you want, but I won't change my mind."

Sam's heart thudded against her chest. There would be no veering Sander off this course; there were no clever lies he would fall for. "I'm not confirming I'm a girl," she said, choosing her words carefully, "but are you planning to tell Tristan you think me one?"

"Not my secret to tell," Sander said. "Although I assumed he already knew. You're a lovely young woman, and he must be half blind not to see it."

She wasn't sure if she could trust in Sander's discretion, but nevertheless, she was angry on Tristan's behalf. "You met me as a woman, Sander, so you can think of me as nothing else. The reverse is true of Tristan." Technically, he had met her first as a young girl, but she wasn't about to divulge that to Sander.

The Uriel leader studied her, his thoughts visible on his expressive face. "Nay, that's not it. He knows, I think."

"Not a chance," she said confidently. "I'd be home back in dresses or hanging in the gallows if that were true."

Sander smiled kindly at her. The damned man was always smiling. "Maybe he hasn't acknowledged it to himself, but he knows on some level. I've seen the way he looks at you. For a man like him, it's easier to believe convenient lies than to face the consequences of the truth. He can't fathom breaking the rules, so he denies the obvious."

"That's a hefty analysis considering you've known him one day," she said.

Sander shrugged his shoulders against the tree. "I'm good at reading people. For example, I know you're terrified right now."

"Terrified? Of you?" Sam scoffed. But Sander was right; she was terrified.

"Aye. But I shan't tell your secret to a soul. I swear it on my wife's grave."

"Why?" She was his captor, not his friend, and he had ample motivation to betray her gender. He had a powerful bargaining chip, and a smart man would use it.

He closed his eyes, his smile turning wistful. "I was born a farmer's son, you know. I very well could have died a farmer, bound to the same plot of land I was born on. But I wielded a quarterstaff far more ably than I drove a plow, and I've always been far better at guiding people than herding sheep. And then I met my Elizabeth, and I found my purpose. It wasn't on a farm." He sighed. "Duty and capability. Perhaps you've found what you're meant to be."

Sam lifted her head defiantly. "I'm meant to be a Paladin."

"Or a Uriel," Sander said with a wink.

Looking at him skeptically, Sam asked, "Do you count women among your Uriel, Sander?"

"No."

Sam smirked. "I thought not."

Sander regarded her thoughtfully. "But I would consider it, for the right woman."

And there it was, the bait to lure her away. "If I were a woman, I'd keep that in mind." She took a few steps backward, physically distancing herself from the spell he wove. "Go to sleep, Uriel. I tire of this conversation."

"As you wish." He tucked his head back into his chest.

Tristan relieved her from her watch a short while later, and she crawled into their tent beside Braeden. She was badly shaken by her conversation with Sander and would have liked to talk to Braeden about it, but she didn't want to disturb his sleep.

Braeden was sprawled out on his back, a thick blanket draped over his legs. He'd undone the tie of his robes, and the black bell sleeves were pushed down to his hips. Bare to the waist, he was savagely beautiful, his lithe body covered by a smooth canvas of golden skin, apart from the ruined ink on his right arm. The wound itself had mostly healed, leaving behind a thick pink scar, but the tattooed glyphs on his shoulder were irrevocably damaged. She wondered if it still bothered him.

She arranged her bedding with as little noise as possible, but Braeden stirred despite her best efforts. He pushed his silver hair off his forehead and looked at her with heavy-lidded eyes. "Sam," he said, his voice raspy from sleep. "What's happened?"

He knew her too well; he saw the tightness of her shoulders and the wrinkle between her brows. For him, that was enough. There was no hiding from Braeden, not anymore. "Sander knows," she said. She wouldn't have to tell him what.

He immediately sat up. "How?"

She pulled her knees into her chest. "He guessed."

"Does he have proof?"

"It's not hard to prove. One merely has to lift up my shirt." Even in the dark, she could see his blush. "Have I offended you with my crudeness?"

Braeden coughed. "No," he said. "What should we do about it?"

Not what should *you* do about it, but what should *we*. She wanted to throw her arms around him and thank him, but their rekindled friendship was too new, the scar on his shoulder too fresh. "Thank you," she said instead. "I don't deserve you."

"Never say that," he half-growled.

She shook her head. "I've caused you nothing but trouble since the day we met."

"Maybe I like your kind of trouble," he said, not meeting her eyes. He pulled his blanket to his shoulders, his broad feet sticking out the other end, and she grinned in spite of herself. The grin turned into a giggle, and she promptly covered her mouth with her hand.

"What?" Braeden asked.

"Your feet. They look funny." Gods, she *never* giggled. Wearing a dress must have addled her brain. Her giggles increased. "Sorry," she gasped, quaking with laughter. "I think I must be overtired."

His lips twitched, threatening a smile, but he suppressed it quickly. "What are we going to do about Sander, Sam?"

"He said he wouldn't tell anyone," she said.

"And you believe him?"

She paused before replying. Could Sam believe Sander? She still wasn't sure. She didn't know what to make of the older man, with his talk of duty and capability. And not that she'd ever really consider it, but she wondered if he'd meant what he said about allowing a woman among the Uriel. "I don't know."

"You need to tell Tristan, Sam," Braeden said, "before Sander tells him for you."

"What difference does it make if it's Sander who tells Tristan or me? The end result will be the same."

"All the difference in the world, Sam," Braeden said. "Hearing it from Sander would be like a knife through the gut. It has to be you."

"It doesn't have to be *anyone*," she said.

Braeden rubbed at his face. "Do as you want."

She watched his hand stroke the pale stubble on his chin, and imagined tracing her fingertip over the strong lines of his jaw. "I always do," she said. You're my only exception, she thought to herself.

They spent the next week on the road, cutting through the Woodmaple Forest instead of traveling through town; Sander was a popular man in these parts, and avoiding people seemed the best way to prevent unnecessary conflict.

The forest was on flat land, and the weather was warmer here than in the mountains, but the air was still crisp and cool with the changing of the seasons. Leaves of every shade of red and yellow hung from the trees and carpeted the ground, crackling under their horses' hooves during the day and cushioning their sleep at night.

The question of whether Sander would hold his tongue hung over Sam like the hangman's noose. But if Tristan stole more glances in her direction than usual, the glances held no malice, so Sander must have kept his quiet—for the time being.

In fact, Sander was a model prisoner: he never threatened escape and was unerringly cheerful. The only complaint he voiced was that Tristan left him tied up whenever demons attacked, which occurred with increasing frequency the further west they traveled.

"I can *help*," Sander insisted. "I feel so damned useless."

"If you think I'll allow you a weapon, you've lost your damned mind," Tristan said.

It was an oft repeated exchange over the course of the week, and the outcome always remained the same. Sam could tell Sander was not used to sitting out a fight and did not enjoy being idle, but he—mostly—kept up his cheery façade. Sam, for one, was disappointed she didn't get to see him in action. The High Commander's skill in battle was legendary, and she wanted to know if the leader of the Uriel was of the same caliber.

It was on the eighth day out from Luca that a man on horseback came to meet them in the middle of the forest. His dark cloak and wide-brimmed hat were nearly identical to the High Commander's spy in Luca, his features as nondescript. The man raised his hand, deliberately curling his first two fingers to his thumb, and then reined his horse near theirs.

"Checking up on me?" Tristan asked with a frown.

"Just making sure you do your part." The man's gaze slid past Tristan and settled on Sander. "I'll inform the High Commander of your success."

"You do that," Tristan said, his tone unfriendly. "Is that the only reason you came, or do you have another message to relay?"

"Nay," the man said. "The High Commander is a few weeks behind you. He'll find you at the Diamond Coast and will take Sander from your custody."

"Did he say what his plans are for Sander?" Tristan asked.

The man fixed him with a level gaze. "He did not, and that is not for you or me to ask."

Tristan's eyebrows rose at that. "I shall ask the High Commander whatever I please. Are we done here?"

"Aye," the man said. "Good day, Paladin Lyons." He tipped his hat in farewell and then galloped past them in a whirlwind of leaves.

As soon as the leaves had settled, Tristan spat on the ground. "Those men are slime," he said. "They should be held to the same code of honor as the rest of us."

"They're not?" Sam asked.

Tristan shook his head. "The Sub Rosa serve the High Commander but are given free rein to execute his orders however they see fit. Their only guiding principle is that the end justifies the means."

"You sound like you disapprove," Sander spoke up.

"I do," Tristan said. "That surprises you?"

Sander shrugged. "To do whatever is necessary is not an uncommon philosophy among men of war."

Braeden, who hadn't cast a friendly look in the Uriel leader's direction since that first night after Luca, turned curious eyes on Sander. "And you? Are you not also a man of war?"

"Aye, among other things," Sander said. "But it is not my philosophy either, and I hope it is not my men's."

Tristan crossed his arms over his chest. "Only moral conduct can produce a moral outcome. It's why rules and law were created, and it's why they ought to be followed."

"Oh, I disagree on that," Sander said. "Sometimes doing the immoral thing is the moral thing to do. I would lie and cheat and steal to protect the ones I love."

Sam and Braeden traded guilty looks, and then their eyes bounced apart. Sam's cheeks burned, and Braeden's face was flushed, too. Damn it, Sander, she thought.

"What do you know of love, old man?" Tristan snarled. "Your wife is dead," Sam winced at the harshness in his voice. His sudden anger had come out of nowhere.

Red crept up Sander's neck, and for once his chronic smile

retreated. "Aye, she's dead," he snapped. "Not a day goes by that I forget it. But my capacity for love did not die at her graveside. I will love her always, and I would cheat the Gods themselves in order to protect our daughter."

"You have a daughter?" Sam asked.

Sander's face softened. "Aye, she's as beautiful as the day is long and as full of fire as her mama."

Tristan passed his reins from hand to hand, and his mouth curved downward. "I didn't know you had a child," he said.

Sander laughed. "A child? Addie is a woman grown, and won't let me forget it."

"Who will care for her while you are . . . absent?" Tristan asked.

"As she reminds me daily, she needs no keeper, though she misses me when I am gone," Sander said. "If I should meet an unfortunate end, I will be sad to leave her alone."

It had not occurred to Sam that Sander was more to anyone than the leader of the Uriel. His grief for his late wife and fatherly love for his daughter did not fit with the image she had formed of him. Unease settled over her, and she questioned, for the first time, whether they had been right to follow the High Commander's orders.

Tristan clucked at his horse. "Come, let's go. I hadn't realized the High Commander was so close behind us. I want to arrive at the Diamond Coast before him."

Kicking her own horse into motion, Sam caught up to Tristan. "It's odd, isn't it?"

"What's odd?"

"You only wrote to the High Commander about Sander's dinner invitation a fortnight ago. If he left shortly after he received your letter, he should be months behind us, not weeks."

"He was probably already headed west. His responsibilities regularly take him away from the fortress." Tristan jerked his thumb at Sander. "I hope your misgivings are not the result of *his* influence."

"I've said nothing," Sander said.

It was true; after the first night, Sander had made no further attempts to persuade her to change her mind about the Uriel. If they talked, it was of small, inconsequential matters. Perhaps he had already shown all his cards and was biding his time. The man was an enigma.

Tristan picked up the pace of his horse, and Sander's by default, and Sam and Braeden fell in line behind them. The forest flew by them till the heavy canopy of trees thinned and finally ended. They were out in the open once more, at the very edge of what Sam thought to be a village, though there was no sign of chimney smoke in the darkening sky.

Tristan's face was a grim mask. "Finchold," he said. "Home sweet home."

CHAPTER 34

$\mathcal{I}$T HAD BEEN more than a decade since Tristan last set foot in Finchold. The village was now abandoned, its human inhabitants replaced by wild ones, the land barren from neglect.

Tristan won his first fight and received his first kiss in Finchold. He stole puff pastries from the baker with his gang of friends, although it couldn't really be called stealing since Master Croft made extra ones just for them. He danced around the Maypole during the Midsummer festival and tugged at Lyndsey's beribboned braids when her back was turned to him. He stood at his brother's side when Danny pledged to cherish and honor his bride for the rest of their lives.

Those were not the memories that replayed in his mind's eye. He did not see the empty, colorless houses, the dried-up waterway, or the sandy road that had lost its shape. Cruel images from the past were superimposed over the present, dark flashes of violence and chaos painting his world red. He saw bodies lying in the street where there were none and heard screaming where there was silence. The stench of death filled his nose and lungs. He thought he would choke with it.

He didn't realize he had fallen to the ground till Sam's hands closed around his shoulders. The world righted itself as Tristan blinked up at him. "What happened?"

Sam sagged backward onto his heels. "You tell me," he said. "You tipped over out of your saddle."

Gods, how embarrassing. But Tristan saw no mockery in Sam's expression, only concern. "I'm fine," he said, pulling himself to his feet.

"You fell off your horse," Sam pointed out. "That's not fine."

"Let it be, Sam," Braeden said from atop his horse. His hat

hung around his neck on a string, and his peculiar eyes pierced into Tristan. In Braeden's unguarded gaze, Tristan could see the same darkness that clouded his own.

"Your concern is flattering but unnecessary," Tristan said, climbing back onto his mare. "Let's find shelter for the night. We'll leave again on the morrow." He didn't want to stay in Finchold any longer than he had to.

The sight of his own house shocked him. From the outside, it looked the same as he always remembered it. The two stories and triangular cross gables were topped by an uneven, sloping roof with slated eaves and a massive chimney. The wood framing of the house was exposed, filled in with beige wattle and daub and tall, narrow windows.

Tristan jumped off his horse and tested the old oak door, which swung open with a slight push. "We'll stay here," he said, ignoring the sick feeling in his stomach. "The stables are in a separate building around back."

"How do you know that?" Sam asked.

"This is the house I grew up in," he said.

Once the horses were settled, Tristan returned to the front of the house. His right foot hovered over the doorway, but he could not make himself enter. Braeden looked at him questioningly. "Sorry," Tristan said. "Give me a moment. You go on ahead."

Sucking air into his lungs, Tristan stepped over the threshold and into the home where he'd spent his formative years. He closed his eyes against the memories that assaulted him. It was no use; he saw blood, so much blood, trickling down pale, pale skin. Human bones that had been licked clean and discarded like the leavings of filleted fish. Flesh riddled with holes where sharp teeth had ripped into it. And then darkness.

He could still hear them in the dark. The screams had faded away till just one remained, and eventually it, too, stopped. The stomp and shuffle of heavy, clawed feet sent vibrations through the walls and floors. Something shattered—glass, by the tinkling sound of it.

"Tristan!" A voice pulled him from far away. "Tristan!"

He took in his surroundings, noting the broken furniture in the front hall and the long dead flowers still in their vase. He made a rueful face. "At least I managed to stay upright this time."

"You look like you've seen a ghost," Sam said, his expression pinched with worry.

"Perhaps I have." He steeled his nerves. "I'll show you to your bedrooms."

He led them to the second floor and opened the door to the first bedroom. Sam threw himself backward onto the four-poster bed—Danny's bed, and for one month, Maira's, too.

"Amazing," Sam sighed. "I haven't slept in a real bed in forever."

Tristan's brother had died in that bed, and his blood still stained the mahogany panels. The sheets had been replaced with fresh ones, though, Tristan had seen to that. He had cleaned everything before he left, scrubbed the floors and walls till his hands blistered and bled.

"Your childhood home is really nice, Tristan," Sam said. "And here I thought you'd grown up a farmer, like Sander."

Life would have been a lot less complicated if he'd been a farmer's son. "My father was Lord of the Manor."

Sam located a pillow and fluffed it behind him, sending a layer of dust into the air. "So we should be calling you Lord Lyons."

Tristan shook his head. "My brother would have taken over Father's title, had he lived. And there's nothing here left to lord over."

Sam's face fell. "I didn't know your brother died. I'm sorry."

Not just his brother; his brother's wife and his parents too. All of Finchold had perished in a single night. Except him. "It was a long time ago." It felt like yesterday.

Tristan tossed the boy a sword. "Sleep with this tonight, and be on guard. Braeden will be in the bedroom beside you and I'll be right down the hall."

"I'll be fine," Sam said, balancing the sword on the bed table beside him. "Goodnight."

Tristan showed Braeden to his room, what had been Tristan's old bedroom, and took the master bedroom for himself and Sander. "You can have the bed," he told the Uriel. He wasn't being kind; he just couldn't sleep in that bed. He wouldn't sleep anywhere underneath this roof. If demons attacked again, this time he'd be ready for them.

"I don't suppose you'd untie my wrists, too?" Sander asked.

"Not a chance."

Sander sat down on the edge of the bed. "It was worth a shot." After a pause, he asked, "Do you want to talk about it?"

"About what?"

"Whatever it is that happened in this house. I know the look of a haunted man."

Tristan leaned against the doorframe. "I'll pass."

"The telling of it releases the toxin, you know. I won't think you weaker for it," Sander said.

Tristan's temper rose. Who was this man to lend his ear without his asking? Perhaps Sander had never been a prisoner before, and Tristan had certainly never before taken one, but he was damned well sure this charade of compassion was not the norm. "Why should I want to talk to *you* about it?"

"I think I'm more likely than most to understand," Sander said. "I left the home my wife and I shared because I couldn't bear to be in it without her. My daughter visits sometimes, to pay her respects, but I haven't gone back since she died."

Tristan sank onto the carpeted floor, his legs suddenly tired. "Look, I know your wife meant a lot to you—"

Sander's eyes grew fierce. "She was my world, Tristan. And when she died, I stopped living. If it weren't for Addie, I'd have given up right then and there."

A heavy weight settled in his gut as old memories resurfaced. "I didn't witness a death or two, Sander. I witnessed a massacre. I don't see why you need me to retell it. The world knows what happened to Finchold."

"Aye, we all heard about Finchold, and Linmoor and Valfort too," Sander said. "But the retelling is for your benefit."

Tristan swallowed. "There's not much to tell." He hesitated, and then the words spilled from his mouth. "It was the dead of night when the demons came. I wasn't asleep because I was fifteen and stupid, and I had it in my head that I was going to sneak out to meet friends." Tristan licked his lips, and continued in strained tones. "Maira—that was my brother's wife—caught me and she brought me downstairs to the dining room so she could give me a proper set down without waking the whole house.

His fingernails bit into his palms. "I heard Danny cry out first." He looked up at Sander. "My brother." He smiled weakly. "Complete shite at fighting. He was always rescuing me from whatever scrape I got myself into and bandaging up my knees and elbows, but he was utter rubbish with a sword. He had no chance, even if he'd kept a knife at his bedside.

"Maira and I rushed upstairs, or tried to. The entire hall was swarming with demons, twenty of them or more. I'd never even seen one before, but Maira had. She asked me if I had a knife, and I produced the one I'd tucked into my trousers. 'They won't die till you cut off their heads,' she told me. 'Remember that.' I told Maira there were too many of them, that there was no way we could win. We needed to leave the house or they would kill us both. She refused. 'I'm going to get Danny,' she said.

"I confess I was a coward. I turned around to go back down the stairs with every intention of leaving. Maira could be a fool if she wanted to; I wanted to survive. But it was too late; the demons were on the first floor of the house, too, and were crawling up the stairs.

"Somehow, Maira and I managed to make it to Danny's bedroom unscathed. We didn't stop to fight; we pushed our way straight through. It didn't matter. Danny was already dead. His corpse lay in the bed he shared with Maira. A hellhound knelt by Danny's side, gnawing at his belly and intestines, grunting and snuffling like a pig.

"Maira grabbed the knife from my hands and ran at the demon. I don't think she'd ever held a knife before except perhaps to clean it, but fear and anger made her strong. She put the weight of her body into the thrust of her knife and drove it straight through the demon's neck.

"That wasn't the end of it though, not by half. Demons poured into the bedroom, attracted by the smell of blood and death. Before I could react, Maira shoved me into a dark closet and closed the door.

"The door had a small keyhole, and I put my eye right up to it. They got Maira, too, eventually, and she died slumped against my closet door. I couldn't see anymore, but I could still hear the demons rip into her.

"I don't know how long I stayed in that closet. I fell asleep at some point, after the screaming had stopped. Daylight filtered through the crack where the closet door met the wall. With some effort, I managed to push the door open and nearly swooned at the sight of Maira's half-eaten carcass.

"The demons were all gone when I emerged from the closet. We had a large household, and none of my family or any of the servants had been spared. The dead were strewn about the house—a few demons, but mostly humans—and their faces and bodies were so mauled that I couldn't identify them.

"I was in shock, I think, but I had the sense to leave my house and go for help. But all of Finchold was much the same. Every home looked like mine, and dead bodies littered the street. The vultures had already come calling, gorging themselves with the demons' leftovers.

"I stayed in my house another week before hunger forced me to leave. There was no food here, and the waterway was tainted with blood and excrement. So I packed up a few spare changes of clothes and my father's sword and what little money I could scrounge up, and I left. This is the first time I've been back."

His story finished, Tristan looked over at Sander to gauge his reaction. The Uriel was silent, pity absent from his gaze. If he had to judge Sander's expression, he'd characterize it as angry. "Say something," Tristan said.

"How did you end up joining the Paladins, after that?" Sander asked.

"The High Commander found me hiding in an alcove just east of Luca. He fed me and brought me back with him to Heartwine. He took me under his wing and saw that I received proper training. He has a knack for guessing at gifts, and he saw that I had talent for the sword."

"That's not what I meant," Sander said. His voice shook with fury. "Where were the Paladins on the night Finchold was attacked? Where were they when Linmoor and Valfort were decimated?"

"I don't know," Tristan said. "Other cities were attacked that night."

"So it was decided that Finchold, Linmoor, and Valfort weren't worth the effort? Why?"

"I don't know," Tristan repeated, gritting his teeth. "I was a boy when it happened, and the Paladins afforded me the opportunity to avenge my family. It was enough."

"You're a man now," Sander said coldly. "It's time to open your eyes and grow up."

———

Tristan sat upright against the wall of his father's bedroom, his head bobbing up and down as he fought to stay awake. He would not surrender to sleep in this house, no matter how hard it pulled at him.

Despite his best efforts, his eyelids dragged shut. His mind drifted, lulled by the sound of Sander's soft snores, and gradually shapes formed in the space behind his eyes. Nightmares from his past: a glistening black snout with serrated teeth, a body with its skin peeled back like an orange, a glowing keyhole that flared to red and then black.

The banging at the door jarred him out of his semi-slumber. One of his trainees? No, the banging was too hard and constant, not at all like a knock. Tristan scrambled to his feet and drew his sword. A fissure ran down the center of the wood panel and then the door splintered apart.

Scraps of wood dangled from three sharp-pointed horns protruding from a bony frill that fanned out at the back of a long, narrow skull. A fourth, shorter horn jutted from the top of a predator's beak. The colossal head was attached to a stout, silver-brown body, creased with thick folds of skin.

The demon shook off remnants of door from its horns and raised its head, staring at Tristan with yellow, reptilian eyes. It pawed the floor with a stumpy, three-toed foot and charged, bowling Tristan over. His sword found its soft underbelly and he dragged the blade through to its neck. Blood and viscera spilled from the gaping split, drenching him with putrid fluid. Even without its innards, the demon must have weighed half a ton, and he had to wriggle out from underneath it.

"Untie me," Sander said. "Untie me now!"

More demons had poured into the bedroom, but not so many that Tristan couldn't handle it alone. "Not likely," he said to Sander, and carved through the nearest beast.

The calm of battle fell over Tristan and he danced with his sword to music only he could hear. A fine red mist followed his movements, saturating the air with the smell of death, none of it human. He slashed and sliced with brutal efficiency. He would see them all dead.

His blade was as much a part of him as an arm or a leg. He had long been beyond sword forms or practiced techniques; his weapon and body moved in complete concert. He killed with a single driving thought: They won't die till you cut off their heads. He slit through throats with the precision of a surgeon. Heads rolled at his feet.

Tristan ran his sword through the last of them and bent over to clean his blade. "Tristan!" Sander yelled. The Uriel was no longer on the bed but backed against it, his leg muscles tensed. "The door!"

Tristan raised his sword, turned towards the door—and froze. The demon wore Maira's face.

Looking into familiar, gold-flecked eyes, Tristan was transported to the past. In front of him, Maira smoothed a stray curl away from her pointed, elfin face—she'd tried a dozen different hair oils, but nothing could tame her unruly locks—and her stern frown turned to a reluctant smile. It was always that way with Maira; she would scold him for his latest misdeed, and he would ply her with ridiculous flattery or a clever joke, and she couldn't stay mad at him. She mothered him because his real mother wasn't much of one and Danny was too busy learning to be Lord of the Manor to pay him much mind. Tristan loved her; some days he thought he loved her more than did Danny.

Maira's smile turned playful and she beckoned with her hand, like she did every Midsummer's festival. He would put his hand in hers and they would dance, just once, twirling and leaping and laughing hysterically. She beckoned again and Tristan reached towards her, eager to claim his song.

He noticed, belatedly, that his outstretched hand held a sword.

What was he doing with a sword? He dropped it at once. Maira gave him enough grief about sleeping in bed with the thing; he wasn't about to dance with it.

Fleetingly, an image of an eyeless face soaked in blood flitted across his vision. No! A steel wall in his mind slammed shut, and it was just his Maira again, brimming with a bright energy that couldn't be bottled.

Danny called his name. Not now, Danny, I'm dancing with your wife. Danny's voice grew more urgent. Stop shouting, Danny . . . no, not Danny . . . another man's voice . . . Sander.

The heel of a sideways-turned foot clipped Maira's chin and her head swung backwards. Her fingers slipped free from his grip. Not fingers—hooked talons as long as his forearm.

"Whoever you think she is, it's not her," Sander said. His breathing was uneven from the effort of his kick. "Pick up your sword." He shook his head in disgust when Tristan did nothing. Tristan couldn't; he was caught halfway between ten years ago and today.

Maira twisted her neck with an audible crunch, and her smiling face was upright once more. "Oh for the Gods' sake," Sander muttered. "Untie me! Untie me if you won't kill it yourself."

A jolt of pain laced through Tristan's side, and he looked down in surprise. Bright red pooled through his tunic. He lifted up the fabric and his blood gushed forth from three deep punctures. She'd stabbed him.

Maira lunged for him, her talons extended. Tristan stood mutely still, watching her clawed hand fly toward him. Sander bumped him hard with his shoulder, and the talons narrowly missed their mark.

The Uriel jumped, and his leg sailed through the air like the blade of an axe. His aim was true and Maira fell to the floor with a screech. Sander stumbled to his knees, his balance thrown without the use of his hands. He stood up awkwardly and then rammed his foot into her windpipes, refusing to let up. "Look at it!" Sander demanded, his chest heaving. "It isn't her."

Reality began to penetrate the cobwebs in Tristan's brain. The broken bird on the floor wasn't Maira. Its face and hair were hers, but its breast and belly were feathered with purple plumage.

Midnight black wings extended out from underneath its back, blanketing the carpet. Thin, scaly legs ended in webbed feet with a clawed hind toe.

Tristan retrieved his sword from the floor. Blood dripped onto the hilt from cuts at his wrists that he hadn't noticed were there. He closed the distance to the demon and swung his sword.

Those gold-flecked eyes held him, and the edge of his sword stopped a hair's breadth away from the demon's neck. The hesitation was enough. The demon knocked the blade away with its wing and sent Tristan sprawling.

Sander kicked the hilt of the sword towards Tristan and crouched beside him. "Who is she?" he asked.

"Maira," Tristan said. "I can't do it." He shook his head helplessly. "I know it's not really her, but—"

"Let me," Sander said. "Untie me and I'll end it."

"You know I can't."

Frustration colored Sander's words. "You can tie me up again when it's dead. I swear to it."

Tristan looked at the man who had very likely saved his life, and made his decision. "Don't make me regret this," he warned, and cut through Sander's binds.

Sander flexed his wrists. "Weapon?" Tristan pulled out a long dagger from his belt and handed it to him.

"That'll do," the Uriel said. "That'll do just fine."

CHAPTER 35

OWN THE HALLWAY, in the room that once belonged to Tristan's brother, Sam had scarcely closed her eyes when she sensed a presence by her bed. "Go away. I'm sleeping."

"I can promise you a nightmare," Braeden said.

Her lids cracked open. He was a shadowy form in the dark of the room, half his face lit by a pale moonbeam. "What do you mean?"

He shivered visibly. "Can you not feel them?"

"Stop being cryptic. Do you mean demons?"

Braeden sat on the edge of the four-poster bed, the mattress squeaking under his weight. "Aye. They're coming, and soon. They'll want you."

So it was to be a repeat of the battle in the Elurra Mountains; she would again have a target on her back. "How do you know?" she had to ask.

"I think," Braeden said, barely above a hush, "it's because my demon wants you, too."

Only now did Sam notice the tightness of his jaw, the strain in his wild eyes. His fingers dug into his hands so hard that his nails drew blood. "Braeden!" she exclaimed, and took his hands in hers. Gently, she uncurled his fists and soothed the crescent nail marks.

He trembled under her fingers. "You shouldn't touch me."

She dropped his hands, hurt. "Sorry."

"I meant not when I'm like—" he cut off, bristling. "They're here." He rose to his feet, drawing a sword from the scabbard on his back.

Sam pushed off her covers and lit the unused candle at her bedside, and almost wished she hadn't. A demon loomed in the doorway, a monstrous blend of horse and man. Equine from its hooves to its withers, it had a human torso and head, with another head—a horse's head—growing out of its back.

"It's mine," she and Braeden said in unison.

Sam said thoughtfully, "It has two heads, you know. Shall we share?"

Braeden's lips curved into an unholy grin. "Gladly," he said, and then his blade was in its human throat. Sam grabbed the sword Tristan had lent her and ran around to the demon's back. The horse head screamed as she hacked through its neck from its vertebrae. Over the demon's headless body, she and Braeden smiled grimly.

The creature was not the last of the demons—far from it. Outside the bedroom, the hallway teemed with them, a sea of monsters. The floor beneath them quaked at the heavy tread of their feet. Braeden squeezed her shoulder, and together they walked into bedlam.

It was impossible to say whether the demons targeted her more than they did Braeden. He was at her back at all times, and their attackers had to contend with them both. Sam and Braeden whipped around each other in a deadly whirlwind of steel, slaying anything within reach.

Sam was beginning to think she wasn't right in the head. Though she knew their lives were in peril, she felt, for whatever reason, safe. Perhaps she had improved her fighting skills, or perhaps it was the perfect synchronization of her sword with Braeden's. Or maybe, a snide voice whispered, it was simply having Braeden in close contact. She silenced the voice and let her weapon flow with his.

They gradually advanced down the long hallway, slowed by the furious onslaught of demons. At the midway point, Sam could see that the door to Tristan's bedroom was in shambles. A piece of door fell down, and a man walked out.

Sander.

Cold fear raced through her veins. Sander's wrists were unbound, and in his hand he clutched a long knife. The blade was crimson from tip to grip. Oh Gods, she thought. Tristan.

Her fear turned to fury and fueled her. She broke away from Braeden, killing the demons in her path without conscious effort.

When she reached Sander, she would cut him to ribbons for whatever he had done to Tristan. Her heart ached, but she brushed it aside. She couldn't let emotion weaken her, not when she had the leader of the Uriel to kill.

Then Tristan stepped out from behind Sander, and Sam's rage instantly became relief. His tunic was torn and bloody, and a makeshift bandage peeked out from behind the ripped fabric, but he moved without noticeable pain. Her knees sagged as the fire of her fury drained out of her.

"Sam, pay attention!" Tristan snapped.

She was so happy to see him alive she didn't even roll her eyes at his rebuke. She did, however, raise her eyebrows at Sander. "What's *he* doing free?" she asked, after thrusting her sword into the nearest demon's gullet.

"I've been given a temporary reprieve," Sander said. He wiped his knife against his breeches and adjusted his thumb over the spine. "If it's all the same to you, I'll fight."

"Have at it," Tristan said with a wry twist of his mouth. His sword was unsheathed, and, by the looks of it, had already been well-used this night.

Sander wasted no more time and hacked into the demons that encircled them. He dodged snapping jaws and swiping claws, uncommonly spry for a man of his advanced years. He made short work of the demons, but there was no finesse, no poetry to his movements. Sam felt foolishly disappointed.

"He's good," she commented, "but not as good as Braeden."

"It's not his weapon," Tristan said.

"Maybe not," Sam said. "I guess I expected more."

"There's only one High Commander," Tristan said. "I don't think Sander's men follow him for his ability to fight."

"Why, then?"

Tristan slashed at a demon that had drawn too near. "You and I were born to fight," he said, decapitating the offending demon as emphatic proof. "That man was born to lead."

"I would never follow a man weaker than I," Sam declared.

"Nor I, but strength isn't only physical," Tristan said. A flush of color crept into his cheeks. "And sometimes even those of us who are strong can be weak."

Sam didn't know where his embarrassment came from, but Tristan quickly shrugged it off. He lifted his sword elbow to his shoulder and pointed with the blade. "Finish them."

Sam didn't need to be told twice. She leaped into the fray, cleaving through demon flesh. A demon butted her with fluted horns, catching her under her rib cage and knocking the breath clean out of her. Panting, she tightened her abdominal muscles against the pain and struck with her sword, separating one horn from its skull, and then the other. Her third strike separated its head from the thick trunk of its neck.

The demons kept coming, from the stairs above and below, and from the bedrooms. "Close the windows!" Tristan shouted.

Sam shifted course and ducked back into a bedroom—the one she'd so recently been asleep in. The window was open wide, letting in more than just the cold. Sam moved to shut it, but not before a winged lynx flew in, squeezing its muscular feline body through the narrow opening. It landed in the bedroom on padded paws larger than a human hand and spread its immense wings, black and webbed like a bat's. Its gray coat was dappled with rust-colored spots, and pale fur lined its chest, belly, and the inside of its long legs. Dark stripes decorated its forehead and a white ruff encircled its neck in a thick collar.

The lynx beat its wings once, twice. The hard edge of its right wing bumped the nightstand beside the bed, where Sam had earlier lit a tallow candle. The candle wobbled precariously and then toppled over onto the floor and rolled under the nightstand.

That's not good, Sam thought just as a tongue of flame licked up the side of the nightstand. "Shite," she swore, backing away. The lynx demon followed her, then screeched as its wing encountered the flames. It beat its wings madly, smashing the nightstand into the wall where it burst into flaming splinters. The entire room was soon aflame.

Sam ducked out of the room while the demon shrieked behind her. "Fire!" she yelled, though her warning was unnecessary. Smoke was already filling the hallway. Within moments, flames were spreading across the ceiling and spilling down the walls in bursts of orange and red. Oppressive heat enveloped her.

"We need to get out of here *now*," she heard Sander say from somewhere amid the confusion of smoke and fighting.

"But the demons!" Sam cried, spotting Sander in the hallway standing in the middle of a pile of disintegrating demon corpses.

"Will keep. You won't," Sander said. "We haven't got long till escape is no longer an option.

"Do as he says." Tristan ordered from somewhere in the smoke behind Sander. "Kill if you have to, but the priority is getting out."

Sam fumbled blindly towards the stairs, the smoke thickening till she could no longer see her own hand in front of her. Wheezing and coughing and snorting, most of it not human, accompanied her slow progress down the hall. Jagged nails scratched at her face, and she gasped at the sharp sting. Liquid rolled down her cheek. Probably her blood.

Something grabbed her wrist, and she spun around, prepared to strike. "It's me," Braeden said. "Can you see?"

"Not a thing. Can you?"

"Well enough." Glowing red orbs cut through the fog like beacons—his eyes, Sam realized. Braeden captured her hand in his. Sam said nothing, ceding to the comfort that his nearness brought her.

Braeden guided her through the hallway and down the stairs, his hand never leaving hers even as he fought off demon assailants. His words guided her, too. "Strike now, to your left."

And then miraculously, they were outside, the cool air a heady balm. Sam peered into the night. "Where are Tristan and Sander?"

"They must still be inside."

Sam cursed. Fire billowed out of the windows and a malevolent cloud of black smoke cloaked the upper stories of the house. "If I could *see* anything in there—"

"Look!" said Braeden. A man staggered out of the flaming doorway, another man draped across his shoulders. Once again, the icy fingers of fear held her heart in its grasp. As Sander approached, she could see Tristan's arms hung limply from their sockets.

"He's fine," Sander said, stumbling towards them. "A bit too much smoke, but he'll come around. Help me put him down."

Braeden jumped to Sander's aid, transferring Tristan's weight before setting him down on the ground.

Sander knelt beside him and gently slapped his cheeks. Tristan shuddered and his chest heaved with great racking coughs. When his coughing subsided, he groaned, and his eyes fluttered open. "Gods damn it," he gasped, looking at Sander. "That's twice in one night you've saved my life."

"You're welcome," Sander said, grinning. He patted Tristan's hand. "Now you rest easy while we take care of the demons that are left."

Tristan scowled, and Sam had to bite back a smile. "I'll guard him," she offered, and he actually growled at her.

"Good idea," Sander said approvingly. He nodded at Braeden. "After you."

They slew demons by the light of the roaring inferno till the first rays of the sun broke the horizon. Braeden beheaded the last of the demons, and Sam sat down beside Tristan with a tired sigh. Together, they watched the fire eat away at the house to the frame, and eventually that burned, too, and nothing was left but smoldering ashes.

"I'm sorry about your house," Sam said.

"I hated that house," Tristan said. "Good riddance, I say." He turned his face away, not fully concealing the wetness of his eyes.

Sam's hand hovered over his, and then remembering herself, she placed it instead on his shoulder. To her surprise, he leaned into it. "Good riddance," Tristan whispered again, this time to himself.

CHAPTER 36

𝔗HOUGH TRISTAN'S FAMILY home had burned to the ground, the stable and horses were unharmed—thank the Gods for small favors. Sam suggested they wait a day so Tristan could recover before departing Finchold, but he insisted he was well enough to ride. He conceded to an hour of rest—two hours at the most—and then they would leave.

The matter of Sander, however, still needed to be settled. Sam had expected him to bolt as soon as the last demon was slain, but he stayed true to his word. Secretly, part of her wished Sander *had* broken his promise; his presence unnerved her. She couldn't understand him: why he'd let them abduct him without protest, why he'd helped them, why he'd saved Tristan's life. There was no other explanation for it other than that he was, well, good. And yet the High Commander condemned Sander as a dangerous man, and she was forced to entrust him with her most dangerous secret. It made her uneasy.

Sander crossed the field from the stables with his stallion and passed the reins to Braeden. He dropped to his haunches in front of Tristan, who was resting against a tree. The Uriel held his wrists out to him, palms up. "What are you doing?" Tristan asked.

"Keeping my promise," Sander said. "You can tie me back up. Although, I'd appreciate it if you would undo my binds during the next demon attack. Doing nothing is damned annoying."

Tristan stared at the brown wrists for a long time. The skin was red and irritated where rope had rubbed it raw. "No," Tristan said.

Sander sighed. "You won't consider it?"

Tristan shook his head. "I won't bind you again. I want you to leave."

Sander cocked his head. "Leave?"

"Yes, leave. Go. Go back to your Uriel."

"You're letting me go?" Sander said slowly. "Why?"

Tristan wouldn't meet his eyes. "You saved my life. Twice. It's not something I take lightly."

Sam looked between the two men in disbelief. True, Tristan was indebted to the man, but still . . . "What about the High Commander's orders?" Sam asked.

Tristan scrubbed at his face. "I think he made a mistake." Sam gaped at him, and even Braeden seemed startled by his declaration. "The High Commander is human, too."

Tristan and Sander stared at each other for several moments. Finally, Sander stood and extended his hand to Tristan. "You're a good man, Paladin."

Tristan hesitated, and then grasped the Uriel's hand with his own, allowing Sander to pull him to his feet. "You too, Uriel. Now go, before I change my mind."

Sander dipped his head, and then vaulted onto his horse. "I'll take the reins now." Braeden surrendered them to him wordlessly. "It's a courageous decision to question authority," Sander said, "and one that's seldom rewarded. If you should find yourselves in trouble—any of you—come to Luca. The Uriel always have room for courageous men." He added, almost as an afterthought, "Or women."

Knowing his last remark was directed at her, Sam studiously avoided Sander's gaze. She hoped Tristan didn't read too much into the careless comment, while a small, secret part of her wondered if Sander meant it.

"Thank you," Tristan said, oblivious. "The gesture is appreciated but unnecessary. My trust in you does not extend to your organization. I fear the Paladins and Uriel will never ally."

"No?" Sander asked pleasantly. "And what will you tell your High Commander?"

"That I owe you my life, and should he want you recaptured, he'll need to assign another Paladin to the task. That's all I can promise you."

A gust of wind lifted Sander's hair from his forehead "That's enough, for now." He gave them a nod, and then winked. "Till next time."

"There will be no next time," Tristan said. "Not for me."

Sander chuckled. "I'll miss you, Paladin. You too, Sam, Braeden." He winked again, and then he was gone, his stallion streaking down the dusty road.

They stood watching him go till not even the flank of his horse was in sight. Tristan swore softly and covered his face with his hands. He waved off Sam and Braeden's inquisitive looks. "It's nothing. Let's saddle up the horses and go."

"Will it be all right?" Sam asked, once they were seated on their mounts.

"The High Commander is harsh, but fair," Tristan said. "He will listen to what I have to say."

"And if he disagrees?" Braeden asked. Smoke and flame reflected in his clear eyes. "What will you have us do?"

"Us?" Tristan shook his head. "There is no 'us', not in this. It was my life that was saved, and I who am obligated to spare him. You have no such compunction."

"But we do," Sam said earnestly. "We would have been lost without you." Braeden glanced at her and then cast his eyes downward at his horse's neck.

Tristan shifted in his saddle, clearly made uncomfortable by her comment. "Nevertheless," he said, "I have known the High Commander a good many years, as well as any man can know him, and he knows me. He knows where my loyalties lie, and he trusts me. I trust him in turn."

"How long will it take him to discover Sander's gone?" Sam asked.

"Not long," Tristan said. "Not long at all."

Not long came six days later in the ghost town of Linmoor. Linmoor, an expanse of uncultivated drab lands with stretches of swamp and quicksand that was now bereft of people, was dreary and foreboding. A lone man in a dark cloak waited for them by a thicket of alders. At first, Sam thought he was the same man who had met them in Woodmaple Forest, but his complexion was swarthier, his nose more aquiline. He displayed his hand against his hip, curling his pointer and middle fingers to his thumb. As he drew closer, boots sloshing through mud, Sam could see a sneer on his face.

"Lyons." The man said Tristan's name like a curse.

"Guenther," Tristan said in a matching tone. "Dare I ask the purpose of your visit?"

"Oh, I think you know why I'm here," Guenther said. "Sander Branimir has returned to Luca."

"Has he now?"

"Don't play dumb, Lyons. The whole of Luca knows you released him. You can thank your friend Sander for that."

"He's not my friend," Tristan said between clenched teeth. "The High Commander—does he know?"

Guenther pulled a letter from a pocket in his cloak. "He knows. This is for you." He shoved the note at Tristan.

Tristan traced his finger over the design of the wax seal holding the letter shut. "From the High Commander?" Tristan asked. Guenther nodded.

Tristan broke the seal and unfolded the parchment. He read the letter, shook his head, and then read it again. "No," he said, white-faced. "No, this isn't from him."

"It is," Guenther said. "You know that seal as well as I. You have one week." He didn't give them the courtesy of bowing before trudging away.

"What does it say?" Sam asked.

Tristan crumpled the letter in his fist. "We have one week to recapture Sander," he said, "or my life is forfeit."

"What?" Sam whispered, aghast.

"The High Commander offers you and Braeden amnesty," Tristan continued, his voice shaking—with anger, Sam thought, and something else. "You cannot be blamed for my treachery, and if I should fail to obey his edict, he will welcome you back with open arms. But if you should stay by my side—" Tristan closed his eyes and took a deep breath. "If you stay by my side, he will name you traitors, too."

"If we succeed in taking Sander back," Braeden asked, "all three of us, what will happen?"

"Nothing, for you," Tristan said. "My life will be spared, but recapturing Sander would be my last act as Paladin. The High Commander has stripped me of my title."

Stunned, Sam's mouth dropped open. The only coherent sound she could make was, "Huh?"

"You heard me." He laughed incredulously. "I'm no longer a Paladin."

Her incoherence faded and a deluge of words rushed out. "But what you said before, about the High Commander listening to you, about your mutual trust, the years you've known each other . . ."

"I know what I said!" Tristan snapped. "He's already made this pronouncement publicly. Every Paladin knows or will soon know that I've been banished. He won't go back on it, not now. That would be tantamount to openly admitting he erred in his judgment, and he won't do that, not even for me."

Sam refused to believe that the High Commander could not be swayed. "Maybe if you just get Sander back—"

"No," Tristan said. "Sander is not the only man who keeps his promises. Whatever else I might think of him or the Uriel, I am in his debt. I cannot in good conscience bring Sander before the High Commander in chains when I can't predict the outcome. I will not be responsible for his death."

"What then?" Braeden asked. "You said our lives would be forfeit, but what does that mean?"

"My life, not yours," Tristan said. "Your lives are only forfeit if you choose not to leave. I imagine it means he'll put a price on my head."

"So what will you do? Hide?" Braeden asked.

"There's no hiding from the High Commander," Tristan said bitterly. "I never thought I'd have to."

"So don't," Sam said. "Confront him! Make him understand."

Tristan slumped in his saddle, despair written across his face. Sam had never seen him look so utterly hopeless. "What makes you think he'll believe me? I would have though the ten years I spent in his company would have afforded me the benefit of the doubt."

Sam drew herself up. "We'll support you," she said. "Braeden and I, we'll confront the High Commander with you."

Tristan turned his horse so he could stare her full in the face. His gaze was furious. "Don't be a fool, Sam. That's signing your own death warrants." He gestured at Braeden. "Talk some sense into him. The Gods know he's never listened to me before." He smirked without humor. "And now neither of you have to. Perhaps they'll assign Sagar as your new mentor. He showed a keen interest in overseeing Sam's corruption."

Suddenly, Sam was mad. Irate, even. She looked at Tristan with a glare that was every bit as furious as his. "How dare you," she seethed. "How dare you presume so little of us. *I* don't want Sagar as my mentor. I want *you*. I don't care if you are Paladin Lyons or just plain Tristan. You're the only man in this whole forsaken kingdom who can beat me with a sword."

"Speaking of presumptuous," Tristan murmured.

She narrowed her eyes to slits. "Shut up, you. You're part of the reason I became a Paladin in the first place. Sander might have saved your life, but you saved mine."

Tristan blinked. "When did I save your life?"

Shite! Of course he wouldn't remember his gallant rescue of her in Haywood's forest. She backpedaled quickly. "Never you mind. The point is we aren't going to desert you. Right, Braeden?"

"I go where you go," he said simply.

It wasn't the answer she'd expected—and she didn't have the luxury of thinking on it right then—but it would do for now. Sam crossed her arms over her chest. "So there you have it. We aren't leaving."

Tristan threw up his arms in exasperation. "Suicidal fools, the both of you." After a moment, he added quietly, "Thank you."

Sam had reached her limit on sentimentality. "Think nothing of it," she said. "What now, Tristan?"

Tristan straightened his shoulders and said with renewed steel, "We continue on to the Diamond Coast. I have a few words to say to the High Commander."

Sam shook her head. "Not you, *we*," she said. "*We* have a few words to say to the High Commander."

CHAPTER 37

*T*HE WIND TRIED to wrest Sam's cloak from her shoulders as she stole her first glimpse of the legendary Diamond Coast. A thousand years ago, Hartwin the Brave and the Twelve had fought and won on this very land, bringing the Age of Shadows to an end. They had sealed the worst of the demons away with magic they'd learned from the Gods. And thus had begun the Paladins' legacy.

In the great tomes in her father's library, Sam had read that long before man or demon walked the earth, the Diamond Coast had been dominated by a massive volcano. One day, the earth moved and the volcano erupted with such force that the entire mountain upturned and crumbled, burying itself in layers of ash and molten rock.

Over the millennia, the lava hardened and the wind swept the ash away, leaving behind smooth and square-topped hills the color of onyx. Deposits of blue-black rock rose in stacks from the basaltic ground and surrounding sea, glittering with diamonds. A man could spend a day harvesting the gems and make a lifetime's fortune. But few would risk the journey to come so far west; the Diamond Coast was uninhabitable, with no vegetation or fresh water for many miles. The nearest village was more than three leagues away.

Tristan shielded his eyes with his hand, bracing against the wind. "There are others afoot."

"People?" Sam peered into the distance, squinting. "I don't see anybody."

"There, ahead," he said, pointing. "Do you see that heap of rocks by the beach?" Sam followed his finger to a cobbled pyramid of rusted-over granite. "That's a shelter, if a crude one."

She gulped. "Do you think the High Commander is here?"

"Not yet," Tristan said. "We made good time after Sander left. We must be at least a few days ahead of him."

"So who is there now?" she asked.

"I don't know," Tristan said, "but we'll find out soon enough."

The loose, slippery rock near the beach was treacherous to the horses, so Sam, Braeden, and Tristan tethered their mounts to stakes in the ground and scrambled towards the shelter on foot. A gap in the rock pyramid made for a doorway just wide enough for one person. Tristan went first to make sure it was safe. "You can come in!" he called out. "No one is here."

"After you," Braeden said to Sam, and she squeezed her way through the narrow entry. Braeden followed behind her.

The inside was dark but airy. Light crept in through the spaces between the rocks, creating a speckled mosaic on the ground. A copper pot was strung over a small fire pit and rumpled blankets lined the perimeter of the shelter.

Tristan ran his thumb along the bottom of the fire pit. The pad of his thumb came back dusted with black coal. "Someone's been here recently."

"Aye, we have."

Sam jumped at the sound of the new voice. No, not new—she recognized that deep, rumbling timbre.

"Sagar," Tristan said. His expression was blank; only his rigid posture betrayed his shock.

The Paladin wedged his broad shoulders through the tight entrance and stepped into the shelter. "Lyons," Sagar said coldly. Acknowledging them separately, he said, "Braeden, Sam. I see there are only three of you."

"Just us three," Tristan confirmed, his mouth pinched into a tight line.

"And where is Sander Branimir?"

Tristan shrugged. "In Luca, perhaps? We have not been in recent contact."

Sander regarded him with a mixture of resignation and regret. "Did you even make an effort?" he asked, rubbing a hand over his face.

"To recapture him? Sagar, the man saved my life. If you would only listen—"

"I have my orders," Sagar said stiffly. "And unlike you, I will follow them, however distasteful I find them."

"Orders?" Tristan asked. "What orders?"

Sagar sighed and put his fist to the hollow between his brows. "The High Commander gave you one week to retrieve Sander. Tristan, it's been a fortnight. What did you expect when you showed up here without him? You know what I've been ordered to do."

Tristan's laughter held an edge of bitterness. "What, the High Commander couldn't be bothered to do it himself? *You're* to be my executioner?" He shook his head in disbelief. "I won't give up without a fight, and you haven't a prayer of defeating me."

Sagar flushed a dull, angry red, his cheeks matching the shade of his beard. "I'm well aware who the superior swordsman is between us, Lyons. But I didn't come to the Diamond Coast alone." He turned to Sam and Braeden. "If you two leave now, the High Commander will forgive you everything." When they didn't move, he added, more sharply, "Don't throw your futures away out of some misguided notion of friendship."

"Is that what you did, Paladin?" Sam asked, enraged on Tristan's behalf. She marched right up to the Paladin, shoving her face in front of his. "Throw however many years of friendship away because of one man's order? And in the time you've known Tristan, has he ever been disloyal or anything less than a Paladin should be? Has he?"

Sagar's face grew darker. "D'you think I want to do this? I was perfectly happy in Catania, minding my own business. Then out of nowhere, the High Commander sends me a missive ordering me to the Diamond Coast. No explanation, but it's the High Commander, so I go. Then, I get here, and I'm told that Lyons is colluding with the enemy, and I'm to see him punished for it. Have you *seen* Tristan with a sword? I've no wish to die."

"Sagar?" a man's voice called out. "Sagar? Are you in there?"

"Aye, I've got Lyons here, too!" he shouted back. Sam couldn't hear the man's muffled response.

Sagar returned his attention to Sam and Braeden. "This is your last chance," he warned them. "No? Then the grace period is over. I hope your friendship warms your graves at night." With that parting remark, he unsheathed his sword and backed slowly out of the shelter.

A tense silence filled the small room. Tristan's face was set in stone. "You should go," he said. "They'll still forgive you if you leave now."

"I already told you, we're not going anywhere," Sam said.

"You might die out there," Tristan said. "Fighting a man—fighting a Paladin—is nothing like fighting a demon."

Sam drew her sword from its scabbard. She grinned wickedly. "Don't worry. I learned from the best."

A long knife slipped into Braeden's right hand and he undid the ties of his robe with the other, letting the empty sleeves flutter to his waist. He slid the dagger into his heart, all the way to the hilt, and pulled it out with a grimace. His crimson eyes burned bright.

"Can't say I didn't try," Tristan said, shaking his head. He lifted his own sword from his hip, a long, two-handed claymore. "I'll go first. Hold your weapons out in front of you as you leave. We don't know what's waiting for us on the other side. Be ready for anything."

They exited the shelter single file, Tristan at the head. Four paladins, weapons at the ready, waited for them. Only one was a stranger to Sam: an enormous giant of a man with a shaved head and a gold hoop earring dangling from his left ear. She had no trouble placing the other two men: Paladin Parsall and Paladin Boyle from Westergo. While Sagar may have been drafted to carry out the High Commander's threat, Sam suspected Parsall and Boyle had volunteered for the opportunity.

"Oh, good," Tristan said. "There are only four of you. For a moment, I was worried."

"There are four of us and three of you," Boyle sneered. "You're outnumbered. I did warn you you'd get your comeuppance one day. And I'm going to be the one to hand it to you."

A snort of air escaped through his nose. "That's as likely to happen as the sun falling out of the sky. You couldn't touch a hair on my head if you tried."

Boyle scowled and bent his front knee. "You have an inflated ego, Lyons. Allow me to cut it down to size." He charged, aiming straight for Tristan's heart.

Sam took that as her cue. "The big one's mine," she snarled, and ran at him with her sword.

The giant met her sword with a heavy battle axe, and her teeth chattered as the vibration ran up her arm. The giant laughed. "I am a god, little boy. You will die today."

Oh, please. Sam flicked her sword against his arm. Red spilled from a shallow cut. "Some god," she taunted. "You bleed like a man."

The giant bared his teeth and swung his axe. She danced out of range, just barely. He was unnaturally quick for a man of his size, and his axe whooshed through the air before she had recovered from his first swing. She threw up her sword to block the axe from plowing into her neck. The impact of his weapon against hers knocked the blade from her hands, sending it spinning to the ground.

Shite. She reached for her sword, but he stepped on the flat of the blade, pinning it beneath him. She tugged at the handle, but he was too heavy. He laughed again. "Over so soon. How disappointing."

Sam grabbed a knife from her belt and jabbed it into the top of his foot. He howled, and then the weight on the blade was gone. She snatched up her sword and thrust, catching him under his armpit. It wasn't a killing blow, but it would hurt.

Enraged, the giant roared and drove his fist into her belly. Sam doubled over in pain, holding onto her sword for balance. He elbowed her in the face, hard. A searing pain spread across her cheek and dark spots bloomed across her vision.

His axe cleaved through the air. She ducked, the bit slicing through strands of her hair. Too close for comfort. She shifted onto her toes and attacked, nicking his side. She had to stay on the offensive for as long as she could; he was too strong for her to parry his ripostes. Every time he struck first, it was a battle just to hold on to her weapon.

Sweat dripped from every pore, and her tunic clung to her like a second skin. Dimly, Sam wondered how Braeden and Tristan were faring with their opponents, but she had no time to worry about them as the giant took advantage of even that momentary distraction and struck her across the knuckles with the knob of his axe. Bone crunched, and her blade dropped to her feet. He kicked it out of the way, sending the sword skittering across the ground and out of reach. "No weapon, little boy," he growled. "You're mine now." He raised his axe high above his shoulders, ready to deliver the final blow.

Sam threw her knife into his throat. "You forgot my other weapon," she said, watching the blood gurgle from his mouth. His axe fell harmlessly from his grip, and he sank to his knees, clutching at the blade in his neck. He shot her a final, hateful glare, and then his eyes glazed over with death.

Sam picked up her discarded sword and poked him with it to make sure he was dead. He fell to his side, unmoving, his blood dripping onto the cold rock.

Sam went down on all fours and vomited. Tristan had been right: fighting a man was nothing like fighting a demon. And killing a man . . . She felt no glory, only deep self-disgust. When she had traded in her silk gowns for a sword, this was not what she had imagined.

After she recovered enough to stand, she surveyed the battlefield. Paladin Boyle was dead, and Paladin Parsall lay nursing a fatal wound. Braeden had split him open from chest to naval, and Parsall was holding his own intestines in his hands. Sagar was at the end of Tristan's sword, begging for his life.

"Please, Tristan, have mercy," he sobbed. He was bleeding from several places, and as he shook his head back and forth, Sam could see he was missing an ear. Had anything remained in her stomach, she would have retched.

Tristan's voice was ice. "Like you showed mercy on me, *friend*?"

Sagar's sobs turned into hysterical wailing. "Please, Tristan, please. Oh Gods, I don't want to die."

Sam staggered to her feet. "Let him go, Tristan."

Tristan's gaze didn't leave Sagar. "Why should I? He would have killed us all if he were halfway decent with a sword."

"Because if you kill him, then we're the monsters that they are," Braeden said softly. He crouched beside Paladin Parsall and stared into his pain-filled eyes. "May the Gods have mercy on your soul," he said, and slit the Paladin's throat.

"Fine," Tristan growled. He dropped his blade from Sagar's neck. "Hand over your weapon and I'll let you go."

Sagar began blubbering. "But Tristan, what about demons? How am I to defend myself?"

"Braeden, come here," Tristan ordered. Braeden obeyed, walking to Tristan's side. "Do you have an extra knife?" Braeden produced a short dagger from his robes.

"Here," Tristan said, thrusting the knife at Sagar. "That's all the mercy you'll get from me. Don't let me see you again. Ever."

Sagar opened his mouth as though he were going to plead for something else, and then thought better of it. He nodded instead, tucked the knife into his trousers, and limped off down the rocky beach.

"Do you think he'll survive?" Sam asked once Sagar was a fair distance away.

Braeden sniffed the air. "The smell of blood is strong," he said, "and Sagar is injured. If he can make it to his horse, and his horse is fast, maybe." He shivered, and the skin on his bare arms rippled. "Then again, maybe not."

CHAPTER 38

SAM, BRAEDEN, AND Tristan huddled together in the small rock shelter. The Diamond Coast was crawling with demons, and had they wanted to, they could have fought well into the morning. But they needed to sleep to survive, and the shelter was as good a place as any to rest.

They took turns keeping watch, and after her watch was over, Sam made a nest for herself out of the blankets in the shelter and drew a sheet up around her neck. With the Paladins' deaths weighing heavily on her mind, Sam fought off sleep, fearful of the nightmares that awaited her. But exhaustion won out, and she finally drifted off and into dream.

═══════════════

The flame in the fire pit had died and the moonlight was too weak to penetrate the rock walls, plunging the shelter into darkness. Sam sat up, her bone weariness gone as though it had never been.

The fire roared back to life, a high, flickering blaze, sending shadows dancing across the room. Braeden knelt beside the fire pit, tending to the coals. He looked up at her, his slit pupils reflecting the orange of the flame. "Sam," he said. The way he said her name sounded strange, though she couldn't pinpoint what was strange about it.

"Is it still Tristan's watch?" she asked.

"Aye." Braeden threw another coal into the fire pit, and the flame sparked and flared. "Are you tired?"

Sam shook her head. She felt energized, like she was going to burst out of her skin.

"Let's go for a walk," Braeden said, "away from the shelter for a while."

"But Tristan . . ."

"Will be fine. And we won't go very far."

Sam nodded. "Okay."

She followed Braeden out through the gap in the rock. Tristan wasn't immediately outside, but she made no note of it. "Where are we going?" she asked.

"To the sea," Braeden said. He hadn't bothered to put his hair up in its usual top-knot or braid, and it fell in straight shocks of silver to his mid-back. A light wind ruffled his forelocks and the strands caressed his face. "It's peaceful there."

In companionable silence, they walked along the beach, clambering over slippery rock till the sea was almost at their feet. The waters were indigo in the night, shot through the middle with white where the moon shone. The tide was stronger now, and waves rippled and foamed before spilling onto the shore.

Braeden found a large boulder that was high enough to be dry and sat down on it cross-legged. Sam climbed up beside him and sat so close to him their shoulders touched. For an instant, a mix of surprise and confusion flashed across his face, and then it disappeared. He smiled at her, a full, honest-to-Gods smile with teeth and dimples. Her heart stopped.

"What?" Braeden asked.

Sam was grateful that he couldn't see her blush. "You're smiling. You never smile."

His smile faded. "Don't I?"

"No! Don't stop smiling on my account." She ducked, hiding her face. "I wish you smiled more, that's all."

Braeden gazed at her pensively, and she could almost see his thoughts whirling. Carefully, he grasped the back of her head and placed it on his shoulder. She froze, unsure of how to react.

He stroked her hair with gentle fingertips, and eventually, she began to relax into him. "Who are you, Sam of Haywood?" he whispered into her ear.

She chuckled softly. "I'm not sure I know anymore. Sam of Haywood? Lady Samantha, daughter of the Duke of Haywood?"

Braeden drew up sharply, jostling her head. She sighed. "If anyone can tell me who I am, it's you."

Braeden resumed stroking her hair. "Sam, do you want me?"

She jerked up, the top of her head catching his chin painfully.
"What?" she squeaked.

"Do you want me? Do you want to kiss me?" Before she could
respond, he said, "I think you do."

And then he kissed her.

Braeden's lips were hard and unforgiving. He tugged her
closer, pulling her onto his lap, and his mouth forced hers open.
His tongue slid in, quick and darting like a snake's, and she
recoiled.

Sam shoved at his chest, pushing him away. She wiped her
mouth with the back of her hand. "What was that?"

Braeden leaned in again, his lips descending towards her.
Sam scooted backwards toward the edge of the rock and out of
kissing range. She narrowed her eyes. "Who are you?" she asked,
her voice cold. "You're not Braeden."

"No?" Braeden asked, or the man who wore Braeden's face.
His lips tilted up. "No, perhaps not."

Sam jumped to her feet, and the man who was not Braeden
did the same. She reached for her sword, but her hand brushed
nothing but hip. She was without a weapon.

His laughter rang out like the chime of bells. "You would fight
poor Braeden? And here I thought you were friends." He clicked
his tongue reproachfully. "He wants more than your friendship,
you know. And we can't have that."

He smiled again, a small, secretive smile that had never
belonged to Braeden. As his grin widened, the angles of his face
softened and rounded, and his skin dimmed from burnished gold
to the color of weathered parchment. Threads of dark brown hair
sprouted between the silver, and half the length fell out in chunks.
His elongated pupils spun into circular points as the crimson
drained from his irises.

When he spoke next, it was in the musical voice of the High
Commander. "I've been wondering what it was about you. And
now I finally know."

Sam took a step back, her feet at the edge of the boulder. "H-High Commander?"

He laughed again, and this time the sound was dark and ugly. "Who would have thought it? Sam of Haywood a girl." He shook his head in mock sadness, and said, almost to himself, "Too much of his mother in him. But I suppose even a masterpiece must have its flaws." He sighed. "No matter. I'll rid him of this disease and then he'll be fully mine again."

"This is a dream," Sam said, shaking. It had to be. "You can't hurt me in my dreams."

"Clever girl, you figured it out," the High Commander said. He pulled her to him as though he were going to embrace her. "But I can hurt you when you're awake."

———————————

Sam snapped awake to the darkness of the shelter. The flame burned low in the fire pit. She almost expected to see Braeden tending to the fire, as he had in her dream, but the shelter was empty of both Braeden and Tristan. It really was just a nightmare.

She rolled her blankets around her and attempted to fall back asleep. She willed her heart to slow down and concentrated on deep, even breaths, but sleep wouldn't come.

Echoes of the High Commander's tinkling laughter sounded in her ear. Ignore it, she told herself firmly. It was a trick of the mind, the result of an overactive imagination. Tristan had said the High Commander was at least a day away . . .

Cold hands closed around her throat, and pain—real pain—engulfed her. She gasped for air and found none. Her body bucked against the heavy weight that pinned her, but as the seconds passed, she felt her strength ebb. Blackness crowded the edges of her vision.

No! I'm not ready to die! Sam summoned the last of her strength and slammed her forehead into her assailant's nose.

The hands dropped away from her neck and she sucked in a burning lungful of air. She then pulled her legs up and planted her feet firmly on the ground. She drove the right side of her pelvis up, rolling on top of her attacker. She stared down into the face of the High Commander.

He laughed up at her. "How fitting, Lady Samantha, that you have a man between your legs." She punched him in the mouth. His bottom lip split, but his laughing only increased.

She punched him again. "Where are Braeden and Tristan?"

"Oh, I've kept them busy for a while," he said. "It's only you and me." His tongue traced over his bloody lower lip. "Perhaps you'd like to steal another kiss?" His grin was wide and bloody. "No? Such a shame." He sighed dramatically and then threw her off him as though she weighed no more than a rag doll. The back of her head hit the rock wall and Sam saw stars.

Shaking off her dizziness, Sam scrambled towards the weapons in the corner of the shelter and retrieved her sword. She held the blade out in front of her, trying to keep her arm from shaking. Her knuckles were broken, her throat was raw, and her lungs burned. The sword felt unwieldy in her swollen grip.

"Ah, yes, Sam the swordsman. Swordswoman. I remember," the High Commander said. "I can play with sticks, too." Twin daggers with distinctly wavy blades slipped into his hands. "I'll let you attack first. Consider it a lesson to my most precocious trainee."

Sam aimed a powerful swing at his head, but the High Commander parried it easily. "Sloppy," he said. "Your footwork betrayed your direction."

Sam glared at him. "Are you trying to kill me or teach me?"

"It's never too late to learn." He caught her with a feint to the right, and then sliced deep into the flesh of her left shoulder. White-hot agony lanced down her arm.

The High Commander attacked again, scoring a shallow cut across her stomach. She hissed and struck out, but her blade slid harmlessly off parry. Faith in blood. She was severely outmatched.

Sam counterattacked with a low thrust, but she held no illusions that she could land the lightest scratch on him. He was just playing with her. Regardless, she tried, attacking again and again, but no matter how hard or fast she struck, she couldn't land even a glancing blow. Gods, her arm ached.

"Enough," he said, and Sam could hear the boredom in his

voice. His daggers flashed silver in the dark and then they were everywhere—against her cheek, jutting into her thigh, scraping the skin off her neck. She could feel the blood running down her arms and chest and legs.

It was all physically too much; her sword fell from numb fingers. "Pick it up," the High Commander said, nodding at the fallen blade. She grasped the hilt and tried to lift it, but she was too weak.

The High Commander frowned. "Disappointing," he said. "I expected better from a trainee of Tristan Lyons. Though you *are* a woman, so perhaps allowances should be made."

He stalked towards her, backing her up against a wall. "Shall I confirm your status as the fairer sex?" He traced the point of his dagger down the center of her chest, tearing through her tunic and binding. "My, what pretty breasts you have. No wonder Braeden is so bewitched."

A blind rage overtook her, and she slapped him hard across the face. The High Commander laughed. "Well there's some fight left in you yet," he said. "And me with my dagger at your heart." He pushed his blade into the space between her ribs—just the tip—to prove his point.

"Why?" she asked. "Why are you doing this?"

"Because," the High Commander said, "I made a toy and you broke it." He drove the dagger in deep, and then pain was all she knew.

As she drifted off into the blackness, she heard a familiar voice call out. "Master, what have you done?"

CHAPTER 39

BRAEDEN SHOVED HIS master out of the way and caught
Sam's limp body in his arms. She was frighteningly pale, her
skin marred by splotches and streams of crimson. Blood foun-
tained from the wound in her chest, pooling in the valley between
the slopes of her breasts. Her body seized. Oh Gods, Braeden
thought. Sam.

"She's dying," his master said. "There's nothing you can do."

Ignoring him, Braeden ripped the left sleeve off his robes and
applied pressure to the wound. Her blood, hot and thick, soaked
through the cloth and coated his hands. "You will not die," he told
her. Glaring at his master, he said, "She won't die. I won't allow
it."

"She can't survive a wound to the heart," his master said.
"She's not you, Braeden."

His master was wrong. Braeden's heart, too, was dying. "I
will never forgive you for this," he said, a hot pressure building
behind his eyes.

"You've grown arrogant," his master said. He bent over and
touched Braeden's jaw. The tip of his finger glistened with a
single, pearly drop. "And weak. You'll come to learn that I've done
you a favor."

Braeden stared long and hard at the man who had raised him.
"Never," he said. "I will *never* think that. Sam was—*is*—all that is
good and right with this world. You tried to destroy that. And for
what?" He felt a rush of wetness on his cheeks, and he knew the
tear his master had stolen from him had been replaced by twenty
more. "You and I are done."

"Done?" his master said. "I *own* you." He made a dismissive
wave of his hand. "Now leave her."

Braeden waited for the familiar tug of compulsion to take over, but it never came. "No," he said. The word tasted strange in his mouth. In the many years he'd lived under his master's roof, saying *no* had never been more than a fleeting thought.

His master's face was a dark cloud. He tore off Braeden's other sleeve. "*What did you do?*" His gaze was fixated on the broken lines of Braeden's tattoo.

Braeden glanced at the still-healing scar that bisected his shoulder. "It met with a demon's tooth and a surgeon's scalpel." Dark suspicion formed and his eyebrows drew together. "You told me its purpose was to seal off my demonic nature."

"I warded you with *my* blood," his master snarled. "To bind your demon, I had to bind you to me. How is it that you haven't slaughtered half the kingdom?"

Braeden lifted his chin. "I don't need it anymore. Just like I don't need you."

They both turned at the sound of clanging and heavy breathing. Tristan pushed his way into the room, blood-spattered and disheveled. "So many demons," he said between lungfuls of air. "I've never seen the like." His eyes went wide, his jaw slack. "High Commander," he said grimly.

Braeden's mouth went dry, and slowly, he turned back toward his master. The man he knew as his master was gone, and in his place stood the High Commander. But Braeden knew better; it was only an illusion. The High Commander's fingers dripped with freshly spilt blood—Sam's blood. His master and the High Commander were one and the same.

No wonder his master hadn't balked when Braeden had asked to leave to join the Paladins; he'd never left him. Braeden had thought that by becoming a Paladin trainee, he would finally be free to live his own life, but instead he had been caught in the web of his master's machinations. Had his master always been the High Commander? Or had he merely stolen his face? His master collected faces like people collected rare coins. Even Braeden didn't know his original form.

"Who is that woman?" Tristan asked, cutting into Braeden's ruminations.

His master—the High Commander—guffawed, slapping his

knee. "Too funny," he gasped, wiping away tears. "You always had more brawn than brains, Lyons. It's why I liked you." He shook his head. "It would have been better for all of us if you had never started thinking."

Braeden looked down at Sam's too-pale face. I'm sorry, he thought at her. It should have been you who told him. "This is Sam, Tristan."

Tristan's sword clattered to the floor. "No." He crossed the shelter in two strides and knelt beside Braeden. Tristan cupped Sam's face with both hands. "Oh Gods, it's really him. Her." He turned to Braeden. "You knew?"

"Aye."

"How long?" Tristan asked, his question edged with a thread of anger.

Braeden dropped his gaze. "For a while now."

Tristan's voice shook. "How could you not tell me? How could *she* not tell me?"

"We all have our secrets," Braeden said. His master smirked at that. "Sam wanted to tell you, but she was afraid."

"Afraid? Of me? She thought I would betray her?" His hurt was evident in his tone.

"She was afraid you would hate her."

Tristan fell silent.

"You don't, do you?" Braeden asked. "Hate her?"

"No," Tristan said hoarsely. "Oh Gods, is she dying?"

"No," Braeden said just as the High Commander said, "Yes."

"*He* did this to her," Braeden said, glaring at his master.

Tristan stood up quickly. "You go too far. Your grievance is with me, and that's where it should have stayed." He reached for his sword.

"No," Braeden said. "He did this to her because of me. This is *my* fight."

The High Commander's musical laugh filled the room. "The prodigal son returns to challenge the father. I will show you no mercy, Braeden."

"I wouldn't expect you to."

"We'll fight him together," Tristan said. "You haven't seen him fight."

"I have," Braeden said quietly. "He taught me everything I know." Before that admission could settle in, he said, "Stay with Sam, Tristan. This is my fight, and she is your bride."

Before he could witness Tristan's reaction, Braeden walked out of the shelter, knowing his master would follow. Outside, he and Tristan had left behind a graveyard of demons, littering the beach with their corpses. It was the sudden onslaught of demons that had taken Braeden away from the shelter, and foolishly, he had thought to let Sam sleep. Now, in retrospect, he realized the demons had been a distraction.

Demons trailed behind the High Commander like obedient puppies. Their obedience was a gift unique to his master, a gift Braeden had once craved. For the price of obedience his master had offered him control, and Braeden, a child who couldn't understand the monster inside him or why it did such unspeakable things, had leaped at the bargain. The berserk rages had stopped, and for a while Braeden had been content. He had allowed his master to shape him into a weapon, and if his master had sometimes been cruel, Braeden had told himself that far fewer would suffer than if he were left to roam the earth unleashed.

His master would disappear for stretches at a time—for a week or a few months, and once, an entire year. During those disappearances, Braeden was free to spread his wings, only to have them clipped. People were cruel, he discovered, if less overtly than his master.

It was after his master's year-long disappearance that Braeden had decided to join the Paladins. Naively, he had clung to the hope that the Paladins were truly the bastion of goodness they presented. It was to be his chance at redemption.

Staring into the grinning face of the High Commander, Braeden now knew he'd been a fool to believe the Gods would give him such a chance, and Sam was the cost of his folly.

The High Commander's daggers still dripped with Sam's blood, and a white ball of fury formed in the place where Braeden's heart had been. Swiftly, Braeden drew his two *katar* from his robes. The short blades were wide and triangular, and the H-shaped hand grips sat right above his knuckles.

"You said it yourself," his master said. "I taught you everything you know. Why fight a losing battle?"

Braeden rubbed his katar together, relishing the rasp of steel against steel. "You reap what you sow," he said. "I'm no longer holding back." He sprinted at the High Commander and thrust with both blades.

The High Commander shifted to the side and clamped his daggers around Braeden's left katar. He wrenched the blade from Braeden's grasp, and then the two of them broke apart. "Give up," his master said. "You're already down to one weapon."

"You can't be serious," Braeden said. A new *katar* dropped into his empty hand. He jumped forward and slashed, raking the High Commander's chest. "If you hope to disarm me, we'll be here all night."

His master sliced diagonally. Braeden ducked and rolled, throwing a katar as he somersaulted. The blade lodged itself in the High Commander's kneecap.

His master pulled it out with a grimace. "Thanks for the extra weapon." As soon as the blade was free of his flesh, he chucked it at Braeden's head.

Braeden snatched the katar out of the air, the tip grazing his forehead. The edges of the blade cut deep into his palm, but he disregarded it. "You're getting slow in your old age," he said, "or perhaps I'm getting faster." Braeden threw the katar, and ran forward, following the blades' trajectory. Another pair of katar slid into his hands as he ran.

Braeden's katar were inches from his master's neck when something barreled into him, knocking him to the ground. Massive jaws snapped near his throat. Braeden stabbed upwards, through scale and skin, and shoved the demon's dead weight off his body. "No fair," he growled, scrambling to his feet.

His master laughed. "If I've taught you anything, it's that there's no such thing as fair fighting, only winning and losing. Anything goes." The High Commander crooked his finger, and two of his demon entourage launched themselves at Braeden.

Braeden avoided the swipe of a clawed paw and cut off the offending claw at its furry wrist. The demon stumbled awkwardly on its three legs and stump, and Braeden put the creature out of its misery with a quick slash.

Jagged teeth took a small chunk out of his shoulder, and Braeden's vision blurred. He flexed his bicep to stymie the pain. The demon attacked him again, teeth first, but this time Braeden rammed his knife into its maw. The next stab of his dagger was into his own heart.

It hadn't been long since Braeden last invoked his demon, and the change came over him quickly. Blood surged through his veins in waves and his muscles pulsed and swelled. A red haze settled over his eyes, while his pupils elongated and twisted. His senses sharpened. He could feel the restlessness of the demons that surrounded his master as if it were his own restless energy.

"Attack!" his master ordered. Lips peeled back and haunches coiled, ready to spring.

No, Braeden thought at the demons. He closed his eyes and concentrated. Behind his lids were malleable blobs of darkness connected by thread to a central point—his master. Mentally, he pulled at the thread. *Obey me.* The demons halted mid-spring, frozen in their tracks. Braeden bared his teeth in a parody of a smile. They were his to command.

The High Commander flinched. "I see you've learned a thing or two," he said. "But can you hold them?" Braeden felt a tug as his master tried to wrest away control. The demons snorted and stomped, caught between the two men as they each vied for dominance.

"It seems we are at a stalemate," his master said through clenched teeth, sweat coating his brow.

"So it would seem," Braeden said, aching under the mental strain. It would be so easy to let go—it *hurt.*

The High Commander held out his hand to him. "Come with me, Braeden," he said. "There's nothing for you in their world. You belong with me, not with those who would reject you for what you are. There's so much more that I can teach you. We can ride the world of dreams together and fashion our own reality. A *better* reality. One without man's stupidity and prejudice—"

"Without demons?"

His master laughed lightly, like a flute on the wind. "Oh, Braeden." He scratched a hellhound behind its ears. "You *are* a demon. My greatest experiment—the best of man and imagination. You're meant to be their king." His voice softened. "Even if your Sam were to survive, she's not for you."

Braeden met the High Commander's gaze and held it. "I know that," he said. "It's enough if she lives."

His master's face turned ugly, lit by unrestrained glee. "You really don't know, do you? Whether she dies by my blade or by demon, you've doomed her."

Braeden's upper lip curled. "What do you mean?"

"This *poison* you feel for her," the High Commander spat, "is a contagion. You're the king among beasts, Braeden, and your desires are theirs. Every time you look at her, every demon within range turns into a lovesick puppy."

Braeden shook his head. "I don't understand. Demons are incapable of love."

His master sneered. "Aye, that they are. But they are capable of *want* and *lust*." He took a step closer to Braeden, his small eyes glittering. "You want Sam, Braeden. Well, so do they. And they won't stop wanting her till you either give up this foolish infatuation or she's dead."

Bile rose in his throat. "No," Braeden whispered. "You're wrong."

"Am I?" the High Commander asked. "Ask yourself this—what do you want more than anything?"

Sam. Her name came unbidden to his lips.

"Concentrate, Braeden," his master said in soothing tones. "What do the demons want?"

Braeden closed his eyes again and felt the pulsating storm of the demons' savagery. There, at the center of the maelstrom, was Sam. Their violence warped his desire, and the outcome was a singular, focused bloodlust. He'd felt their pull towards her before, but never had he made the connection.

"You see?" the High Commander said. "Leave her with that idiot Tristan. Come with me."

Braeden's resolve hardened. "Tristan's no idiot," he said. "And neither am I. Whether I choose to leave Sam or not, you'll try to kill her either way. Tristan, too." His voice deepened with menace. "I won't let that happen."

"Don't be a fool, Braeden," his master said. A line of demons separated him from Braeden—he was too close and yet not close enough. Their stalemate would last the night if they both refused to bend. That suited Braeden just fine—it would buy Tristan time to leave the Diamond Coast with Sam. His master continued, "Women are pathetic, as bad as the male of their species."

This piqued Braeden's curiosity. He'd never heard his master speak of such things. "You don't count yourself among them?" Braeden asked.

His master snorted indelicately. "Humans are ruled by their fear. Me, I rule fear." His neck stretched forward, the muscles straining. "I can show you how to take fear and shape it into living nightmare. Love, Braeden, is a fickle thing, but fear will never desert you."

"I have already had a lifetime of fear," Braeden said. "I have no interest in a lifetime more."

For a moment, his master's composure slipped. "Fool!" he hissed, then reigned himself back in. "You will only ever know fear, Braeden, never love. Your own mother couldn't stand the sight of you."

Shock ran through him at the mention of his mother. "You knew her?"

"Knew her? Your mother was mine to play with: a lesson in the power of fear. Do you know what she was afraid of?" His master let out a singsong laugh. "Me. And so I fashioned a demon in my likeness, or at least the relevant parts. I watched it rut with her till she grew round with you." His laughter turned discordant. "Your loving mother tried to kill you as soon as you left her womb. And when that failed, she killed herself."

Rage coursed through Braeden, and he felt himself teetering over the edge. "You killed her as surely as if you held the knife yourself."

"Aye," his master said. "And you, Braeden, were the knife."

The rage and the blackness that came with it consumed Braeden. This time he welcomed it.

CHAPTER 40

S AM FLOATED IN darkness, swept along by the currents of an ocean so black that no light could reach her. Black ocean melded seamlessly into black sky. Sam saw nothing, heard nothing, felt nothing—not even the weight of her own body. She drifted.

Then she heard it—the beat of a drum—soft at first, and then louder and louder till it thundered in her ears, vibrating in her skull. The waters became choppy and rough. Lightning zigzagged through the stark black of the sky. It struck again and again, and each time, the world flashed brilliantly white. Sam saw glimpses of faces in the white, faces she recognized and faces she did not. Shorn blond hair and a rugged jaw, colorless eyes that held more sadness than any one person had a right to, worry lines across the forehead of a beautiful young woman.

And then there was pain—unbearable, excruciating pain, worse than a hundred broken bones or a thousand seeping cuts. Her body screamed out in agony and her back arched, sharp needlepoints pricking her everywhere.

"Shhh," came a soft, feminine voice. "Shhh, you're all right now." A gentle touch swept Sam's hair behind her ears and something cool and damp was draped across her brow. Then darkness claimed her again and all was silent but for the beat of the drum.

CHAPTER 41

*T*RISTAN RAN HIS fingers through his hair. He caught himself and made an effort to keep his hands to his sides. After the past week, it was a wonder he hadn't gone bald. "Has there been any change?" he asked the doctor, Addie.

She fixed him with a scathing glare. Tristan winced. He had asked the same question twenty times a day since the Uriel had taken over Sam's care, and apparently the good doctor was tired of hearing it. "As I've told you before, you will be the first to know if her condition changes, Master Lyons."

Master Lyons. Tristan still wasn't used to his new station. He was a nobody now, a man like any other. "Thank you, Addie."

She nodded distractedly. "Now get out of my sickroom. You're in the way."

It shouldn't have surprised Tristan that the Uriel's doctor was a woman—and Sander Branimir's daughter, no less—not when his trainee was his own betrothed. Gods, what a shock that had been. He hadn't believed Braeden at first, and Sam's face had been so bruised and bloody that it was impossible to reconcile it with the girl he remembered from his one encounter with the Lady Samantha. But Braeden had no reason to lie to him, and as Sam began to heal, Tristan slowly started to put the puzzle pieces together.

As for Addie, she could scowl at Tristan for his constant pestering all she wanted, but he would be damned if he lost his betrothed for a second time.

Before exiting the infirmary, he took one last lingering look at Sam's pale face. The bruises had faded to yellow and the cuts had healed to thin pink lines, some of which would scar. But it was the wound below her neck that scared him—one hairsbreadth closer and the High Commander's blade would have pierced her heart. Regardless, a deep chest wound was a grave injury, and though her breathing and heart rate were steady, Sam had yet to regain consciousness. Addie changed the dressing twice a day but refused to let Tristan see what lay underneath the bandages. "A woman has to have some privacy," she had said.

"I'm her betrothed," Tristan had insisted, peeling back the thin sheet that covered Sam from neck to feet. Having none of it, Addie had slapped his wrist with the dull end of her lancet. "My sickroom, my rules. Get out."

If she weren't so hell-bent on keeping him out of her sickroom, Tristan would have liked Addie Branimir. She had a no-nonsense attitude and a compassionate bedside manner befitting a doctor. As tall as most men but built with the lush curves of a woman, she was, he had to admit, breathtakingly beautiful—the kind of beauty that caused men to lose their heads and women to hate her on sight. Addie had inherited her father's hazel eyes and dark red hair, though it was impossible to tell its length or texture since she wore it in a sensible bun. Her full lips and straight nose, however, must have been gifts from her mother. But she didn't act like most beautiful women that Tristan knew—Addie was far more interested in mending broken bones than in fluttering her eyelashes.

Tristan sighed. "Goodbye, Addie. I'll check in on Sam again in an hour."

"Please don't," came Addie's muffled reply. She had disappeared into the storerooms, likely to mix some foul-tasting concoction for the next poor sap who fell under her care. "I'll send for you if you're needed."

Tristan left the sickbay and climbed up the winding stairs to his temporary chamber in the Beyaz Kale. The chamber was in an unused, musty corner of the castle and the accommodations were sparse—little more than a bed and an extra pallet. Sander had apologized, explaining the room was the best he could do on short notice. But Tristan was grateful to have anywhere to stay; he'd been unsure of the reception he would receive in Luca, considering the circumstances under which he'd left.

Braeden sat on the edge of the extra pallet, pricking his fingers with a dagger. "I just came from visiting Sam," Tristan told him.

Braeden's eyes lifted and then returned to his fingers. "How is she?"

"The same," Tristan said. He took a deep breath and sighed. "You haven't visited her since you got to Luca."

"I know."

Braeden had always been self-contained and a little aloof, but he'd been even more taciturn since he'd shown up in Luca, two days after Tristan had arrived with Sam. When Tristan had asked him what had transpired with the High Commander, Braeden said simply, in a voice colder than the grave, "He lives." And then he clammed up, tight-lipped and somber.

"You should visit her," Tristan said. "I think she'd like that."

"She's unconscious. She wouldn't even know," Braeden said callously. He resumed pricking his fingers. "Besides, she has you."

Tristan shook his head. He couldn't understand Braeden's reluctance to see Sam; the two of them had been thick as thieves before the events at the Diamond Coast. "You should go," he urged. "You'll regret it if you don't. If she dies—"

The tip of Braeden's knife drove deep into his finger. "Don't even say that," he hissed.

A knock came at the door, breaking the sudden tension between them. Tristan opened it to a young castle servant. "Excuse me, Master Lyons," the servant said. "Doc says you should come. Lady Samantha is waking."

A tidal wave of relief washed over him. "Thank the Gods," he breathed. "Braeden, are you coming?"

Braeden averted his gaze. "I'll stay for now."

"Suit yourself," Tristan said. He grasped the servant's shoulder. "Take me to her ladyship."

———

Sam opened her eyes to a face so beautiful it could only belong to a goddess. Funny, Sam had never thought her death would warrant a personal greeting from the Gods. There were so many souls to be ferried over to the Afterlight, after all.

"Emese?" Sam croaked. Why was her voice so rusty?

The goddess rolled her eyes. "Not the first time I've heard that one, I'm afraid," she said in a brisk, businesslike tone. "I'm Addie Branimir, the local doctor. You gave us all quite a scare."

So she wasn't dead, then? She should have realized; she was in far too much pain to be dead. Sam blinked as the room came into focus. Stained glass windows let in soft light and color. The walls were lined by neat rows of beds, half of which were empty. The others were occupied by men and women in varying states of illness and injury. "Where am I?" she asked. The last thing she remembered was the High Commander's leer as he plunged his blade into her chest. She shuddered at the memory.

"You're in Luca, in the infirmary of the Beyaz Kale," Addie said. "Your betrothed brought you here."

Her *betrothed*? Sam glanced down at herself; she wore a woman's chemise and her breasts were unbound. She blanched. Tristan must have figured out her true identity.

"You're hyperventilating," Addie said. "You need to stay calm."

As though the thought of his name had summoned him, Tristan burst into the infirmary. "Sam!" He ran and skidded to a stop a few feet shy of Sam's bed. "Lady Samantha." He bowed at the waist.

Addie rapped his knuckles. "Stop exciting my patient," she said. "It isn't good for her."

Tristan put on a contrite expression. "My sincerest apologies to both of you." He cleared his throat nervously. "Could I talk to Sam—Lady Samantha—for a few minutes?" he asked. "Alone?"

Addie narrowed her eyes at him, placing her hands on her hips. To Sam, she said, "If he bothers you, just yell and I'll get rid of him."

Briefly, Sam considered pretending to fall back unconscious, but somehow she just knew that Addie would see right through the ploy. "It will be fine," Sam said weakly. Except it wouldn't be—after months of deceit, she finally had to pay for her lies. Gods, Tristan must hate her. How could he not?

"Okay, then," Addie said. She tugged on tasseled drawstrings, enclosing Sam's bed in a maroon velvet curtain. "If you feel faint or the pain worsens, call for me." Addie ducked out through a gap in the curtain, leaving Sam alone with Tristan.

Sam squeezed her eyes shut, bracing for a diatribe of accusations and insults. When none came, Sam cracked open a lid.

Tristan bent down on one knee and clasped her hands in his. "Lady Samantha," he said. "Would you do me the honor of becoming my wife?"

Sam's mouth fell open. After a few false starts, she sputtered, "Is this some sort of joke?" It would be a cruel jest, but it wasn't as though she hadn't earned it.

Tristan's cheeks reddened. "A joke?" he snapped. He gave a slight shake of his head. "I'm completely sincere."

"But Tristan," Sam said helplessly, "you don't even *like* me."

His blush deepened. "That's not true."

"Tristan, be serious. I annoy the hell out of you," she said. "You think I'm selfish and spoiled and disobedient. A day hasn't passed where we haven't squabbled."

Tristan tightened his grasp on her hands. "It will be different now," he said earnestly. "That was when you were my trainee. If I had known—"

Sam pulled her hands from his. "If you had known that I was Lady Samantha Haywood, you would never have allowed me to be your trainee. You would have returned me to my father with a scolding and a swat on the behind."

Tristan flinched, and opened his mouth. She put her finger to his lips. "Don't deny it," she said. "You want a wife that you can come home to, who wrings her fingers while you're gone. I'll never be that woman, Tristan. It doesn't matter if you put me in skirts, fix up my hair, and call me Lady Samantha; I'm the same Sam of Haywood you knew as your trainee. I'm willful and stubborn and I'm damned near as good as you with a sword. I'm not going to sit home and mind the babes while you wage my war."

Tristan rose from his kneeling position and sat on the edge of her bed. He glared into her eyes, his expression fierce. "Don't put words in my mouth."

"I did no such thing," Sam retorted. "You said as much yourself. Right after . . ." She forced herself to say the words. "Right after you found out Lady Samantha was dead."

"You speak of her as though you are not one and the same."

Sam turned her face from his. "I have not been Lady Samantha for a long time. Even before you knew me I had given her up."

"I don't understand," Tristan said. "I have never had to hide who I am to be who I want to be. Would it be so bad to become her once more?"

Sam would be lying if she said she hadn't asked herself that same question. She didn't *dislike* being a woman, just the trappings that went with it. "Yes. If I can't also be Sam of Haywood."

Even as she said the words, Sam reconsidered—not the path she'd chosen, but the woman she'd become. Here, a marriage proposal had fallen in her lap, from a man who'd seen her true colors and still wanted to wed her. Must she only be Sam of Haywood, and never Samantha? And did Tristan—or any man—want a woman with her warrior heart? Pride made her say, "You don't need to marry me because of some stupid promise you made to my father."

Tristan shifted on the bed and took her hand in his again. "I know to you this might seem like it's coming out of nowhere," he said. "But I thought about it a lot over the past week. I thought a lot about you. I was angry, you know, when Braeden first told me who you were. It was bad enough when you were just a girl, but worse when I learned you were Lady Samantha. You let me believe that someone important to me was dead."

"Tristan, I'm sorr—"

Now it was his turn to shush her. "I wanted to yell at you, and I did, for a while. For lying to me, for not trusting me, and for having the damned nerve to get yourself halfway killed. Of course there's not much point at yelling at someone when they're unconscious. And once I realized you weren't going to yell back—that you might never yell back—I got scared. You were barely breathing, Braeden was gone—"

"Gone? Is Braeden okay?"

Tristan gave her an annoyed look. "Aye, we were separated for a few days. He's fine." His frown lines smoothed. "As I was saying, it dawned on me—I've grown accustomed to having you around. Far too accustomed to lose you. I *want* you around." He brushed his fingers over her knuckles. "Say you'll be my wife."

At his words, Sam allowed herself to observe Tristan openly. He was sinfully handsome, the golden prince of every girl's dreams, with the hard muscles of a man who fought for his living. He was strong and brave and good, if not exactly kind. As a young girl, had she not fantasized about just such a man? "Wanting me around is not reason enough to marry me," she said finally.

"Do you remember the night we captured Sander?"

"Of course I remember."

"You wore a green gown," Tristan said, "the exact shade of your eyes. You were resplendent. Looking at you, I felt like a depraved man. You were my trainee, but . . ." Sheepishly, he scrubbed at his cheeks. "I wanted to kiss you when I saw you in that gown." Tristan tucked his thumb under her chin and brought his face close to hers. "Will you wear it again for me, Sam?"

"I burnt it," she whispered.

"I'll buy you a new one," he said and kissed her.

Tristan's lips were warm and soft, and for a moment, she leaned into their comfort, closing her eyes. Behind her lids, she saw the future she could have had—could still have—the handsome prince of a husband, the cherubic blond children, the beautiful, well-loved home. And then she saw *him*—silver and savage and alone. His outstretched hand held a dagger, hilt facing out.

Gently, she pushed Tristan away. "No," she said. "I don't want your gown." She'd never been a girl in need of a handsome prince.

He blinked. "What?"

"I don't want to *wear* a gown. I want to wear armor and a sword." She laid a hand against his cheek. "Tristan, you don't want to marry me. You want to marry the *idea* of me. This person you imagine me to be—she doesn't exist."

Tristan rolled over on the bed, his back to her. "You won't marry me, will you?"

"No," she said. And then, more firmly, "No, Tristan, I won't."

CHAPTER 42

*B*RAEDEN COLLAPSED BACK onto his pallet and stared up at the cobwebbed ceiling, reminding himself for the hundredth time why he couldn't check in on Sam. He peeled the sides of his robes apart and ran his fingers along the raised brand on his chest. The skin was swollen and tender to the touch—soreness was to be expected. His efforts to remove the new tattoo had done him no favors.

Six days ago, Braeden had woken up to find a pattern of dark red ink staining the breadth of his chest. Thin glyphs fanned out from below his collar bone to over the tops of his shoulder blades. Three times, he'd taken a knife to the ink, scraping off layers and layers of skin till nothing remained but raw flesh. And each time, his skin had grown back, the tattoo wholly intact.

Though Braeden had no memory of it, there was no question as to who had given him this accursed mark. The tattoo could only be the work of his master, though try as he might, Braeden couldn't recall the sting of ink or needles. He'd lost a lot of time that night—his first true blackout episode since he was a child. Even when he'd lost control with Sam, Braeden had retained some small part of his humanity. But his master had goaded him beyond his limits.

Braeden could remember nothing of what happened after he'd let his demon out, but the tattoo across his chest was evidence enough that the High Commander lived. Now, once again, he bore the stamp of his master's ownership. If this tattoo held the same compulsion magic as his last, Braeden was a danger to everyone—doubly so to Sam.

He hadn't dared visit Sam in the infirmary, not while she was so vulnerable—let Tristan think him an inconsiderate ass. A better man than Braeden would have put an ocean between them. But she was safe in Luca, even from him. Surrounded by Tristan and thousands of Uriel, even a large demon attack was doomed to fail. Still, Sam was a wanderer and a soldier at heart, and she wouldn't want to stay in Luca forever. Selfishly, Braeden hoped she would stay for a while; when she left Luca, he would leave her.

He would allow himself this one happiness: Sam was *awake*. Whatever else went wrong, Braeden would be grateful for this one right thing. He desperately, desperately wanted to see her, to confirm with his own eyes that she hadn't died because of him.

Braeden was weak, and it didn't take long to talk himself into seeing her. Consequences be damned, he retied his robes and climbed down the several flights of stairs to the Uriel infirmary.

A tall red-haired woman stood just inside the sickroom—Addie Branimir, from Tristan's description. Hiding in his chamber for the past five days, Braeden had yet to meet her. She held his gaze without flinching, and that in itself was a marvel.

"So the other one finally shows up," she said, a hand on her hip. "Do you plan to interfere with my work too?"

"No, Lady Branimir. I'm just here to see Sam."

"Call me Addie or Doc; everyone else does." She jerked her head to the right. "Sixth bed on the left. You'll find her in the company of her meddlesome betrothed."

The word *betrothed* dug into him like the cut of a knife. "Thank you, Addie," he said tightly, offering her a slight bow.

The bed belonging to Sam was roped off by a velvet curtain, and as he crossed the room, Braeden could hear muffled voices. He gripped the curtain, prepared to pull it open . . . And then he heard the squeak of a mattress, and Tristan's voice, loud and clear: "Say you'll be my wife."

Her answer would kill Braeden quicker than any poison. He shut his eyes, and when he opened them again, his face was a controlled mask. He turned from the curtain, walked down the room past the five rows of beds, and nodded politely at Addie. As soon as he was outside of the infirmary, he ran.

CHAPTER 43

*A*FTER TRISTAN'S MARRIAGE proposal, Sam received no more visitors in the infirmary. The first day, she didn't mind the solitude; despite Addie's warning, Tristan *had* overexcited her and she spent most of the day sleeping. But she quickly grew lonely and bored. Addie talked to her sometimes, not only about doctorly things, but funny stories about Addie's father and the men who tried to court her. Addie never asked her about Tristan or why he'd stopped coming, and Sam appreciated her tact. Still, Sam was one of many patients and Addie seldom had more than five minutes at a time to spare for her.

On the third day of no visitors, Sam asked Addie about Braeden. She thought maybe she had missed him while she was sleeping; had their positions been reversed, she would have been by his bedside night and day, if he let her. "Has Braeden come by to see me?" she asked while Addie replaced her bandages.

An uncomfortable look crossed Addie's face. "Aye, he came," she said vaguely.

"Oh," Sam said, and some of the tightness in her chest dissipated. "Was I sleeping? Did he say he would come back?"

Addie applied a cool salve to her wound and didn't glance up. "He came by right after you woke up, and he left almost immediately. He said nothing much to me beyond hello and goodbye."

"Ow," Sam said. Her chest hurt.

Addie furrowed her brow. "That shouldn't have hurt," she said, and finished wrapping Sam's bandages.

Was Braeden mad at her? Sam thought they had mended the rift between them, but perhaps she was mistaken. What awful thing had she done that he wouldn't come see her? She'd almost *died,* and she didn't even warrant a "hello" or an "I'm glad you're not dead"? The more she thought about it, the angrier it made her.

Braeden didn't come the next day, or the day after that. Sam grew angrier and angrier till she thought she would choke with it. Or choke *him* with it, if he ever afforded her the opportunity.

Finally, after six days, she caved. "Addie," she called, "would you fetch me a pen and paper?"

Hastily, Sam scribbled a note:

> *Braeden—*
>
> *Come see me in the infirmary. I miss you.*
>
> *-Sam*

In return, she received:

> *Busy, sorry.*
>
> *-B*

He hadn't even bothered to sign his full name. Sam crumpled his note into a ball and seethed silently.

"I don't envy the man on the receiving end of that look," Addie said. She shuddered. "Scary."

"Men are idiots."

Addie raised an eyebrow. "There's no need to state the obvious." She smacked her forehead with her hand. "Speaking of idiot men, I almost forgot; I have a gift for you."

"A gift? For me?"

Addie ducked out of the curtain opening and returned to Sam's bed a moment later. The doctor held a long, curved object with her fingertips, as though it were filthy. "Here. This is yours." She dropped it on Sam's lap.

It was a sword and scabbard. The scabbard was beautiful, plated in bronze and etched with intricate patterns. The hilt of the sword was likewise beautiful, with a sharkskin grip and a pommel that looked to be made of solid gold.

Sam wrapped one hand around the hilt and the other around the scabbard and pulled them apart. The sword slid out of the sheath with a metallic whisper.

Oh Gods, a paladin's sword.

"A note came with it, too," Addie said. She unfolded a piece of parchment and placed the open letter on Sam's knee.

> *To Sam of Haywood—*
>
> *May this blade serve you well.*
>
> *Regards,*
>
> *Tristan Lyons*

He who would have bought her a gown had instead brought her a sword. Sam recognized the gift for what it was—a peace offering, and one she would gladly accept. She was relieved. She valued their relationship but hadn't been sure it could survive both her lies and the fallout from his proposal. Sam wanted him around, just not in the way he intended. Even without his title, Tristan would forever be her paladin.

Sam slid the sword back into its sheath. "If you see Tristan before me, please give him my thanks."

"I will," Addie promised. "He dropped it off here yesterday, but I didn't want to give you any ideas."

"Ideas?"

Addie put on a mock-stern face. "Don't even think about swinging that thing till you've fully healed."

"Would I do that?" Sam asked innocently. Surely *one* practice swing couldn't do much harm . . .

"You are not to be trusted," Addie said, "which is why I'm taking it back for safekeeping till your stitches are out." She plucked the sheathed sword from Sam's grip.

"Oy!" Sam protested, grabbing for the sword. "Give it back!"

Addie twisted out of reach. "Don't be such a ninny. I'm taking your stitches out in a week. You can come back for it then."

"Come *back* for it?"

Addie smiled. "Aye, you've healed quite nicely, and it's time to relinquish your sickbed to another. I'm kicking you out."

"But . . ." Sam bit her lip, feeling utterly lost and alone. "Where will I go?" she asked. Braeden was avoiding her, she certainly couldn't impose on Tristan, and returning to the Center or to Haywood were not options.

Addie's face fell in sympathy. "Oh, Sam," she said. "You can stay here in the Beyaz Kale, of course. My father was supposed to come by to talk to you about it, but he's been tied up with an emergency."

Reassured, Sam asked, "Will I stay with Tristan and Braeden?"

Addie went crimson. "Will you . . . stay with Tristan and Braeden? Share a room with two men?" She shook her head adamantly. "No, no, definitely not. It wouldn't be proper."

"I've been sharing a room with them for months," Sam said practically. "What difference would it make?"

"You're a woman now."

"I was a woman then, too," Sam pointed out. "Nothing's changed."

"Everything's changed," Addie said. "The world knows you're a woman. You can't go on as you were."

Sam glared at the doctor. "In Haywood there are no women doctors. Some women dabble in the healing arts, but the formal practice of medicine is the prerogative of men. How would you have liked it if your father forbade you from becoming a doctor?"

Addie chuckled. "He did just that. I ignored him."

"Then you should understand."

Addie sighed. "You'll need to make concessions, Sam, as did I. When you're at battle and no alternatives present themselves, share a room with a man, if you must. But here, in Luca, you are a single woman and must observe the rules of propriety as best you can. It is not so big a concession."

"No," Sam said bitterly, "I suppose it is not." She wished she could go back to the way things were. It wasn't as though she had planned to hide that she was a woman forever, but she'd wanted to reveal her gender on her terms.

"You know," Addie said, tapping her chin, "things would be much easier if you were married. Married women can do whatever they please."

Sam groaned. "Not you, too."

"I thought as much," Addie said, more to herself than to Sam. "It was just a suggestion. As for your sword fighting, I would never tell you to give it up, although I don't understand the appeal myself."

Addie looked so repulsed Sam had to laugh. "I'm surprised. You like cutting up things well enough."

Addie sniffed. "Surgery is a precision art. Sword fighting is all . . ." She waggled a fist wildly in the air.

Sam started giggling and went to cover her mouth. She stopped halfway and dropped her hands to her sides. Since everyone already knew she was a girl, she could giggle if she damn well wanted to. And so she did. Loudly.

Leaving with strict instructions from Addie to perform nothing more than light exercise, Sam was escorted to chambers one floor above the infirmary, "just in case". She grimaced at the single mattress covered in lacy pink bedding. That was going to take some getting used to.

"Is the room not to your liking, Lady Samantha?" the servant who had escorted her asked.

Sam winced at the name. "The room is fine," she said. "And please, call me Sam."

The servant looked horrified. "Milady, that wouldn't be seemly. Not seemly at all."

Sam pinched the bridge of her nose in frustration. Addie, who had told Sam in confidence that her real first name was Adelaide, had convinced all of Luca to call her Addie or Doc; Sam would get there one day. But not tonight. "My chest is bothering me. Please leave." The servant gave an apologetic bow and left her alone in her new chambers.

The next morning, Sam opened the closet door to find all of her belongings, in addition to several clothing items that were definitely *not* hers. Gowns of varying cuts and colors hung in between her cloak and her formal tunics. "No thank you," she told the gowns, reaching for a pair of breeches.

After she was dressed, Sam headed outside for the Uriel training grounds. She wasn't going to *do* anything—she'd promised Addie, and though she felt much stronger, she knew she wasn't up to strenuous exercise—she just wanted to see where the Uriel trained. And maybe go for a short run. Addie couldn't object too much to that.

Winter had hit Luca hard in the weeks since Sam, Braeden and Tristan had left with Sander in tow. Sam slogged through ankle-deep snow to the training grounds, which were located on a plateau down a shallow slope from the Beyaz Kale. A line of pine trees dusted with white surrounded the perimeter, serving as a natural fence.

Blowing puffs of cold air from her mouth, Sam broke out into a light run to keep her blood warm. By the time she reached the grounds, she was slick with sweat, her damp clothes molding to her body.

Through the trees, Sam could see men training, dueling each other or flogging and slashing at practice dummies. Included among the men was Tristan, who shifted gracefully between sword forms. He must have seen her, because he lost focus and stopped abruptly. His hand made a jerking waving motion, as though he couldn't decide whether he wanted to wave at her or not.

Tristan jogged to meet her halfway across the training yard. "Sam," he said. His gaze drifted downward and then shot up, his face turning beet red.

"What is it?" she asked warily.

"It's just . . ." Tristan ran his fingers through his hair and turned redder, if that was possible. "I don't know how I didn't realize you were a girl all this time. It's sort of obvious." His eyes dropped lower again before he snapped them back to her face.

That was what Tristan was looking at? Sam smacked him in the arm. "I didn't bind my chest today," she said hotly, her face no doubt as red as his. "It's bad for my wound, and besides, it's bloody uncomfortable."

"It's very strange seeing you in men's clothing while you have—" Tristan traced the shape of an hourglass with his hands.

"Tristan!" she exclaimed, smacking him again.

"Sorry, Sam, I'll get used to it eventually," he said, sounding properly chastened. "How do you like the sword?"

Now Sam felt guilty for hitting him. "I love it," she said softly. "Thank you."

"You didn't bring it with you?" he asked, disappointment

coloring his voice. "I was sure you'd want to take a few practice swings with it now that you're free from the witch woman's lair."

Sam laughed. "You mean Addie? She's really not that bad." She made a face. "Although she *is* holding my sword hostage till my stitches are out. Apparently she doesn't trust me."

Tristan grinned. "Smart lady." He sobered quickly. "Listen, Sam, there's something I need to tell you. I was going to come find you later, but since you're here . . ." He gulped nervously.

Tristan was never nervous. Sam narrowed her eyes at him. "Out with it."

"You know I was worried about you when you were wounded," he said in a rush. Oh Gods, Sam hoped he wasn't going to propose again. "I wasn't sure if you were going to make it, and I thought if I had a daughter—"

"If you had a *daughter?*"

He continued, "If I had a daughter, I would want to know whether she was alive or dead. Even if she had run away from home."

"Tristan, I—"

"That's what you did, isn't it?" Tristan asked. "Ran away from home?"

Sam hung her head. "Aye." He made her sound like an impertinent child.

"Did you tell your father where you were going? Or leave him a letter?"

"No, I just . . . left. I thought it would be better that way. And I didn't want anyone to come after me." Tristan was trying to make her feel guilty, but it wouldn't work. She had *seen* her father in Haywood; that had not been the face of a grieving man. He was more inconvenienced than anything else; the duchy would go to a distant relation, unless he managed to procure himself a new wife and heir.

Tristan scuffed the toe of his boot in the snow. "I thought your father should know what happened to his daughter. So I sent him a letter as soon as we left the Diamond Coast. I told him that you were alive but there was a good chance you might die. I told him I would bring you to Luca, where you had the best hope of surviving."

Sam sneered at Tristan. "What a waste of parchment. You don't know my father nearly as well as you think, Tristan Lyons. He will find your letter irksome, nothing more."

Tristan sighed. "That's what I wanted to tell you. Your father is coming to Luca, Sam. He'll be here in a week."

CHAPTER 44

$\mathcal{I}$T WOULD HAVE been easier for Sam to forget about her father's looming arrival if she were able to train as normal. She was under strict doctor's orders not to touch *any* weapons— not just her new sword—till the end of the week. Still, Sam threw herself into what she could. She used bell clappers and lifted stones to strengthen her upper body and arms. She rode her horse down the sloping hillsides to Luca's westernmost gate and then climbed back up on foot. In the mornings, she ran, till short distances no longer winded her.

For the first few days, the Uriel looked at Sam askance, but no one said anything to her or tried to prevent her from using the training grounds, though they kept their distance. She wished she were in top fighting form so she could *really* give them something to look at. She wanted to prove that she belonged out there just as much as they did. She would, eventually.

As she recovered, Tristan ran calisthenics drills with her and they dined together at night. But Sam caught only flashes of Braeden: a flicker of silver hair or a blur of black robes, and then he was gone as if he'd never been. He was like a phantom, and every stolen glimpse of him was like rubbing salt in a wound. She missed him so much it hurt.

Sam didn't see much of Sander, either, and found herself disappointed. When he had been their captive, Sander had teased the possibility of her joining the Uriel. "For the right woman," he'd said he'd consider it. Even if Sam had been born a man, there was no place for her with the Paladins anymore. If the Uriel wouldn't take her, there would be no place for her anywhere. Perhaps her father would restore her as his heir—it would save him the trouble of producing a new one—but the person she had become in the months since she had run away would shrivel up and die. The Uriel were the only real hope she had.

Finally, the day came for Addie to remove her stitches, although in truth Sam was far more excited about reclaiming her sword. "Where is it?" she asked as soon as she spotted Addie in the infirmary.

Addie steered her to the nearest empty bed. "How did I know that would be your first question? Not 'Will this hurt?' or 'How long will this take?' like a normal person."

Sam shrugged. "The pain can't be worse than getting the wound in the first place. I just want my sword."

"And you'll get it," Addie said. "But first, remove your tunic and lie back."

Sam obliged and settled back onto the thin mattress. Addie unwrapped her bandages and gently examined her wound with her fingertips. "Very nice," she murmured. "You'll have a nasty scar, but only your lover ever need see it."

"Addie!"

The doctor laughed. "You're a prude, Sam of Haywood. And I'm only teasing you. Now, this will pinch." She pulled out thin forceps and scissors from her work apron. Using the forceps to lift up the topmost suture, Addie cut off the black string just below the knot, and Sam felt a minor twinge as the doctor tugged the thread out through her skin.

Twenty stitches later, Addie pulled out the last thread. "There. That's all of them." She cleaned the skin again and rewrapped Sam's chest with bandages. "You're to leave this on for five days and then *carefully* unwind it."

"My sword?"

"So impatient," Addie said, but she smiled as she said it. She slipped out through the opening in the curtain surrounding Sam's bed and returned with the beautiful sword—*her* sword. "It's yours, to keep this time."

Sam reached for it with eager fingers, but Addie held the scabbard close to her body. "Before you go running off to the training grounds, I'm supposed to pass along a request from my father."

Sam's ears perked up. "From Sander?"

"Aye. He asked if you would meet him for dinner after sunset tonight at the top of the Beyaz Kale."

"I can do that," Sam said slowly. "Why didn't he ask for me himself?"

"I've scarcely seen him myself in three weeks," Addie said. "I don't know the nature of the crisis he's contending with, but it's taken up all of his time."

"Will you be there tonight, Addie?"

The doctor shook her head. "My father doesn't involve me in Uriel affairs unless he wants my advice on medicine. I'm afraid you're on your own."

———

After two hours in the training yard, Sam retired to her chambers to bathe and dress before meeting with Sander. She found herself feeling quite nervous. Addie could shed no light on what her father wanted to discuss, and Sam feared the worst.

She stared at the gowns in her closet for a long time before choosing her nicest pair of breeches and a high-necked velvet doublet. Sam did not accentuate her femininity, but she didn't hide it, either. Her hair had grown out to just below her chin, and she left her breasts unbound. In her snug-fitting doublet, Sam would never be mistaken for a man. She would come to Sander honestly. Whatever she did next, she would do it as herself.

In a last-minute decision, she strapped her sword to her side. It gave her comfort to have it there. She would go to dinner as a warrior and she would leave as one, too.

At sunset, Sam made the long climb to the top of the Beyaz Kale. An armed guard waited outside the entryway to the domed tower, a man Sam had never seen before. He gave her a slow once-over, the slight widening of his eyes betraying his shock. The guard was no Uriel or the sight of a woman in men's garb wouldn't have surprised him. Every Uriel in Luca knew who Sam was by now. "Sam of Haywood," she stated clearly.

He must have been expecting her, because he moved aside with no further questions. Sam stepped past him into the tower, and her breath caught in her throat. Four men sat around a long table. Sander sat at the head of the table, Tristan sat on his left, the back of a silver head could only be Braeden, and . . .

"Father," she said.

The Duke of Haywood rose from his seat. "Samantha." His gaze roamed over her, taking in her boyish attire. "You look well."

Sam looked from her father to Tristan, to Braeden, and finally to Sander. She felt the sharp sting of betrayal. Her father was coming to Luca; she'd known that much from Tristan, but she hadn't expected to be ambushed. Was this some sort of conspiracy to send her packing? Why else would the Duke of Haywood sit so calmly at their table? It wasn't so hard to believe such a thing of Tristan—he'd always been high-handed—but Braeden? A month ago, she would not have believed him capable of such a thing, but perhaps he'd had enough of her.

Addressing the three of them, she said, "There are less cruel ways to get rid of me. I did not know any of you to be cruel men." She turned her back to them, facing the doorway. She would *not* cry, not in front of them. She would gather what coin she could scrounge, pack up her belongings, and go . . . go . . . go where? Her shoulders slumped. The world had no want of a woman warrior.

"Sam, wait." The voice belonged to her father, but he never called her Sam. "I did not come here to force you to return to Haywood."

Sam turned back toward him. "No? Then why *did* you come?"

"I came to meet with Sander Branimir."

An ugly laugh broke from her lips. "I am a fool. Of course you did not come to Luca for my sake. What a monumental waste of time and effort that would have been, Your Grace."

"Sam," her father said tightly. "Compose yourself. We will talk of this later."

She dropped into a mocking curtsy, gripping on to imaginary skirts. "Forgive me, Your Grace. How *dare* I air our family drama so publicly? Sander, I do hope you weren't planning to use me as leverage in your business negotiations with the Duke. His Grace doesn't give a fig about me, you see."

"Quiet!" the Duke of Haywood shouted. "How self-righteous you are, you who let me believe my own flesh and blood was dead!"

Sam jeered at him. "Flesh and blood means nothing more to

you than insurance for the family line. I'm sorry for *inconveniencing* you by leaving."

The duke's face paled to white. "Is that really what you believe of me?" he asked quietly. Sam said nothing. He closed his eyes. "Then I have failed you as a father." He straightened, as if remembering himself, and returned to his seat by Sander's side.

Sander pushed back from the table. "Sam, would you take a seat? I did not ask you here for underhanded reasons. Had I realized the . . . shall we say, *friction*, between you and your father"—he smiled apologetically at the Duke—"I would have forewarned you that he would be here."

And now, it was Sam who remembered *her*self. "I was out of line." She should have held her tongue in front of Sander and let the cards fall where they may before rushing to judgment. Perhaps there was hope for her yet. "I would hear what you have to say."

Sam took the seat beside Tristan, positioned directly across from Braeden. He kept his head bowed, so she saw only the silver of his hair. Look at me, she willed. I'm right here. He did not. It was worse than not seeing him at all.

Playing the good host, Sander filled five pewter goblets with red wine and set them in front of each of his guests before reclaiming his spot at the head of the table. He took a long sip, cupping his drink with both hands. "I need the liquid courage," he said with a self-deprecating grimace, "for it is not easy tidings I bear." He ran his finger along the rim of his goblet. "War is coming. It is an inevitability, and one I can forestall no longer. I must find allies where I can."

"You want Haywood's aid," the Duke stated. "What war would you have us fight?"

"A war you will have to fight, one way or the other," Sander said. "When the time comes to choose a side, I ask that you choose mine."

The Duke of Haywood sighed. "Must you always speak in riddles, Branimir? Speak plainly, man."

Sam's brows drew to a point. The duke spoke to Sander with far too much familiarity for a first acquaintance. "Do you two know each other?" she asked.

Her father cut her a glance. "I am a politician, Samantha. I make a business of knowing men of import. Of course I know the Earl of Luca."

"The *Earl* of Luca? You told me you were no aristocrat," Tristan interjected.

Sander waved his hand. "The title is purely incidental. When the old Earl died, he left behind no heir, so the title defaulted to me by marriage. It's a formality I seldom use."

"Then Luca is yours to rule by right," Tristan said. "I had thought you an interloper. The High Commander is mad to have ordered your capture. It's akin to declaring civil war." Realization dawned across his features. "Oh."

Sander raised his drink. "Precisely," he said. "The High Commander of the Paladins has declared open war against Luca, the Uriel, and any who sympathize with our cause." He gestured with his goblet at Sam, Braeden, and Tristan. "You three have officially been named traitors, by the way. By the High Commander and his puppet king."

Sam reeled at Sander's pronouncement. In a matter of weeks, she'd gone from being a Paladin trainee to being a traitor of Thule. All she'd wanted to do was protect the people of Thule, as her mother had protected her. And now she was their enemy.

The duke was the first to speak. "I like you, Sander, and I think you'd make a formidable enemy. But to go up against the Paladins, I'd have to be insane. Why should I risk my neck?"

"Because," Sander said, "the High Commander did not name Sam of Haywood a traitor, he named Lady Samantha, daughter of the seventeenth Duke of Haywood."

A wave of shame and self-loathing swept over Sam. The High Commander had made it so that she didn't belong anywhere—she couldn't be a Paladin trainee *or* her father's heir. And Sander had gravely miscalculated. "I told you not to use me as leverage. His Grace will not go to war on my behalf." For once, she wouldn't even blame him.

Sander's eyes glinted, his gaze latching onto the Duke of Haywood. "His Grace just learned that the daughter he thought was dead is alive. If he sides with the High Commander, he is condemning his daughter to die another death."

The duke leapt up from the table, spilling his wine in the process. "Are you threatening Samantha?"

"No," Sander said calmly. "I'm simply stating the reality. If the Uriel have any hope of winning this war, we will need Haywood's support. And if we lose, your daughter will die. The High Commander will see to that."

"For what it's worth," Braeden said. Her heart jumped at the sound of his voice. "The High Commander is not a good man. If morality factors at all into your decision, Your Grace, then you would be wise to throw in your lot with the Uriel."

The duke glared down at him. "Explain yourself, boy."

"I speak of the demons, Your Grace. They do the High Commander's bidding."

"What madness is this?" Sander asked, his calm façade gone. Apparently this was as much news to him as it was to Sam. "How do you know he can do such a thing?"

Braeden raised his head. For a fraction of a second, his eyes lingered on Sam, and then he looked away. "Because he can make me do his bidding, too."

The duke dropped back down in his chair with a dazed expression, and even Sander seemed rattled. Sam wondered what else she'd missed while she'd languished in the infirmary. What secrets was Braeden hiding? Had he kept them from Tristan, too, or was she in the dark alone?

Tristan rubbed at the back of his neck. "What is it you want with me, Sander? I am no duke, and I have no army I can offer you."

"I do not need you to bring an army," Sander said. "I want you to join mine." He nodded at Braeden and Sam. "All of you."

"Yes," Sam said. Oh Gods, yes. She would have a place in the world again. She would be a Uriel.

The duke scowled menacingly at her and at Sander. "You invite my *daughter* into your army? I forbid it."

Sam lifted her chin. "Too little, too late, Your Grace, for you to pretend to be my father." Her eyes shifted to Braeden. "Forbid whatever you want, but I will follow my heart." Braeden didn't look at her but his cheeks colored under her gaze. She sighed and then stood up from the table, bowing, as a man would. "Sander, I am yours, if you will have me."

"I won't stand by and watch you get yourself killed!" the duke yelled, his face mottled and red.

"So don't," Sander said. "Lend your army's strength to ours."

Tristan added, more softly, "Sam is a fine swordsman, Your Grace. I've seen no better. And if it gives you any comfort, I will join the Uriel, too." He twisted in his seat, facing Sander. "Thank you, sir, for this second chance. But my conscience tells me that I cannot accept your offer without saying this first: The Paladins do not all share the High Commander's vision, whatever it is. I became a paladin because I wanted to fight demons; I have no wish to fight good men."

Tristan was right. The Paladins might be rotten at the core, but that didn't make them all unredeemable. She thought of Will and Quinn; in the short time she'd known them, she'd come to think of them as friends.

"I know that," Sander said. "After all, you, Sam, and Braeden were once Paladins, too. I do not think the three of you an anomaly. I would not fight this war against men if the High Commander had not forced me into it. I cannot promise you that no good men will die by my order, but I can promise I will listen to your counsel and spare lives where I can. Will that be enough?"

Tristan nodded once. He would be a Uriel, too.

"What say you, Braeden?" Sander asked. "Can I count you among my men?"

Surprise flashed across Braeden's features and then disappeared, replaced by an emotionless mask. He drew his shoulders back. "No, you cannot."

"Braeden!" Sam cried. "What are you saying?"

Tristan put a quelling hand on her shoulder. "Peace, Sam. He has the right to make his own choices."

Gods, had she completely misjudged Braeden? No, she didn't believe that. She *knew* Braeden; he was virtuous to a fault and the most noble, self-sacrificing idiot she'd ever met. There was something he wasn't saying, something he held back. "Why, Braeden?"

His mask crumbled into pieces, and finally, finally, Braeden looked at her. "Did you not hear what I said? The High Commander can *control* me. I'm a danger to you all." He ripped open his robes at the neck, exposing his skin to the navel. Sam gasped at the sight of the swirl of glyphs across his chest. What did they mean?

"My master . . . the High Commander has marked me as his," Braeden said. He turned to Sander. "I'm sorry that I cannot join the Uriel. But you needn't worry that I'll jeopardize your cause. I'm leaving."

Fury coiled in Sam's belly like a snake lying in wait. "Leaving? To go where?"

"Away from Luca," Braeden said. His strange eyes held a far-away look. "Across the Rheic Ocean, as soon as I can find a ship that will take me."

She would never see him again. "No," she said. "No! Sander, Tristan, say something!" They said nothing, looking at her with grim faces.

With a scream of frustration, Sam drew her sword from its scabbard and held the point against Braeden's throat.

"Samantha!" her father exclaimed. "What do you think you're doing?"

She ignored him. "Get up," she snarled, rotating around the table till she was on the same side as Braeden, her blade still at his neck. Tristan started to rise from his seat, reaching for his own sword, but Sander stopped him with a look. "Let her go," she heard Sander say.

"Get up," she repeated, and Braeden rose wordlessly from the table. If he was shocked at her actions, he had buried it well. Sam slid the blade forward so that the middle lay on its edge against his neck. She grabbed his wrist with her free hand and dragged him across the room. Letting go of his wrist only to open the door to exit the domed tower, Sam called, "Eat without us!"

"Where are you taking me?" Braeden asked as she hauled him down the stairs.

"Somewhere we can talk without interruption, and somewhere you can't run away." Leading Braeden through a long corridor, Sam dropped his hand and fumbled in her belt pouch for the key to her chambers. "This will do." She fitted the key into the lock, pushed open the door, and shoved Braeden backwards onto the bed.

The corner of his mouth lifted. "Pink sheets, Lady Samantha?"

Her lips threatened to curve. Braeden, imposing as ever in his somber black robes, looked ridiculous sprawled out on her bright pink bed. She schooled her traitorous lips into obedience. "Do I *amuse* you, Braeden? Do you enjoy toying with my feelings?"

His mouth lost its smile. "What are you talking about?"

She stepped up onto the mattress and stood over him, pressing the tip of her sword just above his heart. "You've avoided me for weeks, and now I find out you're leaving. Would you have left without telling me?"

Braeden twisted his neck, looking away. "It would have been easier."

"I hadn't realized I meant so little to you." She cursed the tears that welled up in her eyes and willed them not too fall. She laughed softly at her own folly. "You know, I dreamed of you while I lay unconscious. And then I woke up, and you weren't there. I kept waiting for you to come, but you never did."

"You had Tristan," Braeden said gruffly. "You had no need of me."

"I didn't want Tristan! I wanted you!" The tears she'd tried to will away spilled over. "You promised me once that you'd never hate me. I should never have believed you."

Braeden knocked her sword point off his chest and sat up quickly, grasping her knees. "Now who's toying with feelings? You're to be a married woman, Sam. You shouldn't tell another man you want him." He loosened his grip on her legs. "I . . . overheard Tristan's proposal. Forgive me for not extending my congratulations earlier."

She glared at him. "I'm not marrying Tristan. I said no."

Braeden groaned, thumping his head against her thighs. "Why did you do that? He was supposed to look after you."

"I don't *need* to be looked after, by a husband or anyone else. And why do you think I said no, you great lummox?"

Braeden's crimson eyes flared and then he shook his head. "Sam, you need to let me off of this bed. I have to leave. I'm bound to hurt you if I stay."

You'll hurt me if you leave, she thought. Out loud, she said, "That's shite. You couldn't hurt me if you tried."

Braeden ran his hands through his hair, pulling silver strands loose around his face. "Sam, you don't understand. The High Commander and my master, they're one and the same. This tattoo"—his hand traced the intersecting lines of one of the glyphs—"is my master's work, and it binds me to him, as surely as the last. I can't get rid of it; I've tried. He could tell me to kill you, and there's a very good chance I'd obey."

"I'll take my chances. Braeden, don't leave."

He spoke through clenched teeth. "Maybe you're willing to take risks with your life, but I'm not."

Sam dug her fingers into his scalp and tilted his head back. She bent over him so that her eyes were inches from his. "Get this through your thick skull: I am not some fragile flower. I don't break easily. I can defend myself from anything. Even you."

Braeden growled in frustration. "Gods, Sam, you're not invincible. You already almost died once because of me."

She moved her head so that her mouth brushed his ear. "You're not invincible either, Braeden." A half-baked idea formed in her mind. "I'll prove it to you."

She jumped off the bed and raised her sword. "Fight me."

"Why would I want to do that?"

She held his gaze and kept her sword arm steady. "Because if you win, I'll let you leave, no questions asked. We'll say our goodbyes and that will be it."

"You know, I don't need your permission to leave."

She lowered her sword, hurt. "I know that."

Braeden muttered an oath and then stood up from the bed. "You're still recovering from an injury, Sam. You haven't any hope of winning."

She knew that, she did. She would try anyway.

Braeden sighed, slipping a dagger into his right hand. "On the off chance that I lose, what do you get?"

Sam straightened her shoulders and looked him square in the eye. "If I win, you stay."

CHAPTER 45

$\mathcal{B}$RAEDEN SHOULD NEVER have agreed to fight Sam. She was barely a week out of the infirmary, but even if she were in full health, he would be stronger and faster than she was. He knew what she'd do if he dared say that aloud—she would flamboyantly twirl her sword and accuse him of treating her like a girl. She was as strong and fast as any man, she'd say.

Braeden knew that. Sam was . . . amazing. Watching her fight was like watching a thunder storm—powerful and violent and beautiful. He'd never once doubted that she was a warrior, more than worthy of fighting alongside the most elite men.

What Sam refused to accept was that Braeden was no ordinary man. He wasn't stronger and faster than her because she was a woman, he was stronger and faster than her because he was a monster. There wasn't a man alive who could best him—not even Tristan—except his master, and he was as much a monster as Braeden.

There was no reason for Braeden to participate in this absurd duel—what, would they fight in Sam's silly pink bedroom?—and he'd meant to refuse her. But he was so damned weak when it came to Sam; one look at her crestfallen face and he'd relented.

What was the harm, really? He'd defeat her handily, and maybe then she'd understand the threat he posed to her. Then they would part on cordial, if not friendly, terms. Braeden remembered the last time they had almost said goodbye . . . His cheeks flushed involuntarily. He would not demand another kiss from her. Though she'd asked him to forget it, the memory of Sam's lips on his would torture him for a lifetime.

"Will you fight me, Braeden?" There was a pleading desperation in Sam's eyes—but he had to remain steadfast, and that way lay temptation.

His dagger was already in his hands, but still he said, "This is foolishness, Sam. You will prove nothing."

"I will agree that this is foolishness if you agree that *leaving* is foolishness." Sam stepped closer to him, holding her sword straight out from her shoulder. "I know you don't want to fight me, and I don't want to fight you, either."

Braeden wrapped his hand around her blade and felt the satisfaction of steel cutting into his palm. Sam winced. "Stop it," she said.

"I would rather bleed till my body is dry and empty," he said, "than draw a single drop of your blood. But that choice has been taken away from me."

"I believe in you, Braeden," Sam said. "I wish you'd believe in yourself."

The strength of her conviction gutted him, and his frustration boiled over. "Stop deluding yourself, Sam! You know what I am! I am not the knight in shining armor in some ridiculous fairy tale. Look to Tristan for that!"

"I. Don't. Want. Tristan." Sam enunciated each word. "And if this were a fairy tale, I'd be my own Gods damned knight!"

Braeden let go of Sam's sword and stalked toward her. "If you are the knight, then I am the dragon. Do you know how many innocent lives have died by my hand? Hundreds, Sam. Maybe more. I could rend the world apart, and you would pretend that there is no evil within me. This man—this good and noble man that you imagine me to be . . . I'm not him, no matter how much I want to be." He broke off. When he spoke again, his voice was harsh and low. "I am nothing more than a collared monster, and the High Commander holds my leash. I don't trust myself, and neither should you."

"Coward," Sam spat. "That's what you are. You would give up everything because you're afraid of yourself. I know who and what you are, and I'm not afraid. Fight me, you coward!" She struck out with her sword, sliding it along his dagger.

He growled. "Don't think I'll go easy on you. I'll show you what I really am." He jammed his dagger into his heart and let the transformation take hold. He looked at Sam through a haze of red. "This is who I am. You *should* be afraid."

Sam brandished her blade. "I won't go easy on you either. I'm fighting to win." Without warning, she thrust her sword at his breast.

Too slow. Braeden stepped neatly to the side and swung out with his knife, catching the underside of Sam's weapon. The blade jumped in her hand, but she didn't lose her grip. She brought her sword down, smashing it into his dagger.

It was a mighty blow, and normally, Braeden would have dropped his knife. In his enhanced state, he didn't even flinch. Sam spun, swiping her sword at his knees. Dropping into a crouch, he parried the attack. He rolled forward, closing the distance between them.

A dagger was a close range weapon, and a sword was not. Sam stepped backwards to allow herself more room, but Braeden wouldn't give her the opening. He hit her blade with his knife, first from the left, then from the right. Slowly, he forced her across the room till her back was up against the wall.

Braeden drove his knee between her legs and brought his dagger to the side of her neck. He rested his forehead against hers. "Give up?"

Her eyes flashed. "Not a chance." She leaned into his body and then bit him hard in the neck.

The sensation of her teeth against his skin caught him so off guard that he dropped his knife to the floor. "Shite," he swore. Sam grinned and pushed him off her.

He retrieved another knife from his robes, just in time to deflect her next blow. "That trick will only work once," he told her.

"I've got others," she said, lashing out again with her sword.

Even as he fought her, he could not help but admire her. Her eyes were bright with excitement, her pale skin pink with exertion. Her hair was wild and mussed, twisted locks of sable hugging her face. Sam, his warrior. He would die before he put her fire out.

But this time he would win to save her.

Her sword struck dangerously close, drawing a thin line of blood from the stretch of tattooed skin above his breastbone. The cut sent a searing trail of heat across his flesh. His chest began to burn from the outside in, till he felt flickers of flame touch his heart. He sagged to his knees, darkness threatening to pull him under.

"Braeden, what's wrong? I only nicked you."

But Braeden couldn't see, couldn't speak, not to her. He heard only the sickly sweet voice in his head.

You are mine, Braeden. Now and forever.

Braeden seized involuntarily, like a marionette pulled by invisible strings. *No*, he told the voice, even as his body disobeyed him. *I belong to myself.*

Gales of laughter assaulted his ears. *Foolish boy. My claim is staked into your very skin. I own you, body and soul. And I will do with you as I please.*

No, Braeden argued. *You aren't here. You can't touch me.*

His master chuckled, low and dark. *Do you think I would ever have let you go if it meant I'd lose you? I found you, Braeden. I can always find you.* Fingers of fire danced across the glyphs on Braeden's chest. *And tonight I've come to you.*

In denial, Braeden shook his head—or tried to—but his neck was held rigid.

Don't fight me, his master whispered in his head. *You are meant for greatness, Braeden, you and I together. There is only one thing holding you back.*

A scorching heat coursed through his veins, filling his every pore and fiber. He bucked against the white, agonizing pain, and then his body surrendered, loose and pliant.

A hand caressed his chin—his own hand, and yet not his—and forced his head up. His vision cleared, and he found himself staring into a pair of worried, yellow-green eyes.

You see her?

I do, Braeden thought back. *Sam.*

He could feel his master smile, his own lips curving up in an echo.

Now kill her.

Sam watched helplessly as Braeden convulsed and contorted. She couldn't get near him, not the way he was thrashing about. Faith in blood, what was happening to him?

He writhed against the floor, clawing at his robes till he split the fabric in half. The glyphs on his chest stood out, livid and glowing, as though they'd been set alight. Braeden threw back his head in a silent scream, and then lay still.

"Braeden," she called softly.

His hands twitched, and he rose, first to his knees and then to his feet. He stood awkwardly, as though he were not accustomed to the weight of his limbs. His shoulders drew back, his spine straightening, and he regarded her with a cold intensity.

Fear shivered through her. "Braeden?"

He smiled wide, flashing all of his teeth. "He's mine," Braeden said in a honeyed voice that wasn't his. He drew closer, running the backs of his fingers along her cheek. "But he still wants you."

"H-High Commander?" she stuttered, stepping back.

He laughed. "Some might call me that. Braeden calls me Master. I have had many names, but I think that one is my favorite."

She took another step back and butted up against the wall. "Where is Braeden?" she demanded, holding her sword out between them. "Make him come back."

"Silly girl, Braeden never left. He's here with me, seeing what I see, hearing what I hear." His smile turned feral. "And now he'll watch your death."

Sam shook her head, even as her body quaked with unwilling terror. "You're wrong."

His hands shot out lightning fast, wrapping around her throat. He squeezed, his fingers bruising her windpipe. "This is no fairy tale, little girl," he said into her ear as she started to slump. "No one's coming to save you."

Before her vision could fade to black, she clasped her hands together and drove the hilt of her sword into his gut. He grunted, dropping his hands from her neck.

Gasping for breath, Sam sucked air into her lungs. "I don't need to be saved. I'll damn well save myself."

"You talk too much," the High Commander said, drawing a dagger from Braeden's tattered robes. "I grow tired of hearing you." He lunged forward with the knife. Sam turned and he only grazed her side instead of stabbing her through the belly.

She raised her sword and swung for his fingers in an attempt to knock the knife from his hands. As long as he held a weapon, she didn't have a prayer.

Her sword glanced harmlessly off his dagger. She attacked, again and again, and each time he parried her blows without the least sign of effort. The High Commander in Braeden's body was a formidable match, and she was losing.

In a desperate, final effort, she charged him, swinging her sword in a wild arc. He evaded her strike, and then the tip of his dagger was at her heart.

"It's over now," he said gleefully. "Say your goodbyes."

Sam looked into the crimson eyes of the man she'd come to trust more than anyone else and tried to see past the High Commander and into his soul. He was still there, somewhere—the man who had never once doubted her but had only ever doubted himself. He'd protected her secrets as though they were his own and given her everything of himself. And Gods damn him, she loved him, no matter how pointless and irrational love was.

"Goodbye, Braeden," she said for the second and final time. Gently, she let her lips graze over his. "I love you," she told him, and poured her whole heart into one last kiss.

The knife dropped from her chest. "Oh Gods, Sam. What have I done?"

CHAPTER 46

SAM LET HER sword fall to the floor and reached up, cupping Braeden's face in her hands. "Braeden, look at me. I'm unhurt."

"Sam . . ."

She brushed his hard jaw with her knuckles. "You didn't hurt me. I have a few cuts, nothing more. I promise you."

"He made me hurt you," Braeden whispered. "My master—his voice was in my head and I—I wanted to do it. He made me want to do it."

"But you didn't."

"No," he rasped. "I wanted you more."

Her breath hitched, and she stared at him with wide eyes and parted lips. Braeden groaned. "Forgive me, Sam." He fisted his hands in her hair and took her mouth with his.

His grip on her was firm, but his lips were gentle, tender. He kissed her worshipfully as though she were precious, as though she might break beneath his touch.

Braeden began to pull away, but Sam wrapped her arms around him and pulled him back to her. Her lips were a whisper away. "I'm not saying goodbye," she said. "Not again." Her lashes flickered up and then closed. Tentatively, she placed her mouth back on his.

Braeden made a desperate sound in the back of his throat and crushed her against him. His tongue traced the seam of her lips and then greedily plundered within. Their tongues dueled like swords and their bodies trembled. She moaned, or maybe it was he.

Sam kissed him like she fought, with wildness and passion, and with a little mischief. Her lips left his mouth, latching on to the side of his neck. She bit him, right on top of where she'd bitten him before, and then ran her tongue over the marks her teeth left. He responded with a low rumble, pressing her against the hard length of his body.

Braeden broke away, gasping. He looked at her with unrestrained hunger. "I'm a selfish bastard. I should never have done that."

She met his gaze and let him see her matching hunger. "I wanted you to. I still want you to."

Braeden turned away from her. "You don't know what you're saying. You can't want me."

She glared at his back. "I have always known my own mind," she said. "Who are you to tell me what I want?"

"The man who loves you," he said with soft yearning.

Sam hadn't realized she wanted Braeden to say it till he said it. But . . . not like this. Not with sadness and regret. He told her he loved her in the same breath he pushed her away. "You love me?"

"Being loved by me is no blessing. If I could stop loving you, I would."

She wanted to lash out at the sting of his words. "Am I so unworthy of being loved?"

His head snapped back as if she'd hit him. "Never say that, Sam. You're the best person I know." As if he couldn't help himself, he reached out and coiled a strand of her hair around his finger. "You're irresistible."

Sam looked down at her wrinkled tunic and breeches. Her face was unpowdered and damp with sweat, but even if she were clean and tidy, her nose would still be too long and her face too thin, the lines of her well-muscled body too straight to be fashionable. "I'm not," she said practically.

"You are to me." Braeden let her hair slip from his fingers. "I have no control over my attraction to you."

She didn't *want* him to control his attraction, Gods damn it. "So what?"

"It's not an easy thing to explain." Braeden closed his eyes. "It's my fault the demons are attracted to you."

"Demons are attracted to everyone."

Braeden shook his head. "Not like they are to you. I know

you've noticed it, too. Every time we fight them, they go straight for you. As soon as they sense you, they forget anyone else is there. They want you above all others . . . because—because so do I." He stroked her cheek with a sad smile. "You see, Sam? To be loved by me is to be cursed. Because I love you, I've put you in danger."

Sam caught his wrist with her hand. "Is that a serious objection?"

He blinked. "What?"

Idiot, idiot man. "Do you think I disguised myself as a boy because I wanted to avoid *danger*? Do you think I picked up a *sword* to avoid danger? You say you love me. Just who do you think I am?"

Braeden opened his mouth to speak, but Sam spoke first. "I'll tell you who I'm not. I'm not some princess in an ivory tower. I'm not someone who runs scared from a fight. And I'm *not* the kind of girl who gives up on something she wants because of a little thing like danger." She poked her finger into his chest. "I left home to join the Paladins because I wanted to *kill demons*. I should be thanking you for making it that much easier."

Braeden stared down at the place where her finger met his chest. He grasped her finger and hand and placed it over his shoulder. He pulled her to him, wrapping his arms around her waist, burying his face into her hair. "I love you, Sam of Haywood."

She laid her head against his heart and was relieved to hear it beat as rapidly as hers. "I love you, too, you know." Braeden was a noble, self-sacrificing idiot, but he was *her* idiot.

"You can't love me," he said brokenly.

She squeezed him tighter. "I don't do very well with *can't*."

He stepped out of her arms and sat down on the edge of the bed. "I have to leave, Sam."

She gave an annoyed huff. "Why? I don't mind a few demons, and you proved tonight you would never hurt me. The High Commander tried to get you to kill me, and he failed."

"Because it was you." His mouth lifted in a half-smile. "I trust myself a little more around you. But there's a whole city of Uriel he could command me to kill. Tristan, Sander, anyone. Would you have me risk their lives so casually?"

Braeden was right. He'd been tested against her, but no one

else. She wanted to believe he could resist the High Commander's possession again, but she had never experienced the power of his compulsion. It was a high risk to take and it wasn't her life to gamble. She made a decision. "I understand."

"You do?"

Sam sat down on the bed beside him. "We need to leave till we figure out how to remove your tattoo."

"*We?*"

Sam nodded. "Aye. I'm coming with you."

Braeden's head whipped towards her. "I can't ask you to do that."

"I want to." She looked down at her lap. "If you'll have me, that is."

His hands found the tops of her shoulders. "I love you," he said quietly. "It's why I can't ask you to leave with me. I would no more ask you to return to Haywood as Lady Samantha than ask you to throw away the Uriel for me. You finally have everything you wanted, Sam. I won't ask you to give up your dreams for my sake."

"You didn't ask," she said. "I offered. And I'm not giving up on my dreams; I'm making new ones. I want *you*—" She pressed her lips to the corner of his mouth. "—and I want to be a warrior, too. Wherever we go, I'll have plenty of opportunity to use my sword. The Uriel can wait."

His hand left her shoulder to touch the spot where she'd kissed him. "I really am a selfish bastard."

She gripped his knees and leaned towards him. "Then I'm selfish, too. We can indulge in our selfishness together." And because it was what she selfishly wanted, she kissed him full on the lips. The kiss was hard and fast, a promise.

Braeden returned her kiss, harder, till both of them were panting for air. In between breaths, he said, "We'll need to tell Tristan. Sander, too."

Sam looked up at him. "That we're leaving together?"

He nodded.

She tightened her arms around his neck. "Thank you."

"For what?" he asked.

"For letting me come with you. For loving me."

His fingers trailed down her cheek. "A man once told me I would never know love. I believed him."

She gasped. "Braeden." How could anyone tell this man—this man she would follow to the ends of the earth and back again—that he was underserving of love?

Braeden lowered a kiss to her forehead, to each eyelid, to her nose. His lips hovered near her mouth, and he didn't try to veil the stark emotion in his eyes. "It was enough that you didn't fear me. Loving you, being loved by you . . . you've made me believe that maybe I'm more than a monster. That maybe I'm a man, too."

Braeden had bared his soul to her, and so would she. "Do you know why I love you?" she asked. "When I made up my mind to join the Paladins, I thought it meant I had to give up a part of myself. I had to choose between Sam the warrior or Sam the woman, and I chose the warrior. But you . . . you make me believe that I can be both." She elbowed him in the ribs. "One day I'll get you to stop trying to protect me."

Braeden laughed softly. "That's never going to happen."

Sam scowled. "Fine," she said. "Then I'll just have to protect you back."

Tristan swirled the wine in his goblet, watching the burgundy liquid slosh against the pewter sides. He set the cup down on the table, a little harder than necessary. "I don't understand why you wouldn't let me go after them. Sam had her *sword* at Braeden's throat—"

"Tristan," Sander said. There was a gentleness to his voice that Tristan had never heard before. "You're a smart man. If you think about it, you'll know you need to let them be."

Tristan stared at Sam's vacant chair next to him, and then his eyes moved to Braeden's seat. In his mind, he replayed her passionate plea to force Braeden to stay. Would she have held Tristan at sword point if it were he who threatened to leave? He remembered his ill-fated marriage proposal, when he'd mentioned casually that Braeden was gone. It was like she'd forgotten that Tristan had proposed, or that he was even in the room. "Gone? Is Braeden okay?" she'd asked.

"She loves him, doesn't she?"

"I know only what I observe," Sander said. His gaze held something akin to pity.

It was more than Tristan could bear. He finished his wine in one gulp and pushed back from the table. He stood, bowing first to the Duke of Haywood and then to Sander. "If you'll excuse me," he said.

"Of course," Sander said.

Tristan fled, but not before he heard the duke say, "What's this about Samantha? My daughter is betrothed."

As soon as he was free of people, Tristan found the nearest space of empty wall and sagged against it. He hadn't realized he still harbored a hope that Sam would change her mind. That hope was dashed, now. Sam loved another man. Braeden. Gods.

A delicate cough let him know he was no longer alone. With great effort, he tore his eyes from Addie Branimir's impressive bosom to her lovely face. Her forehead creased with worry. "Are you quite all right, Master Lyons?" she asked.

Tristan forced a smile. "Quite."

She narrowed her gaze. "Don't lie to your doctor, Lyons." She knelt down beside him and wrapped two fingers around his wrist, as if taking his pulse. "As I suspected. You, sir, are gravely ill."

"I am?"

She nodded and stood, offering him a hand up. "I have precisely the cure. Follow me." With a rustle of her skirts, she swept away, not waiting for his reply. Shaking his head, Tristan trotted after her. Better that than wallow in his own pathetic loneliness.

She stopped at the infirmary but didn't ask him to come in. "I'll just be a moment," she said. She returned dressed in a long, hooded cloak of white ermine.

"We're going outside?" he asked.

"Aye." Addie gave him a once over. "Will you be warm enough, dressed like that?"

"I'm warm blooded," he said. "Where is it you are taking me?"

She smiled enigmatically. "You'll see."

It was dark outside the Beyaz Kale, and Tristan felt the bite of cold, despite his claim to Addie. Snow crunched beneath his boots as he plodded along beside her. Addie held onto his elbow for balance; she wore those flimsy silk slippers that were all the rage for women these days but highly impractical out-of-doors.

They passed by several buildings till Addie tugged on his elbow, drawing him to a stop. "In there," she said, pointing towards a bright red door. The sounds of music, boisterous laughter and clinking glasses were audible from the street.

"A tavern," he said slowly. "You've brought me to a tavern. Why?"

"Because, Master Lyons, I've diagnosed you with a broken heart." She pulled up her hood, hiding her face, and slung an arm around his shoulders. "Come on, Lyons, drinks are on me."

CHAPTER 47

IT HADN'T BEEN easy for Sam to tell Sander that she would be leaving with Braeden. It was the right decision for her, she knew, and yet she felt a little ashamed of it. But Sander was a singular man and had been remarkably understanding.

She'd told him together with Braeden, and somehow during the telling of it their fingers had wound together. Sander's gaze fell upon their interlocked hands and his mouth had twitched, not into a disapproving frown but into an amused smile.

"It is not an either or," Sander had said. "As Uriel, you are not bound to this soil, only to the principles that guide us. Duty. Honor. Loyalty. Belief in the goodness of man." He put one hand on each of their shoulders. "Do what you need to do, and come back to us. I told you this once before—the Uriel always have room for courageous men." He grinned at Sam. "Or women."

Telling Tristan did not go as well.

Sam knocked on the door of his chambers in the Beyaz Kale—which was awkward in itself, since he shared the room with Braeden—and asked if he would be amenable to a walk outside. She didn't invite Braeden; she owed Tristan that much.

It wasn't as though she'd accepted another man's proposal after turning his down, but it was close enough. And in the days following their first exchanged I-love-yous, she and Braeden had done a shockingly poor job of hiding their affection. Twice, Braeden had pulled her into a discreet corner and kissed her senseless, and twice Sam had accosted *him*. She blushed just thinking about it.

And thus for the sake of her friendship with Tristan, Sam thought it best she break the news herself.

In uncomfortable silence, Sam and Tristan trudged down the

snowy slope to the Uriel training grounds, stopping when they reached the tree line. They stood apart, watching the Uriel men spar with swords and fists.

When Sam could stand it no longer, she said into the silence, "I'm leaving."

Tristan faced outward into the trees and did not turn. "With Braeden?"

"Aye."

The wind played across his hair, blowing overlong strands into his cobalt eyes. "Where will you go?" he asked.

"Across the ocean," she said, "to Yemara. We're going to pay a visit to the old orphanage where Braeden first met the High Commander. Maybe we'll find some answers there."

Tristan stiffened. "That's . . . far."

"I'll come back," Sam promised. "Both of us will. The war will not be over so soon."

"I don't suppose it will," Tristan said. He looked at her then, really looked at her, his gaze intent on hers. "Is this what you want, Sam? To follow a man halfway around the world on what may amount to a wild goose chase?"

"I love him," she said simply.

Tristan responded with a single nod, and they fell back into quiet. "I could have loved you," he said finally.

She didn't want to hurt him, didn't want to lie to him either. "In another lifetime, I could have loved you, too." She offered him her hand. "Friends?"

Tristan stared at her extended palm. His eyes, blue and wintery, drifted up to her face. "No." The single word shot like an icicle through her heart.

Tristan whipped around, then, and with straightened shoulders, began the long trudge back to the Beyaz Kale. His pride was wounded, not his heart, and one day he would see it.

A quarter of the way, he halted. Slowly, he turned, the frostiness in his stare melted into something else. "Ask me again when you return."

Sam and Braeden rode out early the next morning on borrowed horses. The horses would carry them as far as Southport, and from there they would need to hire a ship with a willing captain and crew to take them across the Rheic Ocean. The horses would find their way back home, Sander had assured them.

But before they could leave Luca, a small troop of armed men blocked their exit at the east archway, where Sam had first crossed into the city months back. They weren't Uriel; they were her father's men.

Sam drew her horse to a halt, and Braeden brought his stallion to a stop beside hers. "What does His Grace want?" she asked the leader among them, a stocky man with a broad, red face.

The leader shifted on his mount. "He didn't say, milady. He only said to ask you to wait here for him till he arrives."

Sam's eyebrows rose. "He *asked*?" The Duke of Haywood did not ask; he ordered.

"Those were his words, milady."

Sam nudged her horse forward. "Move out of the way," she said, "or I will make you." She didn't have time for her father's nonsense. Whatever he wanted, it wouldn't be good.

"Sam, maybe we should wait," Braeden said, quiet enough that his voice wouldn't carry to the others.

She whirled around in her saddle, glaring at him. "Why should we do that?"

"Because he's your father."

Sam snorted through her nose. "Braeden, you met the man. I'm not exactly the apple of his eye. He probably wants to haul me back to Haywood."

Braeden shrugged his shoulders. "Sometimes people can surprise you."

She would have argued further, but the sound of frantic galloping drew her attention away. The Duke of Haywood was bent low over his horse's neck, his graying hair streaming in a wild halo behind him. He slowed when he neared them, pulling short on the reins. The duke sagged against his mount and wiped sweat from his brow. "You didn't leave," he said, panting for breath.

"Not for lack of trying," Sam said. Her gaze roamed over his uncharacteristically disheveled appearance. "Aren't you a bit old to be riding like that?"

His jaw tightened but his voice was even when spoke. "I've not got one foot in the grave yet."

Sam lifted her chin and stared him straight in the eye. "Come to stop me?" she asked, with a hint of challenge.

"As if I could," he scoffed. A reluctant smile flickered across his lips.

She didn't understand the source of his smile or his choice of words. "Well, you couldn't," she said without heat. "Why are you here, Your Grace?"

The muscles of his throat flexed as he swallowed. "Branimir informed me of your plans. It is no small journey, nor an easy one."

"I know," she said, unfazed. "You will not deter me." She glanced over at Braeden, who gripped his reins with white, tight-fisted hands. "I have made my choice, and I am happy with it."

"You have always known your mind, Samantha. I am no longer fool enough to believe you will change it, no matter what I wish for you." The duke sighed. "I came here to tell you that whatever happens on this soil or in Yemara, you will be welcome in Haywood. It is your home."

She shook her head jerkily. She'd left behind her childhood there, but nothing else. "My home is not in Haywood. It's with him." She tilted her head towards Braeden. He reached across the space between their horses and threaded his fingers through hers.

The duke's expression was unreadable. "You are my heir, Samantha. When I die, Haywood will be yours, whether you want it or not."

"What about the High Commander?" she asked. "Surely he would not permit a traitor to inherit."

Her father's eyes flared. "My daughter is no traitor, and any man who says otherwise is no friend of mine, nor friend to Haywood." He raised his voice, as though he were speaking to a large audience instead of a few men. "When war comes to Thule, Haywood will side with the Uriel and with Lady Samantha."

Her breath caught. "Why?" she whispered. In eighteen years, the duke had done nothing to indicate he cared about her beyond her value as his heir. Yet in the war between the Paladins and the Uriel, he'd chosen the side of the underdog. Had he done it because of her?

To her surprise, her father turned to Braeden. "I heard what you said, boy. I will not fight for a man who holds the demons in his pocket."

So it had not been about her after all. Sam bit back unfounded disappointment. "Good of you, Father," she muttered.

As if he read her mind, the duke said, "I have always been a politician first, father second. My hand is forced in this matter." His face softened. "But even if it weren't, I would never fight for the side that named you traitor."

She ducked her head so he couldn't see how his words affected her. "Thank you, father."

The duke cleared his throat. "May I say goodbye to you properly? I would part on better terms than we did last."

"You may," Sam said in a small voice.

The duke extended his arm towards Braeden first, clasping his free hand in his. "It's Braeden, isn't it?"

"Aye."

"Do you love my daughter?"

"Father!" she exclaimed, blushing to the roots of her hair. "Braeden, you don't have to answer that."

Braeden ignored her. "I do, Your Grace."

"And does she love you?"

"So she says, Your Grace."

"I'm right here!" Sam complained. She punched Braeden in the shoulder. "And of course I do, you idiot."

"Good," her father said. "You'll take care of each other then."

Braeden and Sam glanced at each other. "Aye, we will," she said. Braeden squeezed her hand.

The duke turned towards her and bowed his head. "Be safe, Samantha."

"And you, father." She meant it.

After goodbyes were exchanged, her father and his men departed, leaving the road open for Sam and Braeden. Once they crossed the rickety suspension bridge that separated Luca from the mountains, they kept the pace of their horses at a near-gallop, far too fast for conversation. Sam welcomed the solitude; she needed to think, to prepare herself mentally for what lay ahead.

This thing between them was still new and fragile, and Braeden and Sam had been too caught up in the newness of passion to hash out what they were to one another. What did "I love you" really mean, anyway? Were they friends who were lovers? Lovers who were friends?

They would not have the luxury of discovering each other slowly, not alone on the road with only themselves as company. Good or bad, there were no more barriers between them—no secrets, no lies, no misunderstandings, no silly rules of propriety, no people.

A little past dusk, Sam and Braeden dismounted their horses by the small wood hut that Tristan had shown them in the Elurra Mountains. They almost hadn't found it, so covered was it by snow. If winter had hit Luca, it had hit the mountains doubly hard; Sam's fingers were numb with the cold.

She and Braeden dug their way through to the door and pushed into the small hut. And then they were alone, utterly alone.

Sam was shy, suddenly, an emotion as foreign to her as the Rheic Ocean. "Hullo," she said softly.

A trace of a smile touched Braeden's lips. "Hullo." He frowned when he saw her shiver. "Are you cold?"

Sam hugged her elbows to her chest. "A little." She suspected her shivering had less to do with the cold and more to do with Braeden than she cared to admit to him.

Braeden rummaged around in their packs till he located the blankets. He arranged one blanket on the floor and then glanced over at her, as if asking her for permission. She nodded, almost imperceptibly. Braeden carefully laid out another blanket next to the first.

He crawled underneath the blankets, facing away from the door, for which Sam was grateful. She slipped in beside him, lying on her side. It didn't matter that their bodies did not touch; an electrical charge filled the space between them, sending a tremor down her spine.

"I'm going to turn now," Braeden said.

"Okay."

He turned over, so that their bodies faced each other. Wrapping his arms around her waist, Braeden pulled her close, cradling her head to his chest. "Is this okay?"

She nodded, the tip of her nose brushing against the V of tattooed skin at the opening of his robes. The tattoo was smooth now, no longer raised and angry; it had become a part of him. "Do you feel it?" she asked, her fingers following the trail where her nose had been.

The muscles in his chest jumped under her touch. "I'm not dead," he said, his mouth crinkling at the corners.

Sam blushed, retracting her hand. "That's not what I meant!"

"I know." His smile faded. "It's strange. I haven't felt anything since the High Commander ordered me to kill you."

"Maybe he's given up."

"No," Braeden said firmly. "He's biding his time, waiting for a weak moment. My master concedes nothing."

"I wish you'd stop calling him that," Sam said. "He's not your master anymore."

A bleakness entered his eyes. "He is my master as long as his ink is in my skin."

Sam angled herself so that her lips pressed against the place where his neck met his shoulder. None too gently, she bit.

Braeden glared down at her. "What was that for?"

"I'm leaving my mark on your skin," she said, "so you know that you belong to me."

"It will fade," Braeden said.

"Then I shall have to do it again."

Braeden dipped his head and closed his teeth around her earlobe.

"Ouch," she protested. "What was *that* for?"

She felt his lips move against her ear. "You belong to me, too."

Sam and Braeden slept in each other's arms that night, and for many nights after. And Sam, who was both warrior and woman, finally found a place where she belonged.

CONNECT WITH ME

If you enjoyed Paladin – or even if you didn't! – I'd love to hear what you think!

Website: http://sallyslater.com

Twitter: @sallyroseslater

Facebook: http://www.facebook.com/sallyslaterauthor

Wattpad: www.wattpad.com/user/SallySlater